Awakened

Awakened

HIDDEN SOCIETY SERIES BOOK I

J.T. CARROLL

Palmetto Publishing Group, LLC
Charleston, SC

For information regarding special discounts for bulk purchases, please contact Palmetto Publishing Group at Info@PalmettoPublishingGroup.com.

ISBN-13: 978-1-944313-88-3
ISBN-10: 1-944313-88-5

ALSO BY J.T. CARROLL:

Choices: Hidden Society Series Book II

CHAPTER ONE

HOME

Everything to me was so black and white—cut and dry. Why, then, did everything in my life become so complicated? My mom had decided it was time for us to move again, only this time, back to Erving. I don't think any of us were completely ready for it or could understand why we were doing it.

My mom, Laurel, was always a free spirit, and never wanted to be still or to settle in one place for too long. Since March, though, something had definitely changed, and I didn't know if that was good or not. The road trip home in our small Jeep Cherokee was interesting, to say the least. Our destination was our old home, which was my mom's childhood home. We would be staying with Uncle Evan and Grandma Margaret—or Grams, as we liked to call her.

Ever since the death of my father, Erving had never felt like home. I'd always been sure we weren't going to return. I guess life has twists and turns we never expect to happen. That recent revelation was one of those twists and turns out of the many more that were to come. I felt some sort of draw to my roots and to the family we left behind. I couldn't put my finger on it yet, but I knew it may have been an important decision on my mother's part. I felt like she missed home, especially Evan, but she would never say so.

I'd always figured twins had some special bond, but I could not quite figure out their relationship.

The two of them couldn't be more opposite than night and day. They didn't even have the same physical features like most fraternal twins do. My mom, the redhead, and my uncle, with his sandy blonde hair, had the most differences of any set of twins anyone's ever seen. However, the one thing they had in common, besides their dry senses of humor, was their eyes, which were as green as emeralds.

It had been a day since we'd left Billings for a small town tucked away in the northwestern part of Massachusetts. The town was a dream for outdoor enthusiasts, what with the state parks, the lush forests, and the nearby lakes. The population was about 4,500 people, many of which were descendants of the original settlers; one of those families was my own: the Corwens. The town had once been my home, and it was a place where I felt safe—until we left.

I tried not to think of the past so much, but watching the scenery change as we came into New York, the flashbacks started, along with the headaches. The closer we came to our home, the more the images of faces, places, and even smells, would invade my senses. It was like watching a slideshow with random pictures that made no sense at all.

We arrived at Evan's house that Friday morning, only having driven about two and half days, which I think could be a record for the fastest trip of any of our journeys. Driving over the bridge, the "Welcome to Erving" sign greeted us on the opposite side of the road. My headache was a pounding against my temples like a wrecking ball against a building. I could not wait to get out of the car. I could see Alex eyeing me the whole time. I hated when he did that. Who am I kidding?

A mile after the bridge, we continued our journey down a winding road to the place that would be our new residence. It was nestled in amongst the lush landscape of overgrown and untouched trees.

The house was set back about two miles from the main road, surrounded by forest on either side. I could feel the cool breeze of an early spring. It felt like it had just rained. Damp moisture filled the air. The sun was trying to break through the clouds when we came up the drive that eventually exposed the large, colonial house that stood in front of us like a beacon of hope.

The house had been in the Corwen family since they'd emigrated over from Ireland in the early 1700s, according to Evan. It was an off-colored, shade of white with a porch that wrapped around the entire front side with large columns. I started to drift off, thinking about how many times Alex and I had played on that very porch. I tried to avoid the haunting memories, because they were too painful. *Great, there's that pounding again.* I tried not to press my fingers against my temples as eagle eye watched me. If I could put my bare feet on the lush, green grass, I know I could make the pounding stop. My mom told me the earth under my feet was the only way she could calm me down.

Steps on the front porch spread out like a concrete carpet into the circular drive. We pulled up to the front where Evan was waiting to greet us like a doorman. It had been about a year since we last saw him and Grams; I think it was around Alex's and my birthday—last June, up at the lake house.

My brother Alex and I could almost pass as twins ourselves, especially given the fact we had the same birthday, though we were a year apart. I found that phenomenon a little rare in itself. We both had the same color of hair with one noticeable, yet unique feature in our eyes. They were blue, but each of us had specks of gold in one of them. My speck was in the left eye, and Alex's was in his right. This was hard to notice from a distance, but was always a topic of conversation once someone was able to observe close up—something we learned to deal with over time.

From what I had observed recently, most girls found him appealing, being tall and built like a soccer player; just enough muscle without the bulkiness, with a smile that warrants one in return. However, what I saw was that he was warm, caring, and very protective of our family, especially of me. I didn't see him having any problems making friends in our new place. Then again, he'd never had problems in the social department.

I, on the other hand, found myself to be more along the lines of plain and petite, but I did notice the compliments I received from strangers, which were odd to me. I hated the attention, but took it in stride. I just tried to remove myself from it.

My little sister, Allie, on the other hand, was a Barbie doll at the young age of thirteen. Like Alex, she attracted attention with her cute, fair-skinned, oval face, with freckles dotting her checks. You could tell we were all from the same family, even with our slight differences.

"How was your trip?" Evan asked.

He always wanted to know about our latest adventures, like our constant moving was so interesting. Maybe he was that bored that hearing about our travels would spring him from that boredom.

"It was a long drive, but the scenery was beautiful." I winked, feeling that twinge again. He let out a loud laugh, and started grabbing the boxes from the trunk.

Good, he didn't notice, I thought. I just wanted to settle in and take a nap. I had not been sleeping well since our drive back, and the stupid headaches didn't help either.

I walked over the to the passenger side. *Of course, she's asleep.*

"Mom, we're here. It's time to get up." I nudged her a little. She stirred, stretched, and slowly climbed out of the car.

"We're here already? How long have I been asleep?"

"About three hours. Alex took over in New York."

"Hey, Laurel, I think you need to get more sleep. You look horrible."

And there was Evan's attempt at humor. I shook my head. This was going to be a more- than-interesting living situation.

"Ha, ha. Very funny. Where's Mom? I need to talk to her," my mother said.

"She's out back in the garden," Evan said, motioning to the back of the house.

My mom went out back to see Grams while Alex, Evan, and I finished bringing the rest of the stuff into the house. I had no idea where Allie had disappeared to, but I was definitely not carrying her stuff for her.

"Grey, you have the last door on the right. Alex, your room is the second door, next to Grey's. Allie, your room is the third door on the far left," Evan directed us as Allie appeared out of thin air.

I dropped my boxes in front of the door to my room, the boxes making a loud thud. As I opened the large, oak door, I did a double take. I thought for a second that he'd told me to go to the wrong door. I took a moment to retrace my steps, recounting the doors—yup, it was the right room.

The room was large, with dark, wooden flooring and light, taupe-colored walls. The curtains were some kind of sheer material, off-white and almost translucent, and they barely reached the floor. There were two, large windows on the left side of the room and two, large French doors opposite from where I stood. There was so much light in the room it felt like I was outdoors. *This is definitely my type of room—nature encroaching on all sides,* I thought.

I turned to see a large, dark-oak, mission-style bed facing the double doors with nightstands on either side of it. My only request was going to be a desk and a bookcase that could go on the far left of the room. I needed some place to actually study and a place to keep my rather expansive collection of books. I closed my eyes, slowly gliding my fingers along the top of the desk, feeling every knot in it. I felt a pulse of energy run up my arm like a static shock. Letting my eyes take the lead, I noticed directly across was a small door.

I wonder where it goes. The door, to my surprise, led to a walk-in closet with more space than I could have ever imagined. There were drawers and shelves from floor-to-ceiling, all oak, of course. My family was obsessed with it. I'd never really found it odd or even noticed the obsession until now. I definitely thought this closet should have been Allie's, but I would never say that aloud. She has more clothes and shoes than what you find in a store.

I turned back to the double doors, and opened them. I caught a light breeze that lightly kissed my face and danced through my hair. I stepped out to a small balcony looking out over the backyard, Grams' lush garden, and the newest addition to the house, the deck right below. The view was breathtaking.

The forest seemed to encroach upon the backyard seamlessly, like the darkness of night slowly moving across the last of the day's light. In the distance, I thought I could hear the babbling of a stream, which I am sure, carved its way through the trees. My family always commented on how I could hear the littlest things. I guess they were right, given my odd sense of calm when I was around nature, the things I could feel and hear. Yet that sense felt heightened here. I had never really noticed it until now.

Just beyond the house was Grams' garden; a simple rectangle bordered about waist-high by green-hued hedges. In the middle of the hedges, facing the house, was a small, lattice archway sheltering a white, latched gate. If I looked hard, I could see inside of the garden. Toward the back appeared to be a weathered, cedar bench. *Not oak—go figure.* I laughed to myself.

The hedges seemed to enclose and protect the garden of flowers, herbs, and vegetables. There was a large assortment of flowers, I noticed, scanning left: rose bushes, sunflowers, lilies, and daises. Opposite the flowers were several raised, wooden boxes, which enclosed each individual vegetable and herb. There looked to be lettuce, tomatoes, peppers, and zucchini. *Man, I have good eyesight today,* I thought. It was hard to make out any of the other plants that grew there, however. *I will have to check it out for myself later.*

However, I did notice Mom and Grams seemed to be having a very serious conversation. I could tell by their body language and the muttered utterances from them that I'd heard: "Sorry" and "We will help out any way we can." I quickly glanced down when I heard Evan call out to the garden. Out of the corner of my eye, I could see Grams look in my direction.

Damn! She knew I was listening.

I quickly ducked back into my room. Thanks to my curiosity, I was almost caught eavesdropping. I decided that exploring the rest of the house was a better idea for now. I slowed my breath before making my way to the hall.

I walked down the hall toward the bathroom, which was so conveniently located one-room down from Alex's. He stumbled out with the same look of awe on his face that I'd had.

"Can you believe how big these rooms are, Grey?" he asked me.

"No. I can't, but then again, the house is huge." *I never remember it being so big.* I walked back down the hall toward the sprawling, dark, almost-mahogany-colored staircase—but it was oak, of course. I made a mental note to ask Grams what was up with our family and oak.

We finished bringing in our boxes and started to unpack, when I heard Grams call us down for lunch. We stopped unpacking and made our way down to the kitchen.

"Hey, Grams, what are we having for lunch?"

"I thought some sandwiches would be good and quick, Alex. How does that sound?"

"Good, thanks," I responded. He was already eating. At that moment, I noticed for the first time that my headache was gone. *Weird.*

I did not notice that my mom had gone to take another nap after she'd talked to Grams and Evan. She had been sleeping a lot lately. I put it off to her being a wary traveler, and also a single parent. She'd been on her own since our dad's death five years ago. We knew it was hard for her, but she always put on a brave face. I tried to push those memories to the back of my mind so I could finish my lunch.

School was almost done for the year, so there was no point in enrolling for two months. We would enroll at Parker Manning Academy in the fall. Evan happened to be the Dean of Students at the school, so at least I would know one other person there besides Alex.

As usual, Alex was itching for something to do, so Evan had told him about some tryouts at the school this weekend. Of course, on Saturday, he was going to the school to check out the lacrosse team. I would be focusing on more important things, like walking around town trying to find a bookstore so I could further stock my library. I also wanted to find a new journal. Without one, I could not keep my thoughts straight. I also liked to catalog the plants that were around; one of my many oddities, as my brother put it. Allie, on the other hand, found it hard to wait until she could go shopping—what a surprise.

We made our plans around Alex that weekend, as usual, and we drove to the school to drop him off. He was collecting his gear from the car when Mom rolled down the window before he could leave.

"Hey, I'll pick you up at three o'clock." He nodded in acknowledgment. She couldn't help but smile. Turning her attention back to us, I figured it would be the same MO, her and Allie shopping as I tag along bored out of my mind.

"So let's hit the town, girls. Grey, we'll park and you can find the bookstore, while I take Allie shopping. Okay?"

"Okay. I'll meet you outside by the car in about two hours."

"Okay. See you later."

Yup, the exact same. It was always the same. They shopped, while I broadened my mind.

I walked to the small bookstore on the corner. It wasn't hard to find because it was the only one in town. A tiny, brass bell above the door chimed when I opened it. *How quaint.* A middle-aged man—the owner, I figured—greeted me as he looked down through his small glasses. He proceeded to inform me that he could order any book I wanted if he didn't have it in the store. It was a well-known fact in this town that my family had an expansive book collection, so I guess my selection of books were no surprise to him.

I was definitely appreciative of the information, because I was sure that they wouldn't have everything on my list. I nodded thanks, and went about in search of some reading material. Luckily for me, they had most of what I was looking for. I only had to order two books, much to my surprise.

I started to walk down the steps when I felt a shiver run down my back. I looked around at the trees, yet saw no movement from the leaves. It wasn't that cold out, so my reaction was strange, but I shook it off as a cool breeze. *Okay, first the headaches, and now the chills. I hope I am not getting sick.*

I made it back to the car before my mom and Allie, yet again. I decided to sit on the hood of the car and look through my selections while I waited for the wary shoppers to return.

After twenty minutes of waiting, they emerged from their quest with more bags than I thought two people could carry. I saw my mom roll her eyes when she saw me sitting on the hood.

"Grey, how many times have I told you not to sit on the car?"

I didn't answer, considering her question was more rhetorical in nature. I cracked a smile as I hopped down, and jumped in the backseat. I hoped Alex could fit his gear in the car after the lack of space from one afternoon of shopping. I could only image what it would have been like had they had a weekend.

I quickly glanced up when we turned the corner. He was waiting by the fence with two other guys, of course, when we arrived.

It was so like Alex, making friends already. I felt the car come to a stop. My window was down, so I heard them walking over, but I still had my nose stuck in the book. I didn't notice them once they were standing by my door.

"Do you plan on living in the real world today, Grey?" Alex said, trying to coax me away.

"I'm sorry. Did you say something?" I closed the book and looked up at his friends.

"This is Gavin," he said as he pointed to a rather appealing guy with chestnut hair and amazing, hazel eyes—not that I was really paying attention.

I could see the color in Gavin's cheeks as I gawked at the bulges that burst from his shirt. The shirt could have been too small, or maybe he was just fit. I was still undecided. I was finally ripped away from my book when Alex introduced his other friend, Tyler, who was the complete opposite of Gavin, like a before-and-after picture. He was smaller in terms of muscle, and not what I'd call athletic, by any means, but his crazy, spiked, black hair definitely got my attention. I thought I saw blue in his hair for a second. It was the only other thing I noticed, besides his unrevealing, brown eyes that blended into his dark complexion.

I nodded and went back to reading, somewhat unimpressed with the selection of guys in the town so far. Alex shook his head, said his goodbyes, and tried to fit his stuff in the back.

"Hey, be careful of those bags." I thought Allie would tear his head off if her precious clothes got wrecked. He didn't pay attention, and pushed them to the side to make room.

To say their relationship was different from ours was an understatement. In fact, she lived to bug him and he couldn't get enough of pushing her to the edge—the typical sibling, love-hate relationship you'd find in any family. Theirs wasn't at all like the connection between Alex and me. We were different. We, of course, pushed each other's buttons, but we were also in sync with each other somehow. I couldn't quite put my finger on it.

At our mom's request, Alex forced me to go to the field with him. I took my book, and sat patiently in the passenger's seat.

"Can't you leave your books at home for one day?" he asked.

I ignored his comments and cracked open my book to where I had left off. He drove toward the school, mumbling something about my lack of interest—whatever that meant. We pulled in the lot and he turned his focus to me again.

"Grey, please try to look interested. Not that I want to deal with guys ogling you right now, but please," he begged.

I tried to tune him out. It was as if he knew something I didn't. I hated when he acted more like my father than my brother.

"Grey, you may think you're plain, but some of the guys have already been asking about you."

Okay, that got my attention. I also knew this made him uncomfortable, but I didn't care. I continued reading.

"I can't believe I'm saying this, but you are attractive to . . . some. I just want you to try and be social for me, please." He flashed his award-winning smile. I looked up and I couldn't help but laugh.

"Fine, but I can't promise you anything. I'm still bringing my book."

He shook his head while I closed the door to accompany him to the field. *I guess I won that round.* I saw a couple of people sitting there, probably watching family members. I didn't need to deal with everyone today. I let out a sigh before ascending the bleachers. I sat away from everyone, hoping they would keep to themselves. I may have been outgoing with my family and the few friends I had made in Billings, but when it came to meeting new people, I needed Alex more than I thought. My lack of social skills were all due to shyness, and, as Alex put it, because of an interest in my studies more than my own social life. Plus, I never had time for a social life due to our migratory habits—or that's how I justified it to everyone, including myself.

I opened the book and moved the green, satin bookmark to the side. As I began to read the first sentence, I heard someone yell my name. *Great, these must be the friends Alex was talking about.*

"Hey, guys. How's it going?"

I tried to be quick and general with a little wave to Gavin and Tyler. I didn't need or have time for anything right now. Before I retreated into the pages, I noticed Alex talking to someone and pointing to me. *Great, another guy I hadn't met yet, but who I'm sure I would eventually.*

Alex's friends usually became my friends; whether it was because they actually enjoyed my company or not was yet to be determined.

"Hi, do you mind if we sit with you?"

I turned to see two girls coming toward me. I closed my book and waited for the torture to begin. *Just be nice, smile, and try not to say too much.*

"Hi, I'm Quinn and this is Paige. You must be Grey, right?"

Great. They know me, but I don't know them yet. I tried to relax.

"Yes, I'm Alex's sister," I answered, the same as I always did.

Most people knew me as "the sister," so that's what I'd gotten used to referring to myself as.

"Do you know any of these guys here?" I asked.

At least I attempted my hand at conversation.

"Yeah, my brother, Tyler," she said, pointing. "You know him already it seems."

Of course she was his sister; they looked so much alike apart from the fact that her hair was longer and less spiky. I turned and waited for the next introduction, who I guessed would probably be Gavin's sister.

"I'm Paige, and that's my brother Declan."

She pointed to the guy I'd seen Alex talking to earlier.

I was way off. Usually I was good at pegging people, but evidently not today. And now my headache was back. *Great.*

That was pretty much the extent of my involvement in the conversation. I opened my book and briefly interjected when I was asked a question directly. I was relieved when I saw Alex walking to the end of the field.

"Grey, are you ready go?" He stopped and smiled. "Hi, ladies. Grey, are you going to introduce me?"

"This is Quinn and Paige." I pointed to each of them as I spoke, rolling my eyes at his attempt to be charming. He was your typical corny, television-type jock, and that's the level of his charm.

"Hi, I'm Alex. It's nice to meet you." He flashed his smile again. He was so predictable and pathetic sometimes. Of course, they bought his charm. They always do.

I said my goodbyes and pushed Alex toward the lot. I figured I wasn't going to meet his other friends until later. He started the car, rambling on about the girls as we headed home for dinner. I guess chapter three was going to have to wait until later.

The next few weeks flew by at a record pace. Before I knew it, it was already June. We were getting ready to head up to the lake house in Chocorua for the week, and I couldn't wait.

I enjoyed the outdoors and the quiet because I could focus on my reading, photography, kayaking, and nothing else. I was always at peace when surrounded by nature. The fresh air and open landscape called to me, and I felt like I was home.

I'd had good luck this time around because Alex had invited one of his new friends, Gavin Harrington, but fortunately Gavin had already had plans with his family. It was a good thing. I tended to not pay attention to anyone, because I was in my own world when it came to my vacation—and my headache was hitting a ten on my annoyance scale.

The only other thing I had noticed over the last couple of weeks was that my mom was getting worse. She was always tired; her face pained and shallow as if she hadn't slept, even though that's all she did. She was sick and we knew it, even though she wouldn't tell us.

I must've stayed up until morning, looking at the stars and the full moon that reflected on the lake below, because the sun started to rise. I started to fall asleep. *Man, my sleeping patterns are always off up here.*

"Hey, sleepyhead, get up and get downstairs. Mom wants to talk to us!" Alex shouted through the door.

I rolled out of bed and looked at the clock. *Ugh.* I sighed when I saw it was eight o'clock in the morning; I'd slept a total of two hours.

I walked into the kitchen like a zombie, grabbing my tea and bracing myself for whatever she wanted to discuss with us. I hoped it had nothing to do with me meeting people or Gavin's interest in me. Who would have missed it? His interest was so obvious. I looked at her and waited for the talking to start, but this seemed more serious than I'd first thought. She started slowly.

"I just wanted to let you guys know what is going on with me lately," she said. "I'm sick, and I don't know when I'll get better. They found a tumor on the back side of my brain that requires surgery in order for it to be removed. I have declined." She put her hand up to stop my protest so she could finish. "I've had it for quite some time, and that's why I've been getting so tired lately. It's getting worse."

"Mom, why didn't you tell us sooner?" I asked.

"It's not something you can say casually within a conversation, Grey."

"How long?" Alex interjected.

I looked right at him. *How could he be so calm?*

"They don't know. It could be today. It could be a month from now, or even a year. Everything is in order if something does happen."

Great, so we sit here and let it happen. I don't think so. Man, I wished I'd said that aloud. I needed to know the truth, so I demanded it from her.

"So, is this why we came back to Erving?" My headache cranked up to fifteen, and it felt like someone was jackhammering into my skull.

"Yes, that's one of the reasons."

I could see she wanted to explain more, but I didn't let her continue. I was so upset that she'd waited this long to tell us that I couldn't stay any longer. I ran up the stairs to my room. I kept thinking to myself, *How could she do this to us?* The pain increased with every question I asked myself. *How could she keep this from me? We were always so close. We could tell each other everything. Why couldn't she tell me this?* I felt my eyes starting to deceive me as a lone tear trickled down my cheek.

I walked into my room. I changed into my sweater, a pair of jeans, and my hiking boots. I headed out with my journal in hand. *Maybe writing will ease this damn pain.*

Of course, Alex caught me on the way out the door.

"Grey, where are you going?"

I didn't want to answer, but I did.

"I need to go for a walk."

I slammed the door behind me, and headed up the trail toward the other side of the lake.

I walked down the trail along the opposite side of the lake. I found a large grouping of rocks, and proceeded to climb up to sit down to collect my thoughts.

I don't remember how long I was there, but it must've been a while, because the sun was beginning to set over the trees behind the house. The reds and oranges looked like fire cast against the horizon. I looked down at the journal in my hand, and saw that I had only written one word: *Why?*

I guess my thoughts were elsewhere. The need to write them down was too much; the chaos of my thoughts was too much to bear. As I sat there, replaying the whole scene from this morning in my head, I had a strange feeling that someone was watching me. I turned and looked around me. I thought I must be going crazy, because no one was there. I figured it was time to go back, or else I would have to deal with Alex hovering over me for the rest of the week.

I started walking, and as I did, thoughts kept flooding back. None of them made sense. I heard someone coming and I looked up to see Alex halfway down the drive.

"Are you all right?" he asked.

"Yeah," I stated curtly as I continued to the front steps.

My headache started to lessen as he touched my arm. The tiniest shocks tingled their way up my arm toward the back of my neck.

"I hope you can snap out of this, because we—what I mean, is *I*—need you to support me, too."

"Alex, you know you can count on me. We'll get through this like we did when Dad passed. You helped me through a lot back then."

He hugged me, and whispered, "Thanks. It's going to be okay."

At that point, all the pain was mysteriously gone, but it was only for the moment.

Alex was behind me as I walked to the front door. I noticed from the corner of my eye that he nodded his head toward Evan as if to say it was okay.

Mom and Grams were in the kitchen preparing dinner like their conversation this morning was nonexistent. I wasn't ready to deal with them yet, so I decided to help Allie set the table. I was the last person anyone would want cooking dinner.

When everything was ready, we sat down to eat, and for the first time in a while there was no conversation at the kitchen table. I kept thinking to myself how awkward Alex and Allie must feel, but they weren't the only one I was thinking of; it was weird for me, too. Mom was the first to break the silence.

"Everything is going to be okay, Grey."

I couldn't think of anything to say, so I uttered the first words that came to mind.

"I know."

We finished dinner, and I helped Allie clear the table. Once all the dishes were clean, I decided to go out on the deck to collect my thoughts again. Evan was out in the yard with Alex, trying to start a fire in the pit. I sat in the chair next to him.

"So are you ready to get back to reality?" Alex asked, never looking up from his task.

"Yeah, it will be good to get back."

We talked well into the night. I eventually awoke to the sound of pounding rain. I must have fallen asleep outside, yet again, because I'd ended up inside on the couch. Mom decided to cut the trip short due to the weather, but I figured the reason was something else altogether. I sat up, noticing everyone was up scrambling to get things packed. I didn't worry—I'd never unpacked my stuff. I found it made it easier when we up and moved somewhere new.

CHAPTER TWO

CELEBRATIONS

The next week went by like a blur. We'd had five, straight days of rain, so it was good to see the sun that morning. I decided to get up, rolling myself off my bed, and saw someone had slid a note under my door. I picked it up, recognizing Alex's chicken scratch. His little notes always cheered me up, especially today. My sixteenth birthday had come without any fanfare, which is what I'd asked for: no fuss, the family dinner to celebrate my day—or should I say, *our* day—was all I'd wanted.

Alex was turning seventeen that day. He was hoping for only one thing: a car, or *the* car, which was a black Jeep Wrangler Rubicon that he'd dreamed of owning ever since he was five. He had been placing pictures and advertisements around our house—anywhere Mom would see them.

When I was dressed, I headed down for breakfast.

"Happy birthday, sis!" I heard Allie yell from her room as I walked down the stairs.

"Thanks, Allie!" I yelled back as I hopped down the stairs.

Mom was in the kitchen getting breakfast ready. She looked better.

"So what's on the agenda for today, sweetie?" she asked.

"Well, we need to go to the store for tonight's dinner." I smiled, and confessed, "And I still need to get Alex's gift."

Mom and I had begun to reconcile after the bomb she'd dropped at the lake had happened. I was still a little unnerved, but I tried to understand why she'd kept it from us.

"Let me get dressed, and we'll head out after I finish breakfast."

"Fine. I'll give you about ten minutes, and then I'll meet you out front."

I grabbed my muffin and headed toward the hall, when I saw Alex coming down the stairs. The one thing I knew about him was that he found it hard to look at me whenever he was trying to tell me something he knew would upset me. And that moment wasn't any different from the other times.

"Spill it, Alex," I said.

"Don't be mad at me."

That's how all his sentences to me had started since we'd moved back.

"But I invited a couple of my friends over for the barbecue."

That was not as bad as I'd thought it was going to be.

"Okay."

I didn't care if his friends came or not. Evan had come out of his office at the tail end of the conversation. They both stood there in shock. I couldn't understand why. *Am I really that much of a stickler?* I saw Evan smirk, and I wondered if I'd said that aloud.

That day started out as a good day. I did not care if a few more people joined us. At least I knew two of his friends. Gavin and Tyler were becoming permanent fixtures in our home. They were like long-lost friends from another life. According to Alex, they were also here to see me, but I still didn't believe him. It was funny. I figured it was as much Mom's idea as it was his to invite them. I had kept to myself since we'd moved back. They thought I needed to get out more and meet new people, but I found it hard to make friends because we moved so much. Why form attachments if I had to break them?

We got back from town with little time to spare. She brought the food into the kitchen while I hunted Alex down to give him his gift. It wasn't much. He had been dropping hints that he needed some new gloves and a new stick for the upcoming lacrosse season. It was the least I could do to help him out, especially looking back at all he had done for me. I searched for him everywhere, but gave up looking. I put the stuff in his room with a note.

I headed down the stairs, wondering who was coming that night, when I heard the doorbell. I walked over and opened the door to see that more than his two friends had shown up.

They had planned to introduce me to some people so I wouldn't be cooped up with my books all day. *Interesting. Am I that pathetic that I need help meeting people?*

Tyler and his sister, Quinn, showed up first, and, as arranged, Quinn brought her friend, Emery. Tyler was always over at the house with Gavin. Quinn, I briefly remembered from tryouts because she was very talkative. Her mouth hadn't stopped moving from the moment she'd walked into the house. Her friend, Emery, I had not met. She seemed to attract Alex and Tyler's attention with her piercing, blue-grey eyes and unnatural-looking, auburn hair—unnatural in that it was a striking contrast to her pale skin.

I'm sure most people noticed that first, but she seemed to shy away from attention like me. I am sure she would become more comfortable as the night went on. I was trying to reassure myself. I figured I'd disguise my lack of self-confidence with concern for someone else. It work in the past—easy deflection.

Gavin showed up about ten minutes later.

"Hey, Grey! Happy birthday!"

He walked through the door and gave me a big hug and quick peck on the cheek. It felt a little weird, but I managed to get out a thanks as I tried to wiggle free. He took my hand under his arm, escorting me out to the deck. He looked around at everyone, before turning his attention to me when I took my hand back.

"So, I see you've met the rest of the crew—all except one."

"Yeah, they seem very nice." I smiled, and then I caught what he had just said. "Except one? More people are coming?"

"Yeah, Declan and his sister, Paige, are coming."

He was calm, like he thought he would have me all to himself. I waved to Alex, who I'm sure had other plans for me that night, judging from his expression.

"You should know the Watt family. They're your neighbors, after all. They live about five houses down the road."

"I've met Paige once, but I've never met her brother."

I shrugged and shook my head. *How did I not know any of Alex's other friends, especially seeing that they lived closer than Tyler or Gavin? I would have to ask him that one later.* I didn't even notice Gavin was still talking to me. I'm surprised he hadn't noticed I wasn't interested.

"Oh, they probably just got back today. They do a lot of traveling with their family during the semester breaks and the summer."

Well, that at least explains why I hadn't met him and why Alex had never mentioned his name. All I could get passed my lips was, "Oh."

The sun hadn't set yet, but the bugs were starting to descend on the human buffet. Evan lit the torches while Allie and I finished setting the table. I was in the kitchen getting silverware when the doorbell beckoned.

"I'll get it," I said, running to the front door.

I opened it, dropping whatever was in my hand. I didn't hear the clanging on the floor as I noticed his outstretched hand grasping a fork.

"Hi." he said, smiling as he swept his dark, smooth hair back from his face. "I'm Declan Watt, and this is my sister, Paige. Alex invited us."

I looked up, taking back the fork. I had already met Paige, but her brother was what had caught me off guard, with his piercing, gray-blue eyes, and his accent—so swoon-worthy. I felt as if I'd been transported into one of Jane Austen's novels. His accent was that sexy. His eyes reminded me of cloud-swept skies on a sunny day. I must have been lost for what felt like minutes, but was only seconds. Alex came up behind me.

"Hey, Declan. Grey, let them in."

Alex gave me a weird look. I snapped out of my trance long enough to move out of the way so they could come in.

"Come on in. Everyone is out back."

They followed Alex down the hall out to the deck. I closed the door and stood there for a few minutes to collect my thoughts. Beautiful was hardly the right word to use when describing the both of them; they looked like J. Crew models. Declan's eyes weren't the only thing that caught my attention, though his body was something to look at as well. His clothes hugged him in all the right places, helping to define his muscular form. I shook my head and told myself to snap out of it.

Paige looked like a carbon copy of him with longer hair. This made sense, as I remembered Gavin and Alex telling me that Declan and Paige were twins. I was so lost in my own world that I didn't even hear Mom come up behind me.

"Grey, are you okay?" she asked.

"What? Oh, yeah. I'm fine."

I was still thinking about him. It was hard to concentrate on anything else—like walking out to the deck for our dinner. *Snap out of it*, I said to myself again. Mom laughed and dragged me outside, shaking her head.

Dinner was finally ready and everyone seemed to be involved in their own conversations. Evan was putting the food on the table when Alex got up and held my chair out for me. It was a little weird, but I figured he was showing off for the girls. We sat in the middle of the table with Evan and Mom on either side of us. The guests of honor always sat in the middle of the table at all of our family functions.

I tried to listen to what Alex was saying, but I kept thinking of Declan. Every so often I would sneak a glance toward the end of the table. I had never been this fascinated with anyone before, especially one of Alex's friends. I guess I should retract my previous statement from before—there were definitely some guys worth it in this town.

As dinner progressed, Alex gave me the rundown on his friends. I felt like an undercover agent receiving intelligence on my targets.

"So, Tyler and Quinn Ellis live three streets down from us," he said, pointing to them as he spoke. "Their family owns the local café in the center of town. Emery Connors, the quiet one, she lives over by the school. You know her dad. He owns the bookstore in town."

I felt like I should be taking notes. I nodded as if to tell him I was listening, even though I only wanted to hear about one person. I hoped I could remember all their names. If not later, at least by tomorrow, because only one person's name would be in my head the entire night.

"Declan and Paige Watt, they live down the street from us."

As soon as I heard Declan's name, I perked up and interrupted Alex's briefing.

"Yeah, Gavin told me earlier."

Alex shook his head at my obvious obsession and continued with his boring information.

"Their parents are from here originally, but moved to Ireland about a year after they were born because their mother was transferred, or something like that. They moved back here about seven years ago when their grandparents passed away, because their family inherited the house. They did vacation here during the summer, and sometimes around the holidays."

He stopped to take a drink of water, which gave me time to process everything before he started again.

"I'm not sure what their parents do. I didn't get that far yet."

He abruptly stopped when Evan tapped him on his shoulder. I heard someone clear their throat and looked to my right to see Evan getting up.

"So, I would like to say thanks to all of you for coming to celebrate with us."

Evan turned and winked at me, and all I could do was laugh. No one else could figure out our little, inside joke except Alex, who turned to me and smiled. When I turned back to Evan, I noticed Declan smiling in my general direction. I figured he was smiling at Emery who was sitting across from me, and I thought nothing of it, but I smiled back anyway. He quickly looked away, and I found that strange. Maybe my first instinct was correct.

"First, I want to thank my sister, Laurel, for coming back home. Secondly, I want to say that I'm glad that Alex, Grey, and Allie came as well." He laughed and stepped behind Alex and me. "Lastly, I would like to tell the two of you that your present from me, Grams, and your mom will be here tomorrow. I hope you like it, but remember you have to *share* it," he emphasized as he stared at Alex. "Happy birthday, Grey and Alex."

I got up to hug him and whispered thanks. I heard multiple happy-birthday wishes shouted amongst the people table as I sat back down.

Grams came out with the cake she had been working on all day. It looked delicious. It was our favorite: four layers of sin wrapped with shortcake, strawberries, and whipped cream, crowned with whole strawberries. Alex was already grabbing a strawberry off the top before she'd even set it on the table.

"Make a wish, you two," she urged.

We blew out the candles and laughed. The cake was amazing. I didn't think there would be any left for tomorrow, but I could only hope.

"Thanks, Grams. This is great."

"You're welcome, dear."

As we cleared the table, I noticed my mom had decided to turn in early. She had been sleeping most of the time, yet was still tired all the time. The sky began to darken and the stars started to appear, as if someone was flicking on a switch. It was definitely turning into a nice night for some star gazing. Too bad we had left our dad's telescope at the lake.

Even though it was June, once the sun set, it got just a tad cooler. Alex grabbed some wood from the large pile he had stacked earlier, and started a fire. It looked like he was planning on a long night with his friends. I glanced over and noticed Allie wavering in the chair: a perfect excuse to make my get away.

"Allie, I think it is time for you to head up to bed. You're falling asleep," I said softly so she wouldn't get embarrassed.

"No. I'm okay." She yawned and then gave me a look. "All right, I'll go. Happy birthday, sis."

She started inside, and I followed her.

"By the way, here's your gift."

She handed me a small box from the hall closet.

My sister always knew that I loved her drawings; I hoped that this was one of them. I opened the box and saw that inside was a frame that held one of her drawings. It was my favorite, too. The picture was a pencil sketch of the forest with a small stream winding through it—the exact stream from out back.

"This is great, Allie. Thanks."

I gave her a hug and went upstairs to put it up on my wall.

"You're welcome." She yawned again. "See you tomorrow."

I went back downstairs to get some tea before going to bed. I didn't want to bother Alex and his friends. Besides, I was tired anyway. I was staring off into space, waiting for the kettle, when I heard someone say something from the doorway. I turned around to see Declan standing there. I managed to get out a sentence before I freaked out.

"Hi, would you like something to drink?" I asked him.

That was a stupid thing to say. What was wrong with me?

"Thank you. I'm good. I came in to say happy birthday."

He smiled as we stood there in awkward silence for a moment before he spoke again.

"I didn't know you and Alex had the same birthday. Are you two twins?"

His voice was so deep yet soothing that I could not help but want him to talk to me all night. But I needed to be more realistic. He was one of Alex's friends, and in my mind, I felt he was out of my league.

"Thank you, Declan." I blushed. "And no, we're a year apart. Most people often make that assumption."

He turned toward the door as if someone had called his name.

"I have to go," he said. "Again, happy birthday, Grey."

Wow. That was the only thing that kept running through my head. The way he'd said my name . . . my heart had skipped a beat. I shook my head. *Snap out of it.*

His voice was what drew me in. He sounded so worldly, though I couldn't quite place his accent. It was either Irish or British, but they both sounded similar to me. I'd have to ask Alex the next day, but then I remembered him telling me that Declan had lived in Ireland. I hadn't been paying close attention to what he was saying unless it had involved Declan. Even then, my thoughts were elsewhere. At least I did not have one of my famous headaches.

I got my tea and headed upstairs. I closed the door behind me and walked out onto my small balcony. I managed to find a comfortable chair. I sat there looking up at the stars before deciding to go back and grab my book. It was hard to concentrate on Dickens while I sat in the chair listening to the conversations below me.

I changed direction, immersing myself in reading. I could not believe how much I'd actually finished when I looked at the clock on my nightstand. It sounded like the chatter was lower, somewhat non-existent, so much so that I thought they had all left.

I must have fallen asleep, because I felt the warmth of the sun kissing my face. It was definitely morning. I rubbed the sleep from my eyes and stretched, glancing down to see my book had fallen to the ground. In one swift motion, I picked it up and entered my room. I threw the book on my bed as I closed the balcony door. I heard a soft knocking. I figured it was Alex; he was the only one that would be brave enough to bother me so early in the morning.

"Can I come in?" Alex asked.

"Sure. What's up?"

I walked over and sat on my bed.

"How was your night?" he asked

"It was good, especially being able to share it with Grams and Evan."

Alex laughed. I knew he was asking about his friends, but I waited for him to bring it up.

"Oh, I was asking about the rest of the company."

"Your friends are nice, Alex. I hope you had a good time, too."

"Yeah, I did, but I only ask because you went to bed early. Some people were asking about you."

I rolled my eyes. It was way too early for this.

"I was tired. I thought you'd like to spend time with them."

I do not want to know anything else—like who or why.

"Okay." He got up and opened the door. "You're included in that group, too, you know. Don't forget that," he said, the sound of his voice getting fainter as he walked farther into the hallway.

"Oh, yeah!" he yelled. "Mom and Evan want you downstairs in fifteen minutes."

"Thanks, Alex. I'll be right there."

He was more concerned with me having a good time that

he sometimes forgot about himself. That was why I was there to remind him.

I saw my mom running in from the driveway.

"Hey, honey, are you and Alex ready for your gift?" she asked.

"Sure."

I turned to call for Alex, but he was already behind me, giddy with excitement like a kid in a candy store.

As we walked out the front door, my mouth dropped open. I turned toward Alex, who was also speechless. I could have sworn I saw a tear in his eye. Parked in the driveway was a dark silver, almost charcoal-colored, Jeep Wrangler. It was used, of course, but we didn't care. Alex and I had always dreamed of the same car, so for us to share—this was just icing on the cake.

"Thanks, Mom. Thanks, Evan."

I could barely get the words out. Then I heard Alex running toward the driver's side, screaming like a little girl.

"This is awesome!" he yelled.

"Alex, you can take it to practice today. I'm staying home."

"You're the best!" he said, his eyes wide with excitement. "Gavin and Declan are going to freak out when they see this."

I couldn't help but catch my breath a little when I heard his name. What was wrong with me lately? He was one of Alex's friends and he was a normal guy like anyone else.

"You've got to snap out of it," I kept whispering to myself. I turned and walked back into the house, laughing when I saw Evan and Alex jumping with joy.

Later that day, the mail finally arrived and there was a package for me: A long white box with a simple, silver ribbon wrapped around it. I opened the box. Inside, a single white rose with a note attached, written in beautiful handwriting.

Happy birthday, Grey.

It was strange, because the note wasn't signed. I took the box up to my room and found another small box on my bed. I saw the tag and knew that it was from Alex. I opened it to find a small, silver necklace with a triskele pendent attached. The triskele is a triple spiral representing the triple goddess, and an important symbol in my family. It was beautiful: he always knew exactly what to get me. At least I would get more use out of this gift. Alex would be using the Jeep more than me, but that was okay, because I liked to walk anyway. I also liked to see him happy.

CHAPTER THREE

INDEPENDENCE

The summer was just beginning and Fourth of July was around the corner. We were planning on heading back up to Chocorua. The one thing that didn't change was that my mom was still getting worse.

I'd been doing some research online and found that many people could live with brain tumors. Her operation could work, but she'd decided against it due to the risks that could come from that type of surgery. The biggest risk and my biggest fear was the fact that the tumor would continue to grow and put pressure on the arteries in her brain, which would cause an aneurysm. It could burst and cause death. I knew I had to prepare myself for the worst, because she refused the surgery. She was definitely getting worse as time went on.

We left that afternoon and made it up to the lake by nightfall. The next day was the Fourth of July and we were planning to see the fireworks in town. I went to bed without unpacking, as usual, but found that I couldn't sleep very well. My mind was definitely playing tricks on me. The sun was rising. I don't remember falling asleep.

I dragged myself downstairs for what I thought was breakfast, but turned out to be lunch. My sleep patterns and knowledge of basic time was way off. I noticed Mom sleeping on the couch again. She seemed to be doing it all the time now.

The rest of the day flew by—that's what happens when you are reading a good book. Before I knew it, it was time for dinner. It was nothing big because we had to get on the road if we were going to see any fireworks that night. That was when Mom decided to drop yet another bomb.

"Guys, I know you've noticed that I'm getting worse. The doctors are no longer optimistic, because the tumor is growing faster than they first thought."

The pain and agony in her eyes made it worse. I could feel my anger and frustration growing, and consuming all my thoughts. The next thing I knew my glass shattered. Everyone jumped and Alex ran to the kitchen to grab a towel to clean up the mess. I looked up to apologize. That's when I noticed three pairs of eyes staring at me: my mom's, Evan's and Grams'.

"What?" I was a little confused.

"Did you break that glass?" Evan asked in a calm manner.

"No."

"What were you doing just now?" Evan grilled me.

"I wasn't doing anything."

I looked at my mom, wondering why I was being questioned like a suspect.

"Honey, what were you thinking about right before the glass broke?" she asked, rephrasing Evan's question.

"I don't know. I'm angry and frustrated that I can't help you. I wanted to break something. Why?"

It seemed as if Evan wanted to say something, but he didn't. Grams walked over and sat down next to me.

"Grey, has this happened before?"

I had to think for a while, but I couldn't think of anything. All I remembered was the last time we were here. I was walking the trails, I noticed objects in the path, on the ground, like rocks and leaves, and they seemed to move by themselves. *I have to hold back from laughing, because rocks can't move on their own.* I chalked it up to the wind. If I would have told them that they would have thought I was crazy. *Right now, I'm wondering that myself.*

I blurted out the first thing I could think of: "Sometimes."

They all looked at me with curious eyes, but in the way someone would look at you when they were proud of you. It was weird. *Okay, awkward. Alex has got to back me up here.* That's when I noticed Alex was gone, too.

"We need to go outside and talk."

My mom moved toward the deck, followed by Evan and Grams.

Great I'm in trouble. I've broken things before; they just don't know. Alex is always covering for me. Damn, where is he? And why couldn't we talk inside? Was this something that nobody else could hear? Now I'm paranoid.

I looked around the living room one more time for Alex. I sighed, deciding I should face my punishment, whatever it may be. I followed them, and closed the door behind me. I turned, and before I could sit down, the questions began coming. The first one was from Mom. She was acting as if I was sick or something.

"Sweetie, I don't know where to start."

I started to fidget with my bracelets, taking a deep breath. I sucked it up and turned to face the music.

"Just say it. I can take the punishment."

They all laughed.

"We're not out here to punish you." Grams chuckled.

"Then what?"

I was more curious now. I looked at each one of them, noticing Evan was leaning toward me. *Oh man, this is worse than I thought: an Evan lecture. Just shoot me now.* I saw a slight smirk cross his face as he looked at my mom then back to me.

"Where to begin?" Evan started.

I had a feeling this was going to be a long explanation. *This is isn't good, especially when he starts with "where to begin."*

"Our family has a long history, which you already know—but there's more to it."

He paused. I was hoping he was done. Sadly, he wasn't.

"Our family felt it would be safer if they came to settle here. They were escaping persecution from the church when they fled from England to Ireland in 1601. Our family immigrated in the early 1700s, first to Boston and then to Erving. Let's just say, the family thought outside the box."

I looked at Mom, then Grams. *Is he serious?* He cleared his throat to get my attention.

"When the Corwens arrived here in Erving, we were welcomed by other families like us."

Right, the out-of-the-box thinkers. I'd rather have a punishment right about now.

"Our family is well respected here in our community. We kept our 'skills' a secret for fear of persecution here as well."

Skills? What is he talking about? I know Grams practices alternative medicine. She even has a store.

"Are we in the mob or something? Maybe a family with secret powers." I noticed Mom shift in her chair. Oh, I'd hit a nerve.

"Is there something you want tell me or can I go to my room? Seriously, I enjoyed this walk through family history, but I don't get the point, unless you're going to tell me something." *Now I'm getting a little more paranoid.* I started to play with my bracelets again—nervous habit. I started to stand when Evan motioned me to sit.

"Our family is, well, special. We you—aren't like others in the outside world."

Great, I'm an alien. That explains a lot.

"You're not an alien," Evan stated, trying to stifle a laugh. "Okay, how can I put this? Our family comes from a long line of witches."

My eyes widened and I think I was in shock. Now I knew what they meant when they said a "deer in headlights"; I was the deer at this moment. *Wait a minute. Did he just say witches?*

"What are you saying?" I mumbled. "We are . . . I mean, I am a . . . witch?"

"Yes."

"You guys are pulling my leg, right?" I began to laugh. "Mom?" I looked to her for an explanation.

"No, Grey, it's true," she continued. "We all have special gifts we bring to the family."

Gifts? Was she serious? The first person I thought of was Alex, wondering if he knew anything. If he did, he owed me, because we never kept secrets from each other.

"Does Alex know? Is he in on it, too?"

"This isn't a joke, Grey. And to answer your question, yes," I heard him say from behind me. "You and I have the same gifts. We can affect objects with our thoughts. It's called telekinesis."

I stood up and tried to wrap my head around this nonsense. *Tele-what? I'm dreaming, right.*

"This is crazy. You're saying I'm a . . ." I couldn't even say it "A witch?"

Grams grabbed my hands and smiled.

"Yes, you are, Grey. It's in our blood and it's part of our family heritage."

"Okay, well, at least that explains why I always felt like a freak," I muttered to myself sarcastically.

My mom wanted more answers.

"Grey, do you remember anything else that has happened to you? Anything?"

I tried to think of things that wouldn't make me sound too crazy, but it sounded that way when I spoke them aloud. *Oh, because this conversation wasn't crazy enough. Way to drop the bomb. Tell them something, but stick to the truth,* I coached myself.

"I don't know. I feel at home in nature. I always have. It's as if I feel stronger when I'm here, and sometimes I feel people watching me when no one is there. Also, things that are hurt seem to be fine when I touch them."

Okay, the last one hasn't happened in a while because the first time it happened I freaked. I tried to remember that far back. A vague image came to view: it was when I noticed a bird with a broken wing. When I picked it up, it flew away. It was the weirdest thing I'd ever seen.

"That's different," Evan began. "Your father had the same gift. Communing with nature is an elemental gift, affinity for earth. Your Grams is a healer as well, but the other I've never heard of."

He continued to pace as if he was in deep thought.

Great, I'm a freak among freaks. This is crazy.

"My father was a witch, too?" I asked, needing more information.

"Yes, honey."

My mom rose and began to walk toward me.

"We try to marry within our own community. It's safer that way."

Marriage? Now I'm totally freaked out.

"Whoa, this is too much. I need to go right now."

I turned and headed towards the stairs, up to my room. It was all too overwhelming.

Man, what else could happen tonight? Am I going to find out that I can see ghosts, too? I laughed aloud at my own joke. *Who knows? I might be eating those words later.* I heard a knock at the door and I knew who it was.

"Can I come in?" he asked with a sigh.

"Sure, why not?"

"I know it's a lot to take in, but it gets easier."

I was mad at Alex, because he'd kept this secret from me. I couldn't believe he would have done that.

"Really, you couldn't tell me?"

"No. I had to wait for you to start displaying signs," he said, looking out the window. "They wouldn't let me say anything—rules and all. I'm sorry."

"What do we do now?" I questioned, still in disbelief over what was going on.

He started laughing. I couldn't wait to hear what he thought was so funny. It wasn't as if I had to go to school or anything.

"Well, Evan and Grams will begin your studies."

I couldn't believe it. I did have to go to a school of sorts. I was bummed, and you could hear the sarcastic tone in my voice.

"Great, more studying. This just keeps getting better."

"It gets easier. The lessons are more on the craft of healing. You know, being one with nature and stuff like that. That's the family specialty, of sorts."

Wait, the family specialty? Was he serious?

"Okay."

I don't need to go buy a cauldron or stuff like that. That's a good thing, I thought to myself, then I remembered what they'd said about others.

"How many other families are there and who are they?"

"You know some of them. Most of the families in Erving are witches."

I was in a state of shock that a whole community was hidden from the rest of society.

"Do you mean everyone in town?"

"Pretty much. The town was settled to be a safe haven for families like ours."

I wanted to know if anyone else knew, and I was hoping he would tell me.

"Your friends know?"

"Yeah, and they can talk to you about it if you want." His voice seemed to become more excited.

I sat on my bed still in shock, waiting to see what else was going to happen.

"I'll let you get some sleep, okay?" he said as he walked out the door.

The next few days were so hazy I couldn't even remember the fireworks. We would go home the following day and everyone would know, because Alex couldn't keep his mouth shut. It made me feel like an outcast.

I had to suck it up and fake it for now to get everyone off my back. I walked into the kitchen, cheerful and approving. I sat, drinking my tea quietly, noticing mom wasn't up yet.

"Where's mom? Is she still asleep?"

"She stayed up late last night. She needs to sleep." Evan was washing the dishes from the night before. "Are you okay?"

"Yeah, just give me some time to absorb it all."

"You have at least a year to absorb it all." He smiled and leaned in to whisper in my ear. "Your actual lessons don't start until you're seventeen."

I laughed, thinking it was going to take some time. I hoped a year was long enough.

The day passed quickly. It was about four o'clock when I decided to check in on Mom. I knocked on the door, but no one answered. The door creaked as I silently crept in and walked toward the side of her bed. She was still asleep. I leaned over and nudged her, but she didn't move.

"Mom, wake up. Its four o'clock. You need to eat something. You can't sleep the whole day away."

I nudged her again and she didn't move. *Maybe I didn't push her hard enough.* I pushed her shoulder with more force. She didn't wake up. *Okay, don't panic! Who was I kidding? Maybe I should check for a pulse or something. That's what they do on TV, right? Check for a pulse?* I looked down at my hands to see them shaking. *I can't do this! I need help.* That's when I called Evan.

"She's not moving or waking up."

I wanted to scream, knowing at that point she was gone. I was still in shock, because what I feared the most had happened. Grams called the police and explained what had happened. I was comatose. The police arrived with the coroner, who confirmed she was gone. The coroner told us she'd probably felt no pain, that she'd just drifted off to sleep. Alex stayed in my room, trying to console me. He reached out to pull me into a hug, but I didn't want to be touched. I could barely hear him talking. I only heard him say, "At least she is at peace." It hit me at that moment that she was gone. I felt the tears coming and my knees buckled. Alex gripped my arms and I collapsed into him, screaming.

CHAPTER FOUR

NEW BEGINNINGS

My days turned into weeks, and then a month passed by. It was all a blur. I went through the everyday motions and mostly stayed in my room. There were days I didn't even go outside at all. Alex tried to get me out of the house by planning day trips with his friends. A couple times, even Gavin and Tyler tried to persuade me to leave my room. It was hard enough to see the traditional pyre every community goes through after a death of one of their own. I know she isn't there—I mean, her soul is somewhere—but to see her body wrapped and burned was difficult enough.

Today I decided to take it easy and sit on the deck to catch some rays and listen to music—do nothing. I grabbed my iPod and sketchbook as I headed to the kitchen to get some tea.

I attached the iPod to the stereo and hit play. I sat in the Adirondack chair and started drawing, glancing up periodically noticing Grams meandering around the garden. She waved and I waved back. It was funny how I missed the little, daily nuances that happened around here being cooped up in my room.

It was still early. I had the whole day to do nothing without anyone bothering me. Well, I take that back, because as I heard Alex shuffling into the kitchen.

"I thought I heard music coming from the deck and I figured Grams wasn't listening to Carolina Liar."

"So you found me Alex. What do you want?"

"Good morning to you, too, grumpy."

I continued to sketch, trying to ignore him, when I heard two more people in the hall.

"Hey, Alex, are we going or what? Oh, hey, Grey."

"Hey, Declan," I said sarcastically, looking at Alex the entire time.

"Now you say good morning to him, but not to me. I see how it is."

Alex leaned against the railing.

"You see how what is, Alex? You were the one that came out here bothering me, remember?"

I wasn't backing down from this one.

"Um, I'm going to wait outside," Declan said, starting to turn before Alex stopped him.

"Dec, you don't have to go. I'll be ready in a minute, so wait."

Alex stared me down, but he would not win this fight. I had more practice, in part due to my interactions with Allie lately.

"Um, Grey, you are more than welcome to come and watch us practice. Both Quinn and Paige will be there."

"I don't think that's a good idea, Dec, especially when she's like this."

Alex walked down the hall as Declan followed close behind. I ran around the house and caught him coming out the front door.

"I don't want to go to your stupid practice anyway. I've got more important things to do than watch a bunch of guys running up and down a field after a tiny ball."

"Well, you're not welcome then," he said right in my face, looking down at me. "You're not the only one that is grieving. The rest of us are doing what we can to move on like she would have wanted."

He jumped into the Jeep and waited for Declan to get in.

"Grey, I want to say that I am sorry to hear about your mom. If you need anyone to talk to, you can call me."

He touched my arm before walking away. I felt a sense of ease course through my body.

Man, he is so hot I would watch him any day, I thought as I turned and walked around the house toward the garden. I barely knew him, but he was offering his friendship. I needed to stop thinking about him and snap out of it.

I tried to open the gate, but it seemed to be locked. Grams came over to open it for me.

"Sorry, it sticks sometimes. Have you come to help me in the garden today, Grey?"

"I don't have any plans. If you need help, then I'm here."

I walked into the garden and the gate closed behind me. I guess it had a spring latch or something. I kept following Grams until she stopped.

"So, I was thinking you could pick the squash and cucumbers, which are on the other side, and I'll get the tomatoes and lettuce."

She handed me a basket. I walked over to the opposite side and started with the squash.

"How have you been doing, Grey?" she asked.

"Well, I've been hanging in there. You know, taking it one day at a time. How have you been?"

"It's been hard, but I know I can talk to her anytime I want."

She smiled at me. I don't think I'd ever seen her without a smile on her face. I thought to myself. *I wonder if she smiles while she sleeps.* I laughed. I finished on my side and began helping her with the lettuce.

"What's this?" I asked, pointing to the bed next to the lettuce.

"Those are my herbs. There is coriander, thyme, oregano, basil, mint, chamomile, and rosemary," she told me, pointing at each one as she listed them.

"Oh, do we need any of these herbs?"

"No, I have some in the house, but you might want to become familiar with them now. These plants and herbs are part of your lessons. Come now," she said as she stood up and held out her hand. "We're all set here."

She opened the gate with ease and we walked up to the stairs to put the baskets in the kitchen. I shut off the stereo and remembered Allie's birthday was in a couple weeks. Grams didn't need any of my help with dinner, so I retreated to my room to think of something to get Allie.

Before I knew it, it was Allie's birthday. I knew she would want me to be there, and I couldn't miss my sister's birthday. She was turning thirteen years old.

I went down and tried to enjoy her day, but after an hour, the sadness began to creep in again. Her death hit me the hardest, but I was getting through it—I had to. I had to be there to help Alex through it as well, especially after our fight the week before.

As I walked toward the stairs, there was a knock at the door. I turned to answer it, but Evan beat me to it. *Everyone was here for our party. Who else would be coming?* I thought to myself as I turned back toward the stairs. He closed the door, and handed me a long, white box with that same silver ribbon as before wrapped around it.

"This is for you, Grey."

I went further down the stairs, took the package, and returned to my room. *Who'd be sending me a package?* I thought to myself. *It's not my birthday.* I sat on the end of my bed, and slowly opened the box to see another white rose smiling back at me. There was another note, once again written in that elegant handwriting, but, like the first, it was unsigned.

May this small token bring light and happiness back to your eyes.

I had to know who had sent them. When I called the florist, they didn't know who'd sent it—or they wouldn't tell me. This was getting weird. Someone was sending me these flowers and I didn't know who it was, whether I should be scared or flattered.

"I guess someone has an admirer." Alex chuckled at my door.

"A what? I don't know anyone besides your friends."

I wondered who it could be, because I didn't know anybody. Alex laughed as he walked away. I guess I shouldn't worry too much if Alex wasn't thinking much of it.

School would begin in the next two weeks, and I was trying to look forward to that. It would at least be a distraction, especially from the sorrow that had loomed over me all summer. I felt like Eeyore with his little rain cloud. The only thing that kept me sane was the conversations I was having with my mother while I slept, and my brother while I was awake. Alex and I never stayed mad at each other for long. We were too close, and we needed each other now more than ever.

The next day, I decided to walk into town to try to collect my thoughts. It was a beautiful day. The sun was high in the endless, blue sky with a slight breeze that was just enough to cool the air. I reached the center of town, walking past Grams' shop toward the bookstore. The smell of cinnamon and sugary treats from the café was calling my name, but I wasn't ready to face any one that may have been inside. I was hoping to visit the bookstore often during the summer, but due to Mom's death, and my lack of strength to leave the confines of my house, I couldn't. I remembered I had ordered some books when I'd first moved back, and I knew the store was holding them for me.

"Good afternoon," someone said from the second floor.

I nodded and continued toward the counter where a young

girl was standing with her back to me. When she turned and looked up, I realized it was Emery.

"Hi, Grey! How are you feeling?"

She spoke with kindness. She was definitely someone I wanted to get to know further.

"I'm getting along. I'm here for—"

"Your books."

She smiled as she continued my sentence.

"Yes. Thank you."

"How is your brother doing? Haven't seen him lately."

She seemed eager to know the answer. I figured she had a crush on him, or something like that.

"He's fine. He's been at practice all day during the summer. He's so tired at night, he crashes on the sofa. I'll tell him you asked about him."

She looked at me as if I had said something wrong, but tried to change the subject.

"They're working hard, aren't they? I heard that they might win the championship this year."

I played along.

"That's what he keeps telling me."

Now my brother only boasted about his athletic talent to anyone who would listen, especially because he'd been the best keeper the lacrosse team had ever had—or so he told me. However, I he definitely had a reason to brag. He was quite good, from what I saw when we lived in Billings.

"Well, here are your books."

She broke me from my thoughts.

"If you need anything else, just let me know," she said.

I felt as though there was something else behind what she was saying, and it wasn't books. Emery seemed like a good listener; someone you could talk to about anything. It was something I could tell about her the first time I'd met her.

"You know what? There is something." I grabbed a piece of paper and a pen. "Here's my number. Give me a call. Maybe we could do something, or just hang out."

I handed her the paper and smiled as I turned toward the door.

"Thanks, I will." She smiled like she'd just won the lottery. "I'll give you call."

I started walking down the road toward my house, knowing that I'd made my first friend in this town. My mom would be so proud. I'd never really found time to make friends because we'd moved so much. My family was the closest friends I had—and still have.

I was almost there, when I saw the house—Declan's house. As I walked passed, trying not to bring attention to myself, I noticed people arguing on the front porch. Being as curious as I was, I stopped and made it look like I was tying my shoe. It looked like a serious discussion, because it began to get heated between Declan and his sister. Suddenly, I caught his gaze. I was caught off guard. It was as if I could feel all his emotions hitting me at once with his eyes. I had to get out of there—fast—the feeling was too intense. I turned quickly and ran. *I mean, seriously! That's what any sane person would do, right?* I didn't want to be a snoop or get involved. I was so stupid to stop. It was none of my business. My little infatuation was going to get me in trouble. *And what was with that look he'd given me?*

I ran through the front door and almost knocked Allie down.

"Are you alright?" She seemed concerned. "Why are you breathing so heavy?"

"I'm fine!" I yelled back to her as I ran up to my room.

That was the weirdest thing. Why do I always put myself in these positions? I need to stop thinking crazy and concentrate on calming down.

"Grey!" a familiar voice called through the door.

"Yeah." I knew it was Gavin, and probably Alex as well.

"Can I come in?"

So polite. Now I guessed that Alex was probably in the kitchen. "Sure."

I was wrong. Alex was with him, and they both walked into my room. *This is odd,* I thought to myself. *Gavin has never been in my room; let alone, coming in to talk to me with my brother.*

"What's up, guys?" I tried to compose myself.

"I think you dropped this on your way home." Gavin handed me a book. "Declan found it in the road in front of his house. He flagged us down so we could return it to you."

The book was the complete works of Shakespeare. I laughed to myself.

"Yeah, that's my book. Thanks, guys."

"Why don't you come downstairs and get something to eat?" Alex coaxed. "We can make sandwiches or cook on the grill."

I was hungry. Why not, after running to the house earlier, acting all paranoid? I got up and followed both of them to the kitchen. Gavin tried to reach for my hand when I slid past them into the hall. *Seriously, what is wrong with this guy?*

I was in the mood for burgers, so I took the patties out of the fridge and had Alex go start the grill. I also grabbed some vegetables, then yelled up to Allie to come down and make a salad.

She and I brought everything out to the table, and Alex put all the burgers on a plate. It felt nice to sit outside and joke with him again.

"Thanks."

He winked at me and I laughed.

The days—my days—got better as I tried to pull myself out of the funk. Even Grams tried to help by getting me to work a little around her shop. I also got a call from Emery to join her and Quinn for lunch the next day in town.

"Sure, I'll be there."

I hung up the phone, and saw Alex eavesdropping.

"Going somewhere today, sister?"

"I'm going to lunch with Emery and Quinn." I thought, *Who made him the boss of my world? I definitely need to get out of the house.*

I walked toward town and saw the café where we were to meet. You couldn't miss it. It was the only place serving the best food in town, and the Ellis family owned it. From the outside, the café was small—or at least it looked that way. I had to laugh when I looked up at the name. It was so fitting for the town and its occupants. The lettering on the sign, I think, was Old English, which embodied the name, Wicked Brew, to a tee. I walked in and saw Emery and Quinn sitting in the corner near the front window.

"Hey, Grey." Quinn smiled and waved me over.

"This place is great. It looks small from the outside, but it's huge."

I couldn't believe how big the place was; it's size had been deceiving from the street.

We all laughed, and the conversation flowed like we were all friends—and because Quinn would not shut her mouth—the same way it always happened with Alex and his friends.

"So what do you think of the town so far?" Emery asked.

"It's been a while since I lived here, Emery, but it seems the same, like nothing changed."

"What about the guys? Does anyone catch your eye yet?"

"Not really, Quinn, but I have a feeling you'll be the first to know when I do."

We talked for what seemed like hours. It was starting to get dark outside and I had to walk home.

"Thanks, guys. I had a great time. We need to do this more often." I turned toward the door and bumped into someone. "Oh, I'm sorry."

I kept walking without looking up to see who it was. I waved back to them through the window, and headed up the street. As I turned the corner, I saw Gavin leaving the bookstore. He looked like he was looking for someone. I figured it was me. I ducked back around the cafe. I knew he would see me and offer me a ride, but I needed to think and walking helped. I looked back around the corner and he was in his car, pulling out.

I started walking up the street again, and when I reached the Watt's house, I heard a car pull up beside me. I didn't turn to see who it was, but I heard the car window lowering. Gavin. Maybe he was going to see Alex—or at least I hoped that was what he was doing.

"Hey, Grey, do you want a ride?"

I continued walking as he followed me in the car.

"I'm fine. I'm almost home. Thanks anyway." I felt a drop and realized this was not going to be good. Then it started to rain. "Okay, thanks." I felt a shiver run down my back when I agreed.

I slid into the passenger's side. I had that strange feeling of being watched again. I shivered again as I closed the door.

"So what did you do today?" he asked with grin.

I continued to look out the window.

"Emery invited me to lunch with her and Quinn."

I thought to myself, *Why is this five-minute drive taking so long?* And there it came.

"Do you have plans tomorrow?" he asked me.

I didn't hear him, because I was either too preoccupied or—more likely—I didn't want to hear what he'd asked. He repeated his question.

"What are you doing tomorrow?"

"Nothing. Why do you ask?" I already knew his answer.

"I was wondering if you wanted to do something tomorrow."

There it was. The question hung out there. I needed to recover to give him an answer.

"With who?" I began to rethink this car ride. "You and the rest of the gang?"

"No, just me." He turned and winked.

There was that shiver again. At any other time or place, I would gladly take Gavin up on his offer. He was good looking and very nice—but not today.

"Oh." My words were shorter than my thoughts today.

"Did I surprise you? If you don't want to, that's fine. We can go another time." His smile faded when he'd said the last words.

"No. Yeah, I mean maybe another time, okay?" I tried to be straightforward, but it all came out garbled.

"Okay, another time then."

I stepped out of the car and headed for the front door.

"Thanks for the ride, Gavin."

I ran into the house and passed Alex, who happened to be looking out the window at the exact time I was exiting Gavin's car.

"Was that Gavin who dropped you off?" Alex seemed confused. Then he went into big-brother mode.

"Grey!" he yelled to me as he ran up the stairs, opened my door, and stared at me in shock.

"Did Gavin drive you home tonight?" he asked curtly. "I thought you were with Quinn and Emery today."

"Yeah, I was walking home and he happened to pull up when it started to rain. He offered me a ride home."

The less my brother knew about what had just transpired in the car, the better.

"Anything else?" he asked.

What is his problem? I thought.

"No. Now if you don't mind, if you're done with the inquisition, I need to go to sleep." I closed the door on his shocked face.

I knew this was not going to be the end of the conversation by any means, but I had all night to regain my thoughts and prepare for the interrogation the next morning. It was weird, because Alex had never acted like that before. Then again, I'd never given him cause.

I ran to the phone and called Quinn. I had to talk to someone.

"Hello," she answered.

"Quinn, it's me."

"Hey, Grey. What's going on? Is something wrong?" She was either good at reading people or she'd just heard the strain in my voice.

"I was walking home and Gavin happened to drive by and offer me a ride."

I heard her gasp.

"He asked me out." There it was, out, and I was free of it.

"What? Are kidding me? Gavin?"

I felt a little offended, wondering if she'd meant to say it that way.

"Yeah, and Alex doesn't know. Let's keep it that way for now, okay."

"Wow, but I can't say I didn't see it coming." She laughed. "What did you tell him?"

"I told him that now was not a good time." I'd told him no and that was the truth. "What do mean, you saw it coming?"

"Grey, wake up. When I first met you at the field? And then do you remember your party?"

She knew I remembered.

"Every guy was watching you—especially Gavin—all night. I'm surprised you didn't notice, but I think your thoughts might have been elsewhere. Am I right?"

She was right—that night I'd been thinking about my mom, and trying to calm myself down due to a certain guest.

"No, I didn't notice, really." I was a little shocked. "You guessed right—my thoughts were elsewhere."

"I got to go, but I can meet you tomorrow, if you want."

"Sure. How about breakfast? I'll meet you in town around ten o'clock. I'll have to drop Alex off at practice if I want the car."

"Sounds good to me. See you tomorrow."

Well, at least I could talk to her more, and find out exactly

what she saw that night, because I didn't remember much of what
had happened.

It was the last weekend before school would start. I was dressed,
and I headed downstairs to tell Alex that I would need the car
today. The plan was that I would drop him off at practice, then
come back to pick him up. I walked into the kitchen to find him
slumped over a bowl of cereal.

"What's with him this morning?" Evan laughed. "Did you
scratch the car or something?"

Something was right on target, because when he asked me the
question, Alex looked up and glared in my direction, waiting for
an answer.

"No. I'm taking the car today to hang out with Quinn," I stated.

"That doesn't sound that bad. It's your car, too."

Alex turned to stare at Evan. He looked like he was going to
say something, when the doorbell rang. I—quite literally—was
saved by the bell.

Alex walked back in with Gavin.

What was he doing here? I thought I made myself clear yesterday.
You could cut the tension with a knife. *Why was everyone looking at
me now? I didn't do anything.* Evan tried to change the atmosphere of
the room.

"So, Gavin, what brings you by this morning?"

"Well, we have practice today. I thought I might stop by to see
if Alex wanted a ride."

He glanced in my direction, looking for any sign that I'd told
my brother. I shook my head no, but he didn't really seem too
happy about that.

"Grey was going to give me a ride today, but since you're here,
I might as well go with you."

The tension was still in his voice. Hopefully, it was a quiet ride to practice.

"Well, on that note, I'll be off." I grabbed the keys and headed for the door, but I knew I wasn't alone.

"So you got plans today?"

"Yup, Gavin, I'm hanging out with Quinn all day."

I quickly jumped in the Jeep before he could continue with his questions. I have never driven so fast in my life. I turned onto the main road, heading for town.

Quinn was waiting for me behind the counter. We sat down at the same table as before, the one right near the window. I couldn't hold it in anymore I had to tell her what had happened this morning.

"So, you'll never guess who showed up at my house this morning."

"Gavin, right? He is so predictable."

"Yeah, is he really that predictable?"

"Please, I can set my watch by him. He's that predictable. Be careful, Grey. He can cause problems if you let him in. Trust me. I learned the hard way."

"You went out with Gavin?" I was shocked.

"Only once, and that was enough for me."

"He's not really my type, but thanks for the information and the warning."

"Anytime, Grey." She laughed.

We ordered some food and spent the time talking about random stuff, like school, the lack of stuff to do in town, and every so often my brother would creep into the conversation. I had a fun time, but knew I had to go get Alex soon.

"So I got to go get Alex." I glanced over to see her look out the window. "Do you want to come?"

"Sure. Let me go tell my dad. I'll meet you out front."

She was up and around the counter before she'd finished her

sentence. I should have guessed she might have a thing for Alex, but he would never see it—or he had his eye on someone else. I walked toward my car and waited for her.

As soon as she was in, I was sped down the street towards the school. I was late, as usual. I hoped he wouldn't be too mad. We got to the field, but he wasn't there. I guess he got a ride home with someone else, which was strange because I'd told him I would pick him up that afternoon. That's when I saw someone coming up to the Jeep. I'd never seen him before, but Quinn seemed to know him.

"Hey, Jack, have you seen Alex?" she asked.

"Yeah, he left earlier. Got a ride with someone, I think." He smiled as he turned to me. "Hi, I'm Jack."

"I'm Grey." I smiled. He was actually easy on the eyes. *Where has he been hiding?*

"Well, it was nice to meet you Grey. I'll see you around, Quinn." He started to walk off, but stopped and came back to the car. He handed Quinn something, smiling, before heading toward his car.

She turned to me and smiled. She handed me the paper. I opened it to see: "Lunch?" and a telephone number.

She kept smiling, and I tried to change the subject as I slid it into my pocket.

"Do you want to come over for lunch or something?"

"That's fine, but I need to be back at the cafe by five o'clock for the dinner rush." She cringed.

I pulled into driveway. I didn't recognize the car parked there, but Quinn did, and she wasn't going to tell me either. I parked along the side of the house.

"Alex, are you home?!" I shouted down the hall, hoping to

hear an answer.

"He's out back on the deck, Grey!" Evan called from his office.

I headed to the kitchen first as Quinn followed. I looked at her and laughed when I opened the freezer door.

"When we have an argument, we always try to talk it out with ice cream."

"That's a new one. Maybe I should try that with my parents, or even Tyler." She sat down. "So, you gonna call him?"

"What?" I wasn't really listening.

"Jack. Are you gonna call Jack?"

I shrugged my shoulders.

"Come on, he's a great guy—and cute."

I couldn't help but flash back to his green eyes and cute smile.

"I guess so."

I closed the freezer door and reached for the phone. As I talked, I could see her squirming to know the details. I hung up the phone and smiled at her before grabbing the ice cream and some spoons. I walked out to the deck.

"Alex, I thought we could talk."

"I'm a little busy right now, Grey. Maybe later." He smiled and gave me a hug. "Thanks."

I shrugged and turned to go back to the kitchen with Quinn, when I noticed someone sitting on the other side of Alex. I should have left quicker than I had. Sitting next to Alex, was Declan. I heard quiet laughter coming from Quinn. *She knew it was his car out front. Why didn't she warn me or something?*

"Grey, Quinn, how is your day going?"

He seemed charming and polite. I stood there and smiled. Quinn nudged me, but I didn't move.

"Hi, Declan." She answered for both of us, thank god.

I turned and dragged her into the hall. That's when I noticed the ominous, white box with its little touch of color in the form of a silver ribbon. Quinn noticed it at the same time.

"Evan, did I get any mail today?" I asked, knowing the answer.

"Just the box on the table," he said as he appeared in the doorway, smiling. "You definitely have an admirer, Grey."

Tell me about it.

I felt the color rushing to my cheeks as I opened the box. It was the first time I had opened it in front of someone other than anyone in my family. Quinn was just as excited as I was, and I knew it because she was actually quiet for once. There, inside, was the single white rose and a note.

I see that the sparkle in your eyes has returned. It makes my heart flutter with joy.

"Anonymous."

"Yes, Evan." My smile faded slightly. "But I do hope I can find out who is sending them soon."

My cheeks turned a deeper shade of red, and I pushed Quinn upstairs. I was on the second step, when I felt a shiver and a quick push of pain against my temple, making me dizzy. I quickly grabbed on to Quinn's arm so I did not fall. There was concern on Evan's face because it had happened again, and this time he'd been there to see it.

"Are you all right?" he asked.

I shook my head no.

"It happened earlier today, too. I felt like someone was there watching me."

Evan had a puzzled look on his face as he glanced around the room. It was as if he was looking for someone or something. It was starting to freak me out. I could only imagine what Quinn was thinking.

"What is it, Evan?"

"Nothing. Don't worry about it, okay? It's nothing."

He hugged me and proceeded down the hall, toward the deck. Quinn and I continued up the stairs to my room.

"This room is great." She remarked with excitement. I could

tell she was changing the subject. "Where do these doors go?"

"It leads to a little balcony that overlooks the backyard."

She started for the doors but stopped when she heard whispering coming from the deck below. I'd heard it too, but decided I had enough things to deal with today; getting caught eavesdropping was not on my list. She changed the subject when she noticed the other boxes by my desk.

"Do you get these packages often?"

"This is the third one." I glanced out the window. "They are always anonymous and the florist doesn't know who sent them."

"Wow. I wish I got stuff sent to me like that." She grinned while looking at the other notes. "I agree with your uncle. You definitely have an admirer."

We talked for a couple of hours, mostly about my admirer and my date with Jack. It was getting dark and I knew I had to get her back to the cafe. We ran down the stairs and out the door. I happened to notice that Declan's car was still there. Weird.

I got into town in record time.

"Thanks for hanging out with me today."

"Anytime. I'll see you on Monday at school." She laughed and waved as she headed in.

When I got back to the house, his car was gone. I was relieved in some way, but saddened in another. What was the reaction I'd had toward him? I barely knew him. I went upstairs and sat out on my little balcony.

I must have fallen asleep in the chair again because I woke up feeling the warmth I enjoyed so much. The sun was trying to peek through the trees. I got up to look at the clock on the nightstand; it was six o'clock in the morning.

"Ugh. Why am I awake so early?"

Well, I might as well use this time to go for a run. Running always helped me organize my thoughts as much as walking did. I threw on some pants and a t-shirt, then grabbed my sneakers. Alex seemed to have had the same idea.

"Can I join you?"

I nodded and headed downstairs to put my sneakers on.

While running down the drive, we decided to turn last night's ice cream into breakfast. We ran down to the center and strolled into the café. It was crowded, but Quinn got us a table.

Of course Alex started with the hard question first.

"So what's going on with you and Gavin?"

"What do you mean?" I knew exactly what he meant. "Nothing."

He rolled his eyes.

"Well, in that case is there anything else you want to tell me?"

He knew what had happened the other day with Gavin, but at least he wasn't mad at me anymore. I thought he'd found out about Jack, too. I started with Gavin first. I figured that if I didn't get to Jack, Alex would find out this afternoon.

"He asked me out and I said no. End of story." I got up from the table. "I'll be right back. I have to go." I laughed on my way to the bathroom.

When I returned, someone was sitting with him. I couldn't really see who, but as I got closer my pulse started to race. I knew that hair and those hands. It was him. I mean, I'd seen more of the back and side of his head when he was sitting on the deck with Alex than I'd seen his face. Either way, both sides were equally nice to look at.

I gathered myself together, trying to be as casual as I could, but I didn't notice Quinn coming toward me on my left. I bumped right into her and ended up with juice down my shirt.

"I'm sorry, Quinn." I couldn't apologize enough, but she was laughing, so I began to laugh, too.

"It's fine. Don't worry about it. It was your juice, anyway."

I continued to laugh. It helped me calm my nerves.

"Hey, are you good?"

"Yeah, apparently it was my juice. So it's all good, Alex. Don't worry about it."

I couldn't stop laughing to notice his intensive stare or the beautiful smile that accompanied it.

"Would you guys like a ride home?"

Declan looked to Alex, who was still laughing. It was as if they were having a conversation that I wasn't a part of.

"Yeah, sure. It's a little cold outside, and, with Grey being wet, that sounds like a good idea," he sputtered out between laughs.

I was glad to see that I'd amused my brother so much with my little mishap. We walked toward the car when I noticed Gavin out of the corner of my eye. *What is he doing here?* I thought to myself. Declan noticed him at the same time, and proceeded to help me into the car. He gave me his hand as I slide into the front seat. It was weird, but nice. I quickly glanced out the window to notice the uncomfortable glare between the two of them.

"Are you cold?"

Declan turned the heat on as we pulled out. My pulse was racing faster than the engine and I couldn't pull my thoughts together.

"I'm okay."

I stared out the window, wondering what it was about him. *Why me and why now? Then again, why not me, and why not now?* Now I was confusing myself with double talk. What my draw to him was, I couldn't quite understand. But there was definitely something there. Whether it was reciprocated or not was the question. I had to stop thinking about it. I had to get ready for a date.

Alex leaned through the two seats.

"Thanks again, Dec."

"Anytime Alex."

It sounded like he'd meant it not only for Alex, but for me as well. It was as if they were speaking some unknown guy code.

I shook my head, trying to regain my thoughts, and got out of the car.

"Thank you."

I closed the door and went inside. I walked into the closet to change my shirt. I plopped myself in the chair and gazed into space, my usual nightly routine. But then I remembered Jack. At first, I didn't notice they were both below until he spoke. How you could not notice him was beyond me. His voice would probably melt the coldest of days.

Stop, Grey. Stop. You need to control yourself. At least that was what I was trying to say to myself.

They were sitting around the fire when he asked Alex if I was okay or not. Alex didn't answer, so I figured he was too busy with the fire to hear him.

"Did I say something to upset her?" He questioned him again.

"No, man. She's going through a lot of stuff right now. It's not you." He chuckled a little, and I held my breath, hoping he would keep his mouth shut. "I think she likes you, so don't think otherwise, okay?"

Damn it! He said it! Why would he say something like that? Stupid guy, that's why. He never thinks before he speaks. I'd thought he was going to throw out the "It's-not-you-it's-her" speech, but he couldn't help but throw me under the bus sometimes. He laughed, and I assumed rolled his eyes. He then corrected his previous statement.

"You're my friend. She likes all my friends."

I anticipated Declan's response, but not much came out of his mouth after that.

"Oh."

He sounded a tad disappointed, but then again it could have been my wild imagination taking things to extremes. *Was that it? "Oh?" Those are all the words he could get out?* I heard the doorbell, and snapped myself back into reality.

Evan called up to me and I quickly fixed my hair before

coming down the stairs.

"Hey, Jack."

He smiled, and it was contagious.

"So you ready for some lunch?"

He reached for my hand as he opened the door. It actually felt nice, not like it did at all with Gavin. I assured Evan I would be back for dinner. As I turned to walk out, I noticed Alex in the hall watching me with a puzzled look on his face. I didn't care. I needed to get out and clear my head and Jack was a good excuse to do that with.

I had a great time with Jack. Lunch was fun and he had me laughing the whole time with his stories. It was a nice change of pace to get out and not think of anything. I started to change when I heard Alex. He was still out on the deck, and of course he hadn't figured out yet that I could hear him.

Suddenly, I needed to take a walk. I grabbed my camera from the closet as I headed out the back door. I saw Alex staring at me as I passed. He looked a little worried when he glanced up and realized what had just happened.

How could he forget that my room was right there?

"Grey, wait, I—"

He stopped before he said too much. I kept walking into the yard and out of his sight. I needed to be alone. I didn't need an audience. Of course, his actions had just screwed up my nice thoughts from lunch—so typical.

There was one more day before I would meet the rest of the student body that attended Parker Manning Academy—all three hundred of them. That day I thought it would be best if I stayed home and did nothing. Then I heard the doorbell ring. *Oh, man. Please let it be someone for Evan,* I thought.

Evan was at the door before I'd even reached the stairs.

"Another delivery for Grey."

He was amused by my admirer, and because I had no clue who it was yet.

"Thanks."

As I took the box, the door chimed again. The delivery guy had forgotten another package or something. Evan smiled as he turned, and all I could think was *or something.* He handed me a bouquet of white roses with white and black ribbon interlaced between the stems. They were beautiful. I grabbed the card out of Evan's hand. They were from Jack. I smiled as I put them down on the table. I opened the box next. There was that friendly, white rose staring back at me. I opened the note, staring at it.

Thank you.

That's all it said. Evan was just as puzzled as I was.

"Huh, that's weird."

The front door flew open and who I thought was Alex breezed past us and up the stairs. He was in a hurry; must have forgotten something. He came back down the stairs and noticed the box and the bouquet.

"Nice. Someone's special today. Another box. Man, this guy really likes you, huh?" He tried to catch his breath as he read the card.

"Thank you? What does that mean?"

"Your guess is as good as mine."

"Hey, Alex! We're going to be late!" Declan yelled from the driveway.

Alex turned and ran out the door.

"Grey, you got the Jeep. Dec is driving me to practice today."

How odd was that? Since when does Alex spend all his time with Declan? What happened to Gavin and Tyler? They'd been a fixture in our house.

I shrugged it off and lifted the roses up to my nose. *What a great way to start the day.* I happened to glance out the window and noticed Declan as he got into his car. I smiled and went back upstairs to get dressed, and to possibly gather my thoughts. I had to prepare for the next day.

CHAPTER FIVE

SCHOOL IS IN SESSION

When looking back on the summer, it seems like a blur. The months melded together and before I knew it, I had to face the facts. My mom was gone and I was getting ready to begin school without her and in a somewhat unfamiliar place. Oh, not to mention the books of plants and herbs I had to memorize to help Grams in the store. I had to see Jack every time I worked, as his family's shop was two doors down. At least I wasn't going through it alone; my brother and sister were there with me. I finally decided that I should get up and face the day anew.

Alex was already up and ready to go. He'd always been a morning person. I was his polar opposite in that respect. We were so much alike, and being his sister didn't stop him from being one of my best friends. My little sister Allie, on the other, as much as I loved her, I couldn't understand her. She was a little diva-in-training. Everything had to be perfect, including her clothes and hair.

"Are you ready to go yet, or do I have to drag you out of bed again?"

"No, I'm up. You can come in, Alex, if you want."

I was getting the crap out of my eyes as the door swung open.

"You had one of your dreams again, didn't you?"

I nodded. I told him I would be fine and ready to go in five minutes. He shook his head and left. He worried about me more than Mom had sometimes. He knew my dreams had to do with her, but that was all. I couldn't explain everything to him yet because I didn't quite understand it myself. Since she'd passed away, I'd been dreaming about her, and the dreams seemed so real. It was as if she was still there with me, and was trying to tell me something, but I always woke up in the middle of our conversations. I didn't want to worry about that right now. I had to get dressed and face my peers. *This should be fun.*

I headed downstairs to grab something quick to eat before heading off to the first day of a new year. Evan and Alex were deep in the midst of a conversation when I walked in.

"Make sure you guys are not late today. It might look bad if my own family was late."

He looked at me and half-smiled.

"Don't worry, Evan. We're heading out in about ten minutes."

"I'll see you guys later, and don't forget to stop by the office and pick up your schedules!" he shouted as he walked out the front door.

"I hope that I get some good classes," I muttered.

We'd never stayed in one place long enough to actually attend school, except for when we were in Billings. Our mom had homeschooled us most of the time. The problem was that she'd never written anything down, so we had to take placement tests to assess our academic levels. We were beginning our academic careers at Parker Manning Academy at the third-year level. The academy was comprised of five levels, or years. I figured it was a private school thing.

My brother was never one for academics, though. He was smart, but he liked to focus more on lacrosse than on school. Allie placed a little ahead of her peers, and would start as the youngest student in the first-year level.

We pulled onto the long drive toward the school. In the distance, to the right, I could see the school's field and the track. The further down we drove I could see the student parking lot and the school itself coming into view. It looked more like a small college campus than a small private school. The school was huge. One of the larger buildings resembled a large English manor and two smaller buildings farther back from the main building. The main building housed most of the upper-level classes. The smaller building to the right held the main offices and the lower-level classes. The building to the left housed the faculty offices and the library.

We parked in the student lot and headed toward the main office to get our schedules. Once we'd gotten them, I noticed Alex and I only had two together: history and gym. That's great. I hoped that I had some classes with Emery, Jack, or Quinn. I hated saying it aloud, but Gavin, too. We walked toward the main building before going our separate ways.

"See you at lunch, Grey."

Alex waved as he disappeared into the crowd. Just then, I heard a familiar voice. I turned and saw Emery coming up the stairs.

"Thank god, I thought I was going to wander these halls all day looking for someone I knew."

"What do you have first?"

"Um, English literature is my first. What about you?"

One of my favorite classes, but not this early. At least I could look forward to the rest of the day.

"I have history. It's right down the hall from your class, so I'll walk with you."

We walked toward the stairs and up to the third floor. Emery went left and told me my class was the third door down on the right.

I waved to her and headed down to the room. I walked in with no signs of anyone familiar. *This is going to be interesting.* I could feel my shyness coming out. As long as I kept telling myself that I could get through the day, it might work.

The teacher was about to close the door to start his lecture when Declan slid right in and headed toward the last open seat in the back. I felt a weird energy going through my body and set-tling in my stomach. Now I understood what having butterflies in my stomach meant—but mine were more like birds. This would definitely be an interesting class, because now I knew one person in it. I couldn't make up my mind whether that was a good thing or not.

I tried to listen to Mr. Marsh explaining the expectations and some of the material we would cover throughout the year. I also tried—but failed—to not glance over in his direction unless I was looking at the clock.

The class ended and I ran toward the door hoping to catch Emery in the hall. No such luck. I started toward the next class, which was on the first floor. I hoped Advanced Biology II would cheer me up. I walked into class and saw Emery sitting at the long, black, lab table alone.

Thank you, I murmured under my breath. I dumped my bag on the floor and sat on the stool next to her.

"Hey, what happened upstairs? I tried to catch you, but you were gone."

"Mr. Burke let us out a little early. Sorry."

"That's fine." At least I was calming down. "You'll never guess who was in my English class. Declan Watt."

Confused by my expression, she asked, "Really? That's good, right?"

"Maybe. I need to focus on my classes and not my mind rac-ing off somewhere else, though, if you know what I mean."

She nodded to me as Mrs. Warner had already started class. I happened to turn around and I noticed someone else had been lis-tening to our conversation: Paige. *Oh, man. Could this day get any worse?*

I didn't have any more classes with Emery, but she walked with me to art class. I would see her at lunch.

"Hey, I'll see you at lunch." She let out a giggle as she walked down the hall. "Have fun."

I was trying to figure out why she was laughing. I finally noticed the reason. Gavin. I knew he was my brother's friend, but following me in the hall was getting a little weird. I tried not to jump to conclusions too quickly, because he was going to the same room as me.

I walked in and chose the seat in the back near the windows. I turned around to see who was sitting beside me. I liked Gavin and all, but I didn't think it would work. I didn't want to hurt his friendship with Alex. I kept my mouth shut and my thoughts to myself as I bent down to get a pen out of my bag. I looked to my right, noticing someone sitting next to me.

"Hi," I heard a soft, slightly accented voice say. It was Paige Watt.

"Hi."

"So it looks like we have two classes together."

"We do?"

Then I remembered seeing her in biology class.

"Yes, biology." She laughed. "So I didn't get a chance to talk to you at your party."

That was weird. My party had been almost three months ago, but then I thought I hadn't seen her since then. I hadn't really talked to her at tryouts either. I had only spoken to her brother, so I blurted out the first thing that came into my head.

"So how was your summer?" *What a stupid question.*

"It was good, but I wasn't around much, as I was traveling with my mom."

"Oh?" I said curiously. "Where did you go?"

"We were in New York. She had business there."

I turned toward the front. Class had begun and our discussion had proved very interesting, to say the least.

Mr. Haney was a typical art teacher; very thin and dressed casually, the portrayal of an artist you see depicted in the movies. He was very informal, unlike most of the teachers I had met, because he insisted the class call him by his first name. He got right to work our first assignment, which was due at the end of the week. *Negative space, great.* My mind was racing now. *I'll think of something later.* Russell let class out early and I headed to the door.

"So, will I see you at lunch?" It was Paige, and I was relieved.

"Sure, you can sit with me, Quinn, and Emery. I'll see you later."

She seemed so nice, not at all what I'd pictured from earlier that summer. But then again I'd only seen her three times; once at the field, then at my house, and the last time was when she'd been arguing with her brother in front of their house.

The day seemed to drag, especially during trigonometry. I even thought I'd nodded off once or twice, and maybe I should have chugged a coffee or something before class.

Finally, it was lunchtime. My stomach concurred. I grabbed some food and walked over to the table where Emery and Quinn were already sitting.

I began to eat my apple before I'd even sat down.

"Hey, guys. I invited Paige to eat with us today."

Emery looked a little shocked, but Quinn didn't care either way.

"That's fine. The more the merrier," Emery said to Quinn with a smile.

I saw Paige walk in, and I waved to her as she crossed the cafeteria.

"So I heard you have Mrs. Cronin for trig. That must be exciting."

I laughed at the hint of sarcasm in her tone.

"I agree. Real riveting stuff."

"At least you can enjoy the rest of the day," Emery chimed in.

"Yeah, at least there's that."

The conversation flowed with talk of what I thought of the school, what classes we had, and different events from the previous month. Then I saw Quinn and Paige smile as I felt two hands cover my eyes.

"Guess who?" I heard him laugh.

"Um, Gavin, right? Oh, wait. Maybe it's Prince Charming. Yeah, that's my guess. Prince Charming." I laughed and moved his hands. "Alex, I knew it was you. *Please*."

He laughed, but it seemed a little forced.

"So how's your day going, Alex?" I asked.

"Let's just say, I'm looking forward to history class."

"That bad, huh?" I smiled. "Does your presence mean it's time to go to class now?"

He nodded and I got up. I said bye to the girls and headed off to history with him. It was one of our favorite subjects.

We sat toward the back of the room when the teacher walked in. Alex snickered under his breath and I gave him a curious look.

"Good afternoon, class. My name is Dr. Watt and this should be United States History I."

I had a shocked look on my face. Now I understood why Alex had laughed. I closed my mouth long enough to shoot him a quick look. He was still laughing! I tried to stay calm, when all I wanted to do was smack his shoulder. *Ugh.* I took a breath and refocused. I would get him back for this.

Dr. Watt was well dressed, maybe a little too well dressed for high school, private or not. I could see where Declan and Paige had gotten their looks. He was handsome. This class seemed to be the only one that flew by, and I had a free period next before gym.

I decided to walk to the library. Inside, it looked like any other library, old with a musty smell. I sat down in one of the chairs toward the back. I felt like I was in a hunting club rather than a library. The chairs were big and comfortable. They faced a large, unused, stone fireplace and mantle. It looked cold and ominous, more than it did warm and inviting. There was a small table between the chairs and a slightly larger table in front of them.

I took out my Shakespeare book and started reading *As You Like It*—one of my favorites. It was one of his comedies I found not many people knew about, let alone had read. As I reached Act II, I felt a shiver run down my back and a slight twinge against my temple. I turned, but no one was there except the librarian. I must have lost track of time, because when I glanced at the clock I saw I was going to be late if I didn't leave then. I threw my book in my bag and ran toward the gym. I made it just in time.

I changed and ran into the gym looking for Alex. I was a little surprised to see more than one familiar face. Quinn, Gavin, and Declan were in my class as well. That day we would start volleyball. *Sweet!* It was a sport I actually liked. I tried to stay positive about the class roster.

Coach Nelson was a big guy with a deep, booming voice. He was also the lacrosse coach, so some people had this class in the bag. He broke us up into teams. Gavin, Quinn, and several others made up my team.

Me versus Alex. This should be interesting. I smiled, because this was one sport where I had an advantage. He didn't care for volleyball that much. There was more than one problem with the situation, though. I would have to look across the net at Declan, and Gavin got to watch me.

Throughout class, I felt eyes on me from more than one person. And those stupid chills continued to run through my body. *Seriously, can this just be over?* I looked over at Quinn and she gave me a look that said, *I know how you feel.* Thankfully, the class was soon over. I walked to the locker room to change. I was in no rush, because I had to wait for Alex and he had practice after school.

I spent half of practice in the library and the rest on the bleachers. When I arrived, it looked like they were close to being done, so I sat in the bleachers to wait.

I noticed Jack right away, because I knew his jersey number. Alex, he was the goalkeeper. I tried to figure out who was who. It was hard with not being able to see their faces under the helmets. I played the guessing game. Number sixteen was Tyler, number nine was Declan, and number twenty-two was Gavin. And of course, Jack. I remember him telling me his number was seven.

Jack and I had gone out a couple times, but we realized we were better as friends. Everyone on the field all looked the same except for Tyler. I could pick him out easily due to his smaller build. This would be the time to watch Declan without it seeming weird because I was watching a practice. At least that's how I justified it to myself.

"This is crazy," I said to myself.

I changed my mind, took out my book, and started reading where I had left off, at Act II. I glanced up occasionally to see if they had finished, but to also take the chance to look at Declan again.

I heard Coach Nelson call them in, and it seemed like practice was over. They took off their helmets and I was shocked. I watched Gavin.

"Great," I muttered under my breath.

I might have given him ideas, but I hoped he hadn't noticed.

I walked down to the field and Alex came over to meet me.

"Hey, Grey, I need to change, so meet me at the car."

"Okay."

I waved over to Jack as he ran in with Alex. I turned toward the parking lot when I noticed Gavin wink at me. *Oh man, he did notice.* As I turned, I also noticed a quick smile from Declan.

"This sucks big time." I said under my breathe

It was quiet on the way home. I could feel Alex's eyes on me and it was driving me crazy. *Ugh, will this day ever end?* I wanted to eat and go to bed. I needed to sleep, but I also wanted to see my mom again. My preoccupation didn't escape Evan's eye. When I was finished, with dinner, I cleared the table and Alex helped me. I put the dishes in the sink and started to wash while he dried.

"So how was school today, guys?" I heard Evan ask from behind us.

Alex glanced my way and then back to Evan.

"It was fine, except gym."

"You didn't like gym because my team beat yours."

"Well, it was only volleyball. When we play something else, you won't be laughing."

He gave me a shove with his shoulder.

"So school went well." Evan smiled. "That's good."

We finished the dishes and I headed upstairs, but not before Evan called me back.

"What's up?" I asked nervously.

"Did something happen today?"

"No. Why do you ask?"

"You've looked a little preoccupied lately." He tightened his eyes. "Are you sleeping okay?"

What a strange question, but not too far from the truth.

"Not really."

"What's going on? Maybe I can help?"

Do I tell him everything or would I sound crazy? I took a deep breath and began.

"Well, I've been having conversations with mom while I'm asleep." I looked up to see his expression. He was calm, and his face was unchanged. Maybe it wasn't so farfetched or crazy.

"So has she said anything?"

"No. I keep waking up in the middle of the conversation."

"Grey, this may be weird, or even crazy to you, but it's normal to us." He rubbed my arm. "As we told you, our family is different, and some of us can even communicate with others through our thoughts and dreams. That was your mother's gift."

"Thanks for listening, but I'm tired. I'm heading off to bed."

I turned to leave, when he caught my arm.

"Grey, you can come to me with anything. Always remember that, okay?"

He kissed me on the forehead and then headed into his office.

Could this day get any weirder? Maybe I shouldn't think that, because I might get my wish.

I walked past his office, when I heard him talking to Grams about me. I couldn't hear much because they were whispering, but I jumped when I heard the phone ring.

I ran upstairs to my room. I needed to stop being so nosy. It would get me in trouble one day. I guessed the phone was for someone else, and I fell asleep when no one came for me.

It felt like minutes had past when I was on the balcony with her. We talked about my first day and the new friends that I had made over the course of the summer. Her tone suddenly turned serious. She said she needed to explain something important to me. She'd wanted to tell me earlier, but she had passed away too soon.

"Grey, you come from a very prominent family in Erving," she stated with authority. "There are things you need to know about your family and yourself. I want you to remember you are special, and your gifts are great." She repeated this to me every night before I went to bed. "I want you to have this, and you need to trust in what I tell you." She placed a ring in my hand as her voice started to fade. "Listen to Evan and what he is going to teach you."

"Sure, Mom. I will." I woke up on the floor.

"Are you okay?" I heard Alex say through the door.

"Yeah, I'm fine. I must've rolled off the bed."

He opened the door to make sure I was okay.

"Alex, I'm fine. I need to get dressed."

I glanced around him to see Evan on the stairs with a concerned look on his face.

"Okay, I'll see you downstairs." He turned. "You've got ten minutes, or I'm coming back up here to get you."

I grabbed my clothes from the closet and I saw Alex shrug his shoulders toward Evan as he closed the door. I really wanted to go back to bed to hear why it was so important, what I had to learn, but I had to face the real world yet again.

I headed downstairs quickly before they sent the cavalry to my room. Thankfully, Grams had cooked breakfast, and Alex and Allie were at the table eating. Evan was looking over his forms—school business, no doubt. I grabbed a muffin from the counter and headed to the table to sit with them.

Just a typical morning in the Corwen household, I thought.

"Grey, where did you get that ring?" Grams gave Evan a look before turning to me for an answer.

I thought it had been a dream, but on my left index finger was a silver ring with a small amber setting. Inside the stone were small black shapes, almost like squiggly lines, but I didn't recognize the ring. I looked up at Grams, who was awaiting my answer. Everyone in my family knew we didn't keep Grams waiting. I couldn't tell her Mom had given it to me in my dreams, so I lied.

"I found it in my jewelry box. I thought it was nice, so I put it on."

I knew they didn't believe me, especially after my conversation last night with Evan, but she didn't question me any further.

It was a long ride to school at least I could avoid Alex for a couple of hours. The day dragged on, but before I knew it, I was in art class with Paige.

"How's your day going?" She looked concerned.

"Okay. Just a little tired. Rough night."

She gave me a strange look, but dropped it. I don't think I was ready to tell anyone yet about my dreams. I knew they may have been able to help, but I guess I hadn't come to grips with it myself.

How could anyone just go about their life not knowing that they were a witch? I mean, I always knew there was something differ- ent but I figured it was just me. The rest of these families probably knew when they were old enough to talk. I started to think about how long Alex had known, and if the same thing would happen to Allie.

The day was done and I walked around in a daze. My thoughts were somewhere else. I went to the library as I had the day be- fore. I decided to look around for any book on the history of this town. I found a large book toward the back of the library on the second floor. It was covered in dust. I guessed no one had checked this one out in a while, probably because their families had al- ready told them. I wiped the film from the hard, leather cover- ing. I walked over to a small table and turned the musty-smelling, water-stained pages. It was definitely old, and it contained what I was looking for: the history of the town; when it was founded and the founding settlers.

I scanned the columns of names. I recognized some of the families who had first settled in Erving. Four original families had settled it before it was officially founded as a town. The family names were Ellis, Connors, Watt, and Parker. I didn't know the last name. I only knew the Parker family had started my school— or at least that's what Evan had told me.

I'd have to ask Evan more about it when I get home. I glanced at the other names in the registry and found Gavin's family and ours before I put the book back. As I walked away, I heard a loud thud. I turned to see the book on the floor. I guess I hadn't put it back right. I noticed it was open to the page with the Parker fam- ily on it. I did not have to time to look; I closed the book and made sure it was secure on the shelf before heading toward the field.

Thankfully, practice was just ending. That was a good thing. I didn't have to wait. I had no patience when it came to waiting.

"So, where have you been?" Alex glanced my way.

"In the library." I questioned his motives for asking such an obvious question. "Why?"

"No reason. Just making sure you're okay." He smiled. "I'll meet you at the car."

After dinner, I went to talk to Evan. I knocked on the door to his office.

"Can I come in?" I asked.

"Sure, Grey. What's on your mind?" he asked, not looking up from his desk.

"I wanted to ask you about something I read in one of the local history books in the library."

He just nodded as if to give me a sign to continue.

"Well, I had a dream again last night, and Mom was there." I started slowly. "She said we are a prominent family, and there were things I needed to learn from you."

That got his attention and he looked up.

"Is that where you got that ring?" he asked, pointing his pen toward my hand.

"Yes, she gave it to me but I woke up before she could explain why."

"So you've come to ask me?" He crossed his arms and leaning slightly back in his chair.

"If you don't mind telling me." I hoped he wouldn't.

"Well, that ring belonged to your father's family. He gave it to your mother as a gift when he was courting her. The symbol inside the stone is the letter P for the name of his family."

"What was the name of his family? She never told us."

Now I was confused. I thought Corwen was our last name. She'd never told us his last name. It had never come up.

"Your father was a member of the Parker family."

"One of the original families," I muttered to myself.

"Yes, how did you know that?" He was curious now.

I was curious about how he'd known what I was thinking, but I answered anyway.

"The book in the library."

"Oh. Well, your father had a falling out with his brother, your Uncle Sean." He started slowly. "That is why your last name is still Corwen. Your mother kept her family name because he asked her not to change it."

I was even more confused now. What feud? And why there were no members of the Parker family in Erving now?

"What happened?"

"Your Uncle Sean was never one to follow the rules. He and your father were the last of the Parker family line. Your father didn't want the disgrace of his name to be placed on his children or your mother. You see, after certain events, Sean, he went mad. Your last name was Parker, but after these events your father had her change it back to Corwen."

"What did he do?" It was like a plot for a movie. *I wish I had popcorn.*

"He took it upon himself to destroy your father, and in the process he destroyed himself as well. Your uncle died in a car crash."

I gasped. My father had died in a car accident when I was eleven. I vaguely remembered my uncle, but maybe I didn't remember because I'd tried to block out those tragic events in my past. Mom had told us he was trying to help a friend, but it couldn't be the same accident.

Evan saw me processing things in my eyes as I ran through the information I'd just received.

"Yes, it was the same accident." He was now sitting next to me. "The night your father died—"

"He was trying to stop his brother?" I interrupted, trying to remain calm.

"Yes, he ran in front of the car to stop him, but Sean kept driving. Your father was hit hard. Sean swerved and hit a tree. He died on impact, but your father passed away later in the hospital due to his injuries. I know this is a lot to process, but you, Alex, and Allie are all descendants of the Parker family."

"Okay. So what does that mean exactly?"

"As a member of one of the original families that settled here, your responsibility to the town and your craft are important. Members of the original families make up the four members of the town council. Since there were no more members of the Parker family left—or so people thought—the Harrington family has taken their place."

"So Alex will be a member then?"

"Yes and no. It's kind of complicated. But if he's to take your father's seat, it will be when he comes of age and finishes his schooling."

What does that mean, 'if he takes the seat'? Man, all of this is too complicated to think about right now.

"Does Alex know this?" I already knew the answer.

"Yes, we told him last night. We thought we could wait a little longer with you—until we saw your ring this morning." He patted my hand. "Does that answer your questions?"

"Yeah, I think I need to sleep and process this."

I hugged him and walked toward the stairs.

"Thanks," I said.

My night was dreamless for once. I woke up in my bed and not on the floor this time. I got dressed before making my way to the kitchen. Everyone was chattering on about this coming weekend. It was a long holiday weekend and we were going up to the lake. Evan let Alex ask his friends to come with us, so I'd taken it upon myself to invite some of my new friends, too. I didn't want to be in a house full of testosterone all weekend.

All three were coming—Emery, Quinn, and Paige—which meant it would definitely prove to be an interesting weekend. We hadn't been in the house since Mom had passed. I heard both Gavin and Declan were coming. The rest of the day flashed past me, and before I knew it, I was set. I had one more day to prepare for our trip back. The plan was to have Emery, Quinn, and Tyler stay at our house that night and the rest would meet us in the morning.

My art project was due that morning and I quickly sketched the stream in the backyard. I wasn't concerned about my grade because it was only the first assignment and my mind was elsewhere.

At lunch, I had to go over my plan with Emery because we were taking several cars. I pulled her aside to ask for a favor.

"I know Gavin is going to go with Alex because I'll be there." I paused. "But I need you to go with my brother. I need time to deal with this situation. Can I count on you?"

"Sure, I'll have Tyler go with me."

"Sit in the front so Gavin and Tyler are in the back. Once they're in, he'll think I'm riding shotgun, but we'll switch at the last minute."

"Good plan. I'm in." She laughed. "Boy, will he be surprised. But what car will you go in?"

"I'll take my chances in Declan's car with Paige and Quinn."

She gave me a look, hesitated, and then agreed.

"I can handle it as long as I'm in the back." She was as skeptical as Quinn was when it came to me controlling my head around him.

"Okaaay," she said, elongating the word.

The rest of the day I heard Alex talking about what we were going to do that weekend with his friends. I decided to brace for the worst and sit through practice that afternoon. Their first game was next Friday. They were practicing longer this week to make up for the break, which worked out perfectly for us. We worked out the details for that night in the parking lot. Tyler would bring Quinn and Emery over after dinner.

"So are you looking forward to this weekend?"

I sat still, looking out the window but I could see Alex's reflection standing behind me.

"Yes and no."

He smiled, and I couldn't help but smile back.

"It's going to be hard, but we'll get through it."

He squeezed my hand and I tried to relax. Alex always knew how to comfort me. We got home and I ran upstairs to get everything ready. I had to let Quinn in on the plan. I had already let Paige know earlier when I'd been at practice. I ran so fast up the stairs I didn't see the box on the table.

As I came back down, Alex yelled from the kitchen, "You got something!"

There was the white box with a red ribbon. I went over and opened it. Inside, there were two roses—a white and a red one. *That's different. Not the same box*, I thought to myself. I found a note.

Looking forward to this weekend, Gavin.

"Oh crap."

I heard Evan and Alex come out from the kitchen.

"What happened?" Evan examined the box. "That's not the same person, is it?"

"No, it's not."

I could see Alex trying to remain calm before he spoke.

"Who are they from? Jack?"

Calm for now, I thought.

"No, Gavin."

I could see the creases starting to form in my brother's forehead. I still couldn't figure out why he was so mad. Gavin was okay, but maybe it had to do with the Harringtons having the fourth council seat.

"Its fine, Alex. I got it under control. Calm down."

It was weird, because he'd been so cool about Jack and me, even though it hadn't worked out. He tried to look amused by my response, but to me he still seemed mad. I left the box there on the table and threw the card away so he wouldn't see it. I know he wanted to, but I wasn't going to give it to him. It would only add fuel to the fire. I had enough to deal with this weekend. I didn't need his thoughts running through my head as well.

After dinner, Alex was still upset for some reason. I hoped Tyler could get him to calm down. The doorbell squealed. Tyler, Quinn, and Emery came in, and I had them throw their stuff in a side room off the hall.

"What's up with him?" Tyler asked.

"You might want to ask him, Tyler."

I nodded toward Alex, and then I looked at Emery and Quinn as I motioned toward the table. As soon as Alex and Tyler went into the kitchen, I turned to Quinn and Emery.

"He's mad because you got another gift? Or am I missing something?" Quinn looked confused. "I thought he didn't care who they were from."

"Well, it's not the same box. Look." I pointed out the ribbon and the two roses.

"Was there a note?"

"Yes, but I threw it away." I looked into the kitchen and back toward the box.

"Who?" they both whispered.

"Gavin."

The light went off in their heads. Now they knew why Alex was upset.

"Figures. Why did he send them?" Emery was curious.

"The note just said, 'Looking forward to this weekend.'"

I looked at them and we all started laughing. It was nice and flattering to receive flowers, but I didn't want to give anyone the wrong idea.

We stayed up late talking, but it didn't matter because none of us were driving in the morning. Emery and I filled Quinn in on the plan. A couple of times Evan had to come in and ask us to keep it down. Emery fell asleep and I took the opportunity to ask Quinn some questions.

"Do you know anything about the founding families?"

"I know some. Did you have any questions? I can help as much as I can if you want to talk about other things, too," she offered.

"When did you know you were different?" I thought I would start with the easy ones.

"My parents told me when I was seven years old, but only because they caught me moving my stuffed animals around the room."

We both giggled. I could picture a fuzzy teddy bear flying around with a stuffed dog.

"Do you have any other abilities?" I yawned. I guess I was tired.

"No, just telekinesis. What about you? I'm sure you having healing in your blood. I mean, your Grams is the best."

"Yeah, I can heal some, but I haven't really tried since I mistakenly healed a bird when I was ten years old. I have telekinesis as well. Like I said, you're probably all better than me, the late arrival, here."

I brushed it off, as I didn't want to reveal too much—and I didn't know much either. We finally settled down after Alex burst through the door, half-asleep, grumbling something about driving in the morning and giggling girls. I could only make out some of what he was trying to say. I got up and pushed him back toward his room, telling him how moody he was when he was half-asleep and that he needed to go back to bed. He furrowed his brow before closing the door behind him.

CHAPTER SIX

THE LAKE HOUSE

The chiming of the doorbell woke me up. I looked at the clock. It was eight o'clock in the morning. I'd overslept. Everyone was in the kitchen waiting for me.

"Alex, why didn't you get me up?" I asked.

"You needed the sleep." He laughed.

"Whatever."

I grabbed a muffin and headed back upstairs to get my bag. As I came back down, Gavin, Declan, and Paige were coming in the front door. I was pulling my hair up as I had a pastry in my mouth—not the most attractive look.

"Hi, guys. Everyone's in the kitchen."

Paige came up to meet me, when I noticed both Declan and Gavin's faces. They both looked puzzled. I couldn't understand why until I looked down to see that the box was still there. Gavin smiled as he walked into the kitchen, but Declan went outside.

"Damn," I mumbled.

"What's up?"

"It's a long story, but here's the Cliff Notes version," I started as I walked with her into the hallway. "I've been getting these deliveries with the most beautiful notes inside, but I don't know who they're from." I pointed to the box on the table. "But this box isn't from the same person. It's from Gavin."

"Do you know where these flowers came from? You could call and ask them."

"Yes, I already did and they don't know who sent them."

"Do you still have the notes?"

What a strange question to ask, I thought. *Or maybe she knew the handwriting. She did know almost everyone in town.*

"Yeah, they're upstairs." I turned back toward the stairs and she followed.

I went to my journal and took out the notes.

"There are only three notes."

I handed them to her. She looked at each one and I watched her face for any hint that she knew who it was.

"No, I don't know the handwriting. Sorry." She hesitated. I had a feeling she knew who it was, but didn't want to tell me.

"No problem. At least you tried."

I played along. I didn't want her or Declan think that I had someone when I didn't.

"I need to go see if Declan is okay—and let him in on the plan." She laughed at the last sentence.

I followed her to the door, grabbing my stuff to load in the car. As I crossed by the open door, I saw her standing next to a black Jeep. It definitely would fit in up north; it was built for adventure. I was confused, though. I'd thought Declan drove an Audi A4. I guessed it was his dad's car. Then a little shiver went down my back, and there was the slight temple pressure again, but this time I tried to brush it off and not think about it.

Everything was packed and we were ready to go. Grams couldn't make the trip this time because of the shop. I waited for Gavin and Tyler to get into the back of our Jeep, and then I turned to Emery and smiled. She ran and jumped into the front seat and I jumped into the back of Declan's Jeep with Quinn. I could see Emery laughing and the shock on Declan's face. I started to look at Paige, when I caught his steel eyes in the mirror looking back at me. I stopped laughing. I lost my train of thought. His gaze was intense.

Then I heard Paige shout back, "Good plan!"

I snapped out of it. I started laughing again.

"It was a good plan, huh?" *That was weird.*

"Definitely, just to see the look on his face was priceless."

Paige glanced at Declan who seemed to have a smirk on his face.

We finally reached the house by lunchtime. It was still warm. I thought it might be a good night for a swim. There weren't enough rooms for everyone, but we'd already planned it out. Gavin and Tyler would take Alex's room. Alex and Declan would take mine, and the girls would stay in the living room as if we were having a slumber party. I think it was more because Evan's room was right next to the stairs and he could hear everything—even someone coming and going by the stairs.

I had everyone put their bags in my and Allie's rooms. I didn't know how I felt about Declan sleeping in my bed, but I wasn't going to be there, so I decided it was okay—or at least I thought it was. I couldn't stop thinking how it would feel to be wrapped in his arms. *Oh my god! I seriously have to stop this daydreaming.*

"So I thought we could take a walk around the lake and go swimming," I suggested to the girls. "You can come, too, Allie." She smiled and was glad to be included.

After lunch, we changed and headed out.

"What are you guys doing today?" I asked Alex.

"I don't know, Grey. I think we'll stay close to the house. Play cards out on the deck." Alex winked at me.

Okay, I don't know what that means, but whatever.

I laughed.

"Enjoy the scenery."

We reached the other side and set our stuff down on the outcropping of rocks.

"This is great, Grey," Paige said in awe.

"I always feel calm when I come here."

"I can see why. It's so relaxing."

"Hey, kiddo. You're first."

I grabbed Allie and threw her in, but she still had my arm so I went in with her. She screamed as she hit the water. We all just hung out and relaxed. No doubt someone else was enjoying the view.

"Hey guys, you want to play cards or something?" Alex asked.

"Sure, why not?" Gavin answered. Everyone walked out onto the deck and started setting up.

"This is a great telescope," Declan remarked. "Is it yours."

"No, it was my father's," Alex said nonchalantly. "But Grey is the only one who actually uses it."

"Let's play some cards, man!" Tyler yelled at Declan, who was looking through the telescope. "The stars aren't out yet."

They all laughed and he sat down.

We had started walking back, when I saw Evan coming down the drive. *Now where is he going?*

"I need to go into town and get some things we forgot." He smiled. "Can you and Alex behave yourselves for an hour?"

"Oh, please, Evan. I can handle it."

"Okay. I'll be back in one hour. Don't burn the house down."

We walked in. The guys were still on the deck. I went to get changed, then ran back down to the kitchen.

"I'm going to start dinner. Can you tell Alex to light the grill, Quinn?"

Paige and Emery helped me cut the vegetables for the salad.

"Can I help with anything?" I heard someone say from the living room.

"Sure, big brother, why don't you finish the chicken while I check on the grill?" Paige ordered as she left.

Now this was going to be a little awkward. Emery kept looking at me when she turned to Declan. I'm sure she liked him too.

"So you cook, Declan?" Emery looked at me again. I'm definitely not ready to talk to him.

"Actually, Emery, I do. I cook at home all the time." He smiled back at her and I felt I should slip out now to leave them alone.

"Well then, Declan. Get to work on seasoning the chicken. I'll bring the potatoes to Alex." I answered as I gathered the potatoes and ran for the deck.

What was wrong with me? I couldn't even stand next to him in the kitchen? I'm going crazy—if not today, definitely by the end of the weekend. I figured it didn't matter, anyway. He seemed to be interested in her, not me.

As I turned the corner, I heard them talking in the kitchen. *Me and my crazy, supersonic hearing.* I stood there, curious as to what they were saying.

"Does Grey feel okay?"

"Yeah, she's a little tired, but she's good. Why do you ask?"

"Well, every time I'm around she seems to be running off somewhere else."

"She just gets a little nervous. Nothing to worry about."

Great. Now he's going to think I'm crazy or that he makes me uncomfortable.

"Nervous. Did I do something to cause this?"

She started to giggle. I had to stop this conversation.

"He wasn't ready for them yet!" I shouted as I walked into the kitchen. "Do you need any help, Declan?" I'd asked because I wanted him to see there was nothing wrong.

"Sure." He smiled. "Thanks."

I washed my hands and grabbed the rest of the chicken. As

I looked up, I noticed Emery and Quinn had slipped out, but he hadn't yet. *Okay, I guess he wasn't interested in her. That might change everything now. Wait, why do I care? And what is this pull to him? I have to stop asking questions because I may not like the answers.*

"So you cook at home?"

What a stupid question. He already told us.

"Yes, my mom hates to cook and my father can only reheat soup."

His laugh was deep and intoxicating.

"Who taught you?" I tried to regain my senses. He was just a guy—albeit a very hot, sexy guy. *Damn it, Grey, get yourself together.*

"My grandmother, she was a great cook."

He looked up, noticing we were the only ones in the room. I noticed a slight grin forming on his face.

"She taught me everything I know." He began showing me what to do. "Here, pierce the chicken with the rosemary. Like this."

He enclosed his hands over mine. I noticed how much bigger his were than mine, and my mind went places I'm embarrassed to even admit to. His soft touch felt nice. I felt the same prickly shocks running through my fingers and hands. I think we had a moment, but I pulled my hands back when I heard Evan walk into the kitchen.

"How's dinner coming?"

I could feel my face burning. I needed to escape.

"I think we're ready for the grill."

I washed my hands, grabbed the potatoes, and headed toward the deck.

"Here, Alex, put these on now. Declan is bringing the chicken out." My face was still piqued, when Alex looked up.

"Are you okay? Your face is flushed."

That's great, Alex. Why don't you announce it to the world?

"I'm fine." I tried to compose myself. "You worry too much."

I heard the girls laughing behind me. I turned to say something and Gavin looked up. He saw the same thing as Alex had. He glared at me for a while, then went inside. I was hoping Evan was still in the kitchen when I walked back inside to grab the vegetables.

Gavin stopped me on the way.

"Hey, are you okay?"

"Yeah, I'm fine. Why do you ask?"

If one more person asks me if I'm okay, I'm going to explode.

"Your face is a little flushed."

He raised his hand to touch my cheek. I turned as soon as he touched my face. It felt cold, like a shock of arctic air hitting my face.

"Don't worry. I'm fine." I walked into the kitchen and grabbed the vegetables before someone else could stop me.

"Are you okay?"

For the love of all that is holy, would you people just leave me alone! That's what I should have said, but I didn't. I was more polite.

"Would everyone stop asking me that, please?!"

That's when Declan and Evan noticed Gavin standing in the living room. They decided it would be best to go help Alex outside. *Great. Now he probably thinks I'm not interested. Stupid Gavin.*

Declan took over the grilling duties from Alex because Alex was burning the vegetables. Everyone else was playing cards. Evan and I were inside playing chess.

"So what's going on Grey?" Evan asked.

"Nothing's going on, really."

Stupid Gavin can't take a hint, and I think I blew it with Declan—but nothing's going on.

"If it is nothing, then why are you blushing now, like you were in the kitchen?"

He was more observant than I gave him credit for. I found it hard to lie to him, but I also didn't want to talk to him about this.

"You came into the kitchen at the wrong time. That's all."

As I remembered that moment in the kitchen, I heard the door open behind me.

"Everything is done."

"Thanks, Declan. We'll get the dishes and silverware." Evan glanced at me and winked. He knew exactly what I'd been refer-ring to earlier.

Dinner was somewhat quiet, or at least I was quiet. Everyone else was having their own discussions about what to do tomorrow. I started clearing the table, when I noticed Gavin doing the same. *I cannot get a break, can I?*

I walked into the kitchen and put the dishes in the sink. I turned to grab the glasses and Gavin was suddenly behind me.

"Grey, I was wondering if you would take a walk with me?"

"Sure."

I walked toward the back door, making sure someone saw me leave—anyone but Alex. Thankfully, I caught Quinn's attention. Gavin and I walked down to the drive toward the cars. I walked past the bench that was next to the house, when I felt him grab my hand. I turned around to see him motioning me to sit.

This isn't good, I thought to myself.

"So what did you want that you couldn't tell me inside?"

"Did you get my flowers?"

"They were nice, but not necessary, Gavin."

"Well, I was hoping we could talk about this, our situation."

"What situation?"

"Well, I know you're interested in me." He smiled. "I saw you watching me at practice the other day."

Oh man, I was hoping he hadn't noticed . . . I thought he was Declan. This is going to be awkward to explain, but I have to.

"I think you have made an assumption that isn't true," I said, trying to be polite but blunt.

"Are you saying you weren't looking at me, then?"

"I was . . . but I thought you—"

He leaned in and kissed me.

Oh crap, my first kiss was with someone I didn't see in that way! I didn't like him. I pushed him away, and he stopped, thankfully.

"I think we better go back inside now," I said.

He grabbed my hand again.

"I'm sorry if that felt forced. I didn't want to offend you, but I thought you wanted me to."

"It's okay, Gavin, but I don't want to send out the wrong impression."

"You like me, right?"

"Yes, but—"

He didn't let me finish as he put his finger to my lips.

"Then it's all good. I can wait."

Wait for what? I don't like you. Can't you take a hint?

I quickly turned toward the back door, because he obviously wasn't going to listen to me. I swung open the door with a loud thump, trying to make noise so someone would notice me coming back in. That's when I felt him grab my hand again. At that exact time, Quinn looked up and saw him holding it. I gave her a look that said "please come help."

She started toward the kitchen. I yanked my hand back as I headed toward the stairs. She followed, and out of the corner of my eye, I caught Declan's curious stare. She shut the door and sat on the bed next to me.

"What happened?"

"He wanted to take a walk so he could talk to me."

"Talk to you about what, Grey?'

"If I liked the flowers and if I liked him. He caught me staring at him the other day during practice."

"You were staring at him?"

"Yes and no." I took a deep breath. "I thought he was Declan. They all look alike with their helmets on. I confused their jersey numbers."

"Oh, Grey." She hugged me. "Why didn't you tell him that?"

"I tried, but before I finished my sentence he kissed me."

"He, what?!"

I covered her mouth with my hand to keep her quiet.

"He kissed me, but I pulled away and tried to comeback inside."

I looked down and my hands were shaking.

"He kissed you?!" she shouted.

"Aw, Quinn! Keep it down. People can hear you."

There was a knock at the door. Thankfully, it was Paige.

"Hey, is everything okay in here?"

"No. Gavin kissed her."

"Why? Did she want him to?"

"No, Paige, she stopped him."

Hello, I'm still in the room. Why are you talking as if I'm not?

"That's good, but why did he think it was okay to do that? She doesn't like him that way."

I finally sat up and answered.

"Wednesday, at practice, I was staring at him."

"Why?" Paige urged me to continue.

"Well"—I took another deep breath—"I thought he was number twenty-two and your brother was number nine. Their jersey numbers, I mean."

"Oh, you thought you were watching my brother?"

She wasn't as surprised as I thought she should be, which made me think twice about whether she knew.

"It's a common mistake. They were all wearing helmets, and I guessed wrong."

"Now he thinks you like him?" She was still laughing.

"Yup. He told me he would wait for me to be ready—whatever that means."

"He's going to wait for you to have the same feelings."

"I think that's what he meant." I put my head in my hands. "This night sucks."

"Not the whole night," Paige pointed out.

I started to blush. After a few more bursts of laughter, we all went back downstairs. As we walked out on to the deck I saw Paige nod to her brother. Then I noticed Gavin glance in my direction. *Oh, it's going to be a long weekend.*

We sat around the fire well into the night. The plan for tomorrow was to go kayaking on the lake, which sounded good to me—a group outing would be very safe.

The guys headed upstairs and all the girls curled up around the fireplace in the living room. In the brief silence I heard Tyler yell out, "Are you crazy?!"

We all laughed, because we knew what he was talking about. Now Alex, Declan, and Evan were on the outside, and that was a good place for all of them.

I woke up before anyone else. I grabbed myself a cup of tea and headed out to the deck. The fog was rolling across the lake as the sun started to appear in the east through the trees. I could hear the faint sounds of the loons as well—music to my ears. I took a deep breath as I sat down. This time to me was so peaceful, because my thoughts were racing from yesterday and I needed to organize them.

I heard someone come out onto the deck. I was hoping it was anyone but Gavin. I turned to see Declan.

"Good morning. I'm not disturbing you, am I?"

"No. Just enjoying the scenery."

"Are you cold?" He held out his jacket. "I looked for a blanket, but only found my jacket."

"Thanks. That's very thoughtful of you."

I would rather have your arms for warmth, but I guess this will do. Oh my god, I seriously need to get myself under control.

I put my arms through the jacket and felt instantly warmer. His scent was nice, like dew of the morning with a hint of the woods. The smell was similar to that very morning.

"Did you want something to drink?" I tried to be polite and offer.

"What are you drinking?"

"Tea." I handed him my cup. "I hadn't even drunk it yet." *What a dorky thing to say.*

He took a sip.

"This is very good, but I don't want to take yours." I continued looking out at the lake. If I looked at him, I would focus on those round lips.

"I'll get some more during breakfast." I waved off his attempt to return my mug, although I would have loved to have my mouth where his had just been.

"Well, I'll let you enjoy the morning."

He started to get up. I reached toward his hand. *That was a bold move, Grey.* He sat back down.

"Don't. Please stay. I enjoy your company." I smiled.

When I tried to talk to him, I started to feel as if I had butterflies in my stomach. I took a deep breath. It was now or never, and he calmed me.

We sat in silence for a while, which was nice. I didn't have to say a word. I heard the door open again.

"Hey, guys. It's breakfast time," Alex whispered. I could hear the smile in his voice.

"Shall we?"

Declan got up and held the door open. I smiled back.

"Thank you."

As we walked into the kitchen, I caught some curious eyes surveying the scene. I nodded and mouthed the words "later." They laughed as we sat down. I noticed Evan fiddling around by the toaster. This was not going to be good, because Grams did most of the cooking.

"So what's for breakfast, Evan?"

"I don't know, Grey. I just burnt the toast. Sorry."

"I'll do it."

"No, allow me."

Declan was up and at the stove. I smirked toward Quinn and Paige. They just giggled. Gavin noticed and tried to take some interest.

"Do you want some help?" he asked.

"If you want." Declan answered

It seemed like it was not an invitation, and Gavin didn't move. Within about ten minutes, Declan had made scrambled eggs and toast, and had cut up some fruit for everyone.

I don't like scrambled eggs, but I'll eat them because he made the effort, I thought as he placed a plate in front of me.

"I think you might like this instead."

He'd made eggs especially for me the way I liked them. Next to the eggs was a toasted English muffin with strawberry preserves, fruit, and a cup of tea. *How did he know all this? It was like he'd read my mind. Wait, can some of us do that?*

I looked at Alex, who was still smiling. I figured he'd told Declan stuff about me. That could be the only answer. I collected myself and glanced over toward Quinn.

"We need some plates and silverware. Quinn, could you help me?"

"Sure."

"Do you think you could help me today?"

"I gotcha covered girl." She smiled. "No problem. We all will help."

We both laughed as if one of us had told a good joke.

"What's so funny?" Tyler was curious.

"I was telling Quinn that if we don't get these plates to every-one, we might be eating off the table."

I knew it was not funny, but I had to make something up.

We finished breakfast and I started clearing the table.

"Can I help?" I looked to see Declan waiting for an answer.

"No, you made breakfast, and I think I forgot to thank you. It was perfect." I smiled. "Now go get ready for the day trip."

"Are you sure?" He looked right at me. It felt like he was look-ing for something. maybe a signal.

"No, I'm . . . fine. Really."

Evan passed Declan on his way out. He helped me and cleaned the dishes while I dried.

"So it looks like you have three admirers?" He nudged my shoulder.

"What? I don't know what you're talking about." I brushed it off. I didn't really want to talk about it with him.

"Sure, Grey. whatever you say." He emptied the sink. "Let's see your anonymous admirer, Gavin and Declan."

"Really, Evan." I started to blush. "Stop it! I have to get ready."

"Have fun."

I ran upstairs to my room to get dressed, forgetting it was occupied. I opened the door and saw that the guys were half-dressed. I suddenly turned and closed the door.

I'd seen Alex in a towel before, but he was my brother. It was different to see anyone else that way—especially Declan. I was embarrassed when I heard the soft laughter coming from behind the door. I waited on the top step for them to finish.

I heard the door open and Alex came down.

"Grey, you can open your eyes now. We're done."

He kissed my head and headed downstairs. I turned and entered my room.

"Oh, I'm sorry. Alex said you guys were done."

I covered my eyes and turned away.

"I'm done. Just grabbing my keys."

"Okay, I'll see you outside."

I walked to the closet and grabbed my clothes from my bag.

"This is a nice room."

I thought he left.

"Thanks."

I heard him sigh and close the door. I turned around to make sure he was gone this time. I got my suit and threw on my shirt and some shorts.

When I got outside everyone was ready and waiting for me. Evan and Allie were going into town to shop. Poor Evan. I felt bad.

"The lunches are packed and on the table, guys!" he shouted out the window.

I ran in, grabbed the pack, and hurried around the back.

"I'll take this one. It's great." Declan yelled to Alex

Then I heard Alex shout from the shed, "Sorry, Dec! That one's Grey's."

"Hey, guys! We have a couple of tandems and the rest are singles." I yelled back to the group.

I glanced at Quinn.

"That means some of you will have to share a kayak." Alex explained

I helped Alex pull the rest of the kayaks, then I ran up to the shed and grabbed the paddles.

"Okay, the red one is Alex's, and that one is mine." I glanced at Declan and smiled. "So you can fight over the last four."

Quinn grabbed Gavin and asked him to get one of the tandem kayaks. I mouthed thank you, and she winked.

"Paige and I will take the other tandem."

That left the two single kayaks for Declan and Tyler. I put the pack in the hold and pushed off.

"Are you guys good?" I asked.

"You go ahead, Grey. We're fine!" Alex yelled back.

I got out to the middle of the lake and waited for the rest to catch up. I took in the beautiful day that was unfolding. I leaned back and closed my eyes. My mind started to drift back to thoughts of Declan with no shirt on and how close he'd been to me.

I wish I could take a chance and make a move. If I'm not melting when he looks at me, I'm wondering how his lips would feel. I felt a shiver run through my body. I could hear whispers of a slight breeze and the swirl of water dripping from an oar.

"Are you sleeping?" I heard.

"No, just enjoying the day."

I turned and saw Declan coming up on my right. Everyone else was about ten yards back. *Damn, I can feel his eyes on me.* I quickly ran my tongue along my lips like I was dehydrated and needed a drink. Of course, he was it. A smile crept across my face when he pulled up alongside of me.

"Nice kayak." I laughed. It was Allie's. "Sorry you got stuck with the purple and pink explosion."

"Real men can handle it." He laughed as I heard everyone else approaching.

"Alex, I thought we would head toward the west, near the falls, and set up there for lunch!"

"Sounds good!" Alex yelled back.

It took half the morning to reach the other side of the lake. I got out halfway, jumped in the water, and pulled my kayak up on the shore. Once it was anchored, I went back to help everyone else.

"So do you want to eat now or hike up to the falls and eat later?"

They decided to go to the falls first. I ran back to my kayak and grabbed my backpack.

Alex led the way up the trail. I took a moment to get my camera from my bag. He knew I would bring it, so he kept everyone moving. It was the same with my family as well. They were just used to it. I was always way behind everyone else when I was out here. We were almost there when I heard a noise to the west; it was a deer.

"Sweet."

I left the trail and crouched against a tree, trying to be quiet, but something spooked the deer. It froze for a minute and then resumed its activities.

"Beautiful picture, don't you think?" I heard a whisper in my ear.

"It is when no one is around." I snapped the picture and turned back toward the trail.

"I wasn't talking about the deer."

"Whatever, Gavin."

I ran up to the others who had reached the falls.

"Smile, guys." I snapped a picture.

"Come on, Grey. Put the camera down for two seconds." I knew how much he hated my camera and getting his picture taken.

"Spoil sport," I said.

I placed my camera around my neck and started toward the stone steps. I was halfway up the steps, when I lost my footing and fell back. I was lucky, because someone caught me.

"Thanks." I turned to see who'd helped.

"Anytime." Declan smiled back. I was still holding on to him. I didn't want to move or let go, but I had to if I wanted to continue to the top.

"I find it interesting that you seem so at peace when you are outdoors."

"Why is that, Declan?"

"Because you are yourself. It's almost like you don't need to speak to understand what you're saying."

"That's an interesting theory."

I paused to take his picture.

"Now we might have to separate you from that camera, though."

"Good luck," Alex remarked. "Let's eat. I'm starved."

"Fine, give me ten minutes. I have to go back and get the food." I retorted

"Ugh. Why didn't you bring it with you?"

"Oh, please, Alex. I'll be back before you miss me. Chew on some twigs while you wait."

"I highly doubt that."

I laughed all the way down the trail.

As I came back up, I saw everyone had moved to a clearing off the falls.

"Here you go." I handed the pack to Alex.

"It took you thirteen minutes."

I rolled my eyes. I walked over to the edge and sat down on the rocks near the falls.

"Are you hungry?" Quinn came over with a sandwich.

"Thanks."

"So what's the verdict?"

"What do you mean?"

"Are you going to stand by and watch, or are you going to get in the game?"

She glanced over at Declan. He looked up and smiled at me, but I turned my attention back to her.

"I'm not sure yet."

"What's not to be sure of? He's interested. That's pretty evident."

"Yeah, but is that because of Gavin or my anonymous admirer?"

"Good point," she continued. "We'll have to feel it out with someone on the inside." I laughed. "What do you mean, 'someone on the inside'?"

"Paige, of course." She smiled. "I totally got your back."

"Thanks."

She walked back to sit with the others. I finished my sandwich and quietly started moving rocks, just for practice. I decided to move closer to the falls to get some good shots. Luckily, I had my hiking shoes on or I would have slipped on the rocks. I looked across the falls with my camera, scanning the forest for something to shoot.

I came upon some movement in the brush, and it was big, too. Suddenly, I saw a bear lean down to drink from the stream. I started snapping pictures, hoping this moment would last a while, and he wouldn't see me and charge. I moved slightly to my right and lost my footing. I felt a quick tug on my pack, and I regained my balance.

"You need to be more careful, Grey."

"Thank you, again."

"I'm thinking you like someone catching you."

What does that me? I started reading into things that, in my mind, were not there.

I looked across, noticing the bear retreating into the forest, and I at least got some shots. I turned to get up and slipped a little. Declan put his hand out for me to grab on to for balance. He pulled me up and I crashed into his chest. It felt like I'd hit a brick wall.

"Sorry, Declan," I said into his chest. *Oh, I could stay here for hours.* I took that moment to breathe in his natural, woodsy scent.

"Are you okay?"

"Yeah, I'm okay." *Oh my god, this could not get any better unless he kissed me right now.*

We stood there for a moment. There was something between us, but it was something I could not quite put my finger on because it was different. Different than any of the handful of dates I'd had up until that point. It was like the anticipation of something that could happen. He quickly broke away and turned toward the field. I stood there a little dazed, trying to figure out what had happened. I shook my head and started back down to the rest of them.

I didn't think Quinn had been right about his interest. Maybe it was more like the concern of a friend, or even a sibling. I still felt the excitement of what could have been coursing through my body. His hold was strong yet gentle, and it felt natural to be close to him. I couldn't get my hopes up. I needed to snap out of it. I ran ahead of the group, threw my camera in my backpack, and put it in the hold.

I helped everyone push off and saved Alex for last.

"I'll come back a little later, okay? I need to think."

"No problem. I'll see you in a couple of hours. Don't make me come get you, Grey."

"I won't."

I pushed him off. I walked around to the lower falls and sat on the edge of the pool.

The sun was getting lower in the sky and my watch said it was three o'clock. I walked toward the shore and pushed off. I paddled slowly, trying to take it all in.

In the distance, I saw Evan on the deck. It looked like he was shaking his head. He knew me almost as well as Alex did. I pulled up to the house, and he was coming around to meet me.

"How's it going?" He hugged me.

"It's going." I smiled. "I needed time to think."

"Anything you want to talk about?"

"Nope, but thanks for asking." He helped me put the gear away and we headed in for dinner.

"So, Evan, what's for dinner?"

"I don't know. You need to ask Declan."

I walked in the door to find Quinn, Alex, and Declan preparing dinner. I couldn't help but laugh.

"So, Chef, what's on the menu for tonight?"

"I call it burgers with a twist." He made a twisting motion with his hands.

"Okay, but don't let Alex cut anything. He's all thumbs."

I went upstairs to change and noticed a note on my bag.

I would like to apologize for my reaction this afternoon. It was rude to walk away. I am sorry. Declan

I folded the note and put it in my bag, dressed, and headed back into the kitchen. Alex was starting the grill, but Evan, Quinn, and Declan were still there.

"Can I help with anything?" Evan handed me a tray.

"Take these plates and silverware out to the deck."

I shot him a look.

"I'll be back for the glasses."

I put the tray down on the table. I had Emery and Allie set the table while I went back in to get the glasses. Quinn was on her way out with them, when I stopped her.

"I'll take those."

"Okay."

She headed back into the kitchen. Alex was ready with the grill when Evan came out with the burgers.

"Don't burn the burgers, Alex," I teased.

"I'm not cooking them. Dec is."

"Maybe we should have Declan cook all our meals."

"That's fine by me," Declan stated as he walked toward the grill. "I almost forgot." He walked toward me with cup in his hand. "I got this for you, because I stole yours this morning."

"Thank you. That was very thoughtful." I glanced at Paige and mouthed the words "find out, please." She nodded as if she was already on it.

Dinner went quickly. Quinn and Gavin cleared the table while Allie ran in to get the Trivial Pursuit game. I excused myself to help her.

"Hey, Allie. Do you need help?"

"No, I found it." She pulled herself from the closet with the box.

"What's with game night?"

"Alex suggested it."

She giggled as she headed back out to the deck. She was as sneaky as both Alex and Evan. They knew I didn't like board games that much, because Alex was so competitive and argu-ments would break out between us. It was never a pretty sight, playing games with my family. I felt someone come up behind me and I jumped.

"Sorry, I didn't mean to scare you." His voice was like music to my ears.

"No, you didn't."

"So, they're forming teams for Trivial Pursuit. Would you like to be my partner?"

I'd definitely be anything you want me to be. Damn, Grey, snap out of it.

"I don't know. I hate playing board games with Alex. It gets too intense."

"He promised to be good because you have guests." He smiled.

"Why don't you team up with someone else?"

I closed the closet door and walked toward the living room.

"Please, I don't want to play alone."

Why was he so insistent on playing the game? And with me? I gathered myself and gave in.

"I guess I can, but I play a clean game."

He smiled, then chuckled. We walked out to the porch to see Alex awaiting my answer.

"You ready to play?"

"Only if you play fair and try not to be obnoxious." I glared at him and he held up his hands as if he was conceding.

"Do you have a partner?"

"Yeah, Tyler. I do, thanks for asking."

Declan had disappeared. *That was odd. He begged me to play and then he takes off.*

"There he is!" Evan shouted across the table.

How did he know what I was thinking? He is driving me crazy.

"I thought you might need another cup of tea."

He sat down next to me and placed two cups on the table. I raised my eyebrows and managed to mouth thank you to him.

"No problem, Grey."

The game went on well into the night. Evan called it quits about three hours in so he could get Allie up to her room. She had fallen asleep in the chair as usual. I was a little disappointed because we were a late-night type of family. She must take after our dad.

It was midnight when the game ended. Paige and Emery won. I got up and headed toward the kitchen to rinse out my cup.

"Did you enjoy yourself tonight?" I got a cold chill against my neck.

"Yes, I did."

"I thought you didn't like board games."

"I don't, but Alex promised to behave himself." I was curt. "Did you want anything else, Gavin?"

He whispered in my ear, "Yes."

I flinched, and for some reason he took that as a go-ahead. He quickly turned me around and kissed me.

What was with this guy? I heard someone clear their throat. I was finally able to move out of his hulk-like hold.

"I was bringing my cup to the kitchen," Declan remarked. "I'm sorry I interrupted."

I gave him a quick look as I hurried from the room. Alex saw me run up the stairs and, headed into the kitchen.

"Hey, guys. What did you say to my sister?"

"Nothing. I was putting my cup in the sink." Declan gestured toward Gavin.

"Fine."

"Alex, I need to talk to you about our plans for tomorrow."

He pushed him out to the deck. I stayed on the stairs until Gavin walked up to his room. My headache was back, and it felt like little wasp stinging the side of my temple.   On Gavin's way up, he brushed his hand across my face and I flinched at cold in his touch. I walked down the stairs and jumped up to sit on the kitchen counter. Emery, Quinn, and Paige followed me.

"Are you okay?" Quinn asked.

"No, what's his problem?"

What is with the cold jolts I get from him?

"He thinks any movement is an invitation," Emery said.

"He is competing for you, girl, and he knows he's losing, so I guess he upped his game," Paige explained.

"Now I feel bad."

"This is not your fault. Don't feel bad. He's just a jerk." Quinn sat next to me.

"Why do guys do this?" I turned to them. "I didn't give him any reasons for that action."

"Guys think of their own needs first."

"Don't put my brother in that category." Paige glowered at Quinn.

"Let me rephrase. Most—no, some—guys think of themselves first."

We sat in silence. I hopped off the counter and stood in front of the sink.

"We'll give you a minute."

"We'll be right on the deck. Come and join us when you're ready," Quinn pleaded.

I looked out on the deck and saw Alex and Declan talking. The kettle whistled me out of my trance. I grabbed another cup. I walked out to the deck and over to the table.

"I thought you might need something calming."

I handed him the cup, lightly grazing my fingers against his hand.

"Thanks, Grey."

I walked over to the lounge chair and sat down. I didn't notice anyone leave because I was in my own little world again, looking out at the reflection of the moon on the lake.

"Is this seat taken?"

"Huh? Oh, no. Go ahead." I broke from my racing thoughts. "Did you know you can find all the constellations from here?"

"No, really?"

"I like to sit here and take in the beauty of the night."

He sighed and I heard him get up.

"Declan, you can stay you know?"

"I know, but I think it's best if I turned in." He leaned down and whispered in my ear, "Thank you."

"You're welcome. And forgiven."

I heard him chuckle as he walked inside.

I woke up to my warm friend greeting my eyes to a brand new day. I always seemed to fall asleep outside. I laughed to myself, and I sat up and noticed I was wearing a jacket and covered with a blanket. *Someone helped me out last night.* I was grateful.

I heard the door open behind me.

"Hey, sleepyhead."

"Hey, Alex. Is breakfast ready?"

"No, it's still early. I thought I would come and sit with you."

He came around the chair and squished his way in next to me. I turned to the side and rested my legs on his lap.

"Here," he said as he handed me a cup of tea.

"Thanks, Alex."

"So, Grey, how has your weekend been going?"

"As good as can be expected."

"So I noticed some things have been moved around the deck."

"I must have been bored. I'm not ready to talk to everyone about this yet. I mean, I talked a little to Quinn, but my head has been crazy cloudy lately."

"What do you want to do before we leave?"

"I was thinking about going out to the middle of the lake."

"Go now, so you have enough time to get back before we leave."

"Thanks, Alex." I hugged him before heading upstairs to get dressed.

I quietly walked in and around the bed to get my bag. I heard Declan roll over and sigh. I hope I hadn't woken him. He looked so peaceful while he slept. I tried to tear myself away from the formed ridges of his back when he opened his eyes.

"This is definitely something nice to wake up to," he whispered.

I blushed. I was caught looking.

"I'm sorry. I came in to get my bag."

"Are we leaving soon?"

"No, you can go back to sleep." I smiled at him. "I'm just getting my gear to go kayaking."

I started back around the other side when he grabbed my hand.

"You know you don't have to go?"

"I know." I started to pull my hand away, but his grip was too strong. He sat up and pulled me down to sit next to him. "Do you want me to come with you?"

"No, you need to go back to sleep. You have to drive us home."

I stood up and grabbed my bag. He reached for my arm and pulled me toward him. I was closer to him than before. I felt every warm breath across my face. I could feel the little pin shocks up my arm. I looked down quickly and noticed tiny little bumps dotting his arms.

"Is this okay?" he asked permission.

"Yes," I said.

He leaned in and kissed me quickly but gently. The anticipation of what was about to happen was more accelerating than the actual kiss itself. I lost my train of thought and I just froze.

This is what I wanted, right? I think I want this. I don't know. I have to get out of here.

"Grey."

"I have to go."

I stumbled down the stairs, breezing past Quinn and Alex sitting on the sofa.

"Is she okay?" Alex asked

"I don't know, Alex." Quinn seemed confused. "She had her gear with her."

Alex looked up to see Declan standing at the top of the stairs as Quinn watched me run out the front door.

I must have been gone about three hours, because the sun was higher in the sky when I decided to paddle back. I put my gear in the shed, hung up my kayak, and walked up toward the kitchen door. Everyone was ready to go. They were all on the porch waiting for me.

"I'm ready. Let's go." Evan came over and gave me hug.

"We're all packed up. Go put your bag in the car."

I was the last one out. Everyone was in the cars they'd been in on the way up, but this time I'd decided to ride with Allie and Evan. I heard some murmuring as I walked to the car. What hurt me the most was the look on Declan's face. I needed to think some more. I couldn't be distracted in the car.

CHAPTER SEVEN

REALITY

We pulled up the drive and it felt good to be home. Everyone grabbed their bags out of Evan's car.

"Hey, Emery, Quinn, thanks for coming." I hugged them. "I hope you guys had a good time. Maybe next time there will be less drama."

"You're too funny, Grey." Emery smiled. "I'll see you tomorrow."

"See you tomorrow, silly." Quinn hugged me.

"Bye, Tyler!" I shouted toward his car. He waved back. I walked toward Declan's Jeep. Paige was standing by the passenger's side door.

"Hey, I'm really glad you came and for all your help," I said to her.

"Anytime, and I mean that." She winked.

"Let's keep the original plan, okay, Agent Watt?"

We both laughed and she walked over to Tyler's car to say bye to everyone else. I climbed in the passenger seat and waited before I spoke.

"Hey."

"Hey." He turned to me. "Can you tell me what I did wrong?"

"Nothing, Declan. I was caught off guard." I glanced up at him. "Listen, I want to thank you for coming this weekend."

My heart was speeding up. It was now or never to do something to let him know that I'm interested.

"You're welcome." He was fidgeting with his hands. *I wonder what he's thinking. Ugh, I'm taking a chance, and I hope it pays off.* Seriously, this silence was starting to feel awkward, and lately I'd been the queen of awkward.

"I guess I'll see you in English tomorrow." I leaned in quickly and kissed his cheek. "Thanks again."

I jumped out of the car and headed inside.

After everyone had left, I made sure I got rid of some things before I went upstairs.

"Hey, Alex, can you throw this out?"

I handed him the white box. He walked outside and threw it into the trash barrel. I could have sworn I heard him laugh.

"I think I'm going to turn in early."

I headed upstairs and my head hit my pillow like a brick.

I rolled over when I heard a knock at my door.

"Grey, are you up yet?"

"No. Go away." I threw the pillows over my head.

"Ah, come on, Grey. We're going to be late."

"Fine, give me five minutes," I groaned.

What a bad morning, and I do not drink coffee. I needed something to wake me up because I was feeling horrible. I did not care what I looked like. I pulled my hair back, grabbed my bag, and jumped in the Jeep. I had to beep the horn a couple of times to get Alex out the door.

"Someone woke up on the wrong side of the bed this morning," he chastised.

"Shut up and drive." I closed my eyes and prayed for the day to end.

We pulled into the parking lot. I grabbed my bag and headed for class. I glanced back to see him telling everyone to give me space today. I walked up to the third floor into class. I sat in the back right corner instead of my usual seat toward the front.

I walked through the rest of the day in a funk. I dragged myself into the cafeteria and sat down next to Paige.

"So how's your day going?" she asked.

I didn't pick my head up from the table to answer her.

"Not well. I think I'm getting sick or something."

"You should go home then. Alex can get a ride home from someone on the team."

"I think I might do that."

"Just get better by Friday, okay?" Emery said. "Your brother would hate it if you weren't at his first game."

"I know, I know. Thanks."

I went to Evan's office and had him dismiss me.

"I'm not feeling so great, so can you let Alex know to get another ride home?"

He nodded. I all but ran to the student lot. I jumped in the Jeep and headed home.

She was at the front door waiting for me. Evan must have called her.

"I think it's a cold, Grams. Don't worry."

"Get upstairs. I'll bring you some tea, okay?"

I headed upstairs. I fell asleep in my clothes. I was too tired to change and I didn't care. I woke up a couple of times when I heard the phone ringing, but went right back to sleep.

I heard a light knock at my door. Alex walked in and sat down on the bed.

"How are you feeling today?"

I must have slept through the night.

"I'm getting there, but I'm not going to school today."

"I know, because you missed school. It's five o'clock."

"Wow. I slept longer than I thought."

Alex seemed to think that it might be a good time for some friendly sibling banter, but I just wanted to go back to bed. I think he had something else in mind.

"Are you up for company or not?"

After a couple minutes of trying to get me out of bed, I finally gave in.

"Sure. I guess I could eat something or at least get more tea."

He helped me up, and I pulled my hair back into a ponytail. It looks like someone had changed my clothes, because I was in a t-shirt and shorts. It was probably Allie, because I matched.

I walked into the kitchen to waiting concern over my lack of cheeriness.

"Hey, sleepyhead. How are you feeling?" Evan hugged me.

"I'm getting better, Evan. Thanks for letting me sleep."

I sat down at the counter and laid my head on the marble countertop. The cold surface felt good on my face. I then heard a cup placed in front of me it, and it sounded like a trash compactor crushing cars.

"Would you like some tea, dear?" I heard Grams say.

As much as I appreciated their kindness, I felt like I should have stayed upstairs in the quiet stillness of my cocoon I called my bed.

I picked up my head and took a couple of sips. My head was still pounding. I felt like I was wearing a lead suit.

"I think I'm going to go back to bed, thanks."

Alex was helping me back up to my room, when I heard the doorbell.

"I'll be right back, okay?" Alex told me.

I heard the loud clumping of his footsteps end at the door. My sensitive hearing was too much. I wanted to stuff cotton balls in my ears to stop the sound. Alex was talking to someone, and he was not happy about it at all. I couldn't remember much after that, because I covered my head with my pillows and crashed.

When I opened my eyes, it was five o'clock in the morning. I rolled over and sat on the edge of my bed. I was feeling much better. I walked to the bathroom and took a long shower.

When I got out, Evan and Alex were just getting up.

"You look better," Alex said.

"I feel better. Thanks."

"Anytime. Now go get dressed," he said as he pointed to the floor. "You're making puddles."

I got dressed and then bounced down each step on my way to the kitchen. I noticed a white box on the hall table that must have come when I was sleeping. I ripped it open and saw the familiar white aura of the rose and the unknowing note.

I hope to see your beautiful eyes again soon. Your absence has fractured my heart.

I had to find out who this person was. He had kept me in the dark long enough. I walked into the kitchen with the note in my hand. I sat down and drank my tea. About ten minutes later, Alex sauntered in.

"Are you ready for the game tonight?" he asked me.

"Today is Thursday, Alex. Your game is on Friday."

"It is Friday, silly." He chuckled to himself. "You've been sick, remember? You were out for three days."

"Are you kidding me?"

"Nope." He threw a muffin at me. "You need to eat something, please."

"Fine."

The student lot was a welcome presence, and so was the crowd of our friends. Emery and Paige were the first ones to jump me before I even put one foot on the ground.

"Thanks, guys, but I'm okay."

Paige blew the comment off, and hugged me.

"Alex said you were out of it the whole time."

"I guess I don't remember much, except for the phone ringing a couple of times and someone coming to the house yesterday."

"Do you know who it was?"

"I don't know, but I have an idea." I took a breath. "I heard Alex talking to someone and he wasn't happy about it."

They both looked at each other and whispered, "Gavin."

I nodded in acknowledgement.

"Let's go before we're late," I said.

I walked into class. I was surprised to see Declan wasn't there. I hoped he hadn't gotten sick as well. I sat in the back corner again as class dragged on.

I moved slowly to Biology. I sat down and turned to ask Paige if her brother was sick.

"No, he's here," she said, seeming surprised.

"I only ask because he wasn't in English."

"He might have been at the field house. They had a meeting with Coach Nelson this morning."

I was relieved a little. At least he wouldn't miss the game because he was sick. Class proved interesting that day. We'd started the chapter on genetics.

"That was interesting." Paige was talking to Emery.

"Grey, are you ready for art?"

I took a deep breath hoping he wasn't here yet.

"Not really," I said.

We sat in the back near the windows. I tried to hide behind my easel but to no avail. He made his presence known.

"Hey, Grey, you look better." He grinned.

"Uh huh. Thanks, Gavin."

Thankfully, saved by Russell, who was starting class, I looked at the clock to see that class was almost over. I casually reached for my bag and left to go to the bathroom—my ruse to keep him at bay. I knew Paige would fill me in at lunch on any assignments I might have missed. I needed to escape quickly.

I was in the hall, running to the fourth floor for trig as if I had just escaped from the evil wizard. It was no secret that I couldn't stand math class, but it was my safe haven that day. I actually think I learned something. I wasn't that great at trig, but I was thinking it might prove useful if I could switch classes, or at the very least get a tutor. Trigonometry was the wall I needed to scale in order to continue my adventures into my fourth year without having to retake it. It was something to think about.

Mrs. Vachon let us out late. By the time I'd reached the cafeteria, everyone was there already. Quinn waved me over and I all but ran toward them.

"Hey, girl. You look better."

"Thanks, Quinn." I slid my bag onto the back of the chair. "I need to get something to eat."

"Someone already got you lunch." There, on the table, was a bowl of soup and a cup of what I thought was tea. I shook my head, assuming they'd done it, or even Alex.

"Alex worries about me too much." I sat down and grabbed the cup.

"Oh, it wasn't Alex," Paige said, raising her eyebrows.

I'd been wrong. *Please don't let it be Gavin.* I turned to see Alex sitting at the far end of the cafeteria with the rest of the lacrosse team. Declan nodded in my direction and I mouthed thank you. He shook his head and laughed. I turned back to the girls and ate my lunch. Of course, Quinn was talking, but I only heard bits and pieces. My thoughts were elsewhere.

"So do you want to meet at the school before the game?"

I wasn't thinking straight but I decided to take a stab at answering her question.

"Why don't you and Emery pick me and Paige up at my house?" I looked at Paige. "That way we only take one car."

"Sounds like a plan." She looked at her watch. "I'll pick you guys up around six thirty, okay? Be ready."

She got up and left for class. That's when Alex came over and sat down with us. He looked at my empty cup and bowl. I couldn't wait to hear his pearls of wisdom for the afternoon.

"Did you enjoy lunch today?"

"It was okay for cafeteria food." We both laughed.

"Come on, were going to be late for history."

I said bye to Emery and Paige, and unhinged my bag from the chair.

The rest of the day flew by and soon we were heading home.

"Listen, I have to go back to the school after I drop you off."

"No problem. I'm getting a ride with Quinn." I got out of the car. "And if I don't see you before the game, good luck."

"Thanks!" he yelled out the window as he drove away.

I threw my bag on the table and headed into the kitchen.

"Hey, Grams. Where's Allie?" She rolled her eyes.

I knew Allie was upstairs getting ready. You would think we were going to a concert rather than a lacrosse game.

"I'm getting a ride with Quinn tonight, so you'll have the car to take Allie."

"Evan's coming back to get us." I heard a car pull up. "Thanks for letting me know, Grey."

I grabbed an apple and headed to my room to change.

"Hey, Evan." I waved as I climbed the stairs.

"Grey, this doesn't belong in the hall." I ran back down and grabbed my bag.

"Sorry."

I grabbed the first pair of jeans I could find that were clean and ran into Alex's room to grab his extra jersey. *I don't understand how he can find anything. His room is a mess.*

I went back to my room to change and started looking for

my jacket. I remembered I never unpacked from the weekend; it had to be in there. As I rummaged through the bag, I found two jackets. One was mine and the other belonged to Declan. I must have packed it by accident. I figured I'd give it to Paige when she got here. I threw my jacket on and found something in the pocket: the note he'd left me. I threw it on my desk.

Everyone had already left, so I waited in the kitchen for Quinn. I grabbed my travel mug and made some tea. As soon as I was done, I heard a car honk. I grabbed the other jacket and ran to the car.

"What's with the two jackets? It's not that cold." Quinn looked in her rearview mirror.

"Oh, I packed Declan's jacket by accident." I handed it to Paige. "Can you make sure he gets it?"

"Don't you want to give it to him yourself?"

"No. that's okay. You're here now, so I'll just give it to you."

"Okay." I noticed Emery give Quinn a look.

We got to the school, but we had to park at the far end of the lot. I think the whole town had come to watch the game. After a five-minute walk we tried to find seats. Thankfully, Evan had saved us some.

It was a little warm, so I took off my jacket. The teams were finishing their warm-up on the field before huddling up by the bench. Right before they went back out onto the field, Gavin turned and winked. I was starting to feel sick again.

When is this guy going to see there is nothing there but friendship? I heard Evan and Allie laugh behind me, so I turned and glowered at them.

The other team took a timeout; there was no score on either side.

"This team's good."

"So is ours," Evan answered.

I got a chill, so I turned to get my jacket. *I could have sworn I put it on the bleacher next to me.*

"Here, use this one." Paige handed me Declan's jacket. "Allie took yours."

"Didn't you bring a jacket?"

"No, it would wreck my outfit."

I couldn't help but roll my eyes as I turned around. I grabbed his jacket from Paige and put it on; no reason to get sick again. The team went back onto the field. Alex looked up. He just shook his head, and I stuck my tongue out at him as he laughed. Declan looked up to see what was so funny. He obviously saw me wearing his jacket. I could have sworn I saw him smirk as he lowered his helmet and ran onto the field.

There were only five minutes left in the game and the score was tied. Tyler stole the ball and ran down the field. One of the defenseman slammed him down, and the ball flew into the air. Declan scooped it up and hurled it toward the net. Everyone was up on their feet, cheering.

I hope that we could hold them to zero. I couldn't watch the last three minutes. I put my hands over my face and told Allie to tell me when it was over. I heard boos behind me, and then a gasp.

"Did we lose?"

"No, someone is down." She gasped. "A cheap shot."

I started to worry about who it was, but I didn't want to look, fearing it would be him.

"Who is it?"

"I don't know. It happened so fast."

Whoever it was, was being taking away on the cart. I kept telling myself, *Please don't let it be him.* This couldn't be good. The other player was ejected for an illegal hit. The game was over quickly after that. Both teams hurried off the field.

We followed Evan to the field house, waiting outside as he continued into the locker room. He emerged after fifteen minutes.

"Nothing is broken." He put his hands on my shoulders, "Just badly bruised around his chest and shoulder."

"Well, that's good."

Alex, Tyler, and Jack walked out of the locker room.

"So we thought we would go celebrate down at Wicked Brew."

"How can you celebrate when you're hurt?" I glared at him.

"I'm fine. I didn't get hurt."

"Then who did?!" Emery shouted.

The rest of the team came out and I saw Declan in the back. He didn't look injured either, but he was helping someone out.

"It's Gavin." Paige murmured.

I ran over to see if he was okay. Just because I didn't feel the same way as he did about me didn't mean I liked to see a friend injured.

"How are you doing, Gavin?"

"I've been better." I touched his shoulder and he winced. "Thanks for asking."

I felt a quick jolt of energy surge up my arm. I kept thinking I'd done it again. It was the scenario with healing the bird all over again.

"Thanks, Declan." He started walking toward the rest of the team. "Oh, before I forget, here's your jacket." I took it off and handed it to him.

"So are we going to celebrate or what?!" Tyler shouted.

Everyone cheered and headed for the parking lot. I decided to catch a ride with Evan. I was feeling a little tired. Maybe I hadn't fully recovered yet—or it had something to do with what had happened when I'd touched Gavin.

We returned home. I took Allie inside and Grams followed. Evan decided to go to town to keep an eye on things. As he left, he was mumbling something about boys and keeping an eye out. I got

Allie to bed and headed to the kitchen.

"Well, it's late and I'm turning in." Grams yawned.

"See you in the morning, Grams."

I grabbed some tea and went to bed. A few minutes later, I heard a knock at the door. I was about to get out of bed, when Grams answered it. *Who would be coming here so late?* My mind was racing with bad thoughts.

It was a familiar voice, muffled because my door was closed. It sounded like they were looking for me. I heard her say I was already asleep, but before she closed the door, I heard her mumble something I couldn't quite make out. I rolled over and buried my head.

I woke up and glanced at the clock. It was only six o'clock in the morning. I decided to get dressed, and I grabbed my sneakers to go for a run after I'd changed. I rummaged through my desk for my iPod.

No one was up yet, so I left a note on the table saying I'd gone for a run and would be back in an hour or so.

I took off down the drive, heading towards town. I passed the Watt house, waving to Paige who was getting the paper. I got to town in about twenty-five minutes.

I was a little thirsty, and my stomach started to growl, so I headed over to the café. I was lucky because it was still early and not as crowded.

"Hey, Mr. Ellis. How are you this morning?" I sat at the counter.

"I'm good. You're up early." He grabbed a menu. "Everyone is still recovering from last night."

"I went home after the game. I was a little tired."

He gave me a knowing nod. I had no idea what all that had been about.

"What would you like to drink?"

"She'll have a cup of tea," someone said from behind me. I turned to see Gavin slowly making his way to the counter.

"How are feeling, tough guy?"

"I could be better. Overall, feeling pretty good all things considered."

He seemed to be better and he didn't wince when I touched his shoulder. *Damn, it is the bird all over again. I need to talk to Evan.*

"Why are you up so early?"

"I came down to get muffins for the family for breakfast."

"That's nice." I took a sip of my tea. "I'm surprised you're up. I heard it was a long night."

"Oh, well I went home after the game. Wasn't feeling up to it." He smiled. "What do you want? My treat."

"Um, how about a muffin?" What else was I going to get? I didn't want to sit down and eat with him, nor did I want to lead him on.

"Wait, let me guess: blueberry?"

I nodded in acknowledgement because I didn't want to hurt his feelings.

"Here. At least let me carry everything for you." I grabbed the box, my bag, and the tea.

"Do you want a ride home? It's on the way."

"Sure, why not? I can't run with a muffin and a tea in my hands." I held up the bag and cup.

We pulled up the drive and I turned toward him.

"Listen, I need you to be my friend right now, okay?"

"Sure, no problem." He winked. "I can wait."

That's not what I asked.

"Thanks for the muffin and tea."

I closed the door and headed into the house. As I walked into the kitchen, Evan gave me a look.

"What?"

"Nothing. I thought you were going for a run?" He snickered.

"I did, but I got hungry, so I stopped at the cafe to get something to eat." I sipped my tea. "He happened to show up and offer me a ride back."

Why was I explaining myself to him?

Nothing had happened, and for some reason I felt like I was being interrogated. I expected this from Alex, but not from Evan. He grinned, and it was as if he had heard my rant.

"That's fine. You're lucky Alex is still sleeping. So what's on the agenda today?"

"Paige and I have an art project to do. She'll be over in the afternoon."

"Is there anything else you want to tell me?" He smiled.

Damn, he knew.

"When I touched Gavin last night, I felt a surge go through my hand. It's the bird thing all over again."

"Okay, but you do know it is a gift you have there? Not too many of us are born with that talent, so to speak."

"So does anyone else in our family have it besides me?" I think I already knew the answer.

"Your Grams does. I think the next time you work at the shop you might want to ask her about it."

I nodded in agreement. This was all still too weird for me to discuss in such a rational way. I grabbed my tea and muffin and headed out to the deck. I made myself comfortable, leaning back in the chair to enjoy the rest of my morning. I heard leaves rustling from the right side of the deck. I figured it was a squirrel or something. I put my head back and closed my eyes.

"So you're up early," I heard a voice say from around the corner of the house. I opened my eyes to see Declan walking around the side of the house. I guess I'd found my squirrel and he'd found the nut—me. I saw a smile break across his lips.

"I would say the same for you." I took a sip. "Do you want to come up?"

"Thanks." He walked up the stairs and sat in the chair next to me.

"What brings you over so early?"

"Paige saw you running to town, but not back. Did you get a ride?"

"Yes, Gavin happened to be at the café at the same time as me. So he offered."

"Gavin, huh?" His lips tightened.

"He bought me a muffin and tea. I couldn't run home with them in my hand." I took another sip. "Besides, were friends."

Why was I explaining myself to him? What was he to me? I knew what I wanted, but it was too farfetched.

"What a nice offer, but why did he buy you a blueberry muffin?"

I looked down at the muffin I hadn't touched because blueberry would be the last muffin I would choose for myself.

"Why do you ask?" I kept looking toward the garden. He pulled out a cinnamon swirl muffin placing it on the table.

"Isn't this your favorite muffin?"

I turned to look at what he had. *Damn, how did he know that?*

"Lucky guess." I tried not to smile.

"Or I'm very observant." He flashed a smile. "I came by to see how you were feeling. I came by last night, but you were already asleep." Case solved, and my mystery guest from last night, revealed.

"Thank you for the muffin and your concern. Tell Paige I'll see her at eleven o'clock."

"Paige is coming over?"

"Yeah, we have an art project to work on."

"I'll convey the message. Enjoy your muffin."

"Thanks again." I smiled.

He strutted down the stairs, seeming impressed with his good deeds, then paused briefly.

"By the way, the scenery is breathtaking this morning."

And, with that comment, he disappeared around the corner. My heart was racing at full speed now. I tried to finish my breakfast, but found it hard to breathe and eat at the same time. What I needed was a shower. The dew on the bottom of my sneakers caused me to slip a few times walking down the hall, but I eventually made it to the stairs, unscathed—until I saw Evan.

"Grey, who were you talking to on the deck?"

I didn't want to tell him, so I fibbed.

"Just Mom."

"Grey, please." He chuckled. "Really?"

"I was mumbling to myself."

He threw me a cautionary look as I slowly made my way upstairs. I couldn't believe he would find the view beautiful—unless he hadn't been talking about me. I looked in the mirror and saw a sweaty version of me, my hair all knotted. I needed to stop this irrational thinking. I hoped the beads of warm water would wash those thoughts away.

I don't know how long I was in there, but I heard the door open and close.

"Hey, Grey."

I peeked around the curtain.

"What do you want, Alex?" I leaned against the wall.

"Can we talk about something?" *He chose to talk to me now. He couldn't wait?*

"Sure, but it's your sauna."

I heard him chuckle, but he tried to stay composed for whatever he was planning for his lecture.

"I was wondering what you thought of Declan? I only ask because he has."

We're going to do this now, while I'm in the shower.

"Why do you ask?"

"Well, you're my sister and I want to make sure you're okay."

He sighed. "Your friendship is first over any other."

"So you're saying you don't want me to be friends with him anymore?"

"No, I want to make sure that nobody's feelings get hurt or that I'm not in the middle."

Definitely spoken like a true guy. Deep down it was about his feelings and his friendships.

"I don't think you have to worry. I'm sure he sees me as nothing more than a friend." I shut the water off. "Can you hand me that towel on the sink?" I dried off and wrapped the towel around myself. "So I don't think you have to worry. I can see he only regards me as a friend, and my feelings on the matter will stay my feelings."

"What are you talking about now?" He huffed. "You've got to be either stupid or blind." He followed me into the hall. "I don't care either way, Grey."

"Then why do you need to know if it doesn't matter?"

I slammed the door in his face and sat on the bed for a minute. As I got dressed, I heard someone coming up the stairs.

"Can I come in?"

"Sure, Paige, but you're early."

"Well, the light looked good, so I thought I would come earlier." She sat on the bed. "If you're okay with that?"

I wasn't entirely convinced of her explanation, but at this point getting away from the inquisition was what I needed.

"It's fine. I need to get out anyway. Alex bombarded me with twenty questions while I was in the shower."

"Interesting." She seemed to feel awkward. "Maybe he's being a big brother."

"Or a royal pain." I combed my hair out, then gave up and threw on a hat. "Let's go take some pictures."

I pushed her out the door and grabbed my keys.

"I'm taking the Jeep, Alex."

She retrieved her bag from her car and jumped into my car.

"So I was thinking Laurel Lake." I offered my suggestion.

"I was thinking more along the lines of Lake Dennison. There are plenty of trails and no houses along the water."

I took her suggestion because I was still unfamiliar with the area, and my memories were somewhat blurry. It was about a thirty-minute drive from the house. We parked and grabbed our gear. I followed her toward one of the trails.

"I heard you had a visitor this morning." She was straight to the point, like Alex.

"Yeah, Gavin gave me a ride home." I laughed. I knew to whom she was referring. She ignored me and continued.

"You definitely have a hold on him."

"What do you mean?"

"I've never seen him talk to himself before. It's like he's rehearsing lines in his room. Plus, when I'm going somewhere, he wants to know if you'll be there." She stopped. "And I've never seen him worry about what he was wearing or how he looks."

"I don't know what that has to do with me, Paige." I knew exactly where this was going, and I didn't want to go there today.

"You must be blind."

"And?"

"If you can't see how he cares for you, then you definitely need your eyes checked."

"I can but I can't, if that makes sense. He's never straight to the point about it. He's so cryptic."

"Ugh!" she screamed. "My only concern is whether you feel same. He has been through a lot. I don't want to see him hurt."

"I do like him. You don't understand how much. It's strange, because I don't know if it's normal or not."

"Sometimes I wonder about you." She laughed. "At least that mess is cleared up."

Great. Now I would worry whether or not she was going to

tell him. What did I care if she did or not? I was somewhat—or even a little—positive that he didn't see me as anything other than Alex's little sister.

"Are you going to tell him about our conversation?"

"Only as much as you want."

I agreed with her summation and dragged myself up the trail.

"That's settled. Now let's get this project done."

"Hey, Paige, can I talk to you about something else?"

She stopped just short of the fork.

"Sure, what's up?"

I leaned against a tree for support, feeling its strength helping me with what I was about to ask.

"Have you ever known anyone that can heal with a touch?"

Her face said it all. She was surprised, but answered anyway.

"Yeah, your Grams. Why do you ask?" she was staring at me like she was trying to pick my brain or something.

"No reason. Just wondering is all. It's all little new to me, you know? It was just a question."

She didn't buy what I'd said, but went with it anyway. After that, I tried not to talk about anything, including my "talents," as Evan called them.

We must have spent hours out at the lake. I should have eaten more of a breakfast besides tea and parts of a muffin.

"So we can develop these on Monday. I have a free period after history."

"I have class, but I trust you, Grey."

The ride home was quiet. Paige had fallen asleep. I woke her up when we got back to the house.

"I'll see you tonight. right?" She climbed out of the Jeep.

"For what?" I was confused. Had I made more plans?

"Alex didn't tell you?"

"He didn't get a chance to between his lecture on my eye sight and my stupidity."

She laughed. "We're going bowling tonight."

"Sure, why not? It's one of the only sports I can beat Alex at."
I grabbed my gear and headed inside.

Before I got ready that night, I had to talk to Evan. I knocked on
his office door.

"Come in, Grey."

Seriously, how does he do that? I walked in and stood by the window.

"What's on your mind?" He never looked up.

"I need to know who I go to for a tutor."

"Oh, well, what class is the problem?"

"Trigonometry." I spat it out as if I had just tasted something
bad.

"On Monday I'll set up a tutor for your free period, okay?"

That had been simple enough. No pain involved at all. I
sighed and walked toward the door.

"Have fun tonight, Grey." I turned to see him wink at me.

CHAPTER EIGHT

TEMPTATIONS

I must have been blind if everyone else had seen it but me. If I was going to take chances, what would I start with? My clothes, I didn't want to go too drastic. I grabbed a pair of jeans, a cami, and one of my V-neck Henley shirts. I put on my necklace that Alex gave me, and my mom's ring. I was all ready, and if looks could kill, I would hope to be warning someone tonight.

Alex was already downstairs, waiting impatiently. I guess I'd taken longer than I thought.

"Wow, is that what you're wearing?"

"Yeah, does it look okay?"

"For you, it's a little different from your normal attire. But if you want to attract attention to yourself, then I think you might have succeeded," he said.

"Good. I'm ready to go."

We were the last to arrive, thanks in part to my indecision. Everyone was already inside. I heard a couple of gulps and clearing of throats as we walked toward the counter. I could see and feel his protective side was working overtime.

"Relax." I grabbed his arm.

"Easy for you to say."

He pulled me closer like we were heading into a wolf's den. I grabbed our shoes because he was one arm short—the other was acting as a shackle around mine. I happened to notice a certain someone was missing. I felt somewhat diminished.

"He's here, just in the bathroom," Paige whispered behind me. "He's going to die when he sees you."

We set up the teams. They consisted of Emery and I, Quinn and Gavin, Paige and Alex, and Declan was stuck with Tyler.

"I'll go first." I walked toward the lane and grabbed the ball. *Please let me hit something,* I thought to myself. I wound up and released the ball. Seven pins down.

"Sweet!" Emery high-fived me. I heard a scuffling of feet, then a bang.

"Are you okay, man?"

"Yeah, Tyler. I'm fine. I lost my footing." The girls giggled.

"Good one, Dec," Alex remarked.

The game continued and Alex lost. His competitive nature got the best of him and he demanded a rematch. We were up last in the rotation, and I was a little thirsty.

"Does anyone want something to drink?" I asked.

I took everyone's order and headed up to the counter.

"Wait, I'll help you."

"Thanks, Declan, but I got it."

"I insist."

"Well, if you insist." I turned and continued.

I ordered the drinks, but it took a while because they were busy.

"You . . . look . . . nice." He stumbled getting the words out.

"Thank you. So do you." I was trying to be polite.

"Are you having fun?"

"Definitely. It's one of the only sports I can beat my brother at." I smiled shyly. "And the company is nice, too."

I grabbed the drinks and walked back, leaving him speechless for the first time, I think.

"Hey, where's Declan? Did he get lost or something?"

"Back there picking his jaw off the floor, I think." I smirked. "Who's turn?"

"It's yours," Quinn said, pointing to the board.

We finished our game and Alex lost both times. That time I let him know that it wasn't going to get any better and he should give up.

I brought my shoes back to the counter and felt someone touch my shoulder. I turned to see Gavin.

"How's your shoulder, right?" I tried to show concern, but not too much. I didn't want to give him the wrong idea.

"It's better." He placed his shoes on the counter. "You look very nice tonight."

"Thanks." I started toward the doors, and he was at my side as we walked out.

"So what are you doing tomorrow?" *Doesn't he see that I'm not interested?*

"She's spending the day with me." I heard Declan come up behind me. I looked at him and he winked.

"Yeah, he's going to give me cooking lessons."

"Oh, okay. Maybe another time then."

"Sure." I didn't want to give him false hope. Declan walked me to the Jeep. I started to reach for the door handle when he pulled back.

"So cooking lessons, huh?"

"Well, if you're not busy tomorrow. I can't make anything besides tea and a bowl of cereal." I pouted.

"I'll see you tomorrow at around noon then." He leaned in and whispered in my ear, "But please wear something else or I'll be liable to burn the house down."

I laughed. He pulled his face back to look at mine. His lips were so close to mine. I slid my tongue along my bottom lip before pulling in the right corner. I heard what sounded like a low growl coming from his chest.

"You do look beautiful tonight." He raised his hand to my neck. You could feel the electricity in the little space between us. *Oh my god, I think he is going to kiss me.*

"Thank you, again." I could stop staring at his moist lips, wondering how they would taste and feel against my own.

"Well, I've got to go. Until tomorrow."

He leaned in and gently kissed me. I kept my eyes closed trying to relive the previous thirty seconds. I tried to slow my heart from racing to catch my breath. He walked toward his car, laughing to himself.

"Are you getting in or what?" Alex yelled through the window.

"What? Oh yeah." I got in and he laughed.

"So it looks like someone had a good night."

"I sure did. I beat you at bowling."

"That's not what I meant, and I want another rematch."

"I know what you meant. I think you'd get the same outcome. Just drive." He pulled out of the lot, shaking his head. I could not help but laugh.

We walked in the house, and of course Evan was waiting. I couldn't wait to hear what he had to say or what questions he had for me, but I was ready.

"Hey, guys, did you have—whoa!"

"Trust me, you weren't the only one." Alex rolled his eyes.

"You look like you are on a mission, Grey."

"I was."

"Well, from his expression I would say mission accomplished."

I choked on his words a little and that familiar hue flooded to my face.

"Well, anyway, you have mail."

Who would send me mail? Everyone I know is here. I grabbed the two small envelopes from the table and headed to my contemplation corner. *I think I'm going to need tea to read this mail.*

The envelopes were both addressed to me, but they seemed to

have been hand delivered due to the lack of postage. The handwriting on each was completely different. These were definitely from two different people.

I grabbed my cup and poured the hot water in, submerging the tea. I set the kettle down and took my place on the counter. Taking a deep breath, I opened the first envelope.

I enjoyed your company this morning. I hope we can spend time together again. Gavin

I sighed.

What am I going to do about him? I thought I made it clear this morning. Obviously not. The way I was dressed tonight hadn't helped either, even though it hadn't been for his benefit.

I put his note aside and picked up the next envelope. This person had more elegant handwriting than the previous sender did. The handwriting was not the only difference; the letter was sealed with a silver embossed seal. I ripped open the envelope to uncover what was inside. Silver foil adorned the envelope. Tucked neatly inside was a note. I slowly removed it from its encasement like a curator at a museum. I unfolded it carefully. There was more content to this letter than in the previous.

Grey,

There are at least twenty-two ways I could give to show you how I care, but only one reason to stay away. That one reason is that you don't feel the same way. I will wait for a sign before I divulge my true feelings. As always, my heart belongs to you.

Not signed.

"Huh?" Evan came in to check on me.

"What's wrong?"

"One note was from Gavin and the other was unsigned."

"Let me see the unsigned note." He reached for the note and noticed the envelope. "Did that envelope come with it?"

"Yes." I gave him the envelope. "That explains it." He put them on the counter.

"It's from your anonymous admirer, but this time no flowers." The light finally went off in my head. "You're right." I sensed there was more to it, and he wasn't willing to say what.

"Right about what?" Alex chimed in.

"She got another note from her admirer." Evan handed him the note.

He quickly glanced over it, then paused before he spoke—which I found rather odd for Alex.

"Oh."

"What?" I watched his face. He seemed unnerved, but his eyes gave him away. He knew something.

"Nothing." He handed the note back to Evan, but seemed to be pointing to something in the note. Evan's eyes grew wider and he gasped as well.

"That explains it."

"Explains what?" I was angered. "What do you know?"

"Nothing, Grey. I was mistaken." He put the note down and walked out, shaking his head. I turned to Alex and he shrugged his shoulders.

"Come on. It's late." He pulled me toward the stairs. This wasn't over. They knew something that I didn't.

As I lay in bed, my thoughts were racing to connect the dots. Whatever was in the note shouted, "This is who I am. How could you not see it before?" It was almost two o'clock in the morning when I decided I wasn't going to crack the mystery that night. I curled up under the comforter and stared at the wall until I fell asleep.

Someone shouting outside woke me up. I opened my door, but no one was there. *Was I dreaming?* Then I heard it again, but this time it came from behind me. I walked to the balcony.

"Grey."

"What are you doing, Alex?" I glared. "You woke me up."

"It's almost eleven o'clock. Time to get up, silly."

"You suck, you know that?" I stuck my tongue out at him.

He laughed and strolled out of sight. That day was going to be my lounge-around-the-house day, so I decided to stay in my shorts and cami. I was going to relax. For the first time, I had nothing to do. I sauntered down to the kitchen to get something to eat.

"Are you going to get some clothes on?"

"No, silly brother. Today I'm relaxing and doing nothing." I grabbed a bowl from the cupboard.

"Whatever you say." He laughed as he walked back outside.

"Whatever." I grabbed the cereal box and milk. As I poured my milk, I heard the doorbell ring. *Was Alex expecting someone?*

"I'll get it!" I yelled. I opened the door and I wasn't ready for what was there.

"Whoa!" I quickly shut the door, which was rude, but I'd been caught off guard. I heard Alex behind me.

"Who is it?"

"It's Declan. Did you have plans today?"

"No, you did. Don't you remember?"

"Ah, crap."

What was I going to do now? I didn't have time to change. *Think, Grey, think.* I noticed Alex sit down on the stairs, waiting to see what was to come in the next act.

"Are you going to open the door, Grey?"

I ran my fingers through my hair while Alex snickered behind me. I took a deep breath and opened the door.

"Sorry about that, I was caught off guard." Thankfully, he was still there.

"You forgot, huh?" His smile faded.

"I guess I did. Sorry."

"We can do this another time." He turned.

"No, it's fine come in."

As he walked through the door, he whispered, "I thought I told you I didn't want to burn the house down."

And there was my little enemy bringing bursts of color to my cheeks. I turned to close the door in order to avoid giving myself away.

"Hey, Alex, how's it going?" He sat on the stairs next to him. "Are you joining us today?"

"No way. I know how to cook." He didn't buy it.

"You're more than welcome. It's your house."

"No, I'm good, but I think someone should go get dressed."

"I think you're right." His smile became wider and his eyes appraised me.

"Okay, okay." I shooed them out of the way. "I'll be right back."

He winked. "Take your time, Grey."

"Whatever."

I'd totally forgotten. I thought he'd been joking to get Gavin to back off. I threw on whatever I could find. Unbeknownst to me, they were talking about me in the hall, and I did have some paranoia slipping in.

"So, Dec, I have a question for you."

"I hope I have answers for you, Alex. Fire away"

"Are you my sister's admirer?" His tone was still calm.

"Why do you ask that?"

"The note." Alex pulled out the note I'd received the day before, and Declan didn't deny it.

"What gave it away?"

"The number you put in the note." He pointed to the number twenty-two. "It's your jersey number."

"If you wish me to stop, it'll be hard, but I will."

"No, I'm not asking you to stop. I've never seen her as happy as when she receives these deliveries."

Declan smiled.

"Then what do you want, Alex?"

"You need to be careful with her. I think you might want to talk to Evan first. And tell her—she thinks she has three admirers, not two."

"Three. Who else?" His voice was getting more erratic.

"Gavin, the anonymous delivery guy, and you."

"But two are the same person."

"Yeah, Dec. My point." He slapped his shoulder. "You need to do it soon. She's going crazy trying to figure it out."

I started down the stairs when I saw them talking.

"Are you sure you won't join us, Alex?" Declan changed the subject.

"No, I'm good. I'll be on the deck if you need any help though."

"What were you guys talking about?" I knew it was something other than plans.

"How I'm a better cook." Alex shoved Declan.

"Sure you are, Alex." He got up from the stairs. "Shall we?"

"Where are we going?"

"We need to go shopping first." He opened the door.

I walked out to the car and turned slightly to catch Alex mouth something to Declan and Declan nodding back. I dismissed it as my overactive imagination and concentrated on the fact that I was alone with him in a confined space for more than a few minutes.

He parked and we made our way toward the local market.

"What are we making today?"

"I thought we would start simple." He turned. "It's your choice: fish or chicken."

"Chicken sounds good." *Some people in my family don't appreciate fish.* He smirked.

"Good, because you're making dinner for everyone."

"I can't cook. Remember, the only thing I can make is a bowl of cereal and tea."

"After today you can add chicken to that list." We both laughed.

"You overestimate your teaching skills and my cooking skills, Declan."

Now I knew healing properties of most plants and herbs, but when it came to ingredients to cook with, they were all foreign to me. As we maneuvered through the center, I felt the urge to grab his hand a couple of times, but doubted myself, so I kept my hands in my pockets. He was definitely knowledgeable about his ingredients. I hung on every word like a puppet on a string.

Why don't I suck it up and grab his hand? I'm such a chicken.

"That reminds me: We need to get the chicken from the store down on the corner."

It was as if he'd heard my thoughts. He must have, because he reached for my hand as we were picking out herbs. It was natural, and something told me this was something that would happen eventually.

He unclasped his hand from mine to point to the herbs he wanted. While he talked about what he was making with the salesperson, I took the chance to look around and figure out what was what. I was in my own world, rattled free when I heard him talking to me.

"Are you coming?" He shook his head as he stood next to the car.

I jogged over to the car where he was holding the bags, waiting for me. Now it took about an hour to gather all the ingredients, but I couldn't figure out where he planned to go now. "Where are you going?" I grabbed his arm and he smiled.

"We need one more thing. Can you put these in the car and wait?" He handed me the bags. "I'll be right back."

I was puzzled about what he'd forgotten. It didn't concern me, so I put the bags in the back. I climbed in the passenger seat, but as I fastened my seatbelt he was back. *That was quick.*

"Flowers?" I asked, still confused.

"You always need flowers to brighten the table." He put them in the back. "Here, this is for you."

He handed me a single white rose with a cute ribbon attached. His fingers graced my hand as I reached for the stem. I felt a slight pulse go up my arm. He let his fingers trace my wrist before pulling away.

"Thank you. This is very thoughtful." I could hear my pulse pick up.

"I'm glad you like it." He smiled as he started the car.

My thoughts raced through my head like the cars on the open road. *What a strange choice for a flower. What was with the ribbon?*

I glanced over to double check his expression, but it was hard to tell because he had no emotion in his face. Then I looked at his eyes. That's what gave him away. They were soft, almost intent, or maybe he was concentrating on driving. He turned and chuckled. It was a low, almost inaudible, sound. He caught me looking. I needed to recover, but he spoke first.

"What?"

"Nothing. I was thinking about your choice in flowers."

"Don't you like white roses? I can get you something else."

"No, they're great. And yes, it is my favorite." I smelled the rose. "But I was wondering, what's with the ribbon?" Now his expression changed. He looked discouraged, but it still made no sense.

"It was what the florist picked."

"Oh, okay."

I bought the lie for now but the wheels were already turning.

We started to unpacked the bags in the kitchen when he excused himself.

"I'll be right back," I said.

"What are you doing, Grey?" Allie asked.

"I'm getting cooking lessons, Allie. Did you want to help?" She giggled.

"From who? Your secret admirer?" She picked up the rose and smelled it. "Nice flower, but it would be better in pink."

Just then, it clicked. "Thanks a bunch, Allie." I hugged her and ran upstairs.

I grabbed all the notes and looked them over. Then I grabbed Declan's note from the other weekend—the handwriting was the same. *How could I not put this together? Man, I must be blind.* Alex and Evan had figured it out the night before from the previous note. I rummaged through the drawer. It was missing.

I ran to the balcony and yelled down toward the deck.

"Alex, do you have those letters from last night?!"

"What? This one?" He pulled it out of his pocket.

"Yes, throw it up."

"It's too high, Grey!" he yelled back. "Just come and get it."

"Wait." I grabbed my sneaker and undid the laces. "Here, put it in this."

"Whatever. You're crazy."

"Thanks." I pulled up the sneaker and grabbed the note.

Then it struck me like lightening. The number in the note—it was significant somehow. "No!" I shouted. I heard Alex laugh from below.

"It's about time."

The white rose, the silver ribbon, the silver seal, the foil on the envelope, and the number twenty-two were all connected. It was Declan. He was my anonymous admirer. *Was he trying to tell me in the car?* I suddenly felt bad because I'd brushed it off as no big deal, and he was trying to confess.

I felt stupid now. Hopefully he would try again. I didn't want to diminish his actions or his feelings. I needed to know his feelings because I already knew my own. I shoved the notes back into the drawer and went back downstairs for my lesson.

I grabbed my mom's apron from the pantry closet and prepared myself.

"So where do we start?" I winked at him.

"Um . . ." He shook his head. "We need to chop the herbs."

"Okay, give me the knife."

"Once you've chopped everything, put it in this pestle."

"The what?"

He placed a stone bowl in front of me, presenting it like Vanna White.

"The pestle. We need to crush the herbs to release their flavors more."

He was concentrating on something, but I knew it wasn't the preparation. He quickly cut the chicken into cube-sized pieces.

"Now we're going to add a little olive oil into the herbs we—I mean, you—crushed." He poured and mixed it together. He laid the chicken out on a plate.

"Now you need to rub the herbs on the chicken and let it sit." I grabbed the mixture and poured it over the chicken.

"Don't forget to rub it in so the entire chicken gets coated."

He grabbed my hand and showed me, but quickly moved them as if he was trying to maintain his control. My smile faded a little because I relished in every moment he touched me. He washed his hands and put the chicken in the fridge. I leaned against the counter, waiting for the next step, when he closed the fridge.

"What's next?"

"We need to get the vegetables cut, but we can wait on that." He dried his hands. "We have time. The chicken needs to marinate."

"Do you want something to drink?"

"Water would be nice, thank you." He wiped his face and headed outside.

I washed my hands and grabbed a glass from the cupboard. I

grabbed the pitcher from the fridge and took his glass out to him.

"Here you go." Alex was taking in the sun and reading.

"This is a first." I pointed to the book. "I've never seen you studying."

"Ha, ha. Very funny." He wasn't amused. "At least I don't need a tutor."

That had been a low blow, even for him.

"Who needs a tutor?" Declan turned toward me and then back to Alex.

"Grey does."

"Really? I'm surprised."

"I'm not as smart as people think, you know."

"What subject? I know it's not English." He took a drink.

"Trigonometry." He couldn't help but crack a slight smile.

"Ah, the dreaded subject: math."

"Evan's taking care of it on Monday."

He turned to Alex, wondering what to say, but he wasn't any help.

"Well, what do you want to do while we wait?"

"Let's play cards." He jumped up.

"No, Alex. You cheat." He sat back down. "How about a game of chess?"

"Alex, you can watch. I know you hate chess."

"I'm going to warn you now, Dec." Alex turned. "Chess and bowling are the only things Grey can win at."

"I'll consider myself warned." He cleared his throat. "Let's get my humiliation over with, then."

I went to Evan's office and grabbed the chess set on the desk. As I strolled down the hall, I figured they would talk about me again. I wished I could be a fly on the wall to hear what they were saying.

"I highly doubt that, Dec. I wouldn't underestimate Grey."
He leaned forward. "She's smarter than you think."

"I am counting on that."

"Have you talked to Evan yet? I mean, I want to make sure
you know what you're getting into."

"I have. Plus, what Evan couldn't answer, my dad did. It's all
good." He took a big gulp of water.

I walked back onto the deck with the chessboard, knowing I'd
walked into a private conversation.

"So here we go." I put the board down. "Are you talking about
me again?"

"No don't flatter yourself, sis." Declan continued to drink his
water. *Odd.*

"Whatever." I stuck my tongue out at him. "Let's play."

The game lasted a while. He was better than I thought. I was
so used to playing with Evan. This was more challenging, not
knowing every move he was going to make. It was a mystery I
wanted to solve, and I wasn't thinking of chess. With every move,
I quickly glanced up to see his response. He did the same. I got
nothing, and that seemed to amuse Alex to no end.

I gathered it was time to get back into the kitchen when he
stood up and stretched his arms.

"We'll have to postpone this match. We have dinner to prepare."

"Sure, I'll move the board to the kitchen table for later."

I set the board toward the back corner of the table so no one
would move it. I washed my hands and put my apron back on.

"So what do you want me to do now?"

He was taking the chicken out of the fridge when he cleared his
throat. I gathered he'd taken what I said the wrong way, which was
rather revealing. He composed himself and set out to finish dinner.

"We need to cut the same size pieces of each vegetable—your
choice."

I grabbed peppers, zucchini, squash, and onions. He grabbed

the cherry tomatoes from the fridge. I guess it wasn't really my choice, but I could deal with his input.

"Now take the rosemary stems and put the vegetables and chicken like this."

I finished the rest while he started the grill. He came back in to check on my progress periodically.

"We'll serve it with this rice." He grabbed the pot off the stove.

"What is it?"

"Jasmine rice."

"When did you make this?"

"While you skewered the chicken." He sighed.

I must have taken longer to prepare the skewers than it had for him to prepare rice. That thought was rather amusing, to say the least.

The grill was ready and I brought the chicken out. He snatched the olive oil on the way. After he'd shown me how to brush the grates with oil, I placed the skewers on the grill. *Okay, that wasn't too difficult.*

"This should take a couple of minutes on each side." He closed the lid. "I'll get the plates."

He set the table while I turned the chicken on the grill, trying not to burn it. I kept telling them not to burn, like they could hear me what was I thinking. I chuckled to myself over such crazy thoughts running through my head.

"Those look done." He stood behind me, placing his hands around my waist.

Now if you could only put your head on my shoulder, this would be perfect. Wishful thinking on my part, but a girl could hope.

"You'll make me into a good cook yet." I exhaled deeply.

I heard someone clear their throat. I jumped as he removed his hands, stepping to the side. You would have thought we'd been caught doing something taboo.

"Is dinner ready yet?"

"Yeah, Evan. I need to get the rice."

I removed the chicken from the grill and put it on the table, then hurried into the kitchen to get the rice. My imagination was in overdrive because I thought I'd seen Evan wink at him, and then they'd both laughed. *What is going on? Why doesn't anyone tell me anything?*

I spooned the rice into a bowl and grabbed the tongs and the salad. I put the bowls on the table and ran back to the kitchen for the pitcher of water and the dressing.

"Well, Grey, this looks delicious."

"Thanks, Grams, but you should thank Declan."

I couldn't take the credit. He'd done most of the work.

"She did it. I only intervened when she needed help."

"Then you're being modest, Grey." Grams hugged me and I felt a quick surge. "Sit and enjoy."

I sat at the end of the table. I heard compliments throughout the evening. I took each with some hesitation, which seemed to amuse Declan. The eating slowed and the conversation grew, so I took the time to clear the table. But before I could grab one plate, Evan stopped me.

"We'll get that. You cooked, so we'll clean." He eyed Allie and she begrudgingly agreed.

"But first dessert," Declan chimed in. Grams smiled as she grabbed the rest of the plates.

"Dessert? We didn't make dessert." I looked at him. *When did we make dessert?*

"I know I did. It's been in the fridge all day."

So that's why he wouldn't let near the fridge. But how didn't I see it when I took out the pitcher?

Grams brought out the dessert plates and silverware. He followed her with the dessert. He carried out four layers of heaven in the form of strawberry shortcake and set it down in front of me. I felt as red as the strawberries staring back at me from the top of the whipped cream.

"Are you okay, dear?"

Great. If she noticed, then so did everyone else.

"I'm fine, Grams. Can you excuse me for a minute?" I got up and went to the bathroom.

Well, if I was looking for a sign, then there it was, sitting out on the table covered in whipped cream and strawberries. I splashed my face with water to calm myself. *You seriously need to pull yourself together, Grey.* I took the towel to pat the water away and took a deep breath.

When I opened the door, he was standing in the hall looking rather concerned for my well-being.

"Are you okay?"

"Yeah, I had to go to the bathroom, that's all." I walked back out to the deck, trying to be casual—whether it worked or not, I'm not entirely sure. He followed me and shrugged his shoulders when Alex got up.

"This is great, Declan, but not as good as Grams." I winked.

"It's all about the love you put into it, dear." I knew it was as good if not better than Grams'. He must really love to cook.

I tried to prolong his visit by taking my time to enjoy dessert. When I finally finished, I grabbed the plates and headed to the kitchen.

"Here's some more." He placed them on the counter. "We still have a game to finish."

I looked at the board and tried to think of how I could spread out my time with him.

"Well, there's always the next lesson to continue our game." I placed the plates in the sink.

"Next lesson?" His voice raised in curiosity, cracking a little. It was cute.

"You didn't think you could get away with one lesson, Declan? Besides, you can only eat so much chicken."

He coughed. "Well, then I guess I'll leave until next weekend."

"That's not what I meant."

I grabbed his arm. There was that electricity again, crawling up through my fingers. I tried to ignore it, but it was difficult.

"We can make this a weekly lesson. Besides, I have monopolized enough of your time today. Go hang out with Alex before he gets a complex."

I quickly let go. The feeling was beginning to hurt. I was starting to feel tired, too.

He stood there staring at me for a while. He raised his hand and gently brushed it along the side of my face. He tucked a stray hair behind my ear before walking outside. I almost fell. I felt rather lightheaded. I needed to concentrate on not being surprised by what he did anymore. And what was with that tingling in my arm?

"Are you guys done with the board?"

"No, Evan. We're not. It's an ongoing game."

"Fine. I'll leave it here." He walked toward me. "Do you need help with the dishes?"

"No, I'm good." I braced the counter to regain my thoughts.

"Are you sure everything is okay? You look lightheaded."

He placed his hand on my shoulder. I knew he was trying to help, but I was still coming to grips with my so-called new life. I think he understood, because I felt his hand drop.

"Grey, go hangout. I can do the dishes after all you cooked all day."

I hugged him and headed to my room instead. I needed a moment to compose myself. I changed for bed, and sat out on the balcony. I knew I had to talk to someone, but the only person who would understand had mysteriously disappeared. I guess I would talk to Grams soon enough.

They couldn't see me, because I'd dimmed the lights in my room. I saw Declan shiver a little. It was weird, because it wasn't that cold outside. He never seemed to mind being outside without a jacket. It was as if he produced his own heat. I wondered if that's what I looked like when it happened to me. Yet it didn't seem to faze him at all. Alex started the fire and they talked about the game, practice, and school. I think this time he remembered that my room was right above. This time there was no conversation involving me.

A few hours passed and I heard Evan open the kitchen door.

"Hey, guys. It's getting late and you have school in the morning."

I got up to leave when Alex glanced up and nodded toward the front door. He and I were on the same wave length that day.

Damn, I forgot I changed. I was wearing the same thing I had this morning. Now my heart was racing. I timed my descent down the stairs perfectly as they were coming around the corner.

"Thanks for coming, man. I'll see you tomorrow."

"Anytime. Give me a call when you work out the details."

More plans? I walked down the last few steps to meet them.

"Grey, can you ever put clothes on when we have people over?"

I hit him in the arm. I think I hurt my hand in the process.

"I was getting ready for bed, Alex, if you must know."

"Whatever." He ran up the stairs, shaking his head.

"I had a wonderful time today. Thank you." He started to the door.

"You're welcome." I crossed to meet him. "But remember our deal."

He leaned in and whispered, "As long as you wear that, I'll agree to anything you suggest."

My pulse was accelerating. I could feel my face becoming flushed. He pulled back and gently swept his hand from my brow to the nape of my neck. He paused only a second before pulling my face to his. He placed his lips to mine, ever so gently parting them. I could feel the heat of his breath warming mine. As soon as it started, it was over.

"Good night. Sweet dreams."

I stood frozen, but somehow managed to close the door. I was on the verge of hyperventilating when I began to regulate my breathing. I also notice that my hand didn't hurt anymore either. I really needed to practice my responses, but how was I going to do that? He came out of left field with things.

I slept well that night, not worried about anything but trigonometry. Oh, how I detested math. It was the villain in my story.

CHAPTER NINE

NEW DEVELOPMENT

Dressing in a hurry should be ill advised, because you will always manage to forget something. In my case, it was the film
rolls from the weekend. I had one hour to develop all the pictures,
and I couldn't forget them because Paige would never let me live
it down. I hoped I'd have time to finish after school as well.

I ran downstairs and grabbed a bowl of cereal because it was
quick and easy.

"Evan, don't forget about my tutor, okay?"

"Already on it, Grey." He wrote in his planner. Alex was ready
to go, and was waiting for me as usual.

We ran to the main building, and we were all late thanks to me
and my forgetfulness.

"Remember? I got a long practice today."

"I know. I have film to develop. I should be done when you
are." I held up the canisters.

"Okay, see you in history."

I caught up to Emery and trudged off to English.

"So you made quite the impression Saturday."

"You think?" I rolled my eyes.

"Quinn's been telling me that Gavin hasn't shut up about it
all weekend."

"Oh, great." I grimaced. "I told him my feelings on the situation, but obviously he has chosen to ignore them.

"I guess so, especially when Declan came to your aid that night."

"I'm not a prize to be won, you know." I stopped. "I'm a person with feelings."

"These are seventeen-year-old boys we're talking about, Grey. Get a grip."

"You're right."

"I only wish someone would find me that interesting."

"I can think of a couple people—some you even know."

"Really, who?" I shrugged my shoulders and headed off to class.

I could see the frustration in her face. I knew she would pester me the rest of the day, but that was the plan, because I wouldn't be the center of discussion.

English was harder than normal due to the subtle glares from Declan in my direction. I got up and headed for the door, and, lucky for me, I was saved by Mr. Marsh. I caught up with Emery on the stairs and headed for biology. Now it was time to get the real scoop from Paige.

Emery questioned me the entire way to class, but I stayed strong. We took our seats, but she wasn't there yet. Of all the rotten luck, I turned back to Emery's interrogation. I thought Quinn could talk, but I was beginning to change my thoughts on that one.

"So I heard you made quite the impression," she whispered from the table behind us.

"Paige."

"Did you enjoy your lesson?"

"It was all right." I shrugged and tried to play it cool, but I wasn't fooling the two of them.

"Oh, I guess my brother exaggerates then."

"That depends on what he told you."

The game of wits had begun.

"Did you find out anything interesting while you were cooking?"

Ah, two can play this game and I know exactly what she was getting after.

"Yes, I found out that herbed chicken goes great with jasmine rice."

"Aw, come on." She was getting frustrated. "You know what I'm talking about."

I decided to end the game and come clean. I could trust her to divulge only what I wanted him to know.

"I found out who my anonymous admirer is," I spilled.

"Who is it?!" Emery squealed.

"Mind you, I got the last piece of the puzzle on Saturday night. When I got home I had two notes, one from Gavin and the other from my admirer."

"What did Gavin want?"

"What else?"

"What happened next?" Emery was on the edge of her seat.

"The clue was in the last note. I didn't see it, but Alex and Evan figured it out before I did. Then I received two more clues on Sunday. One was from Declan, and the other from Allie. They both used the same object: a flower."

Mrs. Warner was getting ready to begin class, so I quickly finished the conversation.

"I compared all the notes to one I had from someone I know."

"No, Emery, are you crazy?" I slapped her shoulder. "They all had the same handwriting."

"So what's your conclusion?"

"Declan."

"No way!" Emery gasped.

"Finally, it's about time."

"See, Paige, I had a feeling you knew when you looked at one of the notes, but I couldn't be sure."

"At least we know now," Emery said to Paige.

"Please keep it to yourself, though. I don't think he knows that I figured it out yet."

"He doesn't."

"And I don't want him to, Paige." She put her hand up and crossed her heart. "Good."

Now that it was out, I wouldn't be the center of conversation again today. Art class was even weirder and more unsettling than English. Thankfully, Paige switched seats to block my view.

"Don't forget to develop that film."

"I'll start it during my free period and finish after school. I already signed in for the lab space."

"Great. I'll see you at lunch."

Trigonometry went by in a blur, which was a blessing and a curse. It was a good thing because I couldn't stand the class and a bad thing because the awkwardness of lunch was on the horizon. I made a last minute decision to skip lunch and I checked in with Evan's progress on my quest for a savior. I knocked on the door.

"Come in!" he called from his desk.

"Hey, Evan. I stopped by to check your progress."

"It's all set. Your sessions start tomorrow during your free period in the library."

"Who is it?"

"I don't know. They have a pool of students who volunteer. I'm sure it will be fine." He looked at me as if I was supposed to ask him something else.

"Thanks again for your help." I tried to leave while I had the chance, but it just wasn't my day.

"I can't have a member of my family failing a class now, can I?"

"I guess not."

"Aren't you supposed to be at lunch?" His eyes grew wary.

"Yes, but this is more important." I stretched the truth a little.

"Here, take half of my sandwich and go to class before you're late."

"Can you write me a note just in case, please?"

He took out his pad and jotted something down.

"Here, now go."

I ran across the lot to the main building as if I was running from a burning house. I was late to class, so thankfully I had a note. Alex could relax now, because nothing had happened to me. I knew exactly what he was thinking. Class ended and Alex changed his usual route to walk me to the dark room. My theory was that he needed the time to grill me on my whereabouts earlier.

"Why were you late and what happened to you at lunch?"

"I had to talk to Evan about my tutor."

"Well then, I'm satisfied now, but you had people worried."

"Sorry."

"I took care of it. You should be good unless you don't show up in gym."

"I'll be there. Now go to class before you're late, too." I pushed him in the general direction of his class.

"You better be there, Grey!" He yelled down the hall. I grabbed the rolls and locked the door.

This was taking longer than I'd thought it would. I didn't realize how many shots we'd taken. I was glad I'd signed out time after school. I did what I could during my free period and put the rest away for later. It was going to take me some time to clean up.

I ran down the hall toward the locker room, reassuring myself I wasn't going to be late. I changed and booked it into the gym, *Ugh, great. Basketball.*

Alex turned around and smiled. At least he was good. Alex nudged Declan and I waved. You could see the worry fade from his eyes as he turned back around. It was nice to see he cared that much.

Coach Nelson chose Gavin and Alex as captains. *That's just great. I know which team I'm on, thanks.*

He flipped a coin and Alex won, so he had to choose first. No big surprise, he chose Declan. He winked at me, knowing he was going to pick me next. *Guess what, Alex? You didn't think of Gavin.*

When Gavin chose me, I looked over to him and he finally realized his mistake. I lucked out. At least Quinn was on my team. The one thing Gavin forgot to factor into the game was that Declan—not Alex—would guard me.

At that point, I didn't care anymore about the drama. I used my frustration toward him to my advantage in the game. The one good thing was I was too quick for him and Alex. I figured it was due to my size. Gavin and I were all over the place, high-fiving everyone after each shot. The game was turning more into street ball than a friendly game in gym class. Coach blew the whistle and the game ended peacefully with no injuries, but we did beat Alex. I was smug the rest of the day.

"Good game, little sis." He messed my hair.

"All in a day's work," I joked, and of course he had a comeback.

"I didn't think you could play basketball so well."

"When you have the right motivation, you can do anything you put your mind to."

I walked into the girls' locker room with Quinn. I changed quickly, almost knocking people out of the way to get to the darkroom. I must have had a lucky penny in my pocket because the person before me had finished early. I locked the door and got to work.

As it always did when I was having fun, time passed quickly. I hung my last picture to dry and looked at my watch. It was five o'clock. I hoped they were still practicing because I knew how impatient Alex was. I started to take down the dry prints when I heard a knock at the door.

"Yes?" I stood by the door, knowing it was him.

"Hey, Grey, are you done yet?"

"Give me ten more minutes, Alex. I need to clean up."

"I'll be at the car. Hurry up, would you?"

He was definitely upset that I was making him wait. I hurried to clean up, waiting for the last of the pictures to dry. I grabbed them and threw the negatives into a folder. I ran as fast as a jack-rabbit to the parking lot.

"Sorry."

"It's about time. You're lucky. We just finished practice." He peeled out of the lot.

"Calm down, would you? I said I was sorry."

"It's not you. I'm just amped up. I'm sorry."

"No problem. But make sure I get home in one piece, please."

He slowed down and started driving normally. I figured something was up. He wasn't going to tell me so I dropped it for the time being. When we got home, I called Paige to tell her I was done. Her mother answered the phone.

"Hello. Is Paige there?"

"Who's calling?"

"This is Grey Corwen." I stayed polite.

"Hold on, please." That was awkward. She'd seemed curt.

"Hello."

"What's up?" Paige's voice was low.

"Is everything okay?"

"Hold on." I heard a door open and close. I could also hear arguing. "Grey."

"Yeah, I'm here. What's with the arguing?"

"So there was an incident at practice today. Several players got detention for two days."

Of all the days to miss practice, I had to miss the one with the most action. I had to know what happened. If Alex wasn't going to tell me, then maybe she would.

"Who and why?"

"Well, Gavin, Tyler, Jack, Declan, and Alex."

"What?!" I shouted. "Sorry."

"No problem. It happened during a break in practice."

"What happened?"

"I think you should ask your brother that question, because it concerns you."

"What do you mean?"

"Look, I have to go. What did you want?" She seemed hurried. It wasn't like her.

"I finished the pictures this afternoon. I'll bring them with me tomorrow, okay?"

"Super. I'll see you then. And don't forget to ask."

As soon as I hung up the phone, I heard Evan yell for Alex from his office. I picked the phone back up and pretended I was still talking so I could listen. Alex walked past me into Evan's office and closed the door behind him. I kept the phone with me while I crept over to the door and leaned against the frame to listen.

"What happened out there today?" he fumed. "Why did you get detention? I want every detail."

"We were on a break during practice. Tyler and I were getting some water when Gavin came over. Declan and Jack came off the field right behind him." I heard him take a deep breath and exhale. "Tyler asked if Grey was okay, because she wasn't at lunch today. I was about to answer, when Gavin chimed in and asked why Tyler cared. Tyler told him they were friends and that Quinn was worried."

"That doesn't sound like that would cause a brawl," Evan pointed out and I agreed.

"That's not the whole story."

"Then by all means, continue."

"Gavin turned and said that it looked like Grey was friendly with more than one of them. Tyler yelled back that Grey was just a friend. Gavin responded, 'I heard that in my car plenty of times while we were making out.' That's when I charged him, but Dec and Jack held me back. He continued to run his mouth, saying I guess she's easier than most of us expected, and before I could hit him, Dec did. Gavin went down like a rock. He stumbled back to his feet, then punched him back. Jack and I pulled Dec away and Tyler grabbed Gavin. Coach came over, and without any discussion, gave us all detention for two days."

"Well, as a guy—and as your uncle—I'm glad you stuck up for your sister, but I'm gladder that Declan punched him for making such false accusations. As an administrator, however, I don't condone your actions, so the detention stands. Alex, you need to remember to watch yourself. You need to, especially now."

"I know. I'm sorry. I wasn't thinking. It was bad judgment on my part." Alex's tone was somber. Evan said something else that was inaudible. *Damn these oak doors.*

"Now go get your sister off the phone so I can call the Watt household."

I heard him walk toward the door and I ran back to the table.

"Yeah, I'll talk to you tomorrow. Bye." I hung up the phone as Alex walked out, dragging himself upstairs to his room.

"Grey, are you done with the phone?" Evan seemed calmer now.

"Yeah, it's all yours."

I grabbed my bag from under the table and skipped every other step to talk to Alex. I noticed Evan had gone back into his office because I'd heard the door close. I threw my bag on my bed and headed toward his room, but unlike other times, I knocked before I went in.

I cracked the door and saw he was putting his equipment away, mumbling to himself. I walked over and hugged him.

"Thank you."

"For what?"

"You know what."

"You have to stop listening to other people's conversations."

"I know, but it's not my nature." We laughed as he hugged me back.

"You should thank Jack and Tyler. If we didn't pull them apart when we did, I think Declan would have beat him to a pulp—not that he doesn't deserve it."

"I'll thank them tomorrow." I headed for the door. "Are you coming down for dinner I'm not cooking."

"As long as you're not cooking, why not?"

He grabbed my waist and pushed me out. He shoved me into the kitchen. It smelled like Grams had made lasagna.

"I hope you're hungry."

"Can you save some for tomorrow so I can take it for lunch?"

"Whatever you say." He rolled his eyes as he tried to take the whole pan.

"Grams, can you put one piece aside for me now?" I begged. She put one piece into a container and placed it in the fridge.

"Thanks."

The conversation didn't seem to flow as well as it had due to the recent events, so I broke the tension.

"Evan got me a tutor today."

"That's great, Grey. When does this tutor start?" Grams asked. I think she was trying to help as well.

"Tomorrow, so maybe I can have a C average before the break."

"That's wonderful."

Alex left when he was done and Evan went to his office to make the call he hadn't made earlier. Grams, Allie, and I cleared the table and washed the dishes. I knew I needed to talk to Grams, but how was I to do it with Allie standing right there?

"Is there anything you want to talk to me about, Grey?" *Man she was good.*

"The other day I got this weird tingling feeling that started at my fingers and then moved up my arm. I also felt a little light headed, too."

"Maybe you are too stressed." Allie remarked.

"Allie, don't you have homework to do?" She politely looked at Allie. I continued drying dishes until I heard Allie making her way up the stairs.

"Was this the first time it happened to you?"

I looked at her, wondering how she knew.

"I mean, after the bird, Grey." She smiled. *Okay, now that was weird.*

"Well, when I touched Gavin at the game after he was hurt, and on Sunday, when Declan was here."

"All right, well, it's natural to not understand what is going on. What you actually experienced was a transfer of energy or feelings."

She put the dishes down and walked me over to the table. I figured this was going to be a lot to take, so sitting would be best.

"When you touch someone or something that is injured—like the bird—you are actually helping them heal. Your talent is rare, in a sense. All of us in this community have some capacity to heal others in different ways, but in our family, the gift is heightened. You and I are similar in our gift of healing, but yours is a little more concentrated."

Great. I'm a freak among freaks.

"Okay, so does that mean I can't touch anyone?"

"No, it just means you need to have control when you use it." She smiled and I think I finally understood something for once.

After our talk, I dreaded going upstairs, but I had to—my homework wasn't going to magically do itself. I could only wish. I sat at the desk and opened my science book. Then I changed my mind. I took the photos from the bag and plopped myself on the bed.

I must have fallen asleep, because I woke up in a pile of pictures. Everyone except Declan and Gavin was waiting by Tyler's car for us when we pulled into the lot. *What a jerk. I would have punched him myself if I'd had the chance.* I stepped out and headed straight for Tyler. He was the first in the line to thank for yesterday.

"Hey, Tyler. I wanted to say thank you—it was stupid, but thank you."

"No problem, Grey. All in a day's work for a super hero."

"You're too funny."

I walked over to Declan, who was leaning against his car. Everyone seemed to wander off toward the main building—how subtle.

"Are you hurt?"

"Not really. You should see the other guy, though." He grinned and winced when I touched the right side of his face. "My eye is a little sore, but I'll survive."

I leaned in. "This eye?" I pointed to his right side.

"Yes." I leaned in further and gently kissed his eye. I didn't want to chance touching it with my fingers when I hadn't even begun to learn how to control my abilities. I felt tingling on my lips. *Man, when Grams said 'touching' she meant with any part of me. That's just great.* I sighed.

"Thank you, but next time let me fight my own battles, okay?"

I gently ran my fingers over his cheek and down to his chest, where I left them for a minute or so. He didn't say anything. He just stood there with his eyes closed, so I dropped my hand and started to walk away. He pulled me back.

"I need you to answer one question for me."

"What do you want to know?" *Please don't ask me about my gifts. I will answer anything but that right about now.*

"You and Gavin, is it true?" Pain struck his face with every word.

"No." I was angry that he would ever think that. I knew we were not together, but I thought he knew how I felt.

"I ask because of the comments he made yesterday." And there was the crux of it.

"I'll tell you if you want to know the truth." The pain on his face was more evident now.

"Yes, please." I leaned against the side of the car.

"Gavin has made his intensions known from the first time I met him in April, but his advances have happened more often since what happened at practice a couple of weeks ago. It came to a head over the weekend when we were at the lake."

"I know of one incident, but what else happened at the lake?" He opened his eyes.

"He asked me to take a walk and I stupidly agreed. I was hoping that time he would listen to me when I told him again that I didn't feel the same way he did."

"You don't?"

"No, I don't." I grabbed his hand, hoping I could ease some pain. "During our walk I tried to explain that, but he kissed me. I pushed him away and headed back into the kitchen. That's when you guys saw me run up the stairs. When Quinn and Paige followed after me."

"So why does he think there's something there? And what's this thing about practice?"

I was hoping he would forget I'd mentioned the practice, but if he wanted to know everything, then he was going to get it. I felt this odd need to tell him everything.

"When we first moved here, Gavin spent a lot of time at our house. He was a permanent fixture. I treated him more like a brother, but he might have gotten the lines crossed."

I was getting off topic; I tried to pace myself.

"So one of the first practices I went to, I took that time to check you out—without your knowledge. I couldn't tell who anyone was because of your helmets, so I guessed by jersey number and I chose wrong. I found myself glancing periodically at Gavin instead. That's when it escalated. So on Saturday he thought me looking nice was for his benefit. Probably because of concern over his injury and the café incident."

"What happened at the café?" His eyes were wide.

"Well, that morning I went for a run. I got hungry, as you know. I went to the café to get a muffin and tea. Gavin walked in and offered to buy my breakfast and give me a ride home. I couldn't run home with a cup and a muffin. And I thought we were friends, so I said yes. While he drove me home I told him I wasn't interested, but he didn't listen—hence his thought from Saturday night."

He pulled me closer.

"So now that I have the whole story, I want to know one thing. Are we friends, Grey?"

"Yes."

"Just friends?" I lightly touched his lips with the tips of my fingers and he closed his eyes while a soft sigh escaped.

"That's up to you, but being your friend is not enough for me."

I pulled away and hurried off to English. I made it in time, but he never came. I can't say I was surprised. He wanted the truth, but whether he could handle what I'd just dropped on him was another story. I walked into biology with two pairs of eyes staring at me.

"What? What did I do?"

"My brother is walking around like a zombie."

"Okay, so why are you looking at me?

"You were the last one with him," Emery chimed in. "So what happened?"

I wasn't sure whether I should say. Then I decided to throw caution to the wind.

"Well, he asked me questions about Gavin and I told him the truth." I took a breath. "And he asked me some more questions. And that was it."

"What other questions?" Paige leaned forward.

"And be specific. We want every word," Emery added.

"Well, he asked me if we were friends and I told him yes. Then he said, 'Just friends?', and I said that was up to him, but it wasn't enough for me. That's it. Oh, then I ran to class before I was late."

"That explains it." Paige smiled. "He never knew how you really felt and you caught him off guard."

"You don't get the power you have over men, girl." Emery laughed.

Well, at least that hurdle was out of the way, and I hoped the first round of twenty questions was over. Biology went off without a hitch, but art would be another story. I could feel my fist clench when I thought about it.

I handed Paige the pictures in the hall on the way to class. We lucked out because Gavin wasn't there and we got to work on our projects. The time flashed by quickly, and I must have been caught in a time warp because I didn't even remember sitting through trigonometry. It was lunch, and I was looking forward to Grams' lasagna. I walked over to the table and sat down. Quinn was eyeing my lunch and I knew what was next.

"That looks good."

"You can have some. Grams made it." She grabbed a fork and dug in.

"Wow, that's good." She chewed. "You guys got to try this."

"Where is everyone?" I noticed that half the lacrosse team was missing.

"They're in detention during lunch," Quinn answered as she chewed.

We finished my lunch, then I headed to history. I figured I would get stares from some students, but not others. I got a strange look from Dr. Watt when I walked into class, which was definitely weird and made me feel uncomfortable. I couldn't let it bother me, though. My day was just starting to look up. He continued to stare me down, and my pulse started to race. I decided to leave before class started, but Alex caught me in the hall.

"Where are you going?" He pushed me toward the room. "We have class."

"I'm not going." I moved out of the way, trying to level the pounding in my head. The pressure was too much.

"What happened?" He was concerned.

"Dr. Watt gave me a weird look that made me feel uncomfortable, so I left."

I didn't want to elaborate. I wanted it to go away.

"Come on." He was hurting my arm as he dragged me down the hall.

"Where are we going?"

"To see Evan. This is unacceptable. You didn't do anything."

We walked across the courtyard toward the administration building.

Alex knocked on Evan's door and waited.

"Come in!" he called. "Hey, guys. Aren't you supposed to be in class?"

"Yes, but I think there is a problem." *No, there is no problem,* I kept thinking.

"Yeah, you're hurting my arm." I pulled away.

"Sorry." He then turned back to Evan. "Dr. Watt is making it hard for Grey in history." *Great. What is this, kindergarten? I can take care of myself, Alex.*

"What do you mean *hard?*" he emphasized the last word.

"I caught her running out, almost in tears, because he gave her some strange look that made her feel uncomfortable."

"Is this true, Grey?"

"Yes, but it's no big deal. I can handle it."

"Nonsense. I'll deal with this—family or no family. Faculty shouldn't use their authority to make others feel uncomfortable."

"Thanks, Evan."

"Here are notes to get back to class." He handed them to us. "Also, give this to Dr. Watt."

Alex grabbed the folded note and put it in his pocket. They exchanged looks. It looked like they were having some nonverbal conversation that I wasn't privy to.

"Thanks, Alex."

We walked into class and handed our notes to Dr. Watt. Alex smirked as he presented another piece of paper. Something was up, because he actually gulped—even he'd seen trouble coming. At least class went by faster than normal because we'd missed half of it.

"Off to meet the tutor." Alex hugged me and walked away.

"Good luck, Grey. I'll see you in gym."

CHAPTER TEN

TUTORS OR TORTURE

I waited in the library. My tutor was five minutes late. I had started my homework when I heard someone come over to the table.

"Finally. You're five minutes late." I looked up. "What do you want, Gavin? If you know what's good for you, you'll turn around and walk away."

"You're waiting for your trigonometry tutor, right?"

"Don't tell me you're my tutor." *Ugh, could this day get any better? I mean, seriously.* Great!" I started to stand.

"I'm the only trig tutor." He smiled.

"Seriously!" I started to ball my hands into fists. *This is not happening!* I started to shake, and I could feel my whole body vibrating. I opened my eyes and saw Gavin staring back at me strangely. *This is so messed up. I can't believe I have to deal with this. I should just drop the class, but I can't because I need it. Stupid math. Stupid Gavin.* I let out a breath I didn't know I was holding in.

"Fine. Just so we're clear, you're my tutor and nothing else."

"Whatever." He threw his bag down and took out his book. "So let's get started."

It was more painful than I'd thought it was going to be. It was like getting a root canal without the drugs. I guess I would have to get used to it, but the problem was that we had the next class together as well.

"I guess I should say thanks for your help." I found it hard to say the words.

"Well, we have plenty of time to get your grades up." He put his book away. "Your tutoring sessions are every day during your free period."

I cringed when he said that. I threw my books in my bag and hurried toward the door. He caught up halfway to the gym. Everyone was staring. I saw Alex and Declan standing outside the locker room. *Could this day get any worse?*

When we arrived, Alex gave me a look and Declan walked into the locker room. *Man, I can't win today.* Gavin headed into the locker room with a smile on his face. *I guess it was mission accomplished for him.*

"What's with that?"

"He's my tutor, Alex. I had no choice. He's the only trig tutor on campus."

"We'll see."

"Don't start anything, please."

"I'm making it easier for everyone." He looked at the door.

"Okay, fine. See what you can do." I walked into the locker room, changed and headed to the gym.

Only Quinn talked to me because I refused to talk to Gavin, and it seemed that Declan refused to talk to me. I couldn't figure out why he was mad at me. We weren't even dating.

We were still playing basketball and the teams remained the same. At least I could try to explain to him what happened. I guessed wrong. Alex was defending me—in more than one way.

"This sucks," I whispered to him. He fouled me.

"I'll talk to him after class."

I took my shots and we continued on that way until the game was over. Declan left before I could catch him. Quinn put her arm around me.

"Let Alex talk to him, Grey."

"I've lost him before I even got a chance to have him."

Where did that come from? Man, I'm losing it.

"Come on. I'll sit with you during practice."

"Thanks."

We were taking our time walking toward the field when I saw Alex trying to reason with Declan. It looked heated. I wanted to intervene but Quinn held me back. The bleachers awaited me like a death sentence for my misery. Paige was already there, but she hadn't heard yet and I was glad for that.

"So what's going on now?"

"Declan's upset," Quinn told Paige.

"Why?" She looked at me for an answer.

"You know I have a tutor for math, right?" She nodded. "Well, it turns out that the only trig tutor they have in the school is Gavin."

"I don't think so."

"No, that's true. But because he tutors me during my free period, he thinks he can walk with me to our next class—with Quinn, Alex, and your brother."

"Oh, man. He's going to be grouchy tonight."

"I'm sorry." I grabbed her arm. "I should stay away for now until things settle. I still don't understand. We aren't even dating."

"I don't know, Grey. He doesn't see it that way."

"Maybe that's a good idea, Paige." Quinn motioned toward the field as Alex walked by shaking his head.

"This is not good." I sunk into the bleachers.

"I'll talk to him." She pulled me up. "I've got an idea. Let me handle it."

"Okay."

We sat through practice and it was tough to watch. You could see the tension on the field. I felt overjoyed when it was over. It was too painful to watch another minute. We headed to the parking lot while they were finishing up. I waited for Alex by the car, and thankfully he was the first one out. I waved to him.

"I tried." Alex patted my head.

"I know. Paige is my only chance now."

He pulled to a stop and I took it slow as I entered the house. I had no appetite after that afternoon's battle royale on the field, so I retired to my room to change for bed. I walked out to the balcony for a while, and that's when I heard Evan and Alex below.

"What happened? Why did she run upstairs?"

"Well, she met her tutor. Let's say it complicated things with Declan. I mean, they aren't together, but he feels like they are. I don't get it."

"We can talk about that later." Evan quickly changed subjects. "What's wrong with her tutor?"

"It's Gavin."

"What?!" He started pacing. "I can get another tutor for her."

"Apparently he's the only one."

"Well, I'll get her a private tutor, but it will take some time. She has to finish out the week."

I would go through the rest of the week being tortured. I couldn't even enjoy the night sky. I closed the doors and burrowed under the covers. I didn't sleep at all and I looked like it.

The ride to school was quiet. Alex knew better than to talk to me. I got out of the car and Emery came over.

"You look horrible. Did you sleep at all?" She pushed my hair back from my face.

"No, it was a bad night."

"Let's get you something before class." We walked past the group and headed toward the cafeteria. "Here, at least drink this. It might help."

"Thanks, Emery." I took a sip. "I feel a little better."

We were halfway to class when I noticed him walking up the stairs. He glanced to the side and I could see in his eyes that he was miserable. It was horrible. I wanted to touch him and take all his pain away.

"He'll be fine. Paige talked to him and she said to give him some time."

"Okay." I took a gulp.

"I'll see you in biology. Smile, please."

I tried, but only half a smile came out—but I'd still tried. I shuffled into my normal seat in the back corner near the window. No quick glances from Declan that I saw, today. I couldn't deal with that—not that morning. I was up and out before Declan could get up.

I hurried down the stairs to my next class. I slumped in my seat and my only luck so far that day was that we were having a lab. Paige came up behind me and gave me a hug.

"It's okay. He understands. "I still don't understand it, though. We aren't together."

"I know. I don't understand it either—and I asked."

I patted her arm and she went to her seat.

"What did he say?" Emery asked.

"That was the thing. He shut down and went to bed without saying anything."

The rest of the day was much the same. I walked to my classes in a slump and the next couple of days were blurs I wanted to erase.

It was finally Friday, and I could deal with things in silence over the weekend at least. I tried calling him several times, but to no avail. He wouldn't even talk to Alex about it either. I decided to take some action, and I chose to act like I was over it. If he wasn't going to talk to me, then maybe I could do something to get him to reconsider. I needed something to remove me from my funk.

I walked to English class like any other day, but something felt different. I was laughing with Emery on the way up. I had my friends to hang out with, even if one of them was absent. I sat through English with a smile, knowing I was giving him what he needed: space. That didn't mean I couldn't look.

Others noticed my change, but I couldn't tell if he did. I walked past him on the way out and I caught him smile—though he tried to hide it. It might have been working, but I tried not to let him see me peek. I laughed and walked to biology.

"So I think this might snap him from his mood."

"I think it started working already." Paige pointed to the door and I saw him wave.

"Boys are so predictable."

It was sort of funny how a piece of clothing and a change in attitude could change a mood so quickly. But art class was not going to be pleasant. We'd finished the lab from earlier in the week and Mrs. Warner let us go early.

"So are you going to the game tonight?" Paige inquired.

"Yeah, my brother still plays, right< and there's only one more game before regionals."

"Right, right." She mocked me.

Unfortunately, my bad luck returned, because Gavin wasn't in art, nor was he at lunch. I was trying to cancel my tutoring session, which was a joke. He ogled me more than he tutored me. Now I would have to suffer his staring the whole session.

As I walked to the library I felt that shiver again going down my back. I hadn't had one of them in a while. I shook it off and headed inside. Right on time—let the staring commence.

In one week, I knew less about trigonometry than I had when I had no tutor. He followed beside me as I walked to class. And, as with every other day that week, Alex was there to meet me. But that day was a little different, because Declan stood with him.

"Alex, Declan." Gavin was so informal.

"Hey, Gavin." Alex tried to be civil.

I had started to walk into the locker room, when I felt a tug. I was locked in a kiss with Declan. He was not as gentle as he usually was. This had more passion behind it. I guess he was done with his solitary confinement. I heard Gavin growl and Alex laugh. Declan let me go, and walked into the locker room with a huge smile on his face.

"Well, that was interesting. Did you know about this?"

Alex shrugged and walked into the locker room. As I came into the gym, Quinn grabbed me.

"Are you okay?"

"Yeah, I'm good. Just help me to the stands."

She walked with me as I tried to regain my balance due to the shock of recent events. His off-the-cuff actions drained me physically. I needed my balance for basketball today.

"Are you ready to play?"

"I think so."

The more we played, the more I regained my composure. I started to enjoy myself again because I was beating Alex's team.

"Good game, bro. Better luck next time."

"I was saving my strength for tonight."

"Sure you were." I wiped the sweat from his hair and he growled.

I got changed and waited by the car for him to show up, but Quinn came out instead.

"They had a meeting today." She threw me the keys. "He said to move his stuff into Tyler's car."

"What about you?"

"You can drive me home and then to the game."

"How about I drive you home, you grab your stuff, and we go back to my house before the game."

"That sounds better."

She opened Tyler's car and we moved the gear before we took off.

"You do know if they win tonight, the party is still at your house?"

"I know."

Evan had made a deal with the coach that every time they won they could celebrate at the house. It also gave him a chance to keep an eye on everyone, especially after that infamous practice.

Quinn grabbed her stuff and threw it in a bag. We got back to my house with enough time for me to change and grab something to eat. I ran in so fast I didn't notice the box until Quinn pointed it out.

"Wow! It's one of the famous mystery boxes."

Quinn picked it up. There, in her hand, was the elusive white box with the silver ribbon. She handed it to me and begged me to open it. Inside, the box was a little different. The white rose and note were the same, but there was something wrapped around the rose. I pulled out the note first.

My heart was fractured when we were apart. Please take this token as a sign of the end of my imprisonment. By accepting this, you will mend my heart and it shall forever be yours. Number Twenty-two

It was signed this time. I guess he'd decided it was time for me to know, even though I already did. I removed the rose, and there was the token—a jersey, his jersey. *Too cute. So 1950s.* I laughed.

"I guess he wants you to wear it."

Another note fell to the floor when I unfolded the jersey.

You are my lucky charm. Only good things will come when I am around you. Please wear this as a sign of good luck for me. Declan

"Oh, that is so cute! You have to wear it." Quinn pushed me upstairs. I started to change and she stopped me. "Wait, what's his favorite color?"

"Silver, I think." I wasn't sure, but everything he'd given me was silver.

"Just change your top. I know you have a light-grey shirt in here. That's pretty close to silver." She threw the shirt at me. "Give him some happiness."

I put the shirt on and threw the jersey over it. I grabbed my jacket and waited for her to change.

"Just leave your stuff here. You'll be back tonight either way. I think we need a girls' night."

She laughed as she grabbed her jacket.

"Let's go."

We grabbed some lasagna and ate it on the way. When we pulled into the student lot, it was packed, but I knew Evan had saved us seats. I put my jacket on for an element of surprise and grabbed Alex's jersey from the back. We ran to the stands. Paige and Emery were already there.

"Thanks for saving the seats." I threw the jersey at Allie. "It's yours now, kiddo."

"Why aren't you going to wear it?" Emery was intrigued.

"You'll see."

The team finished warming up and huddled by the bench before the game. I took off my jacket and gave it to Quinn.

"Nice surprise," Paige commented. "A gift?"

"It arrived today, actually. With this."

I pulled out the white rose.

"Very nice."

We turned to watch the game. We were down by two when we

called a time out. Right before they headed back onto the field, Declan looked up and smiled. I smiled back.

"Hopefully he saw what I was wearing."

"He saw."

They rolled their eyes. The game continued, and it was down to the wire. The score was tied thanks to Tyler and Jack. I had to cover my eyes. I could not watch. There was only one minute left. Suddenly, I heard screams and cheering and I opened my eyes. They had stolen the ball! Declan and Jack were racing down the field. Declan passed to Jack as he got jammed. Jack then hurled it toward the lower right corner, and it bounced off the ground and into the net. We won! I couldn't believe it. After the team huddled, I heard Quinn sigh.

"What?"

I looked up and saw him climbing up the stands. He grabbed me and kissed me, but this time he was gentle.

"Thanks for my good luck." He ran back down the stands and to the locker room.

"Well, I would say the madness is gone," Paige said to Quinn.

"I would say so, but we might want to drive Grey home now." She grabbed my arm. "Evan, tell Alex to go with someone else back to the house, please."

"Sure. Will do, Paige."

He grabbed Allie and headed down to the locker room.

We stopped at Emery's and then Paige's house so they could grab a change of clothes for the next day. I also snapped out of my trance like state.

"This is going to be fun. I'll let you in on my secret." Their eyes widened with anticipation.

We got home in time to help Grams set up. I went to the deck to start the fire. Quinn threw the drinks in the coolers and every-thing was set. Grams would put out the food later.

We made our way upstairs to change. I took off his jersey and hung it on the end of my bed.

"So here's my secret." I opened the doors to the balcony.

"Your balcony is the secret," Quinn whispered.

"Just wait." The team started to pile in and the conversations started.

"Did you see Emery tonight? She looked hot," said the first male voice.

"I know. What about Paige? Man, she is smoking," said the second male voice.

"Hopefully Gavin isn't a jerk tonight," said the third male voice.

"I think Grey would kill him herself," said the second male voice.

"That's amazing," Paige whispered.

"I know. I can hear everything that is said on the deck and nobody knows except Alex."

"Does he say anything?" Emery asked.

"No, he usually brings people out here when he knows I'm in my room."

"What a great brother," Quinn snickered.

"Let's get ready."

They got dressed while I combed my hair and put it into a loose ponytail. I grabbed my necklace and put on my ring.

"That's a gorgeous ring. Where did you get it?" Paige admired.

"My mother gave it to me." It wasn't a lie. Plus, I'm not sure I was ready to divulge everything. "And my father gave it to her."

She was looking at the black mark inside and I think she was trying to figure out what it was.

"It's the letter P for my father's family name."

"I thought your name was Corwen?"

"It is, Paige, but Corwen is my mother's maiden name. My

father asked her to change it after they were married."

"I'm sorry, but if you don't mind, can you tell me what your father's name was?" They all leaned forward.

"Parker."

"Are you kidding me?!" Paige screamed.

"I knew it!" Emery yelled.

"How about that?" Quinn was actually speechless for the first time.

"What's the big deal?"

"The deal is the Parker, Watt, Ellis and Connors families are the original settlers." She pointed to Emery and Quinn. "And their families have been close for generations. The families only allow marriages within the four families when it is feasible. I think he lucked out on this one."

"Are you serious?" I was shocked that this was what my mom was trying to tell me about the importance of my family name.

"Yup, the only deviation was your family. At the time, the families already had their marriages, but the Parker family still had two sons left. Your family was second in line for one of them. The Harrington family chose Sean and that left your father with your mother."

"I've never heard that before." I was confused. "I thought my uncle was unmarried?"

"Yes, he ended up that way because the Harrington family's daughter married someone else."

"Interesting. I've never heard that."

"Quite. It is interesting. We found you to complete the families."

"It's weird how things work out," Emery commented.

"Not really, because my mom knew. She said her illness was one of the reasons we came back. The other reason must have been this: our friendships."

"Your mother was one smart cookie." Paige gleamed. "But I don't think friendship was the only reason. It's something to think about, Grey."

"Let's go have fun. We can talk later. We have all night." I brushed off her last comment because I didn't want to think about that right now.

We headed downstairs and they joined everyone on the deck. Before I reached the door, Evan stopped me.

"I see your wearing your ring." He glanced down. "Do they know?"

"Yes, I told them and they filled in the blanks as to why my dad's family was—and still are—important."

"How did they receive you?" His eyes seemed scared waiting for my answer.

"With open arms." He hugged me.

"Your mother was right. You are something special." He hugged me again. "Go ahead and have fun with your friends."

I kissed him on the cheek and walked out to the deck. I stood by my friends who were in the corner near the railings. This was the spot where you could see the entire crowd. Paige was sitting on the corner railing and I leaned against her. She draped he arms around my shoulders for balance. We sat and joked around throughout the night.

"I think some people are jealous of me," Paige whispered. I knew the answer but asked anyway.

"Oh really, and who might that be?"

"Well, there's that gentleman over there." She pointed to Declan. "And then Gavin and that young man over there."

"You're too funny, Paige." I hugged her arms. "I think we should raise our glasses to them in a gesture of politeness and show them that we're aware of them."

"And their win tonight," she added.

We held our glasses up and nodded our heads in a gesture to both of them. Gavin was confused, but Declan raised his glass and winked.

"Well, I've never seen that gesture before."

"I think in no certain terms it is what we refer to as flirting."

"Well, Paige, should I impart a gesture back?"

"Oh, do try. This is so much fun."

Suddenly I felt like I was in a Jane Austin book minus the British accents.

"Let's see, what should I do?"

"I got it," Paige whispered in my ear.

"You're bad, but okay. Let's see how this works."

I lifted my index finger and traced around the rim of the glass. Then I dipped my finger into the glass, brought it to my mouth, and slowly sucked off the water that dripped from it. I heard more than one gulp and a clearing of throats, but the best reaction was the look on his face. I think it was shock.

"You're good. You should start a business and sell your tips to those who need it." She laughed and hugged me again.

"Let's see what happens next. This is fun." We all started laughing and waiting for a response. I got one from someone I wasn't expecting.

"Are you crazy or what?" Alex stood next to me speaking in a low tone. "You guys are going to give more than one person in here a heart attack—or worse."

"What's wrong, dear brother, can't take the heat?"

"You're funny. Now give me my sister back."

"She's ours now, Alex." They all laughed and Paige hugged me again.

"Whatever, girls." He left shaking his head.

"Okay, we should stop before someone busts a vein."

"That's fine by me. Alex ruined the atmosphere," Paige quibbled.

"I'm making my move. Goodbye, ladies." Emery walked toward Tyler.

"My brother. Oh man, why?" Quinn gagged a little.

The night wore on and I started to fall asleep against Paige's arms and the railing. Suddenly I felt colder arms around me.

"How's your evening going, Sleeping Beauty?"

"Better now, Declan."

"So were you guys trying to kill me tonight?"

"Come on, you started it."

"I think not."

"I do. We just nodded, but you winked."

"And you sucked your finger." He inhaled and paused. "And what do you think that does to a guy?"

"Well, Alex warned us, but where's the fun in that?"

"You are evil."

"I know."

"You are such a witch," he whispered in my ear. I sat down in the Adirondack chair in the corner and he sat next to me.

"What did you say?" He leaned in and whispered again in my ear, "That's what I thought you said. How did you know?"

"Alex told me after he found out."

"Does Evan know you know?"

"Yes."

I sat on his lap and laid my head on his chest.

"Is that okay?" he asked.

"As long as you don't care, Declan, then I don't."

"I'm a little relieved you are from this family, because it would be harder to leave you if you weren't. You know the rules."

"I guess I'm glad, too, but if you change your mind, there's always Gavin." I chuckled and he hugged me tighter.

"I don't think so, silly girl." He kissed my neck. "I think I'll keep you."

"Can I ask you something?"

"Sure, what do you what to know?"

"What is this, Declan? Are we dating or something else?" He didn't answer right away and I started to panic a little. My pulse started to race and I could tell my breathing was off.

"I thought we were dating, but if you had to ask, then I'm not sure."

"Well, if you'll have me, I think us dating would be a natural progression here." I caressed his arm while I waited for his answer.

"You can't get rid of me that easily." He kissed me on my head.

"Well, you'll have to let me go soon. I have a slumber party to attend."

"Maybe I'll have to crash."

"And how will you do that?"

"I'll be right down the hall sleeping in Alex's room. I was invited to stay here tonight."

"Well, isn't that convenient, you being here the same night as my party."

"I'm not the only one. Tyler is staying, too."

"Well, this is turning a little too kinky for my taste." I laughed and stood up.

"You're so bad. Please come back and sit."

"Unless you want to change your clothes, I think I need to excuse myself for a minute or two." I walked into the house and toward the bathroom.

"So can I come to the powder room with you?" Paige walked beside me.

"I was actually going out for some air."

"I know you were. He gets a little intense sometimes, huh?"

"Just a little. He tends to drive the conversation to intense places."

"Well, I think it would have been tamer if we hadn't had our fun earlier."

"I think you're right." We sat down on the stairs.

"Can I talk to you about something?"

She nodded and I figured it was okay to continue.

"So if Declan knows, then I'm sure you do, too, right?"

"I do, but I also figured you would talk to me about it when you were ready."

"So I also take it you know about my healing talent as well?"

She put her hand on top of mine and I felt that same surge as before.

"You and I are not so different. You may have a little bit more ability in the healing area, seeing as it's your family's forte."

I took in everything she said, but this conversation was beginning to get a little too deep for me. I needed to change the subject.

"Do we turn in now and save ourselves, or do we prepare for the tactical mission they're planning tonight?" She moved her hand, understanding my apprehension.

"I say we prepare now, Grey. If I've learned anything about you and Alex, it is you two are rather competitive with each other." Paige smiled.

"That we are. Listen, I'll go upstairs, because I'm supposed to be in the bathroom anyway."

"We'll come up one by one." She snickered. "I'll come first, then the rest will follow."

"You're sneaky. I knew I liked you."

"Give me about two minutes."

"I'll be on the balcony waiting. Good luck."

She got up and headed down to the deck, and I to my room. I saw her talking to Emery and Quinn. The plan was moving forward—until he grabbed her.

"Where's Grey?"

"She's in the bathroom. Don't get so paranoid."

"I know I got a little carried away."

"I think so. You might want to tone it down a little, big guy."

"What are you talking about?" Then I could see the light click on in his head, probably another nonverbal conversation. "It was too much too fast?"

"Exactly. Chill out and enjoy the party. She's not going anywhere."

She turned and I heard her walking into the hall. She came up behind me and sat down.

"Thanks, Paige."

"Anytime. He needs to be reined in a little, and that's why I'm here."

Quinn walked in, and about minute later Emery entered the room.

"So what do we do now?" Quinn wondered.

"Get changed for bed, of course." I walked into my closet.

I grabbed my shorts and a cami from the shelf and got changed.

"Now I understand why he had a hard time sleeping on Sunday," Paige remarked on my attire.

"Please, Alex sees this all the time."

"But he's your brother."

"Oh, good point. I didn't think of that." They laughed. The rest of them changed, and you would think we were preparing to film a bad sorority flick the way we were dressed.

"So what fun can we have tonight?" Quinn turned to Emery.

"I don't know, but I'm hungry. I think we have ice cream downstairs and some of Declan's dessert is still in the fridge."

"Declan made dessert?" Emery questioned.

"Yeah, the same cake I had at my birthday."

"That cake was so good—definitely get that," Paige whispered.

"Okay, I'll go first and grab what I can. Quinn, you go next and grab what I didn't get.

"Is Allie still up?" Emery asked.

"I don't think so, but I can check. She would be a good look out."

I ran quietly to Allie's room. She was still awake due to the noise outside.

"Hey, kiddo, I need your help."

"Sure, anything!" She jumped out of her bed.

"Okay, I need you to be a look out. We need to get stuff from the kitchen."

"When?"

"Now. Let's go!" I gave her the thumbs up when I reached the stairs.

"Go! The coast is clear." Paige motioned from the balcony.

We ran down the stairs and into the kitchen. I sent Allie to the door to keep watch. I grabbed five spoons, the ice cream, and balanced the cake on top. I slowly moved toward the door and bumped into something. It was Evan.

"Grey, what are you doing?"

"Run!" Allie shouted.

"Nothing!" I ran up the stairs.

"Hey, Allie, what are you doing up?"

"I was thirsty, Evan, but I'm good now." She ran up the stairs to my room.

"Good job, Allie." I gave her a spoon.

Paige waved me to the balcony. I crawled over and listened.

"What was that about?" Alex asked.

"I'm not sure, but I wouldn't worry, okay?" Evan answered. "I think it's time to slow it down. No trouble tonight, Alex." He didn't respond. "I remember the times when you guys had friends over. The tricks need to stay to a minimum. I mean it, Alex."

"Yes, sir!" Alex shouted back.

I looked at Paige. "Allie is our secret weapon."

"You're good at this."

"We've been doing this a long time," I scoffed. "Allie, you know what to do?" She laughed and headed back to her room.

"She knows what to do?" Quinn crawled toward me.

"Yup, she plays both sides, but I know her price and Alex doesn't."

"You're very sneaky."

"I know." I let them in on the plan. "I expect them to try and get in here, but I found a way out and only Allie and I know about it." I walked to the closet, pulled my clothes apart, and pushed the back wall.

"Hey, Grey."

"Hey, Allie." I turned. "This goes to Allie's room."

"There's also stairs that go down to Evan's office," she chimed in.

"This is so cloak and dagger." Emery giggled.

"I'd give them until two o'clock in the morning. That's when the fun begins."

I said bye to Allie, closed the door, and put the clothes back in place. We sat around the balcony, listening and eating. They were still on the deck at one in the morning.

"There waiting us out." I nudged Paige. "It's time to up the ante."

I got up and headed out onto the deck.

"Hey, guys. Alex, Evan asked me to tell you to wrap it up."

"And I'm telling you for the last time to put some clothes on."

"Well, I'm pretty comfortable and you never minded me walking around like this before."

"Because I'm your brother, but these guys are probably picturing you without certain articles of clothing."

"That's fine. You can tell them what I look like in a towel coming out of the shower. I mean, how many times had we had conversations while I was in there." He shot me a look.

"Grey, please go back upstairs."

"I'm not tired, so I don't think so." I sat on the railing.

"So what are we talking about?"

"Nothing now." Tyler looked away.

"How about a game of chess? I can go get the board." I turned and lounged back on the railing.

"Um, I need to use the bathroom. I'll be right back." Declan ran out to the hall. I sat up, and Tyler soon followed.

"I don't know what you're planning, but you won't win." He pulled me off the railing.

"Oh, I think I have the upper hand. The ball is in your court, Alex."

I started toward the stairs when I saw the two of them out front trying to breathe. I giggled and started up the stairs when they came back in. At the same time, Alex came from the deck.

"Can I talk to you for a minute?" Declan walked toward the stairs.

"Sure, what's up?"

"Don't do it, Dec. She's psyching you out," Alex murmured quietly. He waved them off and they reluctantly headed back to the deck.

"So what do you want to talk about?" I sat down next to him on the step.

"You and my self-control, actually. I was wondering how you can cut my legs from under me like you just did."

"Oh, I'm sorry. I can stop."

"Please try to be a little less detailed and a little less exposed."

"Whatever you say." I leaned in and I was an inch from his face. "It's my house, remember?"

His breathing had picked up and I ran upstairs. I walked into my room and closed the door.

"You're evil. I think you're going to break my poor brother."

"I can try." I crawled toward her. "So what I miss?"

"Well, Tyler was apologizing to your brother until he told him to shut up."

"They won't try anything now, I think, but be on guard."

It was close to four o'clock in the morning and half of us were asleep. Quinn tapped my shoulder.

"I have to use the bathroom."

"Okay, I'll go with you."

We walked down the hall to the bathroom. Unfortunately, the old floors creaked in front of Alex's door. She hurried to the bathroom as I stood watch. After what seemed like minutes, I sat down. I heard a door open.

"Oh, man," I mumbled to myself.

Declan walked out. His hair was a mess and he was wearing pajama pants and no shirt. His chest was as defined as his abs; he definitely worked out a lot. I moved my way up to his shoulders. He had a couple of old bruises on his upper arms, which twitched every so often. I tried not to look at his face, but it didn't work when he squatted down next to me.

He traced his fingers along the back of my left shoulder and found it—my birthmark. It looked more like a brand than a birthmark. At least that's what Alex called it.

"What's this?" He leaned around me to look.

"I was born with it. Alex, has the same thing on his right shoulder."

"You mean like this."

He stood up, rolling the band of his pants down and turned. He pointed to his lower back over his left hip. He had the same mark on his back as Alex and I. It was the triskele, the mark of a trinity, but later I found out that in our community it was the mark of a witch, and it dated back to the druids. Also something about a sign of a bonding, but I didn't read too much into that.

"Exactly."

"Intriguing." He pulled his pants back up and sat next to me.

"So, Declan, do you need to use the bathroom?"

"No, I heard a noise and came out to investigate. I don't like the fact that your room is so close to the stairs." He was so cute when he was acting all protective of me.

"So everyone's asleep?"

"Alex gave up about two hours ago. He said you won."

"I don't buy it until the sun comes up."

"You guys get pretty competitive with each other."

"Yeah, it's a curse."

"Funny." We sat for a while, talking. Finally Quinn came out.

"Sorry, I feel asleep."

"Go back to bed. I'll be right there." She shuffled off to my room and closed the door.

"You guys dress to kill, don't you?"

"No, it's just comfortable."

"Uh, huh." He looked toward the door. "I'll see you in the morning."

"Only if you're cooking" He laughed and turned to face me, staring into my eyes. I put my head on his shoulder and he leaned his head on mine and wrapped his arms around me. I felt as though I was being cuddled by a bear, it was warm and inviting.

"I could stay like this all night."

I sighed. "It's not too cold. We could watch the sunrise on the deck."

"I think that sounds very inviting." I grabbed a blanket from the bathroom closet and pulled him down the stairs.

We sat on the two chairs we pushed together. I wrapped the blanket around us. I put my head on his chest as he wrapped his arms around me.

I figured we fell asleep because I heard snickering from above and below. I cracked my eyes open slightly to see the girls peering down from the balcony, and Alex in the kitchen. An audience. *Whatever.* I fell back asleep.

"Don't go out there. You'll wreck it," Alex whispered loudly so I could hear.

"Why not?" Evan peered around the corner. "Oh, I think I do need to walk out there."

"Nothing happened." He grabbed his arm. "They've only been out there for about an hour or so. They were talking and fell asleep. Now leave them alone."

I immersed myself closer into his chest and he reacted by tightening his grip. I felt him leaning down to kiss my hair.

"This is a nice way to wake up," he whispered.

"I don't agree." His grip loosened. "This is." I leaned up and kissed him.

I definitely didn't expect his reaction. He interweaved one of his hands through my hair and the other was around my waist. He kissed me harder and faster when I inhaled to breathe. I had to stop him.

"Well, that was interesting."

"I'm sorry. It will never happen again. I lost my train of thought." He panted.

"It took me off guard, is all." I moved back into his embrace. "The next time I'll be ready."

He squeezed me tighter and let go. "I think I need to get dressed."

"Okay, I guess I will, too."

He leaned back in. "I wish you wouldn't, but it will help me out."

"Sure, anytime, if it helps you out."

He ran upstairs and I heard loud giggling from the balcony.

"Thanks, guys."

"Anytime, Grey," I heard Quinn say.

"You'd better come get dressed!" Paige yelled down.

I wrapped the blanket around me and headed upstairs.

"Morning, Tyler," I mumbled as I passed him on the stairs. He chuckled and headed downstairs toward the bathroom.

"Hey, Grey." Alex walked toward me.

"Yes, Alex, what can I do for you?"

He leaned in and said, "I hope you're happy."

"Why is that, Alex?"

"He is in the shower trying to calm down."

"Do you want me to go talk to him?"

"Be serious, Grey. Behave yourself."

"Whatever you say, Alex." I walked into my room and closed the door. I heard his door slam and we all laughed.

"Seriously though, Grey, you could damage him before you get him."

"I'll be more prudent, Paige." They broke into laughter on their way down the stairs. I got dressed and joined them in the kitchen.

"So what do you guys want to eat?"

"Let's go out to eat. I don't want to trash your house any more than we did last night." Quinn dumped the empty ice cream container in the trash.

"Is there any cake left?"

"Yeah. Here, Paige." We all started eating the whip cream and strawberries with our hands. It was easier than walking over and grabbing spoons.

"Oh, man. I'm not staying here again if they're all going to be here," Tyler said to Alex.

"Guys, can we chill out on the cake?"

"But we're hungry, Alex," Paige said.

"I thought we could go down to the café to eat, seeing as our cook is unable to perform."

We all laughed, but they didn't find it funny. He threw the keys at me.

"Fine, Grey. You take the Jeep and we'll ride with Dec."

"We'll meet you there." I started in on the cake again. "This cake is so good."

I heard a growl and then Alex say, "Get out, girls."

We laughed even harder.

"Maybe we should get going. We have the whole day to have fun." I tried to keep a straight face.

We piled in the Jeep and headed to town.

"So what do you want to do today?" Emery leaned forward.

"I was thinking we could pick up some stuff at the store and have a movie marathon."

"Sounds good to me," Paige agreed. We all agreed. I didn't care what the guys were doing, because this was an all-girls day.

I figured I would give them some time to cool down, especially Alex, so I took a longer route. We walked into the café and spotted them in the back. We took our seats and started looking over the menu. I looked at Alex who was still a little irked about this morning.

"So do we know what we want?"

"Well, I was thinking my dad's great pancakes with whipped cream and strawberries," Quinn suggested.

"I don't know what I want, but it's got to be big, because I'm hungry," Paige smirked.

"All right, enough. You're going to put us in early graves. If you can't behave, then go sit at another table."

"We're just talking about what we want to eat."

"Well, Grey, talk quietly and don't share, okay?"

I got up.

"Paige, if she takes the orders, can you get me some pancakes and tea? Oh, and I think I'm in the mood for some meat, too, so get me some bacon."

I heard Alex slam his hand down on the table.

"Okay, just get me the pancakes and tea."

She laughed and I headed to the bathroom.

CHAPTER ELEVEN

MOVIES AND MAYHEM

We ate breakfast in silence, which was hard. There were a few snickers here and there, but Alex kept reining us back to silence. If he was so concerned about us talking, then he should have moved to another table. Once we'd finished, the girls and I walked down to the corner market to stock up on the needed supplies for a movie marathon—lots of junk food. As we pulled out to head home, I noticed they were behind us. I could only imagine what they were talking about.

I searched the cupboards for some bowls and bounded downstairs to the TV room to watch movies all day. We must have watched at least three movies before one of them came down. Of course it was Alex.

"What are you guys watching?"

"We're getting ready to watch either *Breakfast Club* or *Revenge of the Nerds*."

"Can we watch a movie. We're bored."

I looked around and no one cared.

"Sure, I guess that's okay."

I heard the rest of them clomping down the stairs. There was nowhere to sit because the sofa and loveseat was occupied, so they sat on the floor, which I assume was not very comfortable.

I dropped in *Romeo and Juliet* when the previous movie was finished—it was a girls' day after all. The funny thing was I thought they would get up and leave, but they actually stayed. They must have been bored.

Unaware of what I was doing, I started running my fingers through his hair.

"You might want to stop that." Paige pointed to my hand and whispered. "He might die right here."

We giggled.

"Sorry."

I started to pull my hand away, but he reached for it and pulled it back to his neck. I looked at Paige and she shrugged. I kept it there, mindlessly running my fingers through his hair, every so often feeling the twinge of electricity up my arm.

We all started crying except for a few exceptions, when they were in the tomb and when Juliet woke up. He gently took my hand and placed it on his cheek. He held it there until the end of the movie. I could have sworn I felt tears on my hand, but it could have been sweat. I didn't know.

"We need a break before we finish the rest."

I jumped up and ran upstairs to the bathroom. Paige followed me, then knocked on the door before sneaking in.

"You can't hide out up here the rest of the day. Maybe we should go bowling or something."

"That sounds good. It's not dark, and there'll be lots of people around."

"That won't stop him, you know."

"I know, but I can hope it slows him down a little." It wasn't that I didn't enjoy his company, it was this feeling I had every time I was near him or when he touched me. It was something I couldn't explain, and now I didn't need the intense atmosphere, especially when I couldn't control my gifts.

She hugged me.

"It gets easier, you know."

"Really"

"Really. Let's go and tell everyone else."

I turned the lights on and waited for everyone's eyes to adjust before I cut the movie marathon short.

"Paige and I were thinking it would be a good idea if we went out and got some fresh air."

"What did you have in mind?" Alex was skeptical of my reasoning.

"Bowling." I wasn't sure, but it sounded safe enough, and they agreed.

The girls and I went to change. We hadn't planned it, but somehow we matched. Our attire consisted of your standard pair of jeans, and I had my green V-neck. Emery borrowed my light-yellow one, Paige had a gray V-neck t-shirt, and Quinn had a light-blue, V-neck shirt. It was kind of funny, but I went with it. As we descended the stairs, Alex shook his head and walked out the door.

"I guess we chose the right outfits."

"I think so," Emery replied.

We took our time getting into the Jeep before venturing into the land of balls and pins. When we were walking toward the alley, we bumped into Gavin and Jack outside. I'm sure it wasn't coincidence. I bit my lip, knowing I would regret it later. I liked Jack. We always had fun together, so I invited them to join us.

As I predicted, Alex was not happy when we walked in, but he had to deal with it. We all liked Jack, but unfortunately he was with Gavin, so I had no choice but to invite them both. It seemed as if the teams were already decided. It was us versus them. Someone was looking out for me, because Gavin decided to sit that one out and watch. I guess he was still sore. No loss on my end.

I was having fun. We won three games out of five. It was getting late and I was getting tired, so we had to call it a night. I
couldn't believe how dead-tired I was. Something was zapping my
energy from me. I never used to tire so easily.

"I'll meet you guys at the Jeep."

I walked out as they went to the bathroom, and of course,
Gavin followed me.

"Grey, can you wait."

"What's up Gavin?"

"We used to be friends. What happened?"

"You know what happened."

"Okay, I said I was sorry for that. I was wrong. I know I'm
a jerk."

"You're getting close."

"I'm sorry. Can we try to be friends again? Just friends. That's
it." He smiled.

"I guess I can try."

He hugged me and it felt awkward, like he was planning
something else. I was trying to pull away, when he kissed me. I
pushed away. My instincts kicked in. I threw my hands up, hitting
him across the left side of his face.   I tried to catch my breath
and compose myself, when I heard Paige and Emery.

"Are you okay? What happened?"

Then I lost it and started to ramble.

"He was apologizing. He wanted to try and be friends again,
so I agreed to try. He hugged me when I tried to pulled away, then
kissed me. I slapped him."

"Good for you." Emery hugged me. "Let's get you home.
Paige, you drive." Quinn helped me into the back as quickly as
possible. I think they were trying to avoid a scene.

We drove so fast that I didn't notice they were already helping
me up to my room.

"You need to get in the shower and calm down. Water always helps me refocus. Plus, you don't want Alex to see you like this."

Paige had said Alex, but I also knew who else she was thinking of. I was so drained as they dragged me to the bathroom. That's when I heard Alex come home.

"Grey, where are you?" He heard the bathroom door close. I could hear his footsteps hammering up the stairs as he ran to the door.

"Grey, are you okay?"

"She's fine. We can handle, it Alex," Quinn said through the door.

"What happened? We came out and you guys were gone."

"Alex, nothing happened. Don't worry about it. Go out on the deck and we'll be down shortly," Paige insisted.

"Fine. You've got twenty minutes and then I'm coming back up."

"Give us thirty minutes, okay?"

Quinn turned the shower on.

"Get in the shower, Grey, and relax."

I did what she said, and I eventually climbed in the shower after undressing and crying for a few minutes. I didn't get why I was crying. I think it must have been an effect of pure exhaustion.

"Feeling better?"

"Getting there."

"Do you want us to go hunt him down?"

"No, I think his guilt will eat away at him. Plus, it wasn't just him."

"You're probably right. I do have to say, he got what was coming to him. I would hate to see you in a dark alley" She tried to make me laugh, and it worked just a little bit.

"So do you want to talk about what else is going on?"

"These past couple of days I have been feeling off, like someone is draining my energy or something. I know it sounds weird.

I'm sorry."

"Don't be sorry. If what you say is true, it could be lots of things. You haven't learned how to control your abilities yet. They are sometimes working and you don't even realize it till you feel like you do now."

She placed my hand in hers, closing her eyes as she did. I felt quick pulses running up my hand into my forearm. When she was done, I shut the water off and grabbed a towel from her. I dried off some in the shower before wrapping myself in the soft cotton. She unlocked the door and guided me to my room. Quinn proceeded to tell us what was going on as I got dressed.

"Apparently they came out and we were gone. So were Gavin and Jack. So they were worried, and rushed back here," Emery continued. "They have no clue what happened, and they're expecting answers."

It was like a tag team match, listening to them explain what was happening. Quinn sat me down on the edge of the bed and started to comb my hair.

"What was I thinking?" I put my hands in my face and fell back on the bed.

"You were just being you, Grey. You thought he was sincere."

"No one thought he would pull that crap again," Emery added.

"Hush. Tyler is coming up," Quinn whispered from the balcony.

I heard a knock at my door.

"Um, Quinn, I'm headed home, so if you and Emery want a ride, meet me downstairs."

"Guys, go. I'm fine. I won't let Alex out of my sight. I'm fine. You don't need to worry."

"I'll stay with her. We know he won't leave, and someone has to keep an eye on him, too," Paige insisted.

They didn't know that I needed her to stay for other reasons. Grams was mysteriously missing in action again.

"Okay, we'll call you tomorrow."

"Feel better—and job well done." Emery laughed. They grabbed their stuff and left.

"I feel like watching sappy movies," I informed Paige.

"We still have the Austin classics to watch, and plenty of hot tamales left to eat."

"Let's go." We headed downstairs to the TV room.

I heard Alex come down a few minutes later.

"Do you want company?"

"If you want to join us, you can, and before you ask, I'm fine."

He smirked at me and they sat down on the floor. Paige and I were under the quilt, already settled in. Her calming touch was helping me maintain some sense of reality at that moment.

We watched *Pride and Prejudice* first. I didn't care if they were there or not. I tried to remain calm and enjoy myself for what was left of the night.

"I love that Mr. Darcy."

"Me too, Grey."

I saw Alex roll his eyes and I couldn't help but chuckle quietly. The movie ended. I decided to go with *Sense and Sensibility* next.

"Let me call my dad and let him know we're staying so they don't worry."

"Okay, should I wait?"

"No, I'll be right back." She ran up the stairs and he moved to sit next to me—so predictable.

He wrapped his arms around me as I watched the movie. Paige came back down and I saw her roll her eyes. She took her chances sitting next to Alex. I was so tired, and with Paige gone, I dozed in and out of sleep. I did, however, manage to hear her telling them what had happened in the parking lot. I felt his grip get tighter and heard Alex clench his teeth. I hated when he did that.

Great. Now I can't sleep. I'll have to watch them. The movie finally ended, but everyone had fallen asleep. I eventually dozed off, and every so often I would hear Declan whisper, "I'm sorry for what happened earlier." I cupped my hand to his face to calm him.

He leaned in and kissed my hand and then my wrist, and slowly made his way up to my neck. My neck was where he stayed, making a strange pattern with his lips between the base of my neck and the back of my ear. It got to the point where I couldn't take it anymore I reached for his face and fell back on the sofa.

Our lips locked together, and the anticipation and excitement was evident. One of his hands tangled in my hair and the other hand was on my waist. I slid my hands around his neck and interlaced my fingers into his hair. He pushed my mouth open with his. I could feel his rapid breathing hit the back of my throat, as well as his tongue. He exhaled. I couldn't help but tilt my head back. He moved from my mouth, tracing his way to my neck with the tips of his lips and tongue. His hand slid slowly from my waist, down my thigh, leaving goose bumps behind, finally stopping just below my knee. In one swift movement, he hitched my leg up to around his waist. His breath was becoming erratic and heavy.

It was getting to be too much for me. I had to stop, so I did the first thing that came to my mind. I rolled out onto the floor and ran upstairs. I heard him hit the sofa with his fists, which woke Paige up in time to see me going up the stairs. She instinctively followed me.

I could hear her cursing under breath while I jumped on my bed and tried not to cry.

"What happened down there?"

"I don't know, but I couldn't handle it. It was getting way too intense." She knew what I was talking about, and comforted me.

"He's a gentleman. He understands better than you think." She tried to calm me. "But sometimes his emotions drive his actions."

I continued to lay there with her. I heard a faint knock at the door while I was about to fall asleep.

I heard them a few minutes later out on the deck. She left the doors to the balcony open. Of course, Alex was out there, too, trying to comfort him, not knowing what happened.

"She's my sister and she gets this way sometimes." He had no clue what was going on.

Paige interceded. "Of all nights, you chose this one." I heard her open palm hit his shoulder.

"Your feelings for her are very strong, and so are your thoughts, but sometimes your actions are driven by some other emotions that need to be reined in a little."

"What are talking about?" Alex was still clueless.

"Don't worry about it. Just sit and listen."

"Fine." I could picture the stern pout on his face like he was being punished.

"If you don't know already, her feelings are just as strong for you, then you need to have your head examined. But as much as she wants to give in, she can't right now. Do you understand?"

"I do, or at least I can try. I'm new to this as well. This connection to her is so intense I don't understand it myself."

"Oh, man, are you—"

Paige cut him off. "Calm down, Alex."

"She's my sister, my little sister. I don't want to hear this."

I heard him stomp into the kitchen. It was so typical of him to run when talk of feelings and emotions entered the conversation.

"She'll come down when she's ready, but I think it's best if we leave before she does."

"I need—"

"You don't need to do anything today. You've done enough, don't you think? I suggest you cancel your lesson today. I'll tell her. You grab your stuff and meet me out front."

I heard her run into the hall. In seconds, she was at my door.

"I trust you heard."

"I did. That's exactly what I needed to say—except one thing."

"What?"

"At least let me say goodbye. You don't want him brooding around the house till Monday, do you?" She laughed and grabbed her bag from the closet.

I walked out with her, my eyes still red from lack of sleep, which was finally catching up to me. He was standing at the base of the stairs. He started to talk, but I put my fingers to his lips to stop him. Without thought, I wrapped my arms around him tightly.

"I'll meet you outside," Paige reminded him. He pulled back to see my face as he wiped the tears from my eyes.

"I'm truly sorry for what happened earlier. I get carried away with you."

"I know what you mean."

"Are you okay?"

"I'm fine."

"Then why are your eyes so red?"

"It's a long story, but here's the short of it." I took a deep breath. I was going to tell him what I hadn't admitted to myself until now. "I care for you very much—too much sometimes, for such a short period of time. I don't think sometimes before I leap, and trust me when I say I don't want to stop, but I have to. I can't explain this connection. It goes deeper. There are also things that I need to talk to my family about before I tell you anymore. Do you understand?"

"I understand more than you know." His comment was like a sigh of relief, which I completely understood.

"Good. Now go home and catch up on your sleep."

"You do the same, and I'll see you on Monday?" he asked.

I stretched on the tips of my toes and kissed him. It was short yet sweet.

"Yes, definitely. You can't lose your good luck charm now that you're so close to regionals."

He laughed, hugging me tightly.

"I'll see you later."

He started down the stairs, then sprinted back up. He embraced me, brushing his lips toward my ear.

"I love you, Grey." As fast as he kissed my cheek, he was down the front steps.

I slowly glided back to my room and collapsed on my bed. I quietly said to myself, "I love you, too." It felt strange to say at first, but it was what I was feeling. I was tired but happy—more than happy, even, if that was possible. I eventually drifted off to sleep.

I had to get up early that morning. I had several meetings with prospective candidates for my tutor. I slung my bag into the back and hopped in his car.

"Do you have questions ready for these people?" Evan asked.

"Yeah, I wrote some." I pulled out the paper for my bag. "Thanks for the use of your office."

"Well, I have questions ready, too." He pulled out an index card and I laughed. He was always more organized than I was.

"Let's get this over with."

No one was there yet. It was still too early. The first applicant wasn't going to be there for another thirty minutes. I kept scanning the lot for him.

"How many people are we seeing today?"

"We're only seeing six people total." He grabbed the list from his desk. "Hopefully we can make a decision by tomorrow."

"Sounds good to me."

The first applicant arrived, and I definitely did not like him. His voice was monotone. So much so, he would put an insomniac to sleep. The day dragged on and we had finally finished with every person. There were three possible candidates: a math teacher, a college student, and a student from the school who Evan interviewed without me.

The math teacher, Mrs. Baker, seemed nice, but her schedule was tough to work around. The college student on the other hand, Camden Reed, was a math major at Durham College in the next town over. He definitely did not fit my description of a math geek. He was good looking, and that was an understatement. He might be a distraction, so I would definitely have to deal with that.

Evan interviewed the last candidate. I had to present my project in art class with Paige. Once class was finished, she walked with me to the courtyard.

"So how's the interview process going?"

"Long, but I have three candidates, two are my choice and one is Evan's choice."

"Who's Evan's choice?" I shrugged my shoulders

"I don't know, Paige, but he's a student here."

"Well, that proves my point last week that there was another trigonometry tutor out there."

"You did, and I'll never doubt you again." I chuckled while she rolled her eyes.

"When do you decide?"

"By tomorrow at the latest. I have to go back and go through the remaining candidates with Evan."

"I'll see you at lunch then?" She already knew the answer.

"Probably not." I started down the stairs and headed toward Evan's office.

I walked across the courtyard toward the administration building. I knocked on his office door.

"Come in." Evan was on the phone as I walked in. He motioned for me to sit, then hung up the phone. "Well, that was one of the candidates. Their schedule cannot be worked around, so they have withdrawn their name from the list."

I was sitting there listening to him, but thinking, *Please don't be the college guy. I'm only a teenage girl, and he is too cute. Man, I've got to stop. He could be my tutor and I need to concentrate.*

"Which one?"

"Mrs. Baker. She decided to take on another student whose schedule works better with her own."

Yes, the cute guy is still in.

"So I have two possible candidates to choose from."

"I know one of them." He smirked. "Who's the other one?"

"Your choice. The student that goes here, but maybe we can select both of them." I could picture the wheels turning in my mind.

"Grey, you can only have one tutor."

"Who says? Just hear me out. I can only get two days with this Jackson"—I had to look at the list—"Marsh, but I can get three to four days at the same time with Camden Reed." I can't believe I remembered his name. Maybe that was a sign, a sign that I was being greedy and crazy.

"Okay, maybe we can get both for free, and then I get the whole week of tutoring as well as the possibility of a better grade."

"How are we going to do that?" He smiled as he paced, like he already knew my solution. "We can only get Jackson as a volunteer because he's a student here."

"Credits." I smiled. "Camden needs course credits for experience, right? And you know his course advisor."

"That's not a bad idea. I think it might work. He doesn't start his practice until the end of January."

"What practice?"

"He plays lacrosse for Durham College. He would have to rearrange the schedule, but it could still work." He was already on the phone.

What was with this area and their obsession with lacrosse? Must be something in the water, I thought, when I noticed Evan smirk.

I didn't care, because we'd both gotten what we wanted and I needed all the help I could get. I looked at him and he gave me the thumbs up. I had to go track down this Jackson guy to tell him the good news. I waited for him to finish his conversation.

"So you will have Camden four days a week and Jackson one day a week."

He wrote down the schedule and their phone numbers in case

we needed to make changes to the schedule.

"Jackson will tutor you on Mondays during your free period, and Camden will tutor you Tuesday through Friday at the same time in the library."

"Thanks." I grabbed the paper. "Can you write a note just in case I'm late for history?"

He was way ahead of me. I grabbed the note and my bag to leave.

I hoped Alex would know who this Jackson guy was. I lucked out, getting to the cafeteria with ten minutes left of lunch. I walked through the doors. There was no sign of Alex, so I walked over to the girls and sat down.

"So what's the verdict?" Emery asked.

"I get both of them."

"How did you manage that one?" Paige looked up, but she wasn't surprised.

"I begged, and then came up with an idea of experience credits for Camden."

"Who's Camden?" Quinn asked.

"Her new tutor," Paige whispered to Quinn. "I guess he is dreamy." She giggled.

"I don't know a Camden."

You could see Quinn running names through her head. That girl knew everyone in the entire school. It was like she had a student filing system in her head.

"He doesn't go here. He attends Durham College."

"Nice, girl! A college guy," Quinn squealed. "But who's the other tutor?"

"Some guy named Jackson. He goes here."

"Jackson Marsh."

"Yeah, do you know him Quinn?"

"Yes. It's Jack, silly. He's over there." She pointed to the table where the lacrosse team sat.

"Great. I'll be right back." I got up and walked over to the table. Declan smiled.

"Missed you this morning. Did you come to say hi?"

"No, I'm here to see Jack." His smile faded slightly. "Sorry."

"Me?"

"Yeah, can I talk to you for a minute?"

"Sure."

I could see the puzzled look on Declan's face. I wondered what was going through his head right now.

Jack and I sat a couple of tables away and I delivered the good news.

"So you're going to be my new tutor on Mondays during my free period."

"Super, but I thought you needed a tutor for the whole week?"

"I do, but you're my tutor on Mondays. I have another for the rest of the week."

"If you don't mind me asking, who is it?" It looked like he was trying to remember the other candidates. It reminded me of Quinn a little.

"Camden Reed. He's a student at the college. He's a math major and could use the extra credits." I filled in all the blanks so he would stop asking questions.

"Oh yeah, I remember him from this morning. He was cool. Did you know he plays lacrosse there?"

"I didn't until Evan told me." I got up. "Well, I have class, but thanks. I'll see you on Monday."

I ran back to the table and grabbed my bag.

"I'll see you guys later. I have to make a call before class."

"See you later."

I quickly made my way to the office to use the phone to call Camden. He didn't answer, so I left him a message and headed to history.

The rest of the day flew by. I hitched a ride home with Evan.

The team had extra practices this week and I didn't want to wait.

"So are our schedules all set?"

"I think so. I told Jack and he's all set, but I had to leave a message for Camden."

"Good. Then we should be all set. That was easier than I thought it would be." I could see he wanted to talk to me more about our conversation from Sunday.

"I'm doing better. Still tired, but not as much."

"Have you been doing what Grams suggested?"

"Yes, I'm meditating and I'm drinking the tea she left for me."

"Don't forget to light that candle every time you're in your room." I gave a slight nod of my head, relieved that we were pulling up the drive.

Alex was still at practice, but all of us were hungry and we couldn't wait any longer to eat. We were almost done when Alex strolled in—just in time to answer the phone. He strolled into the kitchen, followed by his bodyguards, Tyler and Declan, which was a little odd. What were they doing here?

"Grey, the phone's for you. Some guy named Camden." They all sat down at the table and I ran to the hall to get the phone.

"Thanks."

I picked up the receiver and proceeded to set my schedule with him. He suggested we work around his game schedule the next day during our session. I hung up the phone feeling excited, and fluttered back into the kitchen. I picked up my plate and put it in the sink.

"So is everything set?"

"Yes, Evan, we start tomorrow and we're going to work out the schedule for his season as well."

"Good. That sounds perfect. See? It all worked out."

"Oh, he also wanted me to thank you for suggesting the credits to his advisor."

"Well, it's a win, win all around." He walked to the sink. "You should go do your homework so he can look it over tomorrow. Also, I want you to go meditate. It will help."

"Okay, I'll see you guys later."

I grabbed my bag on the way up the stairs. I threw it down and changed for bed in case I fell asleep—which seemed to be the pattern lately. I grabbed my trigonometry book and a pencil on my way to the balcony. I thought a session outside might help. I placed my book down and closed my eyes, trying to relax. About ten minutes later, I heard Alex and his band of merry men out on the deck.

"What was that about?" Tyler asked Alex.

"Grey's new tutor," he answered.

"That's cool. At least it's not Gavin, right?" Tyler said. They laughed and I couldn't help but giggle a little, too.

"Sorry she didn't stay, Dec." He chuckled but it sounded forced.

"Its fine Alex. She has a life outside of me."

"Well, on that note, I think we should go. We have a long day tomorrow," Tyler said, motioning toward the door.

"Man, I need to sleep, too."

"I know what you mean, guys."

I heard them get up. I opened my eyes and quickly headed to the stairs—perfect timing again.

"Hey, guys. You leaving?"

"Yeah, I need to get home and sleep." Tyler walked to the door. "I'll see you guys tomorrow."

"Bye, Tyler. Hey, Declan, can I talk to you for a second?"

"Sure." He walked to the stairs and Alex followed.

"I'll see you later, Dec. Get some sleep."

Alex ran up the stairs to his room as I walked down. I pulled Declan outside to sit on the porch.

"So I didn't get a chance to see your smile today."

"I'm sorry. I missed yours as well, but you sounded busy today."

"I hope you get some sleep. You look tired."

I traced circles around his eyes and then down his face with my fingers.

"Sometimes I can't sleep, but I'll try for you."

I moved my hand down to his chest and laughed quietly.

"Try harder, okay? You need your strength."

In one fluid movement, he wrapped his arms around my waist and squeezed me.

"I'll do my best, but I need to leave to do that."

"Okay."

I pulled back and kissed him. It got easier every time I did, and he returned my advances, but this time it was calmer than his previous attempts. He stopped to gaze into my eyes before hugging me. His lips lightly kissing my cheek was a bonus gift.

"I'll see you tomorrow."

I backed into the house and closed the door as he drove down the drive. Alex caught me on the way up.

"Hey, that was nice, Grey."

"I'm trying. I don't want to tease him too much."

"Whatever, silly. Just go to bed." He laughed and pushed me down the hall. I tried to finish my homework before I crashed and burned.

It was colder today. I felt the chill when my toes touched the floor. It was definitely a sweater-and-jacket day.

We walked to the main building and, like every day, I climbed the stairs to the third floor for English. No Declan this morning. Maybe he overslept. He had looked worn down last night.

The day flashed by, so fast that I was in a daze and before I knew it, history class was ending. On a positive note, Declan did eventually make it to school. I at least managed to see him at lunch. Alex tapped my shoulder, releasing me from my mindless thoughts.

"So you meet the tutor today?"

"Yeah, you'd like him."

"Why is that?"

"He plays lacrosse at Durham College."

"What was his name again?"

"Camden Reed. I thought I told you already."

"No way! He's the best attacker on the East Coast. Can I meet him?"

"Do you have a crush?"

"No." He hit me in the arm. It hurt more than it normally did. *What is going with me lately?*

"Sure. I'll invite him to the game on Friday, okay?"

"Thanks, Grey. You're the best."

He ran down the hall like he'd just won the lottery. All I could do was laugh. He was such a little kid sometimes.

I made it to the library in time to see my tutor was already there waiting for me.

"Hey, sorry I'm late."

"No, I was early. Let's get started."

He was definitely something to look at. He had shaggy brown hair like a surfer with tranquil green eyes. His arms were rather muscular and I couldn't help but stare at every twitching movement they made.

"So do you have time to go over the schedule?"

I snapped out of it.

"Yeah," I said.

"So my practices will begin at the end of January, and they end around four o'clock in the afternoon. So I can come to your house around seven o'clock."

"That works. We can use the kitchen or my uncle's office."

"So this time is good for you until January? Then we'll switch."

"Done deal."

"So let's take a look at your work."

I took out my book and we worked through the hour. We eventually packed it in and headed out.

"I'll see you tomorrow then." He started toward the lot.

"Camden, wait." I almost forgot about Alex. "My brother is a fan of yours and he would like to meet you. Could you possibly come to the game on Friday?"

"I have plans later that evening, but I'm sure I can stop by. But can I bring my girlfriend?

"No problem." *Of course he had a girlfriend.*

"Tell your brother I'll be there."

"Thanks, Camden."

I ran to the gym before I was late, changed, and sat next to Quinn.

"How was your session?" She giggled.

"Good. He's coming to the game on Friday."

"What about Declan?"

"What about him? Don't worry. Camden is bringing his girlfriend. Besides, Alex is a big fan."

"Really?"

"I guess he's some top player around here."

We played basketball again, which always made the time go faster, but it didn't that day. It seemed as if everyone was sleepwalking. I must have been those long practices. We finished and headed to the locker room. I was walking with Quinn when Declan passed us. I grabbed his hand and pulled him back.

"Why are you in such a hurry?"

"I've got practice today, remember?"

"Well, I'll be waiting today, so I'll see you later."

"Okay."

He pulled his hand away and headed into the locker room.

"I bet he caught bits and pieces of our conversation, Grey."

"Man, he's worse than me sometimes."

We laughed.

CHAPTER TWELVE

MISUNDERSTANDINGS

We got to the bleachers and Paige was already there waiting as usual, looking rather peeved.

"Hey, girls, who ticked off my brother today?" She pointed to the field. Declan was playing at full force and with what seemed like a lot of anger. I'd never seen him so frustrated.

"That would be me." Quinn sheepishly raised her hand.

"Spill it, Quinn."

"We were talking in gym about Grey's new tutor and how she asked him to the game on Friday."

"Don't look at me like that, Paige. I did it as a favor to Alex, and he's bringing his girlfriend anyway." I shot a look right back. "Your brother needs to listen to the whole conversation instead of the parts he wants to hear."

"Well, then it's his fault and his loss. Idiot."

"More like jealous," Quinn murmured, and we couldn't help but laugh. "Boys."

Practice didn't go for as long that day. They were let go early and given a day off before the game to rest up. I skipped down to the field house to meet Alex and Declan. He came out first and I grabbed his hand.

"Hey, you, where are you going?"

"Home to get some rest." He pulled away and kept walking.

I ran up and grabbed him from behind around the waist.

"Do you want me to join you?" He kept walking toward the lot. "Just stop for one minute. Paige won't be mad." I tightened my grip and he finally stopped. "Thank you." I walked around him. "Now can you tell me what your problem is today?"

"You know."

"I don't, and if you're going to play games and be mad at me for no reason, then you can go home alone." I let go of him and walked away. It didn't bother me either, because he was acting like a child. I reached the lot and waited in the Jeep for Alex.

Dinner was done and I started doing the dishes.

"Oh, Alex, Camden is coming to the game on Friday."

"You asked him? Great."

"Yup, I'm the best sister ever, but you're out of luck, though."

"Why's that?" He put his dish in the sink.

"He's bringing his girlfriend."

"Whatever." He splashed me with water. The phone shrilled and I could only guess who it was. I had Alex answer it.

"Hey, Dec, what's up?!" he yelled. I shook my head—*so predictable.*

"No, she's in the shower. I'll tell her you called, though. See you tomorrow. Bye."

That was one call I didn't want to deal with after that afternoon. I emptied the sink and started up the stairs.

"What was that all about?" Alex walked with me.

"The green eyed monster," I said as I made my way past his room. I noticed him shaking his head as he closed his door. I walked into the bathroom to take a shower.

Both Alex and I woke up late, but we made it to school just before second period. I had a biology test that day I couldn't miss, and we were finishing up our projects in art. I finished my test early, so I waited for Paige outside in the hall.

"So are you ready?"

"Yup. Are you, Paige?"

"Somewhat."

"That's not very convincing. you know."

The class was empty, so we used the extra time to setup our workspace. I grabbed the supplies we needed.

"I won't be at lunch today." I grabbed the knife.

"Why not?"

"I have to make up a trig test I missed when I was sick.

"That stinks."

"Tell me about it." I grabbed my bag and pulled out a note. "Paige, can you give this to Declan?" I handed her the note. "You can come, too." She laughed as she put the note in her pocket.

We got home early for once because there was no practice. Alex went upstairs to lie down until dinner and I prepared to help Grams in the kitchen.

"Okay, Grams, let's make some lasagna."

She made the salad while I prepared dinner. This cooking thing was getting a little easier. I mean layering pasta sauce and cheese wasn't exactly rocket science. I gave Allie the night off and set the table myself.

"So, Grey, how has the meditation been going?" she asked as she passed me the napkins.

"It's helping, thanks. I feel more drained when I'm home than any other place."

"Interesting. Does it happen throughout the day or at certain times?"

"Well, it usually happens when I'm alone, and more so in the late afternoon—especially before I go to bed." I was trying to figure out her line of questioning. "Do you think it has to do with me talking to Mom?"

"No, not so much. Because you say it's more while you're awake, right?"

"Yes." Okay, now she was starting to scare me. What was going on and was this normal?

"I would continue with the meditation, and remember to always light that candle when you are in your room. It is a protection candle; it will not work if you don't use it." She gave me a stern look like she knew I wasn't lighting it. I agreed and finished setting the table.

I was almost done when the doorbell echoed down the hall. I heard Alex bound down the stairs to open the door. As I heard the door close, I looked up to see them all walk into the kitchen.

"Hey, Paige, Declan."

"Is dinner ready yet?"

"Yes, Alex, go sit down and I'll get Evan and Allie."

I walked past Declan and tapped his arm. He quickly grabbed my hand, squeezed it gently, and smiled as I entered the hallway.

"Evan, Allie dinner's ready!" I yelled up the stairs. I went back to the stove and grabbed the lasagna. I started serving everyone before I sat down next to him.

"Let's eat. This looks good." Evan sat down. "Hello, Paige, Declan."

"You made this?"

"Yup, but Grams helped."

"Declan, I just made the salad, dear."

"And it's a good salad, Grams," Allie chimed in. She was such a suck-up sometimes.

"This is really good, Grey."

"It is very good." Declan nudged my foot with his.

"Well, it's not that hard to layer stuff and throw it in the oven."

I brushed off their compliments. The one thing I didn't take well besides bad news was compliments. We finished dinner after several more compliments surfaced about my cooking. Since I had set it, Allie cleared the table.

"Sorry, everyone, but I didn't make dessert. I'm not that good." And with that comment, I at least got a couple of laughs.

We went downstairs to watch a movie while Grams and Allie finished cleaning up. Alex and I had to watch a movie for class.

"What are we watching tonight?"

"Sorry, guys, but your dad has tortured us with homework, so we're watching a documentary on the Revolutionary War."

"Are you kidding me?" I looked at Paige and shrugged my shoulders.

"Sorry, Declan. Not my first choice."

He grabbed my hand and pulled me onto his lap. I tried not to upset him when I moved onto the sofa. "So Dec, Camden Reed is coming to our game on Friday."

"I know, Alex. I heard."

"Now, Alex, I told you not to get all excited. He's bringing his girlfriend." He threw a pillow at me, but missed when I ducked.

"Shut up, would you?"

I picked up the remote and hit play, starting the movie and my evening of torture when he leaned over.

"Sorry."

"You should be. Save yourself the trouble and ask the next time."

"Will do." He held my hand.

"You're stuck with me, buddy."

"That's fine by me." He put his arms around the back of the sofa.

Declan had fallen asleep halfway through the movie, and I didn't blame him. But Alex and I still had to finish watching it. I tried to stay still while he was sleeping because there was one thing that he didn't know—that he would know eventually.

It was getting harder for me to keep the secret when they were getting closer with the more time they spent together. I glanced over and he winked at me. I saw small movements he made with his hands, holding her hand and occasionally putting his arm around the back of the loveseat.

I knew it was hard for him, but it was harder for me as well. I could only imagine what would happen if he found out that I knew and hadn't told him. I was the only one who knew, and that was because I'd found out by accident. How they'd kept it a secret for so long was beyond me, but sooner or later Alex and Paige would have to come clean about their relationship.

Declan fell onto my shoulder, and man, he was heavy. I slowly moved him so he was lying down with his head on my lap. I could see that he was definitely out of it, but I kept brushing my fingers across his face and through his hair to keep him that way. I turned to Paige, letting her know that I had things under control. She got up, and was shortly followed by Alex.

I finished watching the movie while I aimlessly ran my fingers through Declan's hair. I would fill Alex in later on the parts he'd missed.

When the movie was done, I put on Jeopardy. I always felt smarter when I got the answers right. Declan started to stir because I was yelling out the answers like Alex Trebek could hear me through the screen. I looked down and he smiled back at me. He reached up, pulling down on my neck to kiss me.

"Hey, sleepyhead, did you have a nice nap?"

"It was nice. I didn't want to wake up."

"That nice, huh?"

"Yup. But the real thing is better."

He sat up and began kissing my neck, then moved his way up to my ear. I was catching onto his little game. He always knew my weakness and was quick to use it against me before I could defend myself. That time I hadn't said anything, because I couldn't. I was speechless and in the moment.

He slowly moved to the other side of my neck, then up to my

ear again, and I leaned back onto the sofa. We were laying there like before, except he was more controlled and gentle this time, not pushing the limits. I pulled him from my neck and I rolled him onto his back. Then I sat on top of him.

"Is this not fun for you anymore?" I said, referring to his controlled nature.

"Actually, it is now." He pulled me down and we started to kiss again. Thankfully, he hadn't noticed that his sister and my brother weren't there.

"I think we should go upstairs before I push my luck." He kissed me again and got up.

"Okay, that sounds like a good idea if that's what you really want." I was worried about going upstairs now, so as much as I didn't want to, I tried to stall him.

"Don't push your luck, Grey. Please." He turned to go upstairs when he noticed they were gone. "Where are Alex and Paige?"

"They just went to the kitchen, so let's go."

They better come out soon because these cover-ups are stretching me thin. I was running out of things to do or say. I ran ahead of him, reached the threshold of the hall, and started shouting.

"I guess they went to the deck!" He gave me a strange look as he closed the door.

"Why are you shouting?"

"Sorry, I didn't notice. Maybe my ears are clogged." I turned and snickered.

We walked out to the deck. Thankfully, they were out there with their books. I hoped he didn't notice that Alex's book was upside down. I motioned to him as he quickly threw it on the table.

"Paige, we should go?"

"Sure, Dec. I'll get my bag." She walked to the hall and I followed her.

"Paige, you guys need to come clean." I whispered. "This is starting to get out of hand and I can't cover anymore."

She agreed and grabbed my hand, pulling me to the front porch.

"We will this Friday at the game, okay?"

"Fine."

"The bigger the crowd, the easier the reaction from him," she said, pointing to Declan.

"Good idea.' I stopped and quickly changed the subject. "So I'll be ready tomorrow with our presentation."

She looked puzzled until the front door opened.

"Okay, don't forget we need to pass this part, or we can forget about the rest of the project."

"See you guys later."

"Bye, Paige, Declan." I leaned in and kissed his cheek.

I walked into the house and up the stairs. "Alex."

"What?" I heard shower running. I walked in and sat on the counter. "Listen, I can only prepare him so much without telling him. So you better be prepared on Friday."

"I will after the game, okay? I promise." He leaned around the curtain. "Now get out, please."

I scattered, giving him some space. My bed called to me anyway, and I was inclined to listen, especially after tonight. I made sure I lit the candle before hitting the sack.

Friday came and I had never seen Alex so nervous. You would have thought he was having surgery or something. We got out of the car and were making our way to class when Emery met up with us.

"What's up with you, Alex? Nervous about the game?"

"Yeah, the game. It's pretty nerve-racking."

"No, it's because he's meeting Camden."

"Whatever." He gave me a nod to tell her, but no one else.

"Bye, Alex." He walked away.

"What's with him?"

"He's nervous about tonight." I stopped her before we got to the third floor. "If I tell you something, you can't say anything to anyone."

"Okay, you can trust me. I'm not Quinn. I can keep my mouth shut."

I doubted that, but I had to tell someone.

"You swear, not a word—even to Declan."

"Even Declan."

"Well," I whispered, "Alex is going to tell everyone about his girlfriend."

"Alex has a girlfriend?!"

"Shush." I hit her arm. "Be quiet."

"Sorry."

"He's going to tell everyone tonight after the game."

"Who is it? Do we know her?"

"Yes, but I got to go before I'm late."

"You can't do this!" she yelled at me.

"She's close, and you'll see next class."

I tried to sound mysterious, but I don't think it came off that way.

"Paige will tell me. That's not a clue. It's too vague."

I nodded and ran to class before I was late. I could hear her grumbling out loud down the hall. I got to my seat just in time for the quiz I'd forgotten to study for the night before. *Oh, man. I hope I know this.* I glanced over at Declan. He mouthed "good luck" and started his test. As much as I read, I still needed to be thorough in my answers. I was the last one there and it had taken me the entire period to finish. I hated essay questions, so hopefully I'd done okay.

I tripped a couple of times trying to get to biology before Emery could corner Paige for answers. I made it just in time. She was about to turn when I grabbed her.

"Hey, Emery, what are you doing?"

"I'm asking Paige, because you won't tell me."

"Okay, give me two seconds."

"Fine. The clock's ticking." And she wasn't kidding.

I grabbed Paige and whispered in her ear. I explained to her that Alex had agreed, and it would just be Emery for now until after the game. She was reluctant, but she did agree.

"I swear she won't tell anyone or I'll kill her myself." She crossed her heart and pleaded. I moved back to my seat.

"So Alex's girlfriend is someone very close to us," I said, trying to tell her without mentioning names, but I don't think it clicked yet.

"You said that."

"Then listen again." This time I nodded to the table behind me. "She is close to us."

Emery turned to look around behind us. Paige waved to her in acknowledgement. I could see it start to click as she turned back around.

"Do you know now?"

"Yup, she's behind us, right?"

"Yes."

Finally. It had taken a while, but I think she'd gotten it.

"I didn't know he liked Erica." She was surprised and stupid.

"No, not her." I couldn't believe this was taking so long.

"Then who? Because she is the only one behind us and—oh!" It had clicked. She turned around. "Paige?" She seemed shocked as Paige waved to her again. She turned back to the front. "How long has this been going on?"

"Since August, so it's been about four months now. I only found out two weeks ago when I caught them on the deck holding hands." I shot Paige a look. "Remember, no one—even Declan."

"Especially Declan," Paige reiterated.

"Mum's the word until tonight." She sealed her lips and mimed throwing a key away.

The crazy day finally ended, and I could look forward to the weekend because it would be quiet and relaxing, without drama, but I knew in the back of my mind that it was only wishful thinking.

We met at my house before the game. Paige let Quinn in on the secret so she didn't look shocked later. Now three other people knew and I felt a little better. Once we got to the lot, I spotted Camden by the bleachers.

"Hey, Camden, this is Paige, Emery, and Quinn." I pointed to each as I introduced them.

"Hey, girls." He waved. "This is my girlfriend Natalia."

"It is nice to meet you." I said.

"And you as well. I hope your sessions are going well."

"I've only had four sessions, but I got a B on my makeup test. He's a good teacher."

"He is," She laughed as she looked at him.

"You guys are being silly." He grabbed her hand. "That's great, Grey. We'll have you conquering trigonometry before the end of the year."

He laughed and I cringed.

"Great."

We started up to our seats as he introduced Natalia to everyone else. We talked throughout the game. I glanced here and there to see how the team was doing.

The score was tied with fifteen minutes left.

"That attacker is incredible." He pointed to Declan. "Him, number twenty-two."

"That he is."

"It must be a lucky number, because you have the same number. And you're not that bad either," Natalia told him.

"I guess so," he answered. "Do you know him, Grey?"

"Him? Yeah, he's mine. I can introduce you to him if you want."

I'd said it like he was a puppy playing in the field.

"Lucky girl." Natalia winked and then looked at Camden. "These guys and their pride. You need to help them along every once and while."

"Don't get me wrong, Grey. Your brother is doing great as well."

"That's fine. I'm sure he'll appreciate the compliment. He's sort of a fan of yours."

"Aren't we all?" She laughed with me.

"You girls are bad. Now be quiet and watch the game."

That night definitely wasn't the night for us, good luck charms and all, but it was a great game. It came down to the wire. Alex lost sight of the ball when Gavin blocked his view. The other team's attacker scored, ending our season. We still had had a good season and we needed to celebrate that night.

We walked to the field house to wait for Alex, Tyler, and Declan. Camden commented on their performance as Alex walked out.

"Man that was a good game."

"Alex, I want you to meet Camden. This is his girlfriend Natalia."

"Hi, it's nice to meet you." He wasn't convincing in his enthusiasm. I'm sure he was still upset about the game.

"Hey, Alex, it was a good game. If that defenseman didn't block your line of sight, you could have stopped it." Camden tried to boost his spirits. "We could use a keeper with your skills."

"Thanks, man. I appreciate that."

"Hey, number twenty-two!" he called to Declan. "You've got some mad skills. I haven't seen an attacker that good in a while. I'm Camden, by the way."

"Thanks. I'm Declan." He seemed flattered.

"I told you he was good." I winked at him as I talked to Camden.

Declan reached his arms around my waist and kissed my cheek.

"You're too much, you know that?"

"I know."

"So thanks for inviting us, but we have to get back. We have other plans tonight."

"Thanks for coming, Camden. I'll see you on Tuesday. It was nice to meet you, Natalia."

"You too, Grey. Bye." She waved and I turned to Alex.

"So let's go back to the house. You may have lost, but we can still celebrate a good season, right?"

"Right on!" Tyler yelled, always ready for a reason to party.

Declan put his arm around me and we both skipped up to the lot. I jumped in Declan's Jeep. Paige tried to comfort Alex before getting in the back.

"He'll be fine. This always happens when he loses games."

"It wasn't his fault. Gavin is a horrible defenseman."

He had to get his jabs in when he could.

"Remember what tonight is about, okay, Paige?" I said, trying to remind her without raising suspension.

We pulled up and I had Declan park along the side of this house next to my mom's car.

"Okay, so let's have some fun and forget about tonight. It's all behind us now. We need to move on."

Declan pulled me onto his back, which caught me off guard.

"Since when did you become so smart?"

"When I started hanging out with Paige."

She finally cracked a smile as he ran up the stairs and I held on for dear life.

CHAPTER THIRTEEN

THE GARDEN

He let me down in the hall and then we joined everyone in the kitchen.

"So what do you want, food or chips and stuff?" I asked everyone as I grabbed glasses from the cupboard.

"I'm a little hungry. Let's cook something." Alex went to the fridge.

"Okay, you guys go sit on the deck and we'll make something."

They walked out on the deck to relax, but Alex came back in. He looked behind him, making sure he was alone, and grabbed Paige, pulling her around the corner of the counter to kiss her.

"Thanks," he said, and left.

"Aw, that was so sweet," Quinn said.

"I know, but we need to start cooking."

Paige composed herself as I walked to the fridge.

"We can make burgers," I said.

"That sounds easy," Emery chimed in.

Paige started the grill while Quinn and I made the burgers.

"What's all this?" Evan said as he came in.

"We're hungry. Did you want us to make you a burger?"

"Sure. Put some cheese on it for me."

He grabbed the Pepper Jack cheese from the fridge.

"That sounds good." I got an idea. "Hey, Emery, grab me an avocado and a tomato from the fridge."

I grabbed an onion and tried to remember how mom had made these.

"My mom use to make awesome burgers with guacamole and jack cheese. It was her spicy twist on Alex's favorite meal."

I looked at Paige. I washed my hands and started to dice the onions and tomatoes. I had Paige peel and cut the avocados.

"Here you go, Grey." Paige handed me the avocados in a bowl.

I started mashing them until they were smooth, then I slowly folded in the onion, tomato and jalapeño, adding a dash of lime juice. Emery was at the grill waiting for me to bring out the burgers.

"So we're having burgers?" Tyler peered over the chair.

"Yup, do you want cheese on yours?"

"Sure. I'm pretty hungry."

"Look at my girl, cooking. We'll make a chef out of you yet." Declan winked.

"Please, they're just burgers, and Emery is cooking. Not me." I rolled my eyes.

Everything was done, so I grabbed a plate so she could put the burgers on the table.

"Wait! I need to get something!" Alex yelled into the kitchen.

"Grey, we have everything out here already."

I came back out and placed the bowl in front of him.

"Surprise. Your favorite." I hugged him.

"Thanks, Grey. You're the best. This is great. I couldn't ask for anything else right now." He squeezed my arm before kissing my hand.

"Wow! I didn't know you could make guacamole. I'm impressed."

"Don't be, Declan. I've been making this dinner with my mom since I was five years old. It's Alex's favorite."

I had channeled a little bit of my mom during the preparation.

We finished dinner and sat talking about the season. Allie fell asleep as usual, so Evan took her up to her room. I thought it was a good time to clear the table. Alex got up and walked to the corner of the deck, probably trying to figure out when and how he was going to say something. And that small maneuver caught Declan's eye. He turned toward him.

"I'll go talk to him," Declan said.

"No, Paige can do it." I pushed Paige ever so gently, trying to give her the smallest of hints. I grabbed his hand and pulled him toward the door. "I need your help in the kitchen.

"Okay, let's go."

We headed into the kitchen, leaving them alone on the deck. She would thank me later. I put the rest of the dishes in the sink and had Quinn grab some bowls from the cupboard.

"Tyler, can you grab the ice cream from the freezer. It's on the top shelf."

"I'll get it." Declan grabbed the ice cream. As he turned around, he dropped it. Then I remembered Paige and Alex were on the deck alone. Something had to happen and I knew what was going to happen next, but it was like everything was moving in slow motion.

"Oh crap! Tyler, I need you to grab Declan now!" Tyler ran over to him and pulled him toward the front porch.

"We told him, just in case this might happen," Quinn said. They looked apologetic.

"No, good idea." I picked up the ice cream container and placed it on the counter as I headed to the front porch.

"I've got it, Tyler. Thanks."

He let go of Declan and went inside.

"Declan, listen to me. You need to sit down."

I pulled him down to sit on the stairs. His pacing was driving me crazy.

"What the—"

"You need to get a grip. Do you think they planned this? It just happened." I'd said too much, and he looked angry.

"You knew and didn't tell me."

I had called that one earlier. He would be mad at me now.

"I didn't know for a while. They fooled me, too. I found out two weeks ago."

"What do you mean, 'a while'?" His forehead creased. "How long has this been going on?"

"About four months now."

"Man, I can't believe you. Why didn't you tell me?"

"It's not my place to do that. They were going to tell you tonight. They thought you might act this way."

"What?"

"Declan, listen, I know she's your sister, but think of Alex." I took a breath. I could feel the pressure and his anger. "He didn't act like this when he found out about us. You owe him that much at least."

"That's different."

"No, it's the same. I'm his little sister. Do you think it's easy for him to see you ogling me every chance you can? But he deals with it because he knows I'm happy."

"What do you mean, 'ogle'? Come on, Grey."

"Please be serious, Declan. Give it a chance."

"I guess I can try to understand, but it's still not the same."

He reached for my hand, mumbling something along the lines of how he didn't understand how things worked around here. I was still trying to figure out what his last statement was, when I just decided to drop it. I would eventually find out, and it wasn't like this had been planned.

I pulled his chin up and kissed him.

"I think ice cream will calm you down."

"It might, if you have whip cream, too."

"Not now, Declan. Get a grip."

I pulled him up and dragged him back into the house. I held his hand as we stepped out onto the deck. I hoped it would calm him. I think it was working, because I was getting weaker.

"Listen, Dec. I'm sorry. I should have told you."

"No, Alex. It's fine. Grey explained it to me. It's all good."

He hit Alex's shoulder with his open palm.

"Okay, who wants ice cream?" I said.

I ran in and grabbed the bowls, spoons, and every condiment I could find.

"Let's have some fun and relax." I yelled from the kitchen

The tension started to lift and everyone was relaxing when I heard the doorbell ring.

"Who's that?" Alex asked. "Everyone's here already."

"A surprise." I giggled and ran to the door.

"What surprise? And for who?"

"It's not for you. It's for Quinn," Paige said.

"For me? What is it, Paige?"

"Not what, but who." Emery sat up, knowing exactly what she was talking about.

"She didn't, did she?"

"What did I miss?" Tyler looked at Paige.

I walked down the hall and onto the deck.

"Hey, guys, it's Jack." I waved my hands like Vanna White.

"Hi, guys, Quinn." He smiled and I could have sworn I saw her blush.

"Hi. Grey, can I talk to you for a minute in the kitchen?"

She pulled me back inside.

"What's this?" She pointed back toward the deck.

"You said you liked him, and he's my tutor."

"So?" She was a little peeved. I think I might have overstepped my boundaries.

"So he asks questions about you during my sessions."

"Really? He does?"

Now the tides were turning. I knew this had been a good idea.

"Yup, so stop talking to me and go talk to him."

Declan walked in as I pushed Quinn out to the deck. He set his bowl down on the counter.

"You're so nice. That was a good thing you just did."

"I know. I hated having her on the outside of the group."

"What do you mean?"

I pointed to Tyler and Emery. They were holding hands.

"Man, do you know everything lately?"

"No. I don't know why you get so jealous when I'm not going anywhere."

"Please, Grey."

"Oh, I'm right. Just admit it, would you?"

"Fine. I do, but I can't help it. I had a hard time getting you, and I'm going to try even harder to keep you."

"I hope you do—keep me that is."

I wiped whip cream on his nose. He grabbed me, picked me up gently, and placed me on the counter. He leaned in and kissed me hard. I could hear his heart and my breathing accelerating. That's when I heard someone clear their throat a couple of times. I turned my head, feeling a little embarrassed. Evan had seen us.

"Um, Grey, is everyone staying over again? Because there are some rules to discuss."

"I don't know, Evan." I hopped off the counter and followed him.

"Well, let's go ask."

He walked out to the deck and began his speech.

"So here is rule number one."

Everyone looked up. It was odd to hear Evan speak in his current tone. He actually sounded like my parents whenever we'd done something wrong.

"We keep to our separate rooms at all times unless you are out on the deck, watching TV, or using the bathroom as a group."

"And rule number two is what?" I asked.

"I shouldn't have to tell you rule number two, Grey, unless you don't understand rule number one."

"Okay." I wiped the smile off my face.

"So there are sleeping bags in the closet. Keep the noise to a minimum, please."

He turned and walked out.

"That was weird." Alex shook his head.

"I'll call my dad and tell him I'm staying here," Emery said. She went to the phone in the hall.

The rest followed, and their parents seemed to be fine with it. I figured they trusted both Grams and Evan. I also knew there was some more information about our family I wasn't privy to yet. The game plan was to watch a movie downstairs and figure something else out when we got there. I needed to sit down, as I was beginning to feel zapped of energy again. I sat on the sofa and Declan eventually fell asleep on my shoulder. I maneuvered my way out and I quietly made my way up the stairs.

I walked out to the deck and down the back steps toward the garden. I had always wanted to check the place out for myself. I tried to open the gate, but it wouldn't budge. It was like it was locked when there wasn't one. I was about to give up, when I heard a voice beside me.

"Mom?" It felt weird saying it. Maybe I was dreaming, but it felt so real I had to pinch myself to make sure. *Okay, that hurt.*

"Yes, Grey, it's me. You are awake. If you want to enter the garden you need to concentrate to unlock the gate."

"Concentrate on what?"

"You need to concentrate on your ability to move objects."

"Oh, okay."

I tried to think of what I'd done to break the glass. I remembered that I wanted to break something because I was angry. *Maybe I should concentrate on the emotion—or was it the action?* So this time I concentrated on the action, unlocking stuff like doors and windows, but nothing happened.

Why do I have to wait until I'm seventeen to learn this stuff? I thought.

"Concentrate and visualize yourself unlocking the door."

I thought that was what I was doing. This is so frustrating.

"Okay, here we go."

I visualized myself opening the gate. Suddenly, the gate unlocked and swung open. As I walked in, the gate closed behind me.

"Thanks, Mom."

"You're welcome, honey. Enjoy." Her voice faded.

Okay, it was a little weird, but cool at the same time.

I walked to the left toward the flowers. I had noticed Grams out there the other day, picking some of them for the hallway table.

These roses are beautiful.

There were white, pink, and yellow bushes in one row of twos. I remembered when we were little, Grams had told us the colors represented me, Allie, and Alex. She said she'd planted the seeds when we were born, not knowing what would sprout. Those flowers had bloomed. Maybe that was why I liked white roses, because the white rose was a representation of me. I wondered whether the other bushes represented our other halves, because I knew for a fact that Paige loved yellow roses. The petals were smooth and soft as silk. They smelled so fresh. All these thoughts came flooding in. I couldn't control the flash of images bombarding me.

This was really strange. I wondered if Declan liked white roses as well. Maybe that was why he'd sent them to me. It was something to think about. *How did they bloom in the cold weather?* I thought.

The weird thing was that I wasn't cold anymore. It was warm, like the inside of a green house. How was that possible when I could see the sky and there was no roof? I continued to walk around until I reached the bench in the back. On either side were two hand-carved wooden planters filled only with dirt, no flowers or plants. I wonder what Grams was going to plant there.

When I sat down, I noticed my Shakespeare book was next to

me. *Where did this come from? I had never been in here before.*

"Mom?" This was a little weird talking to the air. Good thing no one was around to witness my descent into madness.

"Yes, Grey."

"Did you bring this out here?" I held up the book like she could see it.

"Yes, enjoy your reading, honey." Her voice started to fade again. "Remember your gifts, because you are special."

I guess I shouldn't be surprised at what happened anymore. I sat and read for a while, eventually falling asleep on the bench. I mean, when didn't I fall asleep outside? I also felt a surge of energy, like the garden was giving back to me. *Man, I must be tired. I'm starting to talk crazy again.*

I woke up to someone shouting my name. It was more like yelling, but with it being that early in the morning, I couldn't tell night from day. I opened my eyes to see Grams and Evan running down the stairs. Everyone else was on the deck watching. *Great. An audience for my lecture on being in the garden without Grams present.* They ran in, making it look so easy. *Man, it took me like ten minutes to open that gate.*

"How did you get in here, Grey?" Evan asked.

"Mom told me to unlock the door. Sorry, Evan."

"Your mother. I should have known." He smiled, looking at the lilies blooming.

"Grey, how did you make these flowers bloom?"

Grams pointed to the planters on either side of me. They were filled with white roses and they were in full bloom. *How should I know? I was sleeping.*

"I didn't. They were empty when I sat down and fell asleep."

"Grey, were you thinking of a particular flower while you slept?"

These were definitely odd questions. At that point, I wasn't questioning anything that happened in this family anymore.

"Come to think of it, I might have been, but I can't be too

sure. Why?"

"You made these flowers grow," Evan said.

"How? I was asleep."

Maybe the garden fairies made them grow. I smiled, noticing a hint of a smile starting on Evan's face. *Man, does he hear everything or what?*

"You were thinking of something you enjoy, something that is part of you. And they grew to comfort and protect you while you slept."

"Wow, that's cool."

And it *was* cool—and a little freaky, I'm not going to lie. I actually did two things the previous night that I never knew I could do before.

"I would say so," Grams remarked. "I think we underestimated your abilities. You are definitely original, and you possess special gifts, just like Alex and your father."

I looked up to see everyone still watching us. Only Alex shook his head. *I wish you would just shut up and follow the rules for once.* It was as if he'd yelled from the deck, but his lips hadn't move and the words had been inside my head.

"I don't think so. You shut up."

Evan and Grams watched us, still shocked.

Whatever, I thought.

"Whatever yourself."

Oh, this is cool. How come I didn't see this before?

"Because you're blind, Grey." He laughed.

Now everyone was watching us, not understanding what was going on, or at least that's what I thought. They were not the only ones.

"Are you okay, Grey?" Evan asked.

"Yeah, I'm fine, but Alex needs to stop answering my questions."

I looked up towards the deck. *Seriously, if I have to listen to you in my head, too, I think I might have to scream.*

"I should have known because you guys are so close."

"Are you sure, Evan?" Grams questioned his thought.

Man, everyone's going crazy. I don't understand what's going on right now.

"You will," Evan answered. I looked up and he smiled. "One of my abilities. Pretty neat, huh?"

Of course. Now all the pieces were falling into place. That's how he knew what I was thinking sometimes. *Great. Now I need to sensor my thoughts.*

"I'm hungry, so let's go get some food." Evan's stomach grumbled as he spoke.

Nothing surprised me anymore. It also explained how he knew I was there before I asked a question. I got up and headed toward the gate.

"Grey, wait. I need to open the gate for you!" Grams yelled to me.

It was too late. I got to the gate before them, opened it, and headed up the stairs to the house. Grams and Evan stood baffled yet again.

"We've underestimated her again," Grams told Evan.

Let's see, I want pancakes, eggs, and anything else I can get my hands on. Because I am hungry, I thought as I ascended the stairs.

"Is that all you want? Or do you want the kitchen sink as well?" Declan blurted out.

I turned and looked to him, then Alex. *How did he know? And how had Alex known earlier?*

"Easy." Alex laughed and looked at Declan.

"We are the same in some ways," Declan whispered softly. "I told you there was more to what you knew."

Man, now I have to watch what I think as well as what I say. How am I going to do that?

"That never stopped you before," Evan said as he came up the stairs.

"All you guys stink."

Get out of my head. I stormed into the kitchen.

"I'm lost," Quinn said to Paige.

"Join the club."

They all stumbled into the kitchen.

"Grey, what are you doing?" Paige asked.

"I'm making breakfast, silly."

"I know that, but how? You can't cook."

"Declan is helping me."

She turned to Declan who was on the other side of the kitchen. He waved.

"You've got to be kidding me. That's just great." Paige slumped into the chair.

"Sorry."

"Just stop that, and finish cooking."

We all sat down and tried to eat in silence, but that didn't seem to work too well for Quinn. Declan leaned over and kissed my cheek.

"This is nice. I could get used to it."

"Me too," I said. I grabbed his hand under the table.

After the interesting turn of events, Evan decided that it was time to figure out what else I could do so he could prepare his lessons. I spent all weekend locked in his office with both him and Alex. My plans had been shot for the weekend.

CHAPTER FOURTEEN

SNOW BOUND

The next month flew by and mid-terms were just in time to wreck my December. At least the snow finally came. We could head to the lake for a vacation, maybe even the holiday. I had two days of tests, then I was done. Evan and Alex had figured out the lesson plan, but I couldn't know until my birthday, which made no sense to me. I had already figured out how to do some things thanks to Mom. Evan wasn't too happy about that either. Since that day, my mom had been secretly explaining certain things. I knew if he found out, I was going to be in big trouble, but there was another reason she was helping—but she kept it guarded. She'd told me everything would come in good time.

Evan still had one more week of work left before his break started. He gave us the go ahead to go on our own up to the lake house. There was only one rule, and that was that we had to be back by Monday.

That gave us five days of skiing, snowshoeing, and relaxing, and I was pumped. It would also be interesting because it wasn't just us going—the whole group was going, too. It was weird. I don't think Declan and I had ever been alone since we'd started dating. Someone was always with us and it was strange at times. I felt like I was in a Jane Austin novel, where my father or mother chaperoned my meetings.

Alex and I would arrive on Wednesday and everyone else would be up on Friday. I'm sure only three days was all their parents could tolerate. I mean, who would let eight crazy teenagers go skiing alone apart from Evan? I was surprised they let them go at all. I packed my bags and helped Alex put the gear in the Jeep. We were all ready to leave first thing in the morning. I set my alarm for five o'clock in the morning and I hit the sack.

To our surprise and to the surprise of the local weatherman, it had snowed overnight, so it was a good thing we had off-road capabilities because it looked like they hadn't plowed yet. I got dressed and knocked on Alex's door before heading downstairs.

"Hey, what time is it?"

"It's about six o'clock in the morning. Come on, Alex. Get something to eat so we can leave." I threw him a pop tart.

"I need a shower first."

"For what? It's just us. You can shower when we get up there."

"Fine. My stuff's already in the car."

"Let's go, then. I'll drive up so you can go back to sleep."

I plugged my iPod into the car and plowed down the drive. Alex slept the entire way. They had actually plowed the driveway for once. I figured Evan must have called them after we'd left this morning. I opened the garage door so we could pull in. I didn't feel like cleaning the car off if it snowed again while we were up here.

I woke him up as I grabbed my bag. I slipped by the door on the way out of the garage. Luckily I caught myself on the door frame. *Stupid ice.*

I figured water or some snow had gotten in there during the last storm. Alex was right behind me as I dropped everything in the kitchen.

"Man, its cold in here. Put the heat up."

I ran to the living room to put the heat on before he could complain about anything else. He seemed to be crankier and on edge lately. I brushed it off as having woken him up so early.

"Hey, we have to go to the store if you want to eat this weekend."

"You can go. I'll stay here and start a fire."

He laid down on the sofa and turned the TV on.

"And watch the game."

"And that, too," he said as he was flipping through the channels.

I went out to the garage and slipped by the door again. *Damn.* I grabbed the skis off the Jeep and hung them in the garage before adventuring into town for some food.

When I got back, he was sleeping with the TV blaring.

"Hey, Alex, I need your help bringing this stuff in."

"Hold on."

He grabbed his shoes and coat. We brought the rest of the bags in and started putting everything away.

"Did you get enough stuff, Grey?"

"No, the way you guys eat, I might have to go back out."

He laughed.

"Hot chocolate. Sweet."

"And marshmallows." I threw the bag at him.

"Awesome."

"Hey, don't eat them all. They're for the hot chocolate." He stuck his tongue out at me and ran into the living room with the bag. "You're such a little boy."

"Hey, I'm going to get some more wood outside."

"Grey, put some on the porch so we don't have to walk too far to get more."

"Okay."

Always so thoughtful. Not. I closed the door and started stacking wood on the porch, my thoughts wandering: What did Evan have planned for me? And was I going to be able to handle all the added pressure? Then I thought, *Why am I stacking wood with my hands?* I started to think about how I was picking up the wood and stacking it on the porch. I opened my eyes to see the wood stacking itself. *Man, this teleka-whatever thing is awesome.*

The next two days were colder than normal. We were expecting a storm that night— something I was not looking forward to. I hoped everyone would get here before it hit.

"Hey, Alex are we going skiing today or not?"

"No, I'm tired. We spent the last two days and nights skiing."

"Fine. I'm going snowshoeing around the trail and back." I grabbed my jacket and gloves. "Start a fire, so it's going full steam when I get back. Give me an hour or so."

"Be careful. It's still early and cold out there." He was always concerned about me.

"I will. I got the walkie-talkie with me if you need anything. Bye." I closed the door and grabbed my shoes off the porch.

The trail was deep but I got out and back in about two hours. It was nice to be out there by myself with only the crunching of the snow reverberating off the trees. When I walked in, he was sleeping, but he'd at least started the fire like I'd asked, and it was roaring.

"Hey, Alex, I'm going to sleep for a little while. I'll be in my room if you need me."

"Okay, okay," he mumbled, turning the volume up on the stereo.

It took about fifteen minutes for me to fall asleep. I knew that last trail would wipe me out. I was so conked out I didn't hear everyone come in downstairs.

I thought I heard footsteps. I shivered a little when I felt a slight cold stream of air, but was then warm again. I was having a good dream because Declan was in it, not knowing he was in my bed lying next to me. I felt him put his arms around me and I reacted, thinking I was still dreaming. It started with a kiss on his lips and it became more and more intense. I wrapped my leg over his. He began to kiss my neck and then my ear. My dream was great because it felt so real. I slid off his shirt and pressed my lips along the ridges of his chest and made my way up to his neck.

Wow, I wish I could dream like this more often. I could never be this aggressive in real life.

I felt his hand trace my shoulder and down my side to my waist, which caused me to quiver with excitement. He continued along my neck with his tongue. That's when I rolled on top of him. I started at his neck, then worked my way down his chest and back up again. He grabbed my shoulders and rolled me back on to the bed. His excitement was evident as he started kissing along my shoulders and back of my neck.

My breathing became more erratic, as did his, and I could feel my pulse accelerate. Well, this dream could only end one way, but when would it conclude?

Man, it was getting hot in here.

He moved his left hand up my back while his other hand was entwined in my hair. My hands were gripping the back of his neck while we kissed. He moved along my ear and I exhaled.

At least he didn't speak in my dream. That would be too much. I should definitely dream like this more often. This continued for what seemed like forever, but was only ten minutes. Then I heard the door open.

"Grey, can you—whoa, sorry."

What was that all about? Now she wrecked my dream. I opened my eyes.

"What the—Declan?"

"Good afternoon." He grinned.

"That wasn't a dream, was it?" I asked as I blushed. I looked under the quilt with a shocked look on my face.

"Definitely not my dreams. They are intense, but not this good."

"I thought me . . . but . . . I'm sorry."

"I'm not, so come back over here." He pulled me back to his chest. "Oh, wait."

He grabbed his pants on the floor and put them back on.

"You didn't have your pants on?' I asked.

"Yeah, you threw them off. I was taken back a little, but you kept going. I wasn't going to stop you."

I put my hands on my face.

"This is embarrassing. Quinn just walked in on us."

"I know. Good thing, too." He pulled my hands away from my face and held me tighter. "As much as I wanted to, I think it was best that we stopped there."

I was a little surprised, but not too much, because even though he was a ball of raging hormones, he was a gentleman. But making out with him like that was definitely enjoyable. I would have to remember to not take it as far next time.

"Thanks." I kissed his chest and his body quivered.

"Don't start again, please. I don't think I can take it this soon."

"Sure. Later then?"

"Yes, but not too far next time okay?"

"We should go downstairs."

"Yeah, I'll see you down there." He kissed my cheek and grabbed his shirt.

I laid there for a minute trying to catch my breath. Thankfully, he wasn't expecting anything, because I didn't think I was ready to go there yet. He knew it, too, because I thought about it all the time. I inhaled deeply again and got up. I grabbed my jeans and a sweater from my bag. I ventured out the door and down to the living room.

"Hey, guys, I'm glad you got here before the storm." I said.

"I'm sure you are." Tyler smirked.

I looked at Declan and he shrugged.

"All right, get it out now before I take you each for a long walk from which you don't return."

"I told you not to wake her, Declan."

"You did, Alex."

Everyone started laughing, including me.

It was starting to snow harder now. I worried that we didn't have enough wood.

"Alex, did you use all the wood?"

"Yeah, go get some more. You need to cool down."

I grabbed my jacket and threw his glove at him on the way out.

"Hey, watch it."

I walked back in after a couple minutes to see Alex and Declan in what seemed to be a non-verbal conversation that I wasn't privy to yet again. I looked at him, then told them to cut it out.

"Okay, I stacked a lot more wood. We should be good if we lose power. It's getting bad out there."

"Man, I can't see the deck!" Emery yelled back.

"Hey, Alex, do you want your treat before we lose power?" I walked into the kitchen.

"I ate them all."

"The whole bag?" I was shocked, but not surprised.

"Yup."

"You ate what?" Paige asked.

"Don't worry. I hid the second bag."

"You bought two bags? Sneaky." He got up. "Yeah, make some for everyone."

"Okay, you need to give me five minutes."

"What is she making?" Jack asked.

"It's a surprise, Jack."

I came out with a tray and had everyone close their eyes.

"No peeking."

I gave them each a mug and asked them all to drink slowly, but no one started.

"Don't you guys trust me?"

"I love you, Grey, but I don't know if I can drink this. It might be one of those crazy teas from your Grams." Declan tried to be polite.

"Just drink it, you baby, or you can sleep by yourself in the living room." He took a quick sip and started laughing. *You're so predictable.*

"You're too funny, you know that?"

"Is it that bad, Declan?"

"No, Paige, go ahead and drink it."

Everyone took small sips of the hot chocolate and then they all started laughing.

"You're horrible!" Tyler shouted.

"Hey, Alex, here's the bag." I threw the bag of marshmallows. "You're such a little kid sometimes."

"I know." He grabbed a handful of marshmallows and threw them in his mug.

"Give me that bag back. You've been eating nothing but these all day. No wonder you're tired."

"Alex, you need to eat some real food." Paige hit him.

"Hey, blame Grey. She bought them." He rubbed his arm.

"Grey!"

"Hey, I've been eating food this week. Thank you."

"All right now, kids. I'll send you to your rooms if you don't stop."

"Whatever, it might be fun!" I yelled from the kitchen.

"You walked into that one, Declan." Emery laughed.

"Grey, please."

"Fine. Come help me make dinner then."

I turned on the oven to reheat the lasagna we'd brought up with us. I helped him cut the vegetables for the salad.

"So you've been keeping busy this week."

"Yeah, we mostly went skiing. I hit the trail this morning before you guys came."

"You know, I missed you. I'm really not sorry about earlier."

"I missed you, too. And don't worry about it. Nothing happened."

In some ways, I'm not sorry either, but I'll keep that one to myself for now. Thankfully nothing happened because I was not ready for that big of a step. I think I need to slow things down a little.

He sighed and headed back to the living room.

Damn, I forgot he could hear what I was thinking. I am glad he has to be next to me to hear my thoughts—unlike Alex, who can hear from a distance. I'd learned that little tip from Grams. She'd happened to mention it before we left.

I set the table and called everyone in to eat. Alex was the last one in. He paused a minute, waiting for something. *What?* I looked at Alex.

Is everything okay? Or do we need to sit and eat some ice cream?

I'm fine. Sit down before someone hears you.

Like who? I looked at him, then used my eyes to motion to Declan at the other end of the table.

"This looks good, Grey. Thanks." He sat down.

We finished dinner in time. The lights began to flicker, then went out. Alex went to get more wood and bring it in the house so we didn't have to let what heat we did have out.

"Man, I hope the generator kicks on," he mumbled. "Dec and Jack, can you help me with this wood?"

"No problem, man." Jack got up from the chair.

"Paige, Quinn, can you grab the extra blankets from the closet?"

"Okay." Paige felt her way down the hall.

"Sure." Quinn got up and followed her. It was like the blind leading the blind.

I came out into the living room to get some candles. I seemed to be the only one unfazed by the lack of light. My mom always said I could find my way anywhere, even if was pitch dark, another great trait inherited from my dad.

"Tyler and Emery, you're with me. We need to get all the candles we can find."

We started upstairs to the bathroom and then grabbed all the candles. Emery grabbed more blankets. I ran back downstairs towards the kitchen door, then I felt someone grab my arm from behind.

"Hey, where do you think you're going?" Alex asked me.

"I need to get the stoves from the garage. I'm fine."

"If you are not back in five minutes, then I am coming out to get you." He handed me my gloves.

I trudged through the snow as fast as I could, and finally reached the garage. The door was stuck due to the ice, so I kicked it open. I slowly walked in and I managed to grab the two big camping stoves and started to look for the tanks. *I really wish Evan would keep this stuff together.*

I wasn't watching where I was going and I slipped on the floor again. That time I fell, but I caught the wall. I dropped the flashlight and it rolled toward the Jeep. I thought to myself, *This is the moment in every horror movie when something bad happens.* That is when I started to feel pain in my right hand ruminating from the center outward. Something warm was running down my arm into the sleeve of my jacket. I crawled toward the Jeep and managed to grab the flashlight with my good hand to see what I had landed on.

Crap, I cut my hand on the edge of the hatchet. I had to open my big mouth about the movies. I hurried to the first aid kit on the other side of the garage, avoiding the slick spot.

I held the flashlight in my mouth with my teeth. I threw off my gloves and grabbed the gauze. I looked around to see what I could lean against and took my chances with the Jeep because it was the closest thing. I used the gauze to apply pressure to my hand by leaning it on the corner of the tire so I could retrieve the tape.

At this point, having it tight was not good enough. The blood was still spilling from the wound. I taped my hand again, hoping to slow it down while I ran back to the house.

Leave it to me to keep the drama going this weekend. This is the least of my worries, because he is going to kill me when I get back. I bit my lip, trying not to scream, when I grabbed the stoves and tanks and headed to the house. Alex was at the door ready to come and get me.

"What took you so long?"

"Alex, I need you to get Tyler and bring him back here now."

I remembered Tyler volunteered at the firehouse during the summer. He would know what to do and would not panic in this situation. Then I thought of Paige.

"And Paige."

"Okay, wait here." I noticed Declan start toward the kitchen.

"Hey, what's wrong?"

"Nothing, Dec. Please go take care of the fire. We'll be right back."

He hesitated but went back to the living room to start putting more wood on the fire. *Hurry up, Alex.*

"So what's up?" Alex returned with Tyler and Paige in record time.

"I need Tyler to come with me."

"Where?" Tyler asked.

"To the hospital. It's about thirty minutes away and I can't drive, so you need to." I winced in pain.

"You can't go now, Grey. It's snowing pretty hard." Paige kept looking at my hand.

"I have to. I don't have a lot of time to talk this through, Alex."

"Why?"

"Fine. I fell and sliced my hand open on the corner of the hatchet."

I held up my right hand, trying not to remember that the garage was covered in my blood. It was weird, but ever since I was a kid I'd always hated the sight and smell of blood. Even though I tried to put it out of my mind, I needed to suck it up and deal with it. My hand was dripping blood onto the porch because the gauze and extra tape were soaked through, unable to stop it from flowing anymore.

"Man, Grey, that's bad. We need to go now, Alex."

"No, wait. Let me try something," Paige said.

She put her hand over mine. I felt the quick jolt, then nothing. I don't think it worked and the snow was now red.

"No, I'll go. I can take her."

"No, I asked Tyler because he's better in this situation and he knows more than you," I said.

Alex reluctantly agreed while Tyler grabbed his coat. We ran as fast as we could to the Jeep. He saw all the blood when we got into the garage. His expression said it all, but I had no time to stand there and reminisce.

"Listen, use the four by four. We can get there faster."

"Okay, buckle up, Grey." We backed out of the garage and turned around. We sped off down the drive toward the main road. I noticed Alex with Declan in the living room window as we drove off.

We were almost to the hospital.

"Thanks for doing this, Tyler."

"No problem, Grey. How's your hand feel?"

"It's a little tingly, but it's okay." I winched again. I was trying to figure out why I couldn't heal my hand.

"That not good. You might have hit a nerve," he said. He started to drive faster. "On a positive note, it looks like it is starting to let up."

"Yeah, maybe we'll have power by morning."

And with that comment, I knew Tyler had been the right choice. He calmed my nerves was good at keeping my mind off the pain.

We reached the small hospital in record time, even though it was snowing. Sure enough, I needed stitches—about twenty of them. It was deep, but I'd missed all the nerves. The doctor told me it was very close. He gave me some pain medication and wrapped my hand. I hated taking pills. They made me feel out of it. Maybe, just maybe, I could hide them from Alex.

Tyler was right. The snow had let up and it looked like the storm was fizzling out. We pulled up the drive and parked in the garage. Of course, everyone was nervously at the door waiting, except for Alex and Declan.

"Are you okay?" Paige asked. "He's freaking out, but Alex is with him."

"I'm good. I needed about twenty stitches and they gave me some pain meds that are making me tired—but no nerve damage thankfully."

"That's good," Quinn said as she closed the door.

"Thanks, Tyler." I hugged him with my good arm.

"Thanks, it was no big deal." He was confident but modest.

"I need to lie down for a while."

Emery grabbed the big blanket and put it over me as I drifted off to sleep on the sofa closest to the fireplace.

I felt someone pick me up and lay me back down. I was getting even warmer than I'd been before with the blanket alone. I rolled onto my side. I could feel the electricity emanating from him as he ran his fingers through my hair. I opened my eyes to see him watching me intently.

"How are you feeling?" He leaned in and kissed my forehead.

"Okay. A little tired." I raised my hand carefully to his face.

"You can't scare me like that again." He kissed my hand gently as I winced in pain. "I'm glad you're okay."

I didn't say another word. I didn't want to spoil my time with him. I moved closer to him and put my head against his chest. I listened to his strong yet steady heartbeat and let it lull me to sleep. Everyone else settled in around the fireplace on the floor and in the other chairs and on the sofa.

The power came back on around midnight, or that's what the clock on the mantle said. The heat was coming on slowly and the room was getting warmer. Declan was still asleep when I woke up. The meds where killing my sleep pattern, as they always did. I slowly moved off his lap and he didn't notice, which was good. I noticed everyone had moved up stairs, so I put the blanket on him and headed up to my room. I carefully climbed into bed, covered myself with two blankets, and fell back to sleep.

I woke up sweating. The heat was definitely on now. I tried to take my jeans off, which was rather difficult with one hand. I threw one blanket off onto the floor. I was trying to go back to sleep when I heard a knock on the door.

"Can I come in?" I heard Paige ask.

"Yeah, sure. Close the door."

"Wow, your room is a sauna." She took off a layer and climbed into the bed.

"Yeah, mine and Allie's room warm up the fastest."

"I'm glad you're doing better. You scared us, you know."

"Thanks, but if I didn't get those stoves and the power didn't come back, we would be hungry and cold."

"I know I can handle it, but some of these guys need their food," she said.

"I thought the same thing. Is everyone still asleep?" I asked.

"Yeah, it's still early. You should go back to sleep, too."

"Okay, then later we can make snowmen if the warden lets

me," I said, referring to my ever-cautious and vigilant brother who thought I was accident-prone.

"You're too much, but it sounds like a plan to me." We fell asleep quickly.

I was awaked when I heard everyone down in the kitchen talking and dishes clanging. I decided to stay in bed. I rolled over and smelled something, maybe cinnamon, wafting up the stairs, and my stomach was fighting me to get up.

"Hey, Paige, wake up. I think something smells good downstairs."

"What?" She slowly awakened from her coma-like state.

"The smell. It's coming from downstairs."

"Oh, man. He's freaking out. We better get up."

"I didn't smell that . . . I smelled cinnamon."

"No, Declan cooks when he's agitated."

I rolled my eyes and got out of bed. I grabbed my sweater, jacket, and jeans before we headed downstairs to the kitchen.

"Hey, guys. How's the food?"

"Hey, sleepyheads." Alex kissed Paige. "Grey, how's your hand?"

"Good." I waved it a little, even though it was still sore. "And morning to you, Declan."

I walked over to the stove reached for his face with my good hand and I kissed him.

"You worry too much. Sit down and eat. You need your strength, because we're building snowmen today."

"You're resting today."

"Spoilsport." I stuck my tongue out at him.

"Dec, you do worry too much." Alex winked at him and I laughed. "But, Grey, he's right. You need to rest for at least half the day."

"Fine." I crossed my arms and winced again. What's the point of healing powers if I can't heal myself in the process? *I'll have to ask Grams about that one.*

We finished eating breakfast and I wondered what everyone else was doing since I was on house arrest.

"So what are you guys doing today?" I asked.

"Well, Jack, Emery, Quinn, and I are going skiing." Tyler stated.

I secretly wished I could join them.

"I don't know. I think we can find something to do today, maybe cards or checkers."

"I'm sure we can, Paige."

Alex cleared the table as everyone else went about their plans. As he washed the dishes, I grabbed my jacket off the back of the chair. I slowly opened the kitchen door.

"Hey, where are you going?" he asked.

"To the car. I'll be right back. You can watch me at the door if you want."

It wasn't like I would cut my other hand. *Okay, I need to stop saying stuff like that because it could happen.*

I put my boots on, which was awkward, and headed into the garage. I started to clean up the mess I'd made last night. I think I needed a mop and a hose to clean up the scene. I figured I was taking a while, because Alex was yelling out the back door.

"You got thirty seconds or I'm coming out there!"

I must have taken more time than that, because he was opening the garage door.

"Oh, man. What a mess."

He was shocked by the frozen blood and all the first aid packages all over the floor.

"Good thing no one else saw this, Grey. It looks like a murder scene." He looked at the small pool of blood near the wall and the trail where I had walked around trying to stop it.

"It looks worse than it was."

"I don't know how this looks, but that's a lot of blood." He started to help me pick up the gauze wrappers. "Let's go before people notice we're gone."

I looked around again and saw that he wasn't kidding; it was bad.

We finished what we could and slowly entered the kitchen without raising any suspicions. I winced when I closed the door with the wrong hand. He gave me a look as he walked over to the counter.

"You need to take your medicine."

"No, they make me tired. I can deal with the pain."

"You're in pain. Don't be a hero. Take them now."

He handed me my pills and a cup of water. I took them begrudgingly and headed upstairs to lie down.

What a crappy trip. I got hurt and everyone gets to have fun. Thankfully, I'll be back next weekend and by then I should be a little better.

I heard a knock at the door.

"Come in," I said.

Paige walked in and closed the door.

"How are you doing?"

"Better. The meds are working, but they make me feel so groggy. I'm just going to rest."

"Do you want company in case you can't sleep?"

"Sure, you can stay." I smiled. "What's on your mind?"

"Nothing. Why do you ask?"

"I may not know your thoughts, but I can read your face. What do you want to know?"

She sat down at the end of the bed.

"So you're getting pretty serious, huh?" she asked.

"What?" Then I remembered Quinn yesterday. "No. It was a misunderstanding. I thought I was dreaming."

"But that's not what *his* face said."

"He stopped and I agreed. End of story."

"Well, that's a twist."

"I said the same thing." We both laughed.

"So let's try and get you better." She grabbed the blanket. "Go to sleep. I'll be here."

I turned over and smothered myself with the covers. I fell asleep within minutes thanks in part to my new friend Mr. Pain-killer. I heard the door open and close a couple of times but I pretty much stayed asleep. Alex came in to give me my medica-tion, so I must have been out of it for a couple of hours.

I felt Declan's welcoming arms holding me tightly, but his nat-ural outdoorsy smell was what comforted me the most. I quietly sighed before I spoke.

"Hey, you. How are you doing?" I sighed.

"I'm getting there. You go back to sleep. We leave tomorrow." Declan whispered

I curled up against the contours of his body, watching where I placed my hand because it was still sore. I could feel his lips against my cheek as he pulled me closer against him. I fell back to sleep in the warmth and security of his arms.

I heard the door open and I rolled over.

"Hey, sleepyhead, we're heading out. Are you ready to go home?" Paige asked me.

"Yeah, my bags are already packed. I only need my boots."

"You can sleep on the way home, okay?"

"Thanks, Paige. Sorry for wrecking the weekend for you guys."

I sat up so she could help me put on my boots.

"You didn't, and everyone did what they wanted. Dec and I don't ski, so we enjoyed the company."

"Thanks, again." I hugged her.

"You're welcome, but next time we come up here can we leave the drama at home?"

She helped me up and I grabbed my bag.

"I'll try."

They were all downstairs waiting for us. He locked the door behind me and we headed to the garage. I could see Declan farther up the drive ahead of us. He was the first one there. He opened the door and gasped.

"Grey!" he exclaimed.

"What's wrong?" Paige walked over with me. *Ah, man. I'm in trouble now.*

I remembered only Alex and Tyler had seen the garage since the accident. I walked into the garage with her, waiting for the questions to come.

"Is this all your blood on the floor?" He pointed to the smudges where the pool of blood and the trail of drops throughout the rest of the floor used to be.

"Um, yeah, that's all mine, but it looks worse than it was."

"Grey, he's not going to let you out of his sight now."

I walked to him and gave him a hug. He held me for a minute. As he let go, he kissed my cheek. I figured he wouldn't be the only one. Once Grams and Evan knew I would probably have a permanent shadow.

"You need to get in the car and head home. We will follow you until you get back to the house." His expression was stiff but his eyes were pained.

The drive home was long. I couldn't sleep after seeing his reaction to what Alex referred to as the murder scene. That was the least of my worries. *How would I explain my hand to Evan and Grams?*

"You don't have to explain. I already called them last night."

"Can you stop that for one day, please?" I hit Declan's arm with my good hand.

"No problem." He rubbed his arm. I knew he would still be listening, so I kept my thoughts to myself. A new skill I learned from Tyler on our back from the hospital.

We pulled up the drive and Declan beeped as he headed to his house. Of course, Grams and Evan made a big deal, even though I told them I was fine and the stitches would come out soon. I'd have a big scar on my hand to remind of that weekend. I also needed to ask for help occasionally.

I received the biggest lecture which was preceded by Alex tagging along everywhere I went. Yup, I had a shadow and it was not fun. I looked forward to going back up to the house before the holidays so I could relax, but I wasn't prepared for what their reactions to the scene of the accident would be. I figured after that I wouldn't be let out of anyone's sight. *Ugh.*

I had a couple of days to spend with him before his family left for the holidays, so I took full advantage. The only problem was I had to have my chaperone along for the ride. Not only did Alex not let me out of his sight for a minute, he had Paige and Declan watching me, too. I wasn't that accident-prone. I figured the best thing I could do was to stay home and be bored, because going out anywhere was a nightmare with those three.

Today Declan came to visit. He finally broke the silence in the room.

"What are you thinking?" Declan asked.

"I'm thinking how nice it would be to leave the house without an escort."

"Grey, please don't be like that. I only have a day before I leave. I don't want to spend it like this."

"Sorry, Declan, but what excitement is there to have in my house?"

"I can think of a few things."

He pulled me down onto the bed. *I'm not sure this is what I had in mind when I asked that question.*

"Grey you're ruining the mood." He continued to kiss me, but I wasn't into it that day.

I wonder how much snow they got in the mountains today? I should check the forecast for the weekend just to make sure.

"Okay, you have now officially killed all the romance in this room."

"Declan, are you done with your tirade or should I wait until your head explodes?"

"You are such a—you know what? I wanted to spend some time with you before I left, but now I think that was a mistake."

"So now you're leaving?" I followed him into the hall.

"Yeah, I guess I am. Have a good holiday. See you in two weeks." He slammed the door.

Lately there had been something going on with him and I was not in the know. We'd had little tiffs here and there, but nothing big. When he wasn't with me, he was with Evan in his office, combing over some old books.

I reached for the handle but stopped and decided to let it be. I didn't want to make it worse than it already was. I sat on the stairs for a minute, trying to figure out how irrational I was being when the doorbell rang.

Great. Just what I need. Paige coming to kill me. I walked over and opened the door. Before I knew what hit me I felt his lips on mine in a feverish attempt to appease our situation.

Whatever, I am going to give in for now, so don't get used to it. In the midst of settling our differences, I heard the door close behind us. I pulled myself free from his embrace to see Allie waiting.

"Do you want something?"

"Yes, Grey. I do."

"And what would that something be?"

"A moment's peace, so I can sleep for once this week without you guys causing chaos."

"I'm to blame for this, Allie, and we are truly sorry. I was leaving, so you can go back to bed now," Declan said.

I had to contain my laughter, because he had charm beyond his reach sometimes.

She dragged herself back up to her room and he turned his attention back to me.

"Now where were we?"

"I think we were here." I kissed him. "But now you have to go. You have an early flight tomorrow."

"I wish you could come with me. You would love it."

"And so would you, because I wouldn't be out of your sight for more than a few minutes."

"Please, Grey, don't start this again." He pulled me closer. "I am going to miss you, so please try and behave while I'm gone. I'll try and write to you when I can."

"I will miss you, too, but I can't promise anything, especially seeing as I'm going skiing this weekend. I'll try for you."

I kissed him one last time before he left. I figured two weeks would be nothing, but I was going to find out.

Evan had to cancel our plans for the weekend, but thanks to Alex we would be going skiing with Jack and the Ellis family. We loaded up the Jeep and met them at the café. Jack—and to our surprise—his dog were riding up with us and then back. Alex followed them up while I talked to Jack and played with the dog.

We stayed for the weekend and left on Sunday. Evan had plans that required the whole family to be present. I could only imagine what his plans entailed.

"I'm glad you came up with us. It was so much fun." I stated to the dog

"Grey, I don't think he is going to talk to you anytime soon. I have been telling you this all weekend."

"Alex, he understands everything we are saying. Don't you? What a good boy." I scratched the dog's ears.

"Jack, she has officially lost it and you're my witness. You need to be there when we break the news to Dec."

"Whatever, concentrate on the road or you'll have to explain why I have some broken bones."

He shut up after that and I continued my conversation with Jack and Tucker. It was sad to see him go, but Jack said I could visit anytime. Of course Alex made some off-the-cuff comment, but I ignored it.

The new year was fast approaching. Hopefully next year would be better than the current one was. I was glad for most of the events that had happened this past year, all except one—the death of my mother. That event would require more time to heal.

CHAPTER FIFTEEN

A NEW YEAR

The holidays were around the corner and we would be spending it at the house in Erving.

Everyone was coming to our holiday party on Saturday apart from the Watt family. They had gone to visit relatives in Ireland for the holidays and didn't plan on returning until the beginning of school. Alex and I were less cheerful due to the circumstances, but we got through it knowing the New Year would bring them both home.

We started decorating the house with lights, both inside and out. The tree would go up on Wednesday after we cut it down. Our mom had never cut down a tree for Christmas. We'd always gone to a lot and picked one out. This year Evan was taking us out to cut our own tree down. It was his idea of family bonding, I guess.

We hopped into the Jeep and headed out to the tree farm.

"This should be fun," Evan said as he turned to Allie.

"We need wreaths for the doors and windows, too," she replied. She always wanted the perfect winter scene from the magazines.

"Sure, we'll go all out this year." Evan leaned toward the front seat. "You guys will enjoy this holiday because you're with family and friends."

I chuckled a little at his attempt to bring smiles to our faces. *This year will be different without Mom, but I know she is here in spirit.*

"That's pretty funny, Grey," Alex said.

"I didn't mean it that way, Alex, but it was pretty funny."

This new connection to him proved to be more convenient than before. Sometimes I tried not to think about things to spare him, because he missed Paige as much as I missed Declan. I was so deep in thought I didn't even know we had stopped.

"Are you guys coming or not?"

"We had better go before he has us singing carols."

We found a tree quickly, but I thought it was too big. Evan assured me it would fit in the hall.

"Let's go get the wreaths now." I started back to the main building.

"Grey, wait."

"What?" I kept walking.

"I know this is hard without Mom, but we need to at least try, okay?" Allie asked.

I agreed to try, but it was harder than I thought it would be. Even though Allie was right—I did need to try—I wouldn't let her know that fact.

My afternoon was completely full. We had lunch and then we continued with the decorations. Doing that was the highlight of my day.

"Grey, you got something in the mail!" Allie called from the fridge.

"Thanks." I all but ran to the hall table.

I hoped the mail would cheer me up. Of course Alex followed, hoping for the same thing. I picked up the envelope and brushed my hand across the address. It was from Declan. I opened the envelope to see the beautiful, silver foil smiling back at me. When I pulled the letter out, something else fell to the floor. I picked it up and recognized Paige's handwriting.

"Alex, this is for you." I handed him the note without looking. All my focus was on my letter.

He grabbed it from my hand and headed upstairs. He wasn't one to show his emotions, and I knew it would be hard for him. His room was a safe haven like mine was to me. I concurred with his idea and retreated to my balcony.

Declan's letter was full of beautiful imagery. He talked about the beautiful landscape and his family, but the last paragraph was what made me tear up.

It's been harder than I thought to be away from you. I would say that my heart was hurting, but I know you are keeping it going with your love for me. I miss the touch of your hand and can only imagine it in my dreams. We will be home a week earlier than planned, and the first face I would like to see is yours. I can only see it in the photograph Paige gave me of us at the lake house. Please keep yourself safe until I arrive home to be with you again. You make me complete and happy and I love you. Please keep my heart safe until I return.

I love you always,
Declan

I folded the note and placed it in my desk with the others. He always knew how to make me feel loved and special.

I walked down to the kitchen and sat with everyone for lunch. Alex hadn't come back down yet and I knew it was harder for him than it was for me. We finished lunch and continued decorating, but he never came back down that night. I also didn't want to disturb him either. If there was one thing we had learned from each other, it was that when we needed space, we got it.

The week flew by quickly. Allie and I still had shopping to do, so we headed into town. I'd decided to give everyone my photos, but I needed to frame them first. Allie went to the next store while

I stayed at the frame shop. Thankfully I had a familiar face help-ing me. Some of the photographs I'd taken myself and others I restored. Jack helped me pick out all the mattes and frames for each photograph. Allie had gotten everything done before I had and she hated waiting as much as Alex did.

"You're not done yet?" She was a little irked.

"I have one more, and then we can leave."

I turned to Jack and pulled out my last photograph. This one was the most important because it was for Declan.

"This photo is amazing," he said.

"Thanks." I tried to change the subject. "I want something simple so the photo is the focal point."

He agreed with me, and pulled out some samples. I decided on a matted silver frame with grey and white, double matte. It was quite appropriate for the photo and the recipient, but I was a little unsure.

"I hope he likes it."

"He'll love it, because it's from you. This frame is what he uses for all of his photos anyway." He held up the frame as he talked.

"That makes me feel a little better. So I'll see you and your family tonight, right?"

"We'll be there, so I'll see you later." He started cleaning up the frames. "Grey, your photos will be ready next week. I'll give you a call."

"Thanks, Jack. See you tonight."

Allie breathed a sigh of relief as we walked to the car.

"I thought you liked shopping?" I asked her.

"I do when you are prepared."

Grams had almost finished preparing the food in the kitchen when we got home.

"Hey, Grams, do you need any help?"

"Sure, can you grab the plates over on the table?"

"So are we ready for some fun tonight?"

"Grey, it'll be fun. Your friends will be here, so enjoy the company, please." She shook her head. "I'm good here. Come down in about an hour to help me set up the dining room area. Oh, and remember we have plans later."

How could I forget the decorating of the trees outback for Yule? I looked forward to it every year.

"Okay, Grams." I gave her a hug and headed upstairs.

Alex wasn't in his room. I wondered where he'd gone. I couldn't be bothered with his problems right now. I needed to take a shower before Allie hogged the bathroom. I sat in the steam for a while before I got in. As soon as I jumped into the shower, I heard a knock at the door.

"Grey." *It never fails. He always finds me.*

"Come in and close the door. You're letting the warm air out." I peeked around the curtain and saw him sitting on the counter. "What's up, Alex?"

"I need your help with something." He grabbed something from his back. "Which tie goes, this one or this one?" He held up two ties and they were both hideous.

"Neither," I said.

"Grey, I only have these two ties, so which one?"

"Go in my closet. There's a small box for you."

"Okay, I'll be right back."

I heard the door open and there went my warm air.

I knew he needed a new tie for the party, so I had Allie pick one out when we were in town. She'd picked out a sharp, silk, cobalt-colored tie, because it brought out his eyes. We wanted him to look good in the photos we were taking at the party—not that he wouldn't anyway. He ran back in and closed the door.

"This is great."

"Don't thank me. I bought it, but Allie picked it out."

I heard the door close and him yelling for Allie down the hall. I laughed. He was so predictable. She had also taken the time to pick out something for me, but I hadn't seen it yet.

I grabbed my towel and dried off before heading back to my room. I walked in the closet to get the dress. It was hanging up on the door in a black garment bag. I decided to dry my hair before I took my chances.

I was combing my hair when I noticed a small wooden box on the desk. I slowly opened it to find a beautiful silver bracelet. On closer exam, it had a moonstone in the center with Celtic knots trailing off on either side. It matched my necklace he'd given me for my birthday. There was no note in or around the box. I heard his voice from behind the door.

"You're welcome."

"Alex."

He opened the door and smiled. I held up the bracelet and looked at him.

"Like I said, you're welcome. The bracelet was custom made and it took a while to get it. It was the other half of your present from our birthday, but I decided to hold onto it until Christmas."

"Thanks, it's beautiful, especially the stone." I hugged him.

"It's your birthstone, you know. And it goes with your dress anyway." He pointed to the garment bag.

"Thanks, again."

He left and I finished blow-drying my hair. I took a deep breath before I grabbed the garment bag. I decided to close my eyes while I laid it on the bed. I opened them to see a very simple, dark-silver, V-neck dress. It looked similar to a cocktail dress I had in black.

Even though Allie was younger, she always knew what we looked good in and what made us feel good. Then I nearly choked when I noticed the shoes at the bottom of the bag. She was definitely crazy if she thought I wouldn't kill myself in those heels. They were only three-inch heels, but I would still break my neck going down the stairs. I mean, I couldn't even walk in a straight line with sneakers on.

I finished getting dressed and slowly made my way down the stairs to help Grams finish setting up. Evan was coming out from his office.

"Whoa, Grey. You look amazing."

"You don't look half bad yourself, Evan. I guess we match, your tie and my dress." I laughed because Allie had probably planned it.

"I think he is going to be mad that he missed this. The photograph won't do you justice."

"Let's go help Grams." I pushed him toward the dining room as I tried to hold on to him so I didn't fall.

"Well, don't you guys clean up nicely," Grams said.

"Thanks, but let's thank the resident fashion diva." I heard Allie behind me.

"You're welcome, guys."

We finished setting up just in time as everyone started arriving. Most of the guests were faculty and administration from the school, but also some of the prominent families in the town. Evan made sure I knew everything about the families that were coming—rules and all. Unfortunately, that meant Gavin and his family as well. Thankfully I had Emery, Quinn, Tyler, and Jack to watch my back.

Alex walked into the kitchen, stopping short.

"Wow. Grey, you look just like Mom."

"Thank you, Alex, but I'm trying not to cry tonight, okay?"

"Sorry, but you do. I'm sorry Dec isn't here to see this." He smiled and twirled me around. "I think you would have a personal bodyguard all night."

I laughed.

"Whatever, let's go do our duty." I grabbed his arm. "You can be my bodyguard tonight."

He was laughing as we joined everyone else at the party.

"You clean up rather nicely, Tyler." I said with a smile.

"Thank you. You're not so bad yourself." Tyler smiled back.

"Where did you find this dress?" Quinn asked.

"Allie found it for me. She's over by the kitchen. Go ask her yourself."

Quinn dragged Emery with her to talk shop with Allie. I stayed with the guys.

"Grey, I am going to say this only once, and if you say anything, I will deny it. You look amazing and he is going to be sad he missed this in person," Jack said to me.

"Thanks. I really appreciate that. It means a lot—and don't worry, I won't tell Quinn."

"Tell me what?" *I swear that girl has supersonic hearing.*

"What your present is." I covered myself on that one.

"I can only imagine. Oh, I'll be right back." Her mother was waving her over.

"So what did you get her?"

"A gift certificate to some store she shops at. She basically came out and told me what she wanted."

"It's the thought that counts, right?"

"It's not as great as what you got for everyone. I wish someone would give me something, like, you know—something from their heart."

I had a feeling it wasn't working out with the two of them, but it wasn't my place to say something, so I kept my mouth shut.

"So thanks for coming tonight. I'm really glad you did, and if you need anything just give me a call."

"Thanks, that means a lot." He handed me back to Alex and left.

"That was really nice. I think Dec is rubbing off on you. No pun intended."

I hit him in the arm.

"You're a pain, you know that?" *But he wasn't too far from the truth.*

The rest of the night we continued to receive compliments on the house, the decorations—even a few about my dress. The night was long and we finally went upstairs to bed. We offered to clean up, but Grams had said she was all set and then sent us to bed. I felt like I was five years old all over again.

The photos from the party and the photos that would be my gifts to everyone would be ready around the same time the following week. I had Alex pick them up from Jack because Alex would be in town shopping.

The holiday was fast approaching and before I knew it, Christmas had come and gone. Everyone loved their gifts, especially Evan. I'd given him a restored photo of him and my mom when they were little. The one time snooping around paid off for me.

The only thing I could think of right now was the fact that there were four more days until Declan and Paige came home. I'm sure Alex was thinking the same thing, because he tried to busy himself as much as I did. Thankfully, we had our friends to distract us. Our recent ski trip with everyone was the break we needed. Jack had called to say our photos were ready early, and he'd mentioned they looked great. He told me the photo didn't do any of us justice; that we were all stunning. I laughed a little every time I thought of people's reactions to the three of us. In one of the photos, we had a classic Charlie's Angels pose. It was a fun night.

I had Alex go pick up the photos while I got dinner ready. He was gone a while, so I figured he got to talking with Jack or something. I heard him walk in the front door. He was talking to someone who I figured was Evan or Allie.

"Grey that smells good. Is it done yet?"

"Almost. Why?"

"I invited some friends to join us tonight."

"Okay, that's fine." I was thinking in my head, *Jack, Ty, Emery, and Quinn—or all of them.* It was good, though. The more, the merrier.

"Did you get the photos?" I asked.

"Yeah, and Jack was right. It didn't do you guys justice at all, but you all still look great."

"Whatever."

I turned to get more plates and glasses from the cupboard. After I set them down on the counter, I checked the roast in the oven.

"Hey, Alex, how many people did you invite?"

He didn't answer me. Maybe he'd gone upstairs. I closed the oven and stood up to go out in to the hall—then I froze.

"Two extra people. That's it," I heard Alex say.

I ran to the other side of the counter and nearly knocked Declan over.

"What are you doing here?! Not that I mind, but you're not supposed to be back for three more days."

"We left early. My dad had to be at some faculty meetings, and we were making him miserable being there." He kissed me. "I've missed this."

"I have too, and I'm glad you're home." I kissed him back.

"I am too, but a little upset that I missed this."

He held up the photo of all of us at our holiday party.

"We had fun. Alex was my bodyguard all night, except for when he switched off with Jack—Gavin, you know."

"I heard. I wish I could have been there, because you looked amazing."

He grabbed my waist and pulled me close.

"I have the dress upstairs. Maybe another occasion, okay?" I brushed his cheek with my hand.

We stood in silence for a while when I heard someone clear their throat. I turned and dropped my arms to my side.

"Paige, I missed you. How are you?" I hugged her.

"Better than him right now."

I turned to see a shocked look on his face. I walked over and kissed him.

"We have plenty of time to catch up, so be patient." He laughed and clutched my hand.

"So, Grey, how are you guys? Tell me everything?"

"Well, we cut our own tree, decorated, hung out with the gang, and slept. That's pretty much the whole two weeks. Oh, and we went back to the lake house to ski before the holidays."

I saw him shiver, then squeeze my hand when I mentioned the lake house. I tried to ignore it.

"Well, what about you guys?"

"We saw family and stayed home most of the time. Nothing really exciting. We wanted to be home."

"We all missed you guys, too."

I hugged her and headed around the counter. I opened the oven and took the roast out. It was pretty much done. I placed it on the counter to cool before I cut it.

"Grey, tell me one thing, please." Paige asked.

"What is that?"

"When did you learn to cook?"

"Oh, well, Grams was showing me some things, and then other times it's just come to me. Weird, huh? Why?"

"Well, I think you don't need lessons anymore."

"I'm far from a good cook, so a few more lessons wouldn't kill me." I winked at Declan.

"I missed this," she said.

Me too, Paige. Me too, I thought.

We finished dinner. Evan cleaned up while we went downstairs to look at the pictures. Declan hadn't left my side since they'd gotten here. It was nice, but he was being intense again. I hoped Paige would see, and then get him to chill out. I knew it was because of the distance that had been between us the past two weeks, but I tried not to dwell on that.

I brought out the albums and the photo sets that Alex had brought home. I started going through the photos with Paige.

"Wow, you look amazing. I'll have to see that dress soon."

"Okay, I looked nice, so let's move on, please."

I'd almost forgotten about their gifts when Declan commented on the photo on the wall.

"This photo is incredible. Who took it?"

"Well, Dec, it's my gift from Grey." He pointed to me. "She took it."

He turned to me and smiled. The photo I'd given Alex was of the mountain trail by the lake with the elusive bear in the background by the water's edge. I had taken it back on the rocks. I remember it had been right before I slipped, and he'd caught me.

"That reminds me. I have something for you guys." I got up and went to the closet to grab their gifts. "Here we go."

Paige opened hers first. It was a photo of the trail near Lake Dennison. The day we'd taken shots for our project, we had piled up stones on a larger rock near the water. So Zen of us.

"This is great, thanks." She hugged me. "What's yours, Dec?"

He was speechless. She grabbed the frame and sighed.

"It's beautiful," she said. I could see a small tear roll down her cheek.

"It's nothing. Just a photo. Don't go getting teary-eyed."

"It's more than that, and you know it."

Alex grabbed the photo because he hadn't seen it yet. It was a shot I'd taken of two white roses intertwined with a silver ribbon. The roses were simply floating on the water's edge near the lake like a cloud in the sky. I'd done it in black and white because it looked better that way. Jack had been right; the silver frame matched perfectly.

"Don't downplay your talent, Grey." He handed the photo back to Declan.

"I'm not. I put thought into all my photos."

"I see. And the frame?"

"Jack helped me. I thought the frame should be simple. It helped the photo pop more," I explained. "He also said it went with all the other pictures you have."

"Can you come here, please?"

I walked over to him and looked back to see Paige smiling. He leaned in and brushed my cheek with his lips.

"It's more than simple, and I love it. It shows me what I mean to you—that our lives are intertwined."

I pulled back and wiped a tear from his face.

"You got me. But please be happy."

"These are tears of joy."

"So give her the gift, Alex."

"What gift?"

"Now, Paige, I got you something, but it's no big deal. So don't think you need to give me anything in return, okay?"

He pulled out a small, white box and handed it to her.

"Thanks, Alex."

She opened the box, and inside was a silver bracelet with a light-green, inlayed stone in the center. The stone was a peridot, her birthstone, and it was beautiful.

"It's kind of like mine."

"Let me help you put it on."

"This is beautiful. Thank you, Alex." She kissed him.

"I have something for you, too. As long as we're giving gifts," Declan said.

It was like Christmas all over again.

"What gift?" I said. "Please, you don't have to give me anything. You're my gift, and that's all I need. I don't need anything else."

"Please accept this, because it will keep me in your thoughts when I'm not around."

He handed me a small, black box. Inside was a silver ring. He placed it on my right hand next to the finger on which I wore my mom's ring.

"This is a knot ring."

He took a breath as he looked at my hand. It was a somewhat strange sigh, like he was thinking of something else when he'd placed it on my finger. Not that it freaked me out too much, but it did make me wonder.

"The intertwined knot symbolizes two souls bound by everlasting love and affection."

I stood there, lost in the moment. I embraced him for what seemed like minutes. It was the most beautiful gift I had ever received from him, besides the flowers and the notes.

"Thank you," I said.

He kissed the tears from my face.

"You're welcome. You now have both my heart and soul with you."

"Okay." I collected myself. "Let's go through these photos."

He held my hand while we sat on the sofa. They watched one of the bowl games on TV while Paige and I went through the photos.

"I love this one of the two of you. Can I have it?" Paige asked. She held up the photo of Alex and I on the stairs.

"Sure. I'll have Jack make me another copy from the negatives."

"Thanks." She put it on the table. "Where were these taken?"

I looked at the pile and saw the photos from the ski trip with Jack and the Ellis family.

"Oh, these were from a ski trip we went on a couple of days after you guys left."

"The weekend after . . ." I felt Declan squeeze my hand and then kiss it.

"Yeah, by then the pain was almost gone—and my gloves were pretty thick."

"This one's funny. What is Jack doing?"

"Quinn and I tried snowboarding and fell into a pile of snow. He pulled us up and carried both of us back to the lodge like a caveman."

"Yeah, it was funny. You could only see their butts and Jack laughing. That was a good time."

"You like it because I actually fought him the whole way— and fell again when he put me down."

"Oh, this is my favorite." I handed her a photo of Alex. "He fell asleep with Jack's dog, Tucker, on the sofa."

"When did you take that?" Alex grabbed the photo.

"The second night there. You know, the day we played hockey on the rink."

"Hockey?" Declan asked.

"Yeah, it was pretty funny to see Grey checking Tyler. I think there was retaliation later that night."

"Well, he deserved it when he hip checked me by the net and he only thought he got me. The whip cream fight was funny that night."

"Aw, I like this one the best." I pulled out a picture of me, Jack, Alex, and Tucker. "Man, I loved that dog."

"Yeah, and he followed us everywhere. He slept mostly with Grey. You would have thought it was her dog, not Jack's."

"I had to keep warm somehow. But the licking in the morning was not fun."

We started laughing and then Paige stopped to say something.

"So I guess you guys had fun then?" Paige asked.

"Only when we weren't missing you guys."

I sat back into Declan and he kissed my hair.

"It's fine. We don't ski anyway," he whispered. "But it seems I have some competition with Tucker."

"No, there's no competition. He wins, hands down." I laughed. He put his arms around my waist, and before I knew it, Declan licked my face.

"Oh, man. Dec. That was gross. Grey, are you okay?"

I wiped my face with my sleeve.

"Declan, that was a little gross," I said.

"Well, I guess I can't compete then."

"Please, I like your kisses better than doggie breath." I kissed him.

"Maybe later then?"

"Please pace yourself."

"Fine." He sighed.

We finished telling them stories about the trip and then moved on to the party over the weekend.

"I can't get over that dress. You definitely look great in that color, too," Paige said.

"Thanks. Allie picked it out for me."

"She should pick out my clothes, too."

We continued sifting through the photos from the party. I don't remember much after that apart from Declan excusing himself for a minute at one point. I must have fallen asleep, but it wasn't a deep sleep because I could still hear the conversations going on.

"How did it go after we left?" Paige asked Alex.

"It was weird, but we were so busy that Declan and Paige being gone only crossed our minds when we were alone or with each other. She put on a good face for me, but we missed you guys."

"And you guys?" Alex asked.

"Dec was a mess. He wouldn't even go to the rugby matches with the family. It was hard to see. He missed her so much."

"It must have been hard to watch."

"It was, but he was happier when we landed. He all but ran to your house tonight." She giggled.

"So I'm glad you guys came home early. I did miss you. I also missed Dec's conversations," Alex said.

"Thanks. I'm definitely glad to be home, too."

I heard Alex kiss Paige, then I heard footsteps on the stairs coming closer to me.

"I come home and she falls asleep. That's perfect," Declan said.

"Don't, Dec. Let her sleep. She's been on the go all day. Go sit with Alex," Paige said.

"You know what, Paige? Maybe we should go home and get some sleep, too. They'll be here tomorrow."

"Yeah, we missed you guys, but you just got in and you need some sleep."

"That's probably for the best. Should we leave her here to sleep?"

"No, I'll carry her to her room," Alex said.

"I'll do it before we go." Declan replied.

I felt someone pick me up and then start walking. Before I knew it, I felt my soft, inviting comforter. I heard more footsteps by the end of my bed, then the creaking of my balcony doors whenever they were being opened. The doors closed after a minute and the footsteps came closer to my bed.

"So do you listen to everyone from here?"

"Maybe."

"Get some sleep. We'll talk later. I really missed you, sweetie."

He kissed me and left.

CHAPTER SIXTEEN

FOUNDER'S DAY

I rolled over and covered my face with my pillow to drown out the sounds of the birds singing. *I'm starting to regret putting a feeder outside my window.* I forced my eyes to open, as it was too comfortable and warm in bed. I peeked out from under the pillow. I saw I'd woken up late; the clock said it was noon. *I must have been tired.* I got up and headed downstairs, still in my clothes from the previous day.

"Hey, sleepyhead, you got some mail," Evan said.

He was eating his lunch. He handed me what looked like an invitation. It was addressed to me, but with a last name Parker, not Corwen. *That's weird. No one knows me by that name except the family.*

"Why is this addressed to Miss Grey Aven Parker, Evan?"

I gave him the envelope. Not too many people knew my middle name and I wanted to keep it that way. I guess my mom hadn't wanted to stick to names that started with an A, but compromised in making my middle name begin with it. I'm glad she stuck to her guns on that one.

"Because you are a Parker. Alex and Allie got the same thing." He paused and smiled. "You know, I still love your middle name."

Great. This is not what I need right now—another trip down memory lane.

"Grey, it's a beautiful compliment. Also, you should feel lucky, because your parents wanted it as your first name."

He laughed as I swatted him with the letter. I didn't need this so early in my day.

I opened the invitation and read it, but didn't really understand what event it was actually for.

"So we're invited to attend the Founder's Day Ball? What's that? We never went to this before."

"You did. You just don't remember. The Founder's Day Ball is held every January 22 to celebrate the founding of Erving and the town's traditions. All the families are invited to attend the event. The rest of the week is filled with fairs, games, and fun stuff like that."

"Well, at least I can wear my dress again." I sat down.

"Actually, every family must be represented there, especially the families who were the original settlers. You're going to have to represent the Parker family by wearing the colors that are part of the family's crest."

"What are the colors then?"

"The Corwen family color is white, and your individual color is green."

"Why is my color different from yours and Grams? I'm a Corwen. Why aren't I represented by that color?"

"You, Alex, and Allie represent one of the original families now. The Parker family's color must be represented by all of you. I understand this is a lot to take in all at once, but it's your duty now."

Wonderful. Not only are we an important family, now we have duties to uphold. Ugh.

"Do you know what the other families' colors are?" I asked. I was curious, but I also wanted to change the subject before I received a family history lesson.

"Well, let's see, our family's is white and the Parker family's is green; the Watt family's is silver; the Ellis family's is gold; the Connors' is blue; the Marsh family's is black and the Harrington family's is red."

I chuckled a little thinking about the fact that silver was the Watt family's color. Now I knew where the inspiration for the silver ribbon and the silver envelopes had come from. If I'd known that information before, I would have figured out who had been sending the flowers sooner.

"Fine. It looks like I need to take Allie shopping." I got up and headed to Allie's room.

"Wait, Grey. There's more."

"More?"

"Yes. Because you're not married, you must be escorted to the ball by your father or a male family member. I will be escorting you, and Allie will be escorted by Alex. Once we are there, you and I have to dance the first dance together. Then you guys can go your own ways."

"Man, so many rules I have to learn." I sighed.

"It gets easier, Grey."

He hugged me and went to his office; probably to dig up books for me to study before the big night.

I ran upstairs to get dressed and grabbed Allie on my way.. We both needed new dresses and I needed all the help I could get. She would never pass up a chance to shop. We hopped in the Jeep. I needed to make a stop first before we got in to town.

I walked up the stairs and knocked on the door. An older woman answered the door, who I assumed was their mother.

"Hello. Is Paige here?" I asked.

"May I ask who you are?"

Oh, right. She's never met me.

"I'm Grey Corwen."

"Hey, Grey! Did you miss me already?" I heard Declan say from the hall. "Mom, I got it, thanks."

"She's not here for you, Declan. Now go get your sister, please," she said sternly.

He looked a little shocked, but winked at me as I headed up

the stairs to get Paige.

"So you're the girl who's captured my son's heart?"

"Yes, Mrs. Watt. I suppose I am."

"Well, I should congratulate you, because no one's done that since Emma."

"Oh, I don't know Emma. Sorry."

"She was very beautiful. She was *right* for him."

I started to unravel inside. I felt the strange need to leave immediately. It was weird how I'd never heard of Emma. No one, including Alex, had told me about her, and I couldn't help but wonder why they hadn't.

"Please tell Paige I'll be in town . . . if she could just meet us there. Thank you for your time."

I turned and ran down the stairs. I skidded out of the driveway and headed toward town. I could feel the tears welling up in my eyes, but I tried to keep my composure in front of Allie. I still didn't understand what was upsetting me—then it hit me. *I wasn't the only one. I was a backup.* Where had that thought come from? It was like someone was putting ideas in my head, almost like they were my own.

"Grey, are you okay? Where's Paige?"

"I don't think she was home, so I left a message for her to meet us in town." I took a deep breath. "And I'm fine."

"You don't look fine."

Sometimes I didn't give Allie enough credit, but this was not something I wanted to talk to her about. I didn't think she would even understand, but I needed to tell someone.

"I was just told that I wasn't right for Declan, and that I wasn't his first choice. I was the backup plan."

"Oh, man. Why someone would say that to somebody?"

"I don't know why. Maybe it's true? I don't know. Let's talk about something else."

I removed my ring and put it in the center console. I didn't want to be anyone's backup plan. Maybe I deserved better. I tried to look forward to spending the day with Allie.

We pulled up to the small boutique and headed in. Allie took all of ten minutes to find me a dress. It was similar to the silver one I had, but the color was a beautiful, emerald green. We then got Alex his tie and left.

As I drove home, I had Allie grab an envelope from the glove compartment. I stopped to place the ring inside and to write his name on the outside of the envelope. Allie gave me some paper from her planner. I then wrote a short message.

Declan,

> *I am sorry to hear that I was your backup plan. I'm sure you want to be with Emma at the Founder's Day Ball; like you were meant to be from the beginning. You can have your heart and soul back.*

Grey

I sealed the envelope and pulled up to their mailbox. I had Allie get out and put it inside.

When we got home I didn't want to talk to anyone, so I headed straight to my room. Allie told Alex and Evan not to bother me—especially whenever Declan would call or come by.

I sat in my room for hours, thinking about how stupid I must be. *How could I let this go so far? But my feelings were still there, and unchanged. I love Declan, even if I was his second choice.*

I kept wondering why he'd chosen me anyway. Of all the people in the town, it had to be me. I needed to calm down, so I decided to let the water wash it all away. I started down the hall. I caught sight of him in the hall downstairs with Alex.

"Grey, wait! Please!" he yelled as he ascended the stairs.

I ran to the bathroom and locked the door. I turned the shower on to avoid conversation.

"Grey, please come out and talk to me. Tell me what I did."

"Go away, please. Just leave me alone. It is over."

I got in the shower and cried. Alex started shouting through the door.

"Grey, come on! Open the door! We need to talk this out." He was starting to get agitated when I hadn't yet opened the door. "You can't stay in there all night."

What he didn't know is, though, is that I didn't have to. There was a passage in the closet that led to Mom's old room. I'd found it a couple of weeks before, when I was bored. I would sleep there tonight—and until they left me alone. I shut the shower off and dried my hair.

"Grey, please come out and talk to us."

I walked through the closet. I soon fell asleep in my mom's bed. I could still hear them trying to get me out. Finally, Evan unlocked the door, explaining as he did that I wasn't in there. He'd figured out where I was, but respected my wishes to not let anyone else know about the passageway. I used the passages to move about the house until Declan eventually stopped coming over. I had a flood of emotions raging through my mind. Most of them didn't feel like my own, but in a sense they seemed very real. The pressure in my head began again. It felt like someone was trying to push through. I hadn't had the headaches in a while, but they'd come back with a vengeance.

A couple of days had soon passed. I was getting sick of hiding out in my own house. Allie gave me the all clear, so I snuck downstairs to grab something to eat. I double-checked to make sure I was safe from an ambush. I was sitting on the counter, when I heard Alex on the deck talking to someone.

"Damn it!" I said.

I ran to Evan's office through the passage behind the wall and up to Allie's room.

"Hey, I thought the coast was clear," I said to Allie.

"It is. No one's here except you and me."

"Then why is Alex on the deck with someone?" I pointed to the window.

"I don't know, but let me find out."

"Allie, wait. Go to my room through the passageway so you can listen on the balcony."

"Okay, I'll be right back."

Please don't get caught. Whatever you do, don't get caught.

She left the same way I'd come in; hopefully they were still out there. I kept watch out the window to make sure they were still there. That's when I heard Alex call up to the balcony.

Damn it! She got caught.

I opened her door to see her stumbling, but she waved me back. I closed the door and sat on her bed for a half an hour, waiting, before she finally came back.

"What happened?"

"Grey, it's Paige and Declan. I think you should go talk to them."

"No, I can't." There was that odd pressure again.

"Listen, Paige knows about the passages, so think about it."

Suddenly I heard noise coming from the hall toward Allie's room. I ran into the passage and I heard the knock at Allie's door. I closed the wall and then turned to sneak down to Evan's office. I was suddenly startled by someone, and I think my heart stopped for a split second.

"Paige, what the heck?" I said to her.

"Why are you avoiding me?"

"I'm not. Just Declan and Alex."

"Why? What happened a couple of days ago?" she whispered. "You came by to see me, and when I came down my mom said you'd left."

"She didn't give you the message to meet me in town?"

"No, she said you couldn't wait, that you had to leave."

I was getting a little peeved, knowing now that her mother hadn't given her the message.

"Did she say anything else?" I asked.

"No, was there anything else?"

"Take Declan home with you and you guys talk to your mom."

"She's gone on a business trip until Friday."

"Then talk to her on Friday. I'll see you at the ball that night, and you can tell me what she said."

I pleaded for her to go. My head was pounding. All the chaos was driving me nuts. *I wish things would go back to the way they were before I came here.*

"Sure, but tell me, please. He's going crazy, and frankly, I am too."

"Please talk to her and. I'll see you Friday night."

She hesitated, but left through my room. She knew she wasn't getting anything else from me that day. I was sure she might try again, but with the way my thoughts were jumbled at that moment, I didn't think I would be able to tell her what was real and what was not.

I heard them run toward the office door thinking it was me who was going to exit. Paige told Declan they "had to leave—no questions asked." They would see us on Friday.

I decided to sleep in Allie's room the rest of the week, and I made sure I had my candle, just in case. Alex never came in there, so I was safe for another two days. Allie continued to bring me stuff to eat, and when Alex would go out, I would eat downstairs.

When I woke up, it was late afternoon on Friday. She gave me the go ahead to take a shower as she grabbed my dress from my room. Alex and Evan had gone out for some last-minute things, which was probably part of her plan. I finished my shower and headed back to her room. She did my hair, then her own. As we got dressed, I noticed her staring at me in the mirror.

"You look great, Grey, like Mom. Green is definitely your color. It's no silver, but it'll do."

"I miss her too, Allie. You look very nice yourself. Let's go before we're both a hot mess."

As we slowly made our way toward the stairs, I noticed I'd forgotten my jewelry. I had Allie wait as I went to get it. Opening my jewelry box, I heard Evan and Grams outside in the garden. They were worried about the flowers. I peeked around the door and saw that one of the white rose bushes was bent over and its flowers were wilted, which was weird, because the other bushes were fine.

I grabbed my necklace, bracelet, and my mom's ring. Allie and I walked out to the hall and down the stairs together.

"Grey, Allie, you girls look great," Evan said to us.

"Please can we do this, and then go home?"

"Relax, Grey. We'll leave at a reasonable time. Remember, you need to do this."

"Okay, but when we get home I want to see this book that you keep quoting from."

The ride over was quiet. Alex and I were fighting. I hated it, and as far as I saw, he hated too. I walked into the large hallway with Evan. We abruptly stopped in front of two large oak doors. I was confused.

"Why are we stopping, Evan?"

"You have to be announced to enter the ballroom."

"More rules? Do you think people will be shocked to hear the Parker name announced?"

"Yes to both questions, Grey. Are you ready? Here we go. Smile, please."

The doors opened. Then they announced me: "Miss Grey Aven Parker, escorted by Mr. Evan Corwen." They announced Alex and Allie right after. *I can't believe they used my middle name. Ugh.* I saw Jack and Quinn out of the corner of my eye, and waved.

"What do we do now, Evan?"

"We wait for the music, and then we dance." He pointed to the band.

"Fine." I stood there, waiting, as everyone else entered. I could hear the hushed whispering, and I concluded it had something to do with us. The town hadn't heard the Parker name in over five years.

The band started to play. I danced with Evan and tried to enjoy myself. The song ended and he turned me over to Jack.

"So how are things going?" Jack asked.

"Okay. Have you heard otherwise?"

"Well, word has it that you and Declan are done."

"You are correct." I was curt. "Why?"

"I would watch out tonight. Gavin is on the prowl."

"Thanks for the warning. So how do you cope with all these rules?"

"I've been doing this since I can remember. I know it seems strange, but if you ever want to talk about it, I would be happy to help. I kind of wish the situation was a little different, but I'm still your friend. It may not have worked out in the end, but always remember that, please."

I needed that right then. The song ended and I hugged him before he disappeared into the crowd. I heard someone ask me to dance, and I turned around to see Declan.

"I don't think that's a good idea," I said. "Thank you for asking, though."

He grabbed my hand.

"Just one dance, please."

The music started. I couldn't stand there, so I started dancing. *This is so awkward.*

"It's only awkward if you make it so. Can you tell me what's going on?"

I think I need to go. I'm sorry. He looked amazing—that had been hard to say.

Turning him down made it feel as if my heart was splintering into pieces. I walked away and bumped into Gavin on my way toward the doors.

"Would you care to dance, Grey?" he asked.

"Sure, Gavin. Why not?"

I didn't care. I just wanted to go home and go to sleep. We started dancing, and then I heard a low growl from the crowd. *Great. Do I live amongst wolves, too?* I saw Declan standing next to Jack and Alex. He was upset. His eyes were fierce, and they were on me the whole time.

After the dance I couldn't wait to get out of there. *Some fresh air would be great right about now.* Gavin escorted me out of the room. It was getting too intense in there for both of us.

"Please, Gavin, I'm not interested. Unless you want a black eye, don't think about it."

He agreed, so we continued to walk to the bench in the courtyard.

"What's the deal, Grey?"

"I found out I was Declan's second choice—a backup plan. I wasn't as important as his first choice."

"Who told you that? Did he?" I could see Gavin's fists clenching.

"No, his mother told me earlier this week."

"Here." Gavin reached in his jacket and handed me a tissue. "Its fine. Don't cry, Grey. Please. Did you talk to him or to Paige about this?"

"No, but I told Paige to talk to her mother today." I wiped the tears from my face.

"Then I would wait to find out the truth." He saw me shiver. "Here, take my coat."

"Thanks, Gavin. I appreciate it." I took his coat and put it on. "Why are you being all nice to me now?"

"I've always been nice. Maybe a little too forward, but in the end your friendship means something."

I couldn't help but think our friendship had more to do with my family—not with me.

I didn't say anything as I leaned my head upon his shoulder. We sat in silence for a while and then he stood up taking my hand.

"We should get back before they send the search party out."

I took his arm and we walked back to the ballroom. I let go as we entered. All eyes were on us as we crossed over to a table.

"Thanks for listening, Gavin. You can be a good guy when you want to be." I kissed his cheek and thanked him again.

"Thank you, Grey. I hope you've enjoyed tonight. I'll see you in school."

I gave him back his coat and then he left. I sat down and then realized Quinn had just sat down next to me.

"What was that? You go from Declan to him?"

"No. He was being a good guy, by listening."

"Gavin? Really?"

"I was shocked, too. But he can be nice when he wants to be."

We laughed. I saw Declan and Alex again as I glanced toward the other side of the room. Declan looked simply crushed—by what, I had no idea. He was the one who'd hurt me with his lies.

"Hey, Grey, do you want to go?" Evan asked me.

"Yeah, thanks." I got up and turned back to Quinn. "I'll talk to you later."

"Sure, but what happened, Grey?"

She grabbed my arm and suddenly I felt the familiar surge again. It was as if she was willing me. Without a thought, I whispered the story in her ear.

"Can I talk to Paige about this?" she asked me.

There was that pulse again.

"Sure, but no one else. I'll talk to you later."

I walked out of the room with Evan, feeling drained again. *Okay, I really need to get my hands on some of my lessons.* We met Allie at the car and headed home.

"Thanks, Evan."

I kissed him on the cheek and headed upstairs.

I woke up late again, but this time I felt like someone was watching me.

"Good morning," Alex said to me.

"What are you doing here?" I rubbed my eyes.

"We need to talk today."

Quinn!

"Fine. What do you want to talk about?"

"What's been going on with you, Grey?"

"Nothing. Why?"

"Nothing? You gave Dec his ring back, you've been avoiding him and Paige, and then you were with Gavin last night."

"It's complicated. Leave it alone, Alex. It doesn't concern you."

"It does concern me, Grey. You're my sister, and I care about what's going on with you. I also have friends I need to help. Don't make me choose, please."

"You don't have to. I'm fine, really."

"Grey, it's going to be awkward when he's here. I don't want to put either of you in that position."

"Then tell me when he's coming and I'll leave. Don't worry about it."

I got up and went to the closet to get dressed. I saw Declan's jersey on the wall and I took it down. I walked out with it in my hand.

"Alex, can you please give this to him for me?" I handed Alex the jersey and turned toward the door. "I'm taking Allie to the mall, so you can invite him over if you want."

"Grey, what changed? What did he do?"

Quinn didn't tell him. Great. Now I have to.

I walked back over to Alex and whispered details of the day's events in his ear. He was as shocked as Quinn had been last night.

"Bye. I'll see you at dinner."

I knew Alex would ask Declan or confront him about the situation today. I'd overheard Alex rambling on in his head about rules or something. *What is with this community and their rules? Rules that I just don't understand.*

Allie and I got back in time for dinner, but there was no sign of Alex. Grams was out, so Evan ordered pizza. We ate downstairs while we watched a movie. I heard footsteps coming down the stairs. *Damn. No escape this time.*

"Hey, guys. Watching a movie?"

"We just finished. There's pizza in the kitchen."

"I ate at Dec's house. Can we join you?"

"Well, I'm headed upstairs to take sleepyhead, here, to bed. But I'm sure Grey wouldn't mind."

He shot me a look. *Be nice, Grey.*

"Okay, I'll see you later."

I saw Alex and Paige walking toward me. They sat down on either side of me.

"So what are we watching?" Paige asked me.

"I was going to watch Jeopardy, but if you want to watch a movie, I can leave."

"No, please sit. We'll watch that."

I sat back down and began watching TV again.

We sat in silence for a while, but I could see that Alex was itching to say something.

"Spit it out, Alex," I said.

"Grey, I talked to Paige and Dec about what you told me."

"And your point is?"

"Please listen to me before you interrupt."

"Fine. Continue then."

"They had no idea what happened until I told them. It's not true. Listen to me. Declan went out with a girl named Emma once, sometime back around April of last year. It was one date—that was it. He couldn't stand her. He said she was boring." *We also didn't know if the family was coming back here, so our parents had to have a plan,* he continued, this time communicating telepathically.

"Then why would she say that to me?" *And what are you talking about, having a plan? More rules I don't know about.*

Paige sat next to me on the sofa and put her arms around me.

"We asked her, but she couldn't give us an answer. That's when we left. Dec was furious. So was my dad when he heard."

I continued to lean into her shoulder without saying a word.

"I'm sorry, but it really hurt me. It was harsh thing to hear from someone who doesn't know me."

"Don't be sorry. It's not your fault. Our mother had some issue with your mother and your Uncle Sean—or she *did* have a problem. That's the argument I heard on the way out." *There was also an argument about the alternative plan.*

"Maybe this is for the best," I said. "This makes two fights now that Declan has had with your parents over me."

"Don't be stupid, Grey. My father is on your side this time."

Great. So that means he wasn't on my side before.

"Grey, I think we need to talk to Declan," Alex said.

"No, I've got a better idea."

CHAPTER SEVENTEEN

CONFRONTATIONS

I ran out the front door, jumped into the Jeep, and sped to the Watt's house. I pulled in the drive and walked up to the porch. Paige was already at the door, waiting to open it for me. I walked into the living room and stood there in front of her parents.

"Can you please tell me why I gave up something wonderful? Because I'm curious," I said to them.

"I'm sorry, Grey. I didn't mean to take it out on you—my frustration, that is. When I saw you, it brought back some past issues; you look just like her. I had issues with her. And it was wrong for me to say those things to you. I didn't want my son to be hurt. I'm truly sorry."

"I would never hurt him, but because of you, I did. Well, that's all I wanted, so I'm going to leave before I create more turmoil for you."

I pulled out and drove away. I didn't know where I was going, but driving seemed to help me clear my head. I got back to the house around one o'clock in the morning and entered to a few angry faces. Alex got to me first.

"Grey, where have you been?"

"You're in serious trouble, young lady." Evan said sharply.

"I'm sorry. I needed to clear my head. I should have called.

I'm really sorry."

"You're grounded for a week. No questions asked. Good night."

"Good night."

I headed upstairs and went to sleep.

A few days had passed, and that morning I woke up early, only having gotten a few hours' sleep. I decided to stay in bed that day and think about how bad I'd messed things up. It was going to be hard, but I thought Declan and I could be friends. If he wanted to, of course. When I saw him, what was I going to say or do? *I'm sure he's mad, and I don't blame him.*

The rant in my head was interrupted when I heard people talking out on the deck. I got up to listen on the balcony. It was Paige and Alex.

"Do you think she'll see him today?" Paige asked.

"I'm not sure. We can always ask her."

"I'm worried about whether they'll find their way back to each other. Dec can't live without her. He loves her too much. This crazy thing between our parents doesn't help. He's a mess right now. He won't talk to anyone. I'm afraid we need to know how she feels."

"She loves him just as much, but she has doubts about their relationship—and him—because of your mother's remarks." He sighed. "She also hasn't been told everything just yet, so we need to cut her some slack on this one."

"I know. I'm sorry she did that. She feels horrible. He refuses to speak to her still."

"Let's go see. It doesn't hurt to ask if she'll see him today."

I heard their footsteps in the hall and I jumped into bed and hid under the pillows. They rapped on the door.

"Grey, can we come in?" Alex whispered through the door. "It's me and Paige."

I heard the heavy door creak open and then someone sit down on my bed.

"Grey, I know you're awake."

"What?" I rolled over. "Oh. Hey, Paige. Is it time to get up?"

"Sure, it's only noon." She smiled. I missed that.

"Wow, it's lunch time already."

"Can we ask you something?" Paige said.

"Sure, why not? Bring on the questions."

I knew what the questions were, I just wasn't sure of my answers yet.

"Can you see him today?"

I sat for a minute, pondering my decision. *I love him deeply. I can't see him alone. Maybe they could stay with me? What could I do to rectify my mistake?*

"Yes, he does. And we can," Alex said.

"Alex, please. Not now."

I hated when he did that.

"I'll go call him. Have him meet us, okay?"

Alex was downstairs before I could protest.

"Did you answer him?"

"Yes. He's taking care of it." I nodded my head to the hall. "Paige, I'm sorry for confronting your family like that the other night."

"You had every right. She behaved badly, all because of a past situation. Declan's still mad at her, you know." She pulled me out of bed. "He mopes around all day, mumbling to himself. He's a mess, Grey."

"I'm sorry for that. I thought it was all true. Can you see my side, even just a little?"

"I can. It would hurt me as well. Let's take this one step at a time, okay?"

"Deal."

"So can you tell me what happened with Gavin the other night?"

"Nothing. We danced and talked. He listened to me, and gave me his coat because I was cold. We sat for a while, then came back. He was polite. He didn't try anything."

"But Dec saw you kiss him."

"I gave him a friendly peck on the cheek, like I would with you or Allie. It meant nothing and he knew it." *Your brother saw what he wanted to see.*

"Okay, but you need to explain that to both your brother and to Declan. They think you moved on."

"Please give me some credit. I would never move on that soon, and definitely not with Gavin. Maybe Jack," I said, joking.

"Not funny, Grey. And I think Quinn might have something to say about that. Now you need to convince him. You know how his imagination can make this stuff up out of thin air."

"I'll do my best, but I can't guarantee anything, Paige."

"You'll both come around. Maybe not today, but soon. Stranger things have happened."

Oh, I knew all about strange things these days. Welcome to my daily life.

We strolled into the kitchen. I needed to get something to eat. Alex was still on the phone. *Why is it taking so long?*

"Sorry, guys. It took longer than planned." He grabbed an apple.

"When?"

"He wants everyone to meet him at the fair today."

"Are you kidding me?" Paige said.

"Nope. He insisted."

"Okay, let's go then." Suddenly I wasn't hungry anymore. "He wants witnesses. That way he'll have them."

Alex had already called everyone else and they had agreed to go. It was just the three of us who still needed to head to the fair grounds. I climbed into the backseat of the Jeep as my heart began to race. I felt sick.

"Are you okay, Grey?" Paige asked me.

"It's nerves. I'm okay," I lied. And Alex knew it.

"It'll be fine. Just keep breathing normally."

I noticed Alex smile in the mirror. He knew something, but he wasn't going to tell me.

I can't wait until this week is over. As much as I like green, wearing it all week was a pain. I want my brown, silver, and gray clothes back.

"You look fine, so stop worrying, would you?" Alex laughed. "I feel the same way."

I laughed as Paige gave us both dirty looks warning us to stop.

When we arrived, everyone was waiting at the entrance for us.

"Hey, Grey, how are you doing?" Tyler asked me.

"I'm good. And you?"

"Could be better. Emery's sick, so, you know?"

"Well, I'll be your date today—at least until I have to talk to Declan."

"Thanks."

I grabbed his arm and we walked into the fair. It felt weird not being there with Declan, but being with the gang definitely boosted my mood. We stopped to play the ring toss game, and it eventually came down to Jack and me.

Okay, Jack. No cheating. I know you, and I have the same abilities. Let's keep them at bay.

He laughed, but got the message loud and clear.

"Jack, she's pretty good at this game. I mean, she used to practice at home just for fun."

"I'll take my chances."

He threw his ring and it waivered a little around the edge before falling to the ground. I was getting ready to throw, when I heard his voice in my ear. I froze.

"You look beautiful in green, but I prefer you in silver," Declan whispered.

"Thank you."

I took a breath and tossed the ring. I turned around and saw him standing there, looking past me toward the bottles. I threw the ring, and then everyone gasped. *Success!*

"You won! I guess you're lucky!" Quinn shouted.

"No, it's just practice." I turned back to the game. "Quinn, your choice. What do you want?"

"Thanks, but don't you want it?"

"No, I don't need it."

"She always gives her prize away," Alex said.

"Why?"

"Because, Jack. I don't need some prize to know that I won," I said. "Besides, someone else can enjoy it."

I walked with Tyler to the next game.

"So, Tyler, how are things going?" I asked him.

"They're good." He took a breath. "Grey, we all know what happened. It was wrong, but give it a chance, please."

I felt like my relationship with Declan wasn't only important to me, but to those around me as well. I really had to sit down and have that conversation with Evan.

"Listen, if anyone deserves you, Grey, it's him. And vice versa. Please give it a chance."

"I will, Ty. I needed a moment to clear my head."

We sat down on a bench as everyone slowly walked toward us. Declan approached me.

"Hey, Tyler, can I talk to Grey for a minute?" he asked.

"Sure, Dec. She's all yours."

I hope so. I, myself, hoped for the same outcome.

He sat down next to me and sighed. There was only the sound of people enjoying themselves at the fair. The silence between us lasted for several more minutes until he finally spoke.

"Grey, I'm truly sorry for what happened. But it's not true." He took a deep breath before he continued. "I've never felt this way before—about anyone. I didn't like Emma; my mom set me up on the date. It was awful. We had nothing in common. It wasn't like the times I spend with you."

"Declan, I understand, but you need to see my point. She shattered my heart that day, and she didn't even know me. I don't know why I believed her, but I did. And I'm sorry for that."

He started to reach up to wipe my tears away, but I beat him to it and he quickly dropped his hand. We sat for a little while longer, not knowing what to do or say. *I want him to know that I still love him. I need him back in my life.* I felt his hand on top of mine and my heart started to race.

I miss this feeling. I wonder if we can get past this mess? I really hope we can, because it was hard without him. I felt something cold on my finger, and looked down to notice my ring.

"It's yours. I gave it to you as a gift, so it belongs to you," he said.

I sat there, speechless, staring at the ring. Then he stood up.

"I wanted you to have it back," I said. "It makes me sad when I look at it, so please keep it."

He turned to walk away.

"Thank you for everything."

I started to cry as he left. Why didn't I stop him? Why didn't he fight for this?

Alex heard me, and ran over to my side as Paige grabbed Declan. I could see them talking—or should I say, I saw her yelling at him as he half-listened to her and glanced back at me every once in a while. Alex knelt down in front of me and grabbed my shoulders.

"Are you okay, Grey?" he asked. He was trying to block my view of Paige and Declan, but it didn't work. I could still feel and hear them. "Grey?"

"I'm not okay," I whispered for the first time.

He seemed shocked, shocked because I hadn't given the answer I usually did: "Fine. He sat down and held me.

"It's going to work out, Grey. Please don't give up now." *This is important,* he continued. *We all need this. You have no understanding of what this could do.*

He was right. I didn't understand. I didn't understand why there was such importance placed on a teenage crush. I just cried into his shoulders as he continued to talk.

"The roses are dying, Grey. The bond is breaking. Only you can fix this."

I looked up. Now I actually understood something for the first time. I knew what he was talking about. I remembered the garden, and what Grams had said: Only I could set things right. What was I waiting for? An apology that wasn't necessary?

I stood up, wiped the tears from my face, and walked toward them. Without hesitation, I acted on pure emotion. I grabbed his arm, turned him around, and kissed him. He was shocked. I had never put that much force and passion behind my advances. His reaction was what I'd hoped for, what I wanted him to do. He embraced me tightly. We stopped hugging briefly so we could both catch our breath. I rested my head on his chest as he whispered in my ear.

"I've missed you so much. Please come back to me. I need you more than you know. I love you, Grey."

I pulled back and looked into his eyes before I spoke.

I needed him as much as he needed me. Our lives were intertwined. If one of us broke, we both broke. We were stronger—and whole—when we were together. That's how it had to be. How had our bond gotten so strong in such a short period of time? I didn't care. I loved him more than I could have ever imagined, but should I say that? Or show him?

"Please do both," he said.

I'd forgotten that he could hear my thoughts. I stopped thinking then, and just reacted. I placed my hands around his face and then parted his lips with mine. It was the most amazing feeling to back in his arms again. I pulled back momentarily, and whispered to him, "I love you, too. Please forgive me."

"No, Grey. There isn't any reason to forgive you, because you didn't do anything. This wasn't your doing. Please understand that."

He embraced me. We stood there for what seemed like forever. I heard Alex clear his throat and I looked up to see him smiling.

"It's about time," Alex said. "Now can we have some fun?"

"Actually, I had something else in mind," I answered.

"Really?"

"Please get a grip, Declan," Paige said to him. "I'm hungry, so let's eat before we continue."

Paige laughed, and I noticed his smile drop slightly. I missed that, too—his funny, little quirks.

"Ty, is your café open right now? I want a burger." I asked as my stomach growled

"Yup, let's go," he said.

I turned to walk with them to the café and he gently grabbed my hand.

"Thank you, Grey." He held my hand and kissed it hand as we walked. "Now we can go."

CHAPTER EIGHTEEN

SPACE IS OVERRATED

Things slowly went back to normal before the ball, but it was a little different. It was more intense than before, more serious. I'd never gotten around to talking to Evan; I hadn't had a chance because I was never alone for more than a second. That coming Friday, after school, I would get a break from it, though—a girls' night out. We were planning on having dinner and going bowling, and then back to my house for the rest of the night.

I slowly got back into the swing of classes and my tutoring sessions continued; although they were only with Jack, because Camden's schedule had changed. Camden had invited us to some games of his, and Alex was pretty happy about that. Thankfully, the week went by quickly. I needed a break from reality for at least one night.

I decided to walk through the garden before I went to pick up Paige. I noticed the rose bushes were now blooming again, and they were looking healthier than before, stronger even. It was weird how the flowers were so connected to all of us. I slowly walked around the garden, and then I felt another shiver. I looked around, but no one was there. At that moment, I decided it was time to leave before something else happened.

I knocked on the Watt's door. Their mother answered again.

This is great. Can't I get a break?

"Is Paige ready, Mrs. Watt?"

"She'll be down in a minute. Would you like to come inside and wait?"

"Sure."

We sat in the living room as I waited for Paige. Mrs. Watt started to say something, but then stopped suddenly.

"Hello, Declan," she said.

I turned and saw the lack of expression on his face. He was still mad about what had happened. He pulled me up so I was close to him, and then leaned in and kissed me. It felt forced, and I felt a little uncomfortable around his mother, so I stopped him. He kept his arms around my waist with his chin resting on my shoulder, which seemed like it was an attempt to demonstrate his commitment to his mother. I shook my head and smirked before returning to the topic of what she'd been about to say.

"I'm sorry, Mrs. Watt. You were saying something?"

Declan held me tighter.

"I wanted to apologize again. I spoke harshly, and without thinking. I'm sorry for that."

"It's fine. We all make mistakes—but we learn not to make them again in the future."

I felt him squeeze me tighter. He kissed my cheek.

"Thank you," I whispered.

Paige came downstairs, and I could tell that she felt the tension in the room as she hurried to the door.

"Well, I'm ready to go. Come on, Grey."

"I'll see you tomorrow, Declan," I said. I kissed him goodbye on the way out the door.

We stopped at my house to drop off her stuff. She climbed

back in and then we sped off toward town.

"You'll actually see them tonight." Paige said.

"What? I'm not ready for a battle with Alex again."

She started to laugh as we pulled up to the café. I felt a shiver run down my back again, but I headed inside without a second thought. I was hoping she hadn't noticed. That feeling seemed to be happening more frequently.

We finished eating and then hopped into the cars for some fun at the bowling alley. As we walked in, I noticed Gavin with someone. *Well, at least he'll leave us alone tonight.* I laughed to myself, and of course Paige had caught that.

We got to our lane and started to play. Quinn went first, and was followed by Paige. I decided to go last, because I was enjoying my time out with my friends. It was the breather I'd needed—no responsibilities or having to deal with family issues. I got up from my seat and rolled the ball down the lane. I landed a strike.

"Nice shot, Grey!" I heard Gavin say behind me.

I turned to thank him and saw him standing on the stairs next to his date. Before I could thank him, I happened to notice the looks on everyone else's faces. They looked upset.

I thought we were passed all this. I looked back to Gavin and his date. She was definitely attractive, tall, with long, black hair and piercing, hazel eyes. *What was she doing with him? Finally, I can be free from his advances.*

"Thanks, Gavin. It was a lucky shot."

"Oh, where are my manners? Grey, this is my girlfriend."

"Nice to meet you." I stopped. "I'm sorry, what did you say your name was again?"

"I didn't," she said. Her voice was soft and melodic. "I'm Emma."

"Oh."

I knew I'd heard that name before. I have to say, she was downright rude. They deserved each other. I stepped back and took a breath. Then I saw Gavin nod, as if to confirm my suspicions.

"Well, it was nice to meet you, but I have to get back to my friends."

"Have fun. I'll see you on Monday." He smirked as they walked to the door. I turned and walked down the stairs to our lane.

"Quinn, it's still my turn right?" I asked.

"Yeah, but we can stop, Grey."

"No. We're here to have fun, so let's have some."

I took my frustration out on the poor pins.

We finished the game and decided to head back to my house. It seemed like Gavin had sucked the fun out of the night.

I walked in behind everyone as the girls headed toward the kitchen, where we found the guys playing cards.

"So how was bowling and dinner?" Alex asked us.

"Dinner was good."

Everyone remained silent as I slammed the cupboard and the kettle down on the stove. I turned the stove on. Declan had come up behind me and wrapped his arms around me.

"Can you make me some tea, too? I think I might need it," he said.

He kissed my neck.

"Sure. Does anyone else want anything?"

"No, we're good, Grey," Paige said as she sat down.

"So how was bowling?" Alex continued with his questions.

"Well, Grey had a perfect game. She creamed us." Emery laughed.

"Those poor pins didn't have a chance."

We were all laughing, the girls, but the guys just looked confused.

"Can someone let us in on the joke?!" Tyler yelled over the

laughter.

"Fine. I'll tell you." I looked at Paige and she nodded. "Well, we bumped into Gavin at the alley."

"That's not that funny," Declan said.

"I'm not finished, Declan," I said. I held his hand and continued. "He was with his girlfriend."

"He introduced her to Grey personally," Paige said slowly.

"So you met his girlfriend? Maybe now he can stop harassing you," Jack said.

Come on, Jack. I know you can figure this out.

"Paige, what happened?" Alex said as he turned to her, but I answered first.

"I met his girlfriend, Emma."

I heard Tyler slam his cards on the table and I saw Alex ball up his fists. But I wasn't ready for Declan's response. He let go of me and stormed out the front door. The guys all got up and ran after him. I heard Declan's Jeep peel out of the drive. Jack came back in, and was out of breath.

"I couldn't catch him, but Alex and Tyler jumped in before he peeled out."

"Good. They'll need to calm him down before he does anything rash," Paige said as she sat back down.

I poured my tea and sat on the floor next to Tucker. I turned to look at Jack.

"Thanks for bringing him tonight. He relaxes me as much as tea does," I said.

"No problem, Grey. I didn't want him to be alone. Evan said it was fine, that you enjoy Tucker's company."

We must have sat there for at least an hour. I got up to take Tucker outside for a walk and sent everyone down stairs to watch a movie. I walked Tucker around the drive before heading back inside; it was really cold out there.

"So what are we watching?" I asked and then noticed what

was on the tv

"Good choice." I sat down and Tucker followed me.

I eventually fell asleep on the sofa, and I felt a blanket being draped over me. I looked up and noticed Alex.

"Hey, how is he, Alex?" Paige asked.

"He's fine. We calmed him down, but keep an eye out, okay?"

I started to stir and I decided to get up. I couldn't sleep. I looked over at Alex and Paige who were standing by the sofa.

"Hey, Alex, is everything okay?" I asked groggily.

"He's calmed down a little, but he needs time."

"Time? Whatever. He can have time when he sleeps!" I shouted toward the stairs. I turned to see Tyler and Declan walking down.

"You go sit down. And you"—I pointed to Declan—"Come sit here now."

I was sick of this alone time, and I wanted answers.

"Calm down, Grey," he said.

"No, Declan. You can sit and keep me company. Just because someone introduces me to someone, there's no need to get bent out of shape. And wreck my driveway," I added.

"I'm sorry. I thought it was vindictive. I needed some air," he said as he grabbed my hand.

"Well, think before you act next time. You can see Gavin on Monday if you want to talk to him."

"If you were this aggressive, I'm sorry I missed you taking your frustration out on the pins," Alex said.

"Whatever." I stuck my tongue out and scowled at him. "I can show you. Tell me where your lacrosse ball is."

Declan pulled me back down and held my hands.

"Easy, Grey. Alex was joking."

Declan made me sit me down on his lap.

"Fine."

"But keep it in mind for later," he whispered in my ear. I started to relax.

"Please, Declan. You wish." I hit his arm.

"I do all the time."

Paige shook her head as she sat down next to Alex.

We watched a couple of movies and talked late into the night. I started to get tired, so I laid down against Declan. It was comfortable, natural, and it felt like the first time he'd held me. It made me feel at home. He wrapped his arms around me and continued talking with everyone. I fell asleep within minutes to the echoing of his pulse. It was a long day and night.

Why couldn't we just hang out without something happening to someone? I thought about it and I decided I wouldn't change it, because it made things interesting.

I woke up to dog breath. Tucker was panting in my face. *Oh, man. My neck and shoulder hurts, and no one is here but me and the dog.* I sat up and tried to stretch. I must have slept on my neck wrong, because there was a huge knot and I could feel it. I called for Tucker and then headed upstairs. I put my hair back while I walked to the kitchen.

"Well, there's sleeping beauty and her royal aide," Alex said.

"Whatever, Alex." I winced and grabbed my neck.

"What's wrong?"

"Someone left me downstairs and I slept on my neck wrong. Now it's killing me. I think it's knotted up pretty good."

"Sorry, I didn't know it was my job to do that."

"It's not, just wake me up next time, okay?"

I grabbed my neck again, and that time it really hurt. I picked up a washcloth, ran it under hot water, and put it on my neck, hoping it would help.

"Grey, sit down. I'll get you some tea."

Alex pulled me over to the chair.

"Thanks, Alex, but could you also make me something to eat?" I begged, making puppy-dog eyes at him.

"I'll try, but I can't promise that it'll be edible."

I rested my head on the table and tried not to move. I felt his cold yet welcoming hands on my neck as he tried to massage the knots out.

"Is this better or worse?" Declan asked.

"Both," I mumbled into my arm. "Better, because it's you. And worse, because Alex is burning something."

"Damn, Alex! That smells horrible. You're going to burn down the house."

Declan stopped and headed toward Alex.

"Sorry, Grey," Alex said. "I promised I would try."

"What's that smell?" Quinn laughed.

"Alex tried to cook," I mumbled again.

"What is wrong with her?" Paige asked.

"No one woke her up, so she slept downstairs on the sofa."

"It's my neck," I said. "Don't worry. It should get better as the day goes on."

I tried to pick my head up, but I shouted in pain. *Well, I'm not doing that again.*

"Sorry, Grey. We should have come down to get you," Paige said as she sat down next to me.

"Yeah, but your bed was so comfortable," Declan said to me.

"You slept in my bed? So where did everyone else sleep?" I tried to turn my head.

"Well, Quinn and I slept in your mom's room," Paige said. "Emery said she wasn't feeling well. She went home and Tyler and Jack slept in Alex's room."

"Declan, did you enjoy your good night's sleep?"

"I did, thank you. Now I know why you never want to get out of bed in the morning."

"Good, because it's the last time you'll be in my bed."

"Not nice. We forgot, so cut everyone some slack," Declan said. He started to rub my neck and shoulders again, but it didn't seem to be doing any good.

"I need to take a shower. I'll be right back." I grabbed his hands and moved them. "Paige, can you please help me?"

"Sure. Here we go," she said as she went to help me up.

We walked up the stairs to the bathroom. She got the shower ready while I went to close the door.

"So how did you divvy up the rooms?" I asked her.

"Well, we took Emery home, and when we got back we found Declan in your bed, asleep—and everyone else in Alex's room.

"We didn't know you were still downstairs," she said, apologizing again.

"That's fine, but I don't understand why he was in there in the first place."

I stepped into the shower and changed the shower head to massage setting.

"He wanted to be close to you, so he thought your bed would be the best choice."

"Well, it's a little weird because I was downstairs."

"He thought you might come up, but you didn't. And, well, we fell asleep."

I laughed at the thought, but then grabbed my neck again. It was getting better, but I needed skilled hands. I wished Mom or Grams had been there, but I figured the next best thing would work.

"Tell Alex I'll be right down for the touch," I said as I peeked around the curtain slowly.

"The touch?"

"He'll know what you mean."

I heard her leave as her footsteps echoed down the hall. I got out of the shower and dried off, and then hurried to my room to get dressed. My mom had been the best at healing anything. She'd taught us some things, but Alex was definitely better than me. I'd thought it was magic, and I guess I was right in some way. I mean, he could get any knot out of my leg after a run—so fast that I could get up and run again when he'd finished. I slowly made my way into the kitchen.

"Are you ready?" I said

"Yup, let's go down stairs." Alex guided me out into the hall.

I heard everyone following us, probably because they didn't know what was going on. I took off my sweater and laid it on the table. Thankfully I had remembered to put on my tank top, which would make it easier for Alex to work around my neck and shoulders. I didn't feel like giving everyone a show that morning.

"Ready, Grey? It's probably going to hurt. You're pretty tight." He started to cup his hands and placed them onto my shoulder. I felt a surge of pressure as he pressed his fingers deeper into my shoulder.

"Oh, man. That hurts. Not so deep at first, okay?"

Baby, I heard Declan say silently. I decided not to respond. Payback would come.

"Sorry. Hold still."

I heard someone walk around me and stop right in front of my face. I raised my eyes up to see Paige bending down in front of the table.

"So this is the touch?" Declan asked

You don't think I could have helped you upstairs? he again asked silently.

"Yup. She taught us everything she knew. I still think he's better at it than me," I said.

"Really?" Paige said.

"You're pretty lucky," I told her. I winced as a deep shock pulsed through my neck.

"I would say so," she responded.

"Grey, this is really bad," Alex said to me. "It's all in your shoulder. I'm going to try and find Grams."

"Okay."

I could hear him upstairs asking Evan if our grandmother—who had been missing in action for a while—was around. She

was at the store, of course, and I didn't really want to walk down
there given the state I was in. I heard the click of clasp from the
corner of the room. I knew then Alex was taking out the healing
stones. These stones go back generations in our family, or so I'm
told. The stones are infused with healing powers from multiple
generations of healers.

"Stones?" Paige looked toward Alex.

"Evan gave me these stones. They are Grams. We need to
place them on Grey's shoulder, and then down her spine. Then
we let them do their magic." He would place the stones by color
along my shoulder. Each stone has various hues of black, gray and
beige as well as druid ruins. The darker black stones are placed
first then the gray and beige stones.

"Does it hurt?" Paige asked.

"No, you get used to it." I smiled. "So where is Declan?"

"He's behind you." Paige responded

"So you've been holding out on me, huh?" Declan chimed in.

"You never asked. But if you want lessons, I can help. Or you
can ask Alex."

"Maybe I'll take you up on those lessons."

"Here we go. Are you ready?" Alex asked as he rubbed some
sort of nasty goop between his hands. He began to place the stones.

Man, that stuff stinks. I scoffed.

"Yup." Alex stated.

I flinched a little. I could feel the pulse with each stone. I think
Alex had put more of his energy into it than was needed. It was
painful, and I was starting to think it had nothing to do with my
muscles. I was thinking the pain had decided to move from my
head to my body. Something or someone was trying to get to me,
but of course I had no clue as to why. Why was I apparently so
important?

"All set. I'll be back to remove them in about twenty minutes,"
Alex told me.

"Thanks. Maybe you should work with Grams." *I guess we all have some type of healing ability,* I thought as I laughed to myself.

Alex smiled back and shook his head. I always knew what his talents were, but he would routinely brush them off. It was hard for him to help me, because it was something we'd done with Mom. Her healing touch always made everything disappear.

I thought about Declan's last comment. He didn't know much about me, nor did I know much about him. Our relationship was going so quickly that it seemed like we'd skipped the traditional getting-to-know-you period.

I must have fallen asleep, and I woke up when Alex came back.

"Wow, where did you get that scar?" Paige asked as she touched my shoulder.

I felt a quick pulse before she moved her hand. I wondered if she'd felt it as well, or if it was it just me and my freakishness.

"I was born with it—or so our mom told us."

"Us?" she said, her voice rising a little.

"Yeah, I have one on my left shoulder, and Alex's is on his right shoulder."

"He has the same mark?"

"Yup," I said. "Show her."

I heard him sigh as he began to show her. She gasped.

"Wow, you weren't kidding," she said. "It *is* exactly the same."

"Okay, Paige, enough with ogling Alex. Let's get Grey up and around, please." Declan asked.

Alex finished removing the stones. He placed his hands on my shoulder.

"How are you doing?" he asked.

"I've been better."

"You better have her better by Tuesday!" Quinn shouted down the stairs.

"Oh, I forgot." I closed my eyes. "Please do your best."

"What's Tuesday?"

"Nothing. I'll tell you later. Now, please."

I couldn't let him know, nor could I even think about it. I would have to wait until everyone left.

"Well, I'm going to be no fun today, so why don't you guys go out and do something."

"We can't leave you here alone," Declan said.

"I won't be. Evan and Grams are here. I'll watch Tucker until you get back, okay?"

"Fine. But it won't be that fun."

I pulled him down and kissed him.

"Declan, please try and enjoy yourself."

I kissed him again.

"Okay, I'm done," Alex said. He helped me up. "How does it feel?"

I moved my neck. It was okay, but when I picked up my arm, I felt a small twinge. I winced and sat back down.

"Okay, that hurt, but I'll have Grams look at it later."

Alex helped me up the stairs so I could lie down on my bed.

"Are you sure you don't want me to stay?" he asked.

"No, I'm fine. Have fun."

I pushed him to the door with my good arm.

"Bye, we'll be back soon."

"Just go." I laughed as he closed the door. I sat back down and then I heard a knock.

"Alex, please. I'm fine. Just go." I threw my pillow toward the door.

"Hey, what was that for?" Declan asked as he grabbed the pillow.

"Sorry, I thought you were Alex."

"It's okay. I came up to say bye."

He sat on the bed. I pulled him down to lay next to me.

"I thought I wouldn't be allowed in your bed again."

"Oh, be quiet." I hugged him.

"Are you sure you don't want me to stay?"

He tightened his grip and lightly touched my lips with his.

"I'm not sure, but I won't get better if you're here."

I brushed the hair from his face, cradling my hand around his cheek. I tried to ease his paranoia. I was getting good without having had lessons.

"Okay, I'll go. But I'll be back to make you dinner." He kissed my hand.

"Have fun. Let me rest, that way I can be up for that dinner."

I rolled over and tried to sleep. Eventually, I did. It was a rough night, though. I was in pain and I hoped it would subside soon.

CHAPTER NINETEEN

THINK SHAKESPEARE

When I woke up, the light was dancing off the windows, creating little rainbows along the walls. I wondered how long I'd slept. I rolled over to look at the clock and I saw a note that was attached to a rose. I picked up the rose. It was beautiful—and white, of course. I reached for the note.

I didn't want to wake you. You need your rest, so I'll be back tomorrow. Thank you for keeping my heart safe.

I love you always,

Declan

He always knew the right words to say, and that morning I needed them. I slowly got up and headed to the shower. I was still sore, but not as much as I had been the day before. I would have to remember to never sleep on that sofa again.

I finished my shower and slowly meandered back to my room to get dressed. As I passed by the stairs, I heard Evan talking to someone in his office. I didn't think much of it. I figured it was probably Alex or Grams or he was talking about something having to do with school.

I walked into an empty and quiet kitchen. That was when I noticed nobody else was home. I grabbed a bowl and the cereal. I climbed up on the counter and ate my breakfast. I heard a door close and footsteps coming toward the kitchen. I looked up from my cereal and noticed Evan in the doorway of the kitchen.

"Hey, how are you feeling this morning?" Evan asked.

"Better. It's a little sore, but I'm fine." I took a bite of cereal. "Where is everyone?"

"They're out. Did you need something?"

"No. It's just weird. When will they be home?"

Okay, I said the wrong thing. I can feel the questions coming.

"'Weird,' how?"

"Umm . . . well, I've been getting those headaches again. I think my neck was due to the sofa. I feel tired all the time. I've been lighting Grams' candle, but I don't know if it's working."

Man, that felt good to get out.

"I'm not sure, but they should be home soon."

He never actually responded to what I'd said.

"Okay, I'm going to lie down and rest up for Tuesday."

I cleaned out my cereal bowl.

"What's Tuesday?" he asked.

"Volleyball tryouts. Quinn talked me into it."

"I can see that." He hugged me. "Go rest. And good luck on Tuesday. Oh, and we need to sit down and have a conversation sometime soon."

As I walked to the stairs, Alex came through the front door.

"Hey, where were you?" I asked him.

"I was out. Don't worry about it."

"Okay. Sorry I asked."

I continued up the stairs, but changed my mind. I started to go back down to watch some TV. I walked down the hall and heard Alex talking to Evan.

"Is he okay?" Evan asked.

"He had a hairline fracture in two places, but he's fine. The doctor said it'll heal quickly."

"Are you going back there later?" Evan asked

"Yeah, I'll go and pick them up. They're coming here for dinner tonight."

"That's fine, Alex, but what are you going to tell her? She'll see it herself."

Evan sounded concerned.

"I'll go and tell her now," Alex responded.

I heard Alex walking toward the hall, so I ran downstairs and turned on the TV. I started watching some FIFA match. I heard his footsteps behind me and I turned around.

"There you are. I thought you were upstairs."

"No, I decided to watch some TV. I was getting bored."

"Can I talk to you about something?" he said. He muted the TV.

"Sure. What's on your mind?"

"We ran into some trouble last night when we were out."

"Is everyone okay?" I asked, worried. "What happened?"

I always thought the worst. I couldn't help it.

"We went to the café and then bowling. We kind of ran into Gavin outside as we were leaving."

"What happened?" I asked again.

"He tried to taunt us, but we kept walking. He yelled something at Dec. He stopped dead in his tracks. Jack grabbed him."

"Well, that sounds like Gavin." I said.

I felt a strange surge of rage. *That's weird.*

"There's more." He paused and then continued. "Gavin thought it would have been better if you hadn't moved back to town. Tyler ran toward him and then Jack grabbed him, but Jack forgot that he'd had to let go of Declan."

"So you stopped him, right?"

"No, they got into it, and when we pulled them apart, it was bad. Declan had a busted hand, and it was covered in Gavin's blood. Gavin had some pretty nasty cuts on his head and his face. They both had to be taken to the hospital."

I sat there, fuming. I could feel the breaking point coming. The rage felt forced—it wasn't like me at all. Something was happening and I couldn't control it. During the whole conversation I had fought to keep control of what little patience was left.

"He's fine. I need to go pick them up at the hospital. Listen, there's more I think you need to know."

What else could go wrong? I didn't want to know.

"Evan probably wanted to tell you himself, but I'm beating him to it."

"Just spit it out, Alex." He was always so long winded.

"Our family is very important and is very prominent in this community. It has something to do with the council, but I really can't get into it right now."

Then why tell me? I thought.

"Because there are things that have been in place since we were born. These things are now being challenged. The balance can't be altered. Do you understand?"

"No, not really. Does this have anything to do with Gavin and Declan?"

"More like the Harrington, Watt, and Parker families. Listen, it's complicated to explain, and I need to get back to the hospital."

He started up the stairs.

"Can I come with you so I can kill him myself?" I asked.

"I don't think that's a good idea."

"I don't care what you think. I'm coming."

I grabbed my shoes and opened the door easily, without a thought.

"Whoa, remind me to never get on your bad side."

He turned onto the main road and drove to the hospital as I

mumbled to myself out the window. Alex didn't talk because he thought I would unleash my frustration on him. It was something more, though, and I couldn't quit put my finger on it.

Alex and I walked down the hall together at the hospital until we eventually saw both Declan and Gavin sitting in the waiting room. Declan was smiling when he saw me, but his smile eventually faded when I got closer and he saw my expression. I could hear Alex behind me, telling them to run, but no one moved. It was too late.

"What are you thinking? Seriously, tell me. I want to know." I didn't give him a chance to answer. "You can't go around fighting people who say stupid things about me just because they want to get a rise out of you." I took a deep breath and waited for an answer. I saw Gavin smile. "Oh, I'd wipe that smile off your face, because you're next." Suddenly I felt a pulse of rage when I looked at Gavin. Was he doing this? Was this his ability?

"I'm sorry, Grey. It was stupid. I'm sorry. I wasn't thinking, and you have every right to be upset."

"Whatever. 'Upset' doesn't even come close to what I'm feeling right now." I was still ticked off as I turned to Gavin.
"You need to control your mouth and keep your thoughts to yourself. So you never got me—deal with it! I'm sure your girlfriend is pretty upset about this." *And whatever this stupid family feud is about, it needs to stop. I don't want to be involved.*

"Actually, I'm not," I heard someone say behind me. I turned to see Emma as she walked over and helped Gavin up.

"Don't you have anything better to do than stick your nose in other people's affairs? I hope you're done." Emma chimed in.

"Actually, this was about me. And I'll do whatever I want," I said. I was reaching my threshold.

"Are you done with your tirade?" Gavin snapped.

I had reached the breaking point. His comment had put me over the edge.

"No. One more thing," I said.

I punched him in the face, which sent him falling back into the chair. Alex threw me over his shoulder and proceeded to run.

"I'm done now!" I yelled down the hall.

"What the hell were you thinking?" Alex asked.

I didn't answer. When we got to the Jeep, I climbed into the back seat. My hand was killing me, but punching him had felt good. We still had to wait for Paige and Declan to come out.

"Seriously, you talk about Dec controlling his emotions. You should take your own advice." Alex was clearly upset. "I guess your shoulder is fine now. You better hope the council doesn't find out about this. How's your hand?"

"It's fine, Alex."

Paige and Declan finally came out. They got in the Jeep and we headed back home.

"Alex, I think it's best if we drop Paige and Declan off first," I said as I continued to look out the window.

Paige concurred.

"That's a good idea." *Girl, what were you thinking?* she asked silently. *I don't know what 'feud' you were talking about back there, but that punch was the last thing I expected out of you.*

She reached for my hand. I turned to let her know that I was fine. I turned back around so I could continue to stare out the window.

"I'll see you tomorrow in biology," I said.

"Grey, I'm sorry, again. I don't know what else to say," Declan said to me.

He reached for me, but I stopped him. I grabbed his hand.

"Don't say anything, please. Go get some sleep. I'll see you in English tomorrow."

I kissed his hand.

When we arrived home, I headed straight for the kitchen. I was hungry, and I was zapped of any energy I'd had earlier. I had started to make myself a sandwich when Evan walked in. He looked at Alex and then at me.

"What's with her?" he asked Alex.

"She's on a rampage."

"Oh, what happened?"

"We went to get Dec and Paige at the hospital."

"Where are they?"

"At home!" I yelled from the fridge.

Evan turned back to Alex, waiting for an answer.

"She yelled at Dec, Gavin, and Emma. Then she punched Gavin. I think she broke his nose. I had to drag her out."

"Grey!" Evan exclaimed.

"He had it coming, Evan. And so did his girlfriend. They're lucky Alex grabbed me when he did. This stupid thing between the families has to stop now."

He didn't look too happy that Alex had told me.

I hopped up on the counter and ate my sandwich. We sat in silence for a couple of minutes while Evan paced.

"Here's what is going to happen. Grey, I think you need a break. You can hang out with the girls, but Declan is off limits for a week." He turned to Alex. "And you can hang out with your friends, but no one can come to the house unless one of you isn't home. Agreed?"

"That's fair," I agreed. They both looked at me in shock. Reluctantly, Alex nodded in agreement as well.

"Everything is settled. Well, that was easier than I thought. I don't know why your mom always made it out to be so hard." He walked to the fridge. "Oh, Alex. I need to speak with you later in my office," Evan said. He then looked at me. "So are you ready for Tuesday?"

"Yup. All ready to go."

"What's Tuesday?" Alex asked.

"Nothing that concerns you, Alex, so butt out," I said as I hopped off the counter.

I went to my room. I needed to finish my math homework and catch up on my reading for English. The problem was that I needed help with my homework—and someone to talk to, so I went back downstairs to talk to Evan. Alex was on his way out, looking like he wasn't too happy.

"Evan, I need a favor," I said to him.

"What, Grey?"

"I need help with my math homework. Can I call my tutor and have him come over?"

"That's fine. Go call him."

"Thanks, Evan."

I ran to the phone and called Jack.

Alex was in his room when Jack came over. We used Evan's office to do my homework.

"So, just to let you know, Alex and I are both off-limits to each other's friends for a week—except for you, because you're my tutor."

"Really? That stinks for everyone else." He smiled.

"I think it might be good for some of us. Besides, I'll be busy anyway."

"Oh, right. Tuesday. Quinn told me. I'm sure you'll make the team—I've seen your spike. You may be short, but that one move you two do is incredible."

"Thanks. We needed something to distract everyone, but other than that one move, I'm not too good on my feet." I laughed. "Now back to trigonometry."

Jack left, and my homework was complete. I hadn't gotten a chance to talk to him about the feud. Yet another eventful day at the Corwen household.

I finished my tea, brushed my teeth, and jumped into my cozy bed. Monday would most likely be interesting—if Jack hadn't already called everyone and told them about the punishment Alex and I were going to have to endure. I heard the phone ring. It was for Alex. I only needed one guess as to who it was. I rolled over and tried to fall asleep.

The ride to school was quiet. Alex was still mad at me, and at times I couldn't blame him. I got out of the car and took my usual walk with Emery to the main building. We parted ways in the hall and I told her I would talk about what had happened in biology.

The day was flying by, and lunch was already right around the corner. I walked to the cafeteria and sat down. There was a note for me on the table. It was from Declan. It was short; all he'd written was "I'm sorry." I got up and threw the note away.

"So are you ready for tomorrow, Grey?" Quinn asked excitedly.

"Yup. All ready. Do you guys want to come and watch?" I asked Paige and Emery.

"Sorry, but I have to work after school. When you make the team, I'll come to the matches." Emery apologized

"I can, but I need a ride home." Paige stated.

"I'll drive you. I'm taking my mom's car tomorrow." I replied.

"Good deal." Paige responded.

We finished lunch and I trotted off to history. I had my tutoring session with Jack later that day, and before I knew it, it was time for gym.

As I walked into the gym with Quinn, Coach Nelson saw us and waved me over.

"Grey, Coach Greer wants to see you now."

"Okay. Bye, Quinn," I said.

"Good luck, Grey."

I ran up to the offices and waited for Coach Greer. He was a tall, lanky man with no hair. He shaved it because most of his hair had already gone. He'd once said that having no hair made people take him seriously. I thought he looked like Mr. Clean—without the muscles.

"Hey, Grey. Come on in." He opened the door for me. "Have a seat."

"So I hear you're trying out tomorrow. I don't think you'll have any problems. Coach Nelson told me about some crazy move you and Ms. Ellis invented."

"Thank you?" I was unsure how to answer.

"Well, I want to see it tomorrow at tryouts, okay?" He stood up. "I'll see you tomorrow. Good luck—but I don't think you'll need it."

"Thank you."

I headed toward the student lot. This had to be one of the more bizarre days I'd had in a while.

Dinner was quiet, just like the car ride to school and back.

"So, Evan, I need to use Mom's car tomorrow so Alex doesn't have to wait for me after school."

"That's fine, Grey. Just be careful."

I had finished my dinner and was putting my dish in the sink when I heard the doorbell. I headed to the front door. Thankfully it was Paige. I didn't know if I could deal with anyone else at that moment. I walked out to the porch.

"Sorry, you can't come in. Alex is home. It's one of the things we agreed to."

"That's okay. I came to see you anyway."

We sat down on the steps and she started the conversation.

"So, I would first like to say, that was crazy how you flipped out on Emma and Gavin."

"No problem. They had it coming. There's a 'but' coming right?"

"But your deal is killing Declan. I also heard my dad talking to Evan—concerning the council."

"He needs to learn to deal with it. It's only a week, Paige."

I don't want to know about the council either.

"I know, but that's not the problem here. It's your lack of forgiveness."

"What? Because I won't accept his apology? Please."

I was getting upset.

"I think it's stupid, too," she said. "He needs to deal, but he's all over me lately. He's driving me crazy."

"Fine. Hold on a minute."

I ran inside to grab a pen and paper from Evan's office. I wrote a note, forgiving Declan, and handed it to Paige.

"Here. This should help for now," I said. "I'll see you tomorrow."

"Thanks. Oh, can I get a ride with you tomorrow? I'll walk to your house."

"That's fine, but be here early."

"Thanks. See you tomorrow."

As she waved, I saw Alex in the window. *Pathetic.*

I dragged myself up to my room and tried to go to sleep. It was a bad night. I dreamt of my father, or at least it felt like a dream. I hadn't dreamt about him in almost two years.

I heard a knock at the door and I rolled over to look at the clock. I was late, and the knock was probably Paige.

"Come in!" I yelled from the closet.

"Hey, Grey. Running late today?" she asked.

"Yeah, sorry. Let me grab my clothes for today."

I grabbed my bag and backpack and then we jumped in the car to head to school.

"Sorry I was late. I had a rough night."

"No problem. I'm only missing gym, which is fine with me."

"Well, okay. Then let's at least make it to art today."

We made it to art right before the bell, and the rest of the day ended up flying by because we'd missed half of it.

"So are you ready for this afternoon?" Quinn whispered.

"As ready as I'll ever be."

"You remember the move, right?"

"I do, but don't worry. Let's worry about gym right now."

Alex was still upset, but a little curious about the secret Quinn and I were keeping. I noticed him talking to Declan and Jack. Jack knew what I was doing, but he'd said nothing as far as I knew.

Quinn and I rushed to change for tryouts. We got back into the gym just in time. I quickly scanned the stands to make sure the boys weren't there.

"Okay, girls, let's get started." Coach Greer blew his whistle. "We're going to do some drills so I can assess your skills. Let's split up into two teams. Quinn and Grey, I want you on the same team. I want to see that move."

We ran through a couple of drills until Coach Greer wanted to see the move. I had Julia, one my teammates on the front line, set us up. Quinn dropped one knee and I stepped up and twisted to my left side for the fake. I spiked the ball toward the back corner on the opposite side of the court—for the kill.

"Nice move. I'm very impressed. Okay, girls, let's finish this tryout so we can get the team together for Thursday's practice."

"Nice move," Julia said to me.

"Thanks. It doesn't work without a good set up. I gotta make up for my height somehow."

We laughed as I set back up for drills. The rest of the tryouts were brutal. I tripped over my feet every now and then, but I made it through.

I got changed and went to meet Paige outside the gym doors. We talked about the tryouts all the way back to her house.

"Good luck. You should make it, though. See you tomorrow," she said.

She ran up to the porch and I pulled out.

I was pulling into my drive when I saw Declan's Jeep and Tyler's car. *Great. Now I would have to go somewhere else.* Evan heard me; he peeked out the window and waved me in. I parked the car and ran into his office.

"Hey, thanks." I tried to catch my breath.

"How were tryouts today?"

"I think they went well, but I'll see tomorrow."

"We need to talk about what happened."

"There isn't really anything to tell except that I felt an overwhelming sense of rage—especially when I looked at Gavin."

"Mr. Watt made sure the council wasn't informed, but you really need to watch yourself."

"Why is it so important? I mean, it's not my seat to win back."

"Actually, it is yours, now that the council has gotten an update on your newfound skills."

Great. Now I wish I didn't move back. This is too much pressure.

"You can go out there. You're probably hungry. I can bend this one rule."

I figured he was done, but he wasn't finished.

"Fine. But you come with me so Alex doesn't freak."

We walked into the kitchen. The guys were playing cards at the table.

"Hey, guys. How's it going?" I said, trying to sound casual.

"Fine. Just playing cards. And you?" Alex said shortly.

Yup, he was still mad at me.

"I'm getting something to eat. Do you guys want me to make you something?"

"No, we ordered pizza," Alex responded.

I heard the doorbell and Alex got up to answer it. I took advantage of the opportunity to see Declan.

"Hey," I said.

I put my arms around his neck.

"Hey, yourself."

He kissed my hand.

"Did you get my note?" I rested my chin on his shoulder.

"Yes, thank you. It helped a little."

"Okay, I'm glad. I'll see you later."

I kissed his neck and went back to making my dinner. When I was finished, I hopped up on the counter and ate my sandwich as I hung out with Evan.

"How did things go today? I heard you were late." he said.

"Sorry, I woke up late. Paige came to get me. It won't happen again."

"Good, because I got this email."

He held up a piece of paper.

"What is it?" I reached for it. "No way! Are you kidding me?"

I hopped off the counter and hugged him.

"You can't be late again okay?"

"I won't! Can I call Quinn?"

He nodded and I screamed at the news.

I was yelling into the phone at Quinn as she continued to excitedly scream back.

"What's that all about?" Alex asked.

"The tryouts," I said.

"What tryouts?" Alex looked at Tyler and then at Declan.

"You mean to tell me you guys didn't know?" Evan laughed.

"No, Grey and I haven't been talking a lot lately." Alex said.

"Here. This is why she kept it a secret. She didn't want anyone to know until she made the team." Evan handed the team roster to Alex. I wasn't on the starting lineup, but I was still on the team. I stood in the doorway of the kitchen after hanging up with Quinn.

I heard Evan silently communicate with Alex. *Alex, I asked her to be a normal teenager. You should understand. Once you start your training, there isn't much left.*

"I think you need to apologize to her," Evan finished.

"I'll be damned," Alex said, nodding, as he handed the paper to Declan.

"Well, Alex, now we're going to cheer her on."

Declan handed the paper back to Evan and Alex walked over to me.

"I'm sorry. I've been a jerk," he said.

I couldn't help but smile back. I hugged him.

"You're forgiven, but don't let it happen again."

He nodded and sat back down at the table.

"I guess we're going to your matches now, if you don't mind."

"Wait until you see this move she and Quinn have," Tyler added. "It's amazing."

"What move?" asked Declan.

"You'll have to come to the matches to find out for yourself."

"Oh, I'll be there. Don't you worry about that."

I finished my sandwich, kissed Evan good night, and headed to my room to finish my homework.

I heard someone call my name. I noticed my father sitting at my desk. I must have fallen asleep, because he sat there, not saying a word. He was smiling like he'd done whenever he was proud of me. I lay back down, closed my eyes, and fell back to sleep.

We had our first team meeting after school and that was when we received our uniforms. Luckily, I had gotten my number, eleven, and Quinn had gotten the number seven. Our first match was a scrimmage that following Saturday, so we had practice the rest of the week and Saturday morning. I definitely needed to get more sleep if I was going to be at practice for hours after school.

I decided to take my mom's car so Alex wouldn't have to wait. I only thought that was fair.

The next couple of days were a blur. I was dead-tired, and pretty much all I did was eat, sleep and go to practice. I now knew how Alex felt during his seasons.

I woke up early that day because I had to go get Quinn.

"Alex, I'm taking the Jeep today."

"That's fine. I'll have Dec pick me up." Alex sipped his juice. "Good luck today, Grey."

"Thanks, but I got number eleven, so I don't need it. See you later."

He laughed as I walked out.

Practice was light that morning because of the scrimmage that was happening later in the day. We had time to go eat something and then we would come back for the game. Quinn and I decided to go to the café for a quick lunch.

"Hey, Grey, is that Declan over there?" Quinn said as she pointed out the window.

"Yeah, what's he doing down here?"

I kept watching. A car pulled up and someone got out of the passenger's side. I couldn't make out who it was, but that someone was definitely female.

"Who is that, Quinn?"

"I don't know. I've never seen her before."

We walked out to the Jeep slowly, and he caught my eye as I got in. His expression was unreadable at the distance from which I stood. I put the gear in reverse, then started to back up slowly. That was when I saw him hug her before she returned to the car. I almost hit the car as I was backing out after it had taken off so fast. I hadn't been paying attention. I stopped for a minute, looking back. I then backed out quickly and gunned it toward the school.

"Damn, you almost hit him, Grey."

"Sorry, I lost track of time. We're going to be late."

"Oh, then floor it." She put her seat belt on. "Who was that woman? Do you know her?"

"No, but I'm sure there's a reasonable explanation."

"When did you become so calm?"

"When I had to say the same thing to Declan. Remember when Cam was my tutor? Also, since I've moved back, I've realized that stranger things have happened."

"Good point. We've got five minutes, so let's get ready."

We ran to the gym and got dressed, and we made it in time for warm-ups. I pulled my hair back and put my band over my head to keep the rest of the hair out of my face. I looked up and saw Allie, Evan, and Paige. But where was Alex, Tyler, Jack, and Emery? I knew where Declan was, but I didn't know about the others. I walked with Quinn to the bench.

"Where's your brother?" I asked.

"He's going up the stands with Emery, Jack, and Alex," Paige responded.

She pointed toward the stands. I looked up and saw Declan sitting with everyone. *That's weird, but whatever.*

We huddled up for Coach Greer's pep talk, then headed to the court. I was serving first. The game progressed quickly, and the other team was good. It was tied at that point, with each team having won two games. I'd played in the first set, but my fancy foot work had left me out of the second set. We were behind by two points when Coach Greer called for a time-out.

We broke afterward, and Coach sent me in as a substitute. I had Julia setup behind us for the move. It might have worked, but we had to use the move sparingly, or teams would eventually practice the block against it.

We lost three sets to two, but got a good idea of how to fix our errors for the next match that was on Wednesday. Quinn and I came out of the locker room to see everyone waiting.

"Hey, that was the best move I've ever seen!" Alex said as he picked me up then hugged me.

"Thanks, but can you put me down, please?" I asked him as I tried to squirm out of his grip.

"No, we're going out to eat at the café tonight. Evan's treat."

Alex carried me as we walked toward the Jeep and everyone followed. I didn't see Declan again. Alex put me down so I could unlock the door. He jumped in the backseat and Quinn sat in the front. As I got in, I noticed a white rose on my seat.

"He'll meet us there," Alex said. "He had to do something first."

"That's fine. Let's go."

I started heading toward town. I was calm for once, because I was sure what I'd seen earlier had been nothing—and I had no reason to think otherwise.

We got to the café and walked in to meet everyone. Declan didn't show up until after we'd ordered. As he sat down next to Alex and Evan, I tried not to draw any conclusions. When I got up to use the restroom with Quinn and Paige, I first stopped and kissed him on the cheek. He caught my hand and pulled me back.

"We need to talk now."

"Okay, I'll be right back. You can meet me out front."

I walked to the bathroom, not worried, because if something was about to happen then I would have already known. I walked out front to talk to him.

"So what's so important that you couldn't talk to me inside?" I sat down. "Wait, first, I want to say, I'm sorry for almost hitting you. We were going to be late."

"That's okay. I thought you were mad," he said, holding my hand.

"Why would I be mad at you? What you do in your free time is none of my business."

"No, they were friends of my father. They came to visit, and Lily had to give me something I forgot when we left over the break."

"That's fine." I was calm, because I knew it was nothing. "So you couldn't tell me this inside?""

"No, it's kind of personal."

He pulled out a small pouch and handed it to me.

"What's this?"

"I got this for you when I was on vacation."

"Something else? You already gave me the ring."

"No, I found this and had it blessed for you," he said. "Open it, please."

I opened the pouch and took out a clear, flat case. There were three shamrocks displayed inside the glass case

"Thanks. It's very nice."

"It's good luck, because it has three of them," he pointed out. "The number three is considered good luck in Celtic lore. You're my lucky charm, so I thought you should have one. Oh, and it's green."

We walked back inside and finished dinner. As we finished eating, Evan got up to speak.

"Who wants dessert?" he asked us.

"I don't know." I said as I sat back in my chair.

"I bought ice cream to make sundaes at the house."

"Let's go." Alex stood up.

"I can't wait to see what happens when we win," I said to Quinn.

"Me too." She laughed.

We all headed back to the house to finish celebrating our team's loss.

CHAPTER TWENTY

LOVE AND LONDON

I had two weeks to plan for Quinn's birthday. February 15 was coming up quickly. Paige and I finished making the reservations for dinner and Paige turned to me.

"So do you know what Alex is doing for me for Valentine's Day?" she asked.

"I don't know. He doesn't come to me about that type of stuff. You should go ask Allie."

"Allie?"

"Yup, she's better at romance than I am. I swear, she should go into business as a love counselor or something."

"You would have thought you'd picked up some things from my brother by now."

"I haven't. And, well, Alex hasn't messed up yet, right?"

"No." She laughed. "Allie's good." Paige said.

"So where do we take her after dinner?" I said, getting back to the subject.

"You don't want to know about your night?" Paige asked me.

"No. I'm sure it will involve white roses, dinner, and . . . I don't know. That's one thing your brother doesn't need help with—the romance department."

"You crack me up. He may have a surprise or two for you,"

she said.

I didn't really want to think about it, because I didn't have much to give him in return. I needed to focus on Quinn's birthday, and leave the other stuff to him. And I had enough to worry about with having to keep up appearances for the council.

"I'm sure he does. Now where are we going after dinner?" Paige wondered.

"I was thinking we could take her to this club down the street from the restaurant. She loves dancing." I responded.

"Good idea. I'll call and get us a table." I wrote down our plans.

"You're good at this." Paige stated, looking at my notes.

"My mom used to work with an events coordinator." I said.

"Your mom sure did have a lot of careers," Paige said.

"I told you she was a free spirit." I replied.

We both laughed.

"Great. Maybe you should do this as a job." Paige said.

"Maybe I will. You'll have to wait and see." I stated.

"So we're all set. I'll meet you on Saturday around two o'clock in the afternoon. It takes an hour to get there." Paige said and then stood to leave.

"Okay, have fun on Friday." I said.

"I will, and you do the same." Paige said.

I grabbed the phone in the hall to call the club as Paige slipped out the front door. I got us a back table in the VIP section and sorted out anything else we needed. As I hung up the phone, I heard Alex come up behind me. I didn't even know he was home

"So, going dancing?" he asked.

"Yeah, for Quinn's birthday on Saturday." I answered.

"Oh, okay. Sounds fun." Alex stated.

I knew what he was *actually* thinking. I could see in his eyes and it was written all over his face.

"Don't even think about it. Don't bother us. This is for Quinn—not you guys."

"Whatever," he said as he started up the stairs.

"I'm serious, Alex. Don't wreck this. It took a long time to plan."

"Fine."

I wasn't convinced, but I needed to focus on my test tomorrow: the dreaded pop quiz that happened every Thursday in math class. Unfortunately, the only part of my day that didn't fly by was when I was in that class. It seemed like I was in the twilight zone, or an alternative dimension where time drained slowly. At least I could look forward to practice today. We were preparing for our first match of the season that Wednesday before the break.

When I walked in the door, I thought I was at a florist shop. As soon as I turned around, I couldn't hold back from sneezing. It was ridiculous. These plants needed to go somewhere else. I yelled for Evan.

"What's up with this, Evan?!" I yelled.

"Ask Allie. They're all hers!" he yelled back.

"Allie!" I yelled up the stairs.

If I took another step into the abundance of arrangements, my allergies would go into overdrive.

"Yeah?!" she yelled over the railing.

"Where did these flowers come from?"

"A couple of people! But the pink roses are the only ones that count in my eyes."

"The what?!" I yelled back. "Allie, come down here! I'm not yelling anymore."

She came down the stairs to the hall.

"These flowers are the only ones that count," she said, pointing to the pink roses.

"Oh, then do something about the rest of them, because my allergies are going haywire."

"I will later," she said, and ran back upstairs.

I followed her upstairs and went in my room. I opened the doors to the balcony so I could breathe in the fresh air. I'd down to do my homework and to work on the plans for Saturday when the doorbell rang. I peeked over the railing in the hall and yelled downstairs as Evan was answering the door.

"If those are more flowers, we don't want them." Evan laughed. "It's just Paige—without flowers."

"Oh! Send her up before she dies at the hands of those things."

Paige came running up the stairs as I walked back into my room.

"So when did your house become a florist shop?"

"When Valentine's Day came around, because Allie can't say no to free gifts."

"That's funny."

"Yeah, when you're not allergic to them it is, but not today."

"How was practice?" she asked.

"He's not here." I responded.

"I didn't ask that."

"I know, but you would have eventually. So what's up?"

"I came here to give you this," she said as she handed me a note.

"Thanks. Your brother's plans, I assume?"

I opened the envelope.

"You guessed it."

I unfolded the note and started to read what I saw was my invitation.

Grey,

Please be ready at four o'clock in the morning and have a small bag packed with your passport and that silver dress. It's all worked out with Evan and your coach. We'll be back in time for Quinn's dinner, so don't panic.

Love,
Declan

"Do you know about this, Paige?"

"Yup, so you better get packed and set your alarm, because he's serious."

"Fine. What do I need?"

"Just the dress and a change of clothes. That's it. You pack while I figure out this alarm clock. So do you mind if I ask you something?"

"Yeah, what's on your mind?"

"You, actually," she said as she sat on the edge of my bed. "I think it's time we have a conversation about your family."

What is it with this town and my family?

"Okay." I said. "What do you want to know?"

"Well, I know you have telekinesis, and you also have some major healing powers like your grandmother does. But I was wondering if there are any other abilities of yours you might want to fill me in on."

I didn't see that question coming. She'd caught me off guard. I really wasn't ready to tell everyone my secrets.

"No, I think you covered it."

She didn't seem like she believed me, but didn't push the issue.

This was crazy. I went back to figuring out what Declan had planned. Why did I need a passport. Paige helped me get my clothes packed and then headed home. I had to get some sleep if I was supposed to be up and ready that early.

It felt like I had just fallen asleep when my alarm went off. I almost turned it off, but I remember the reason I had such an early wakeup call. I grabbed my bag and headed downstairs. Of course,

Evan was up and caught me in the hall.

"Have a good time, Grey."

"Okay, I'll try. But I don't know what it is we're doing."

"You will, and you'll love it." He hugged me. "Your car's here."

I opened the front door and some guy was standing there on my front porch ready to take my bag. I climbed into the back and saw Declan sitting there, smiling. Even at four o'clock in the morning he looked good. Every time I saw him my heart beat faster and I couldn't help but smile.

"Happy Valentine's Day," he said, handing me a white rose.

"Thank you, but did you have to pick four in the morning as our meeting time?"

"It'll give us plenty of time for my plans and for you to return for yours."

He leaned in to kiss me. I could always feel his emotions when he kissed me. Lately he had been gentle, but this morning there was more heat behind his actions, or maybe it was because of the holiday. But I didn't care. Any chance to touch him was more than I could have ever wanted.

"Do you have your passport?" he asked me.

"Yup, right here."

I held it up. It was a couple of years old, but it was still valid.

We arrived at the airport. I figured we were going to Canada because where else would go for a short weekend trip but I wasn't sure. That was the only thing I could think of that would require a plan and a passport.

"A private plane?" I asked as I stepped out of the rental car onto the tarmac.

"Just for you. My mom pulled some strings."

"Nice."

I could tell she was trying to make it up to him, but it was more than I'd expected.

"Thank you," I said.

"You are very welcome."

He buckled me into the plane first and then situated himself. He leaned in to kiss me a couple of times, holding my hand the entire flight. I could feel how nervous he was just from holding his hands. I hated feeling emotions sometimes. I wanted to be surprised, not knowing before it happened. He always had to be doing something to keep his mind occupied. I found it cute in a way, but the more nervous or anxious he was, the more apparent it became. The whole time he was tracing my hand with his fingers and playing with my rings. It was a long flight, so I'd figure out we weren't going to Canada. I managed to fall asleep half way there—to wherever we were going.

When he woke me up, he was dressed in a very sharp black suit.

"I need you to get dressed," he said. "We're here."

I got up and headed to the bathroom to change and fix my hair. Thankfully, Paige had packed my toothbrush. I came out with my bag and saw that Declan was gone.

"You can leave your bag there, Miss Parker," the pilot said. "You're taking this plane back tonight."

Wherever "here" was, we wouldn't be staying any longer than a day. Interesting.

I walked off the plane and saw Declan waiting by a car, another rose in his hand.

"You look amazing." He embraced me. "Get in the car before I change my mind, please."

He handed me the rose and told the driver we were ready. I disliked surprises, but it seemed like he'd put a lot of thought into the day, so I sucked it up and put a smile on my face.

"Where are we going and where are we?" I asked.

"We're going to dinner. And we're in London."

"England?" I was shocked. That's a seven hour flight. I'd been a sleep for longer than I thought.

"That's where London is, right?" He smirked.

"This is too much, Declan. I would have been fine with dinner and a movie at home."

I grabbed his hand.

"And where would the fun be in that? Besides, you know how much I like spoiling you."

"Yes, but this is too much."

"Only the best for you." He kissed me.

The car pulled up to a small restaurant and Declan helped me out. We walked inside toward the hostess.

"Watt," Declan told her.

She took us to the smaller side of the restaurant. I sat down and saw there was another white rose on the table. I shook my head and smiled.

"Never too much. You remember that," he said, reaching for my hand.

"We could have had dinner in Erving, Declan."

"This is just dinner. Your surprise is *after* dinner."

"There's more?"

"Yup, now order before we end up being late."

We ordered quickly and ate, enjoying the quaint restaurant. The table was lit with two candles and someone was playing a piano in the other room near the bar. I tried to take it all in, but it was too much for my mind to comprehend at that moment. It was like I was dreaming and I didn't want to wake up.

"Declan, this is too much."

"Grey, listen. I fly so much that this trip was pretty much free. Don't worry so much. I only want the best for you."

"I don't really have anything to give you."

"You are the only thing I need. My gift is your happiness."

We finished, then left the restaurant, and got back in the car.

"I need you to close your eyes, please," he said.

"What?" I was nervous.

"Just close your eyes."

I closed my eyes, not knowing where we were going yet again. I supposed I wouldn't have known anyway since I had never been to England. We drove for a couple of minutes and then I felt the car come to a stop. I heard the door open. I felt a cool breeze and then Declan's hand pulling mine. I could hear water in the distance.

"Keep them closed."

"Declan, I can't see where I'm walking."

"That's what I'm here for." He helped me out of the car. He guided me up what sounded like stone steps, then I heard a door open.

"Can I open my eyes now?" I pleaded.

"No, not yet." He laughed.

I felt him guiding me down a ramp and then what seemed like an aisle. I could tell when my hand slowly worked its way along the tops of each chair.

"Now sit down, please, and open your eyes."

I did the opposite, of course, and I opened my eyes and sat down. We were in a theatre, and were standing a little off-center in what looked like the tenth row. The theatre was older but still beautiful.

"These are great seats. What are we seeing?"

"Thank you. They weren't the seats I wanted, but what I could get. These seats belong to someone you saw me talking to last month."

"Oh, Lily, right?"

"Yes, these are her and her husband's seats. When I found out this play was running, I had to take you."

"We could have seen a play back home."

"Not this one. I've never seen it in the United States—a professional production of it, that is. I've seen it twice here in London; only these actors could pull it off," he said, and kissed my hand. I was taken back by his comment. Does he jet set often?

Is this who Declan really is, a guy who thinks he walks on water because of his family name? *I hope he isn't.*

The lights flickered and everyone took their seats. As soon as the curtain was raised, I started to tear up. He had taken me all the way to London to see *As You Like It*, one of my favorite of all of Shakespeare's plays. He wiped the tears from my face. I leaned in and whispered in his ear.

"Thank you. This is the best surprise ever, even though you know I don't like surprises. I love you," I said before I kissed his cheek.

"You're welcome."

We watched the entire play and still had time enough to go on a little tour before we had to head back. We walked down the street toward Waterloo Rail Station and then over to the aquarium after we'd stopped to see the London Eye. He had someone take our picture in front of it. I could see the Houses of Parliament across the river. It was all too much to absorb, and it still felt like a dream. We walked back to the car and headed to the airport.

"This was wonderful. Thank you, again," I said, resting my head on his shoulder.

"Anytime, Grey. Anytime."

He kissed my forehead and wrapped his arms around me. We boarded the plane and the pilot let us know we would be heading out in twenty minutes.

"Grey, why don't you change? You'll be more comfortable."

"Is that for your benefit or mine?"

"Whatever you want. It's your night."

I grabbed my bag and walked to the back. Paige had packed my tank top, jeans, and one of his jerseys.

Smart girl. I'll have to thank her.

I put them down and sat in the back until we were airborne so I could then move around to change. We finally took off, and about twenty minutes later, the captain turned off the seatbelt sign. I got up and put his jersey on and left my jeans on the seat. I walked up the aisle, but as I got close, I stopped.

"Can you close your eyes, please?" I asked him.

"For what? Just come and sit with me," he said as he started to turn around.

"No. Please trust me. Close your eyes," I said, using his words against him.

"Okay, they're closed."

I double checked to make sure and then started walking toward him. I sat on his lap and I began to kiss his neck. He moved his hands down my back and then abruptly pulled me back.

"Grey, why aren't you wearing any pants?" he said, looking down.

"I'm more comfortable this way."

"And why are you wearing my jersey?" He swallowed loudly.

"Sorry, here you go."

I took it off and handed it to him. I sat there in only my cami and my shorts.

"Grey, can you please put your clothes back on?" He sighed.

I could hear his heart racing, and I knew it was working.

"Okay, fine, if you want it that way."

I got up and walked back to the bathroom. I had practically thrown myself at him and he'd turned me down. Gentleman or not, what the heck?

I felt his arms around my waist.

"It's not for lack of trying. It's just not the right time. Trust me, you've tempted me since dinner, but I tried to control myself. And right now, it's starting to wane."

"I would say sorry, but I'm not, so I'll say thank you instead."

I turned and kissed him.

"Grey, here, you can have this back."

He handed me the jersey. I put it back on, along with my jeans. I grabbed my sneakers from my bag and went to sit in my seat while he changed. I buckled myself in and leaned back. I fell asleep about two hours into the flight. He woke me up when we landed. I was still out of it, so he helped down and into the car.

We got back to the house and he carried me up to my room.

"Sweet dreams, and thank you. I love you." He kissed me and left.

I rolled over and grabbed my blanket. My father didn't come to me, nor did I dream. I was too tired to dream.

I woke up and rolled over to look at the clock. It was eleven o'clock in the morning. I had to be ready in three hours for Quinn's dinner. I started to freak out as I ran to the shower because I didn't have enough time to get everything together. I leaned against the shower wall for a few minutes, letting the water settle my nerves. Yesterday felt like it had been a flash or a dream. *Did I really just go to London with Declan?*

Thanks to Allie, I had a new outfit for the night. I pulled it from the garment bag, and there, on the hanger, was a silver halter top and black leather pants.

Oh, come on, Allie. What the heck are you thinking?

I put the top on and then looked in the bag to find black boots. *What? Am I a biker tonight?* I finished drying my hair and headed to the hallway.

"Allie."

"Wow! That looks great. When I saw it I thought it would look great, but I've outdone myself this time," she said giddily.

"Are you kidding me with this?" I said.

"Grey, it's fine. For what you're doing tonight, you'll fit right in." She spun me around. "Wait, where's the coat?"

"There's a coat, too?"

I'm going to regret this. She ran to my room and back into the hall.

"Here we go," she said.

She handed me a black, hip-length, leather coat. *Well, at least I could wear the jacket again. It was respectable.*

"I look like a biker in this, Allie."

"Please get with the fashion times," she said as she pushed me down the stairs.

I put my coat over the railing and headed to the kitchen to wait for Paige. As I grabbed a glass of water, I heard the doorbell ring. I walked toward the door as Alex was coming down the stairs and Evan making his way from the office. They'd always had perfect timing and it always freaked me out—until I found out how they did it.

"Whoa! You look amazing," Paige said as she pulled me further in to the hall to look at my outfit. "It's very nice."

"Allie picked it out. Not my choice."

"Um, don't forget your coat," she said, handing it to me from the railing.

"I thought you were going to dinner and then dancing," Evan said to me.

"I am," I replied.

"You look—I can't say it. What's the word?" Alex said, trying to speak.

"Wicked hot!" Declan shouted from the doorway. "Damn! Where have you been hiding this outfit?"

"Down, Declan," Paige said as she pushed him away.

"I gotta go, so I'll see you guys later. Paige, come on," I said. "Let's get Quinn and Emery before we get mauled."

"No, before *you* get mauled." She laughed. "I need Allie to shop for me."

"You can have her," I said.

CHAPTER TWENTY-ONE

OLD FRIENDS

W̶e picked up Quinn and Emery and then headed to the restaurant. I got the same reaction from them when I took off my coat.

"I can see I'm going to get that a lot tonight," I said between bites.

"You think?" Quinn said sarcastically.

"Happy birthday, Quinn," I said.

Laughing, we toasted her.

After we finished dinner, we ordered the triple-chocolate dessert Quinn requested. The employees sang to her, making her blush, but she loved it.

"Are you ready for some more fun?" I said.

"There's more?" Quinn asked.

"Yup, we're going dancing at the club down the street," Paige said, and snickered.

We left the car in the garage as we skipped down the ramp toward the club. There was a long line to get in, but thankfully I'd called ahead to set everything all up.

"Grey, we'll never get in," Quinn said.

"Just follow me." I walked to the front of the line to the bouncer. "Corwen. Grey Corwen, with three guests."

He looked at the clipboard and then moved the ropes to let us in.

"How did you do that?" Emery asked.

"It's a gift," I said as I opened the door.

"Grey, you need to share now," said Quinn.

"You just have to call ahead and schmooze with the manager." I laughed as they looked shocked. "No, my mom knew Scott way back when."

"You are too much, girl," Quinn said to me.

"Come on, Quinn let's go dance the night away. It's your birthday. Live a little." Paige said.

We put our coats in the booth and headed to the dance floor. We danced for about three hours before we all had to sit down and rest. We'd had enough fun for one night. I had to say my goodbyes before we left and I walked down to the bar to say thanks.

"Scott thanks for your help."

"No problem, Grey. Anything for an old friend."

"What do I owe you?" I asked.

One thing my mom had taught me was that if you were working at a club, you got crappy tips. I'd kept that in mind when I decided to give him a fifty-dollar bill.

"Well, hope we see you again soon. Don't be a stranger, because I want to meet this young man of yours," Scott said.

He was one of the good guys. He'd taken a chance, hiring my mom, who'd had no experience. But it had worked out in the long run.

"Okay, bye."

I hugged him, opened the door, and walked down the stairs toward the Jeep and got inside. Paige took off down the road.

We dropped Emery and Quinn off and headed back to my house. I was so tired that Paige helped me up the stairs and into the kitchen. After walking and dancing all night, my legs felt like spaghetti.

He was still there when I woke up. I stretched to kiss him. He woke up and returned my advances.

"This is definitely the way to wake up in the morning," I said.

"I think so, too. Did you sleep well last night?"

"No, not really. It was a little difficult to sleep in your bed with you here."

"You're too much. Now go back to Alex's room. I can hear Paige coming."

He stole one more kiss and headed through the entrance of the passageway. About a minute later, Paige came back through the passage.

"How was your night?" I asked.

"It was great. And yours?"

"I don't know. I fell asleep, so I guess it was restful."

I got up and headed to the bathroom. I could hear her laughing as I walked down the hall. I got into the bathroom and the shower was on. *Alex must be in here already.* I closed the door and went to the sink to brush my teeth.

"So, Alex, I heard your night was fun."

"What did you say?"

"Oh, crap! Declan, what are you doing in here?"

"Taking a shower. What are *you* doing in here?"

"I always come in here when Alex is taking a shower, and vice versa. We have the best conversations in here . . . " I was getting off topic.

"Are you kidding me?" he said.

"No, I'm not."

I decided to take a chance and put my toothbrush down.

"Grey, are you still there?"

I didn't answer him. I was really going to be taking my chances with this one. I opened and closed the bathroom door. Once he realized that I'd "left," I locked the door and ran back to the shower. He pulled back the curtain to make sure I was gone, but I got in fully clothed. I didn't want to take too many chances that morning.

As he was fixing the curtain, I stood there at the other end of the shower, staring at his gorgeous, muscular body; even his butt was cute. *Built.* Each ridge defined his stature like someone had carved them out of clay. I slowly wrapped my arms around him and began to stroke his chest with one of my hands. He started to shiver as I moved my hand along his arm. He turned and threw me against the wall.

Not really the reaction I was hoping for, but I'll take it.

He instinctively kissed my neck, then moved his way to my lips. He seemed to be a different person, more impulsive. I guessed what I'd decided to do had crossed the line, because he was definitely not going to stop this time. My shirt was half-off when I heard a knock at the door.

"Hey, Dec! Are you done yet?" Alex called through the door.

I jumped out and grabbed a towel from the closet. I closed the door and headed down the passageway as I heard Declan answer Alex.

"Yeah, give me a minute. I'll be right out."

"Okay, I'll be downstairs." Alex said.

I waited for him to pass, listening for his footsteps going down the stairs, before I slipped out into hall. I looked both ways and ran to my room. I leaned against the wall, trying to regain my composure and calm my racing pulse.

"Hey, what happened to you?" Paige asked. She was getting dressed. "Why are you wet?"

"Keep your voice down. I did something that crossed a line."

I told her what had happened and she tried not to scream at me. I knew she was irked, because she slapped me on the shoulder.

"Thanks. I needed that reality check."

"Anytime. You're going to push too far one day, and it won't stop."

"I know. No more chances. I'm done," I said.

I got dressed and then dried my hair.

"I think I need to go for a run," I said suddenly, changing my mind. "I'll be right back, okay?" I changed clothes again and grabbed my sneakers.

"I'll give you thirty minutes," Paige said.

"Okay. Be right back. I'll just go around the neighborhood."

As I ran down the stairs, Paige right behind me, the bathroom door opened.

"Paige, you up?" Declan asked.

He didn't see me.

"Yeah, do you need something?"

"Come talk to me for a second, and then you can go back downstairs."

I ran out the door and down the drive. I'd made it five blocks before I realized what a stupid idea that stunt in the shower had been. *What was I thinking? I know, I wasn't thinking. That's for sure.* I ended up downtown, so I decided to make it up to Declan with some muffins. *Nothing says I'm sorry like pastries.* It took me forty minutes to run downtown in total. I made it back to the house in time to see Evan walking down the stairs. I closed the front door.

"Hey, what do you have here?" Evan asked.

"Muffins, Evan."

He followed me into the kitchen, took his muffin, said thanks, and left.

"Hey, I bought muffins to say I'm sorry—and that I was stupid," I said, looking at Declan.

Alex thought I was talking about the club. He had no clue, which was a good thing. He got up and grabbed a blueberry muffin and a chocolate chip one for Paige. I put the kettle on to make some tea. Declan came over and assumed his regular position, arms around my waist with his chin on my shoulder.

"I forgive you, but let's not try that again, okay?" he said, kissing my neck.

"Okay, here's your cinnamon muffin."

I handed it to him and he sat down. I grabbed the kettle and poured two cups of tea, and then walked over to the table.

"Here's your tea, Declan."

I put the cup on the table and started to walk back to the counter.

"Come back here."

He pulled me down to sit on his lap. I almost spilled the tea, but I froze before it could fall. *That was weird.* I'd quickly grabbed the cup before anyone noticed.

"Please warn me the next time you decide to do that, okay?"

I put my cup down, along with my muffin. Allie walked in and over to the fridge to get some juice.

"Allie, I got you a chocolate chip muffin."

"Thanks," she said. She grabbed the muffin and sat on the counter. "I heard your outfit caused quite the scene at the club and at dinner."

"What?" Alex turned to her. "Tell me what you heard."

"Allie, shut up," I said through gritted teeth.

"No, Allie. Tell me."

I made a silent deal with her, and it was going to cost me big time.

"I heard she turned a lot of heads, got some numbers, and got some guy thrown out of the club."

"I know that already," he said. "Tell me what I don't know."

"That's all I know. Thanks for the muffin," she said to me.

She jumped off the counter and headed towards Evan's office.

"You got some phone numbers, huh?" Declan asked.

"Yes, but we left them on the table—especially the paper swan."

"Someone sent you a paper swan with their number on it?" He chuckled. "How lame."

"Whatever."

I tried to get up, but he pulled me back down.

"Chill out and eat your muffin," he said.

"You know, I think I need to take a shower."

"Not funny." His smile faded and he stopped laughing. "Just sit down. I'm sorry."

"No, really. I stink. I need a shower. I just ran to town and back."

"We thought you drove," Alex said, seeming surprised and impressed.

"Nope, I needed to get some air this morning." I looked at Paige. "And now I need a shower, so let's go, please."

I turned to Declan, leaned down, and spoke softly in his ear.

"Go, Grey. We'll be here when you get back." He sighed and helped me up.

I ran upstairs and headed straight to the bathroom. I took the quickest shower anyone in that house had ever known. I walked toward my room, dried off and got dressed, deciding to let my hair air dry.

I strolled back into the kitchen and sat on his lap.

"So is my tea still warm?"

"Well, I like the look," he said, ignoring my question and running his hand through my wet hair. "I didn't know your hair was curly."

There's a lot you don't know about me. Paige shot me a quick look.

"Yeah, when I blow dry it I can straighten it, but if I let it air dry, it's wavy."

He leaned in and whispered in my ear.

"You wish," I said. "Maybe you should go home."

"If that's what you want." He laughed.

"You guys need to grow up," Alex snapped as he went into the hall.

"What's up with him, Paige?"

"I don't know, but I can find out."

I turned to Declan and put my head on his shoulder.

"So what do you want to do today?

"I can think of something to do."

He began kissing me. I heard someone come into the kitchen, but we didn't stop.

"Can you guys seriously get a room or something?" Alex demanded.

"Sorry, Alex." I jumped up and put my cup in the sink. "What's up?"

"Shut up!"

He grabbed his keys and stormed out. I knew his moods. I had seen them before, but last time, it was me experiencing them. But I couldn't figure out if the reason for his mood was me, the fact that he no longer had a chance at the council, or what. I knew I had to back off.

"Declan, can you go talk to him? I don't want him doing anything stupid."

Declan ran after him. I went up the stairs and heard Paige in my room.

"Paige, what happened?" I asked.

"He's a little upset, so give him some space."

I knew Alex, and space was not what he needed.

"Why is he mad? Did we do something wrong?"

I sat next to her on the bed, knowing the answer already. Alex was just as predictable as me at times.

"No, it's about last night."

She stopped and inhaled. I didn't want to know the details so

I quickly said the first thing that came to mind before she could speak again.

"Paige, its fine. Declan is with him." I tried to comfort her. "This is totally something outside of my realm of expertise."

My brother had the hardest time expressing his emotions. We were like each other in more ways than I'd thought. But maybe Declan wasn't my first choice as far as who I would talk to about Alex's problems.

"It's okay."

"Listen, let's take Allie to the mall. I owe her."

"Sounds good. I need some fresh air."

"Allie, we're going to the mall. Meet me downstairs!" I yelled down the hall.

"I'm ready. Come on," she said from behind as she stood by the door.

How the heck did she do that?

I opened Evan's door and peeked in.

"We're going to the mall and Allie's coming with us. Let Alex know where we're going, okay?"

I didn't want Alex to worry about anything after that morning.

"Sure. I'll let him know."

We headed to the car and out the drive to the mall.

Allie always tells me shopping can make anyone happy. Hopefully this will work for Paige.

We spent most of the day shopping. We'd had lunch and were getting ready to leave when something caught my eye—or rather, *someone.*

CHAPTER TWENTY-TWO

BILLINGS COMES
TO ERVING

"Grey? Grey Corwen?" he said.

"Yes. Do I know you?" I said as I tried to remember his face.

"Travis. Travis Cole from Jackson Middle School."

Now I really had to work hard to remember. The only school we'd attended was in Billings. My brain was working overtime trying to figure it out.

Then it hit me. Art class, seventh grade. He had definitely changed. He'd gotten taller. He was bigger than Alex, but still had that blond hair and green eyes. And I couldn't believe I'd forgotten about those cute, little dimples.

"Wow, Travis. Of course I remember you! Art class, right?"

"Math and Spanish, too. Remember how much you hated math?"

Oh, great. A blast from the past—just what I need today.

"She still does," Paige interrupted.

"I'm sorry. Paige, this is Travis. We went to school together in Billings."

"It's nice to meet you," she said.

"And this is my little sister, Allie," I said as I pulled her close.

"I remember you. Grey used to write your name everywhere."

I nudged her to shut up, and gave her a look before I turned back to him.

"So what are you doing here?" I asked him.

"Oh, we're out on break and my family is heading east to visit some relatives."

"Really? Where? I mean, what town?" I said, trying to stay polite. *Don't say Erving. Don't say Erving*, I kept repeating to myself.

"Erving." He answered. I hoped he was visiting relatives in Turner Falls or Greenfield. Any other town close to the mall but Erving.

He'd said it. *Crap.*

I didn't know you had relatives there."

"My uncle and his family moved there about ten years ago. I haven't seen them in years," he said.

"Who's your uncle? I mean, what's the family's name?" Paige asked before I could.

"Brooks," he answered.

Paige leaned toward me and whispered, "Not like us. They're one of the few who don't know the true origins of the town."

I knew then to keep my mouth shut about anything that concerned me, my family, or the town.

"So what are you girls doing here?"

"Shopping," I said. I laughed as I held up our bags.

"If I remember correctly, you hated shopping. You would have rather ridden bikes on the trails than shop."

"Yeah, this is more for Allie than for me." I said, looking to Paige for help.

"Do you need a ride back to town, Travis?" she asked him, which didn't help me at all.

"No, I have my uncle's car. Grey, can I call you while I'm here?"

"Um, I don't know."

"Sure. Here's her number," Allie said, butting in. "She has a game on Wednesday. You should come."

Allie handed him a piece of paper. I could have killed her, and trust me when I say that Paige wouldn't have stopped me.

"Thanks. I'll give you a call. I'll definitely come see your game on Wednesday."

I told him goodbye.

"Nice to meet you, Travis," Paige said.

What was that all about? Well, I know one thing for sure. Allie better pray on the way home.

The ride back was a little too quiet. I tried to start a conversation, but everything seem to lead back to the mall.

"So you had a thing for Travis?" Paige asked me.

"I did, but that was in middle school. He's changed a little, and I moved."

I looked in the mirror at Allie. The truth was that he hadn't changed at all. He looked the same, but older and a little cuter.

"And then I met your brother, so case closed," I said as I continued to look at the road.

"Not really, thanks to your sister. She opened the door again."

"Not on my end. He's passing through, and he was a good friend."

"He's going to call you. You know that, right?" she added.

"I know, and if someone had let me finish back there, he wouldn't have had any hopes when he calls, nor would he be coming to my game."

I shot a look at Allie in my mirror.

"Whatever," she huffed, like she was five years old.

I wished I could tell her why we couldn't see random people—especially people who weren't like us. Some rule stated that it was

forbidden. A mix of the bloodline was the only thing I could remember at that point.

We pulled up to Paige's house and Declan's Jeep was there,
thankfully. I figured whatever was with Alex had been settled by now.

"I hope you had fun today. I'll see you tomorrow." I said to Paige.

"I did, thank you. See you tomorrow. Bye, Allie."

Paige closed the door and walked up to the house as I pulled
out and began driving toward our house. I was sure Allie could
feel the tension in the car. When we pulled into the drive, she all
but jumped out and ran inside. I turned the car off, and walked
in with my bags.

"What's wrong with Allie?" Alex asked as I walked in.

"I bumped into someone from Billings, and she did something
stupid."

"Who was it?" he asked.

It seemed like he was in a better mood.

"Travis Cole. She also invited him to Wednesday's game."

"Oh, crap," he said, clearly peeved.

"I know, Alex. I started to tell him and she interrupted me. I
know the rules, so don't get all rule-police on me."

He ignored my last comment.

"What's he doing here?"

"Visiting his family," I said. "They live here in Erving."

"Who?"

"The Brooks family. Paige said to keep quiet . . . because they
aren't like us."

"I know, so be very cautious."

"He's only here during his break, so he'll be gone soon." *At
least I hoped he would.* "He knows I live here, and he might want to
hangout. But we can do that in a big group. We'll go bowling or
something. Don't worry, Alex. I'll take care of it."

"You better, for your and his sake. If Dec finds out, you'll
never be alone again."

I knew Declan's protective side. It was something I would rather not deal with again.

He was stern, but then he smiled.

"So did you get me anything?"

"Yes, I did, but Allie has it. And Paige has the rest."

"You are horrible," he said playfully as he shoved me up the stairs.

"I learned from the best."

I put my things away and prayed that Travis had lost my number. My homework was done and I was ready to sleep, but not before a little more practice. Unbeknownst to anyone, I had been practicing my skills, opening and closing doors, the drawers to my desk, trying to turn the pages of my book with my thoughts. The only thing I hadn't tried in a while was talking to my mom. I thought I'd better leave that for another time; telekinesis was draining enough. I needed my sleep, because we were having longer practices the next two days.

I pulled into the lot behind Alex. Paige and Emery were waiting for me, but so was Declan. I needed to get to Paige before class. I got out of the car and started toward her, but he grabbed me first.

"Good morning, sunshine. I missed you yesterday." He kissed my cheek.

"I only went to the mall, and if you let me talk to Paige right now, I'll wear one of the outfits tomorrow."

He let me go and quickly kissed my hand before walking over to Alex. *He was so easily persuaded.* I caught up to the others.

"So did you talk to him last night?" Paige asked.

I knew who she was referring to.

"No, he didn't call. And I was busy with homework and stuff."

"Good." She smiled. "So I talked to Dec last night and he explained everything, so we're good now."

"That's good, but I haven't said anything yet."

"And if he doesn't call, you won't have to." Paige winked at me.

I knew she hadn't said anything, but if Travis did call, Alex would say something if I didn't.

Thankfully the day passed by in a blur, and before I knew it, I was at practice.

"So we had some cute guy in the café last night," Quinn said.

"Oh, yeah? What about Jack, silly?"

"Oh, he was asking if we knew you, and where he could find the school for the game on Wednesday."

"Great," I said as my smile faded.

"Who is he?"

"He's a friend from Billings. We went to school together. That's it."

"I don't think he sees you that way." She laughed. "You better warn Declan."

"Oh, I will. Don't worry."

The problem was that I didn't get a chance tell Declan about Travis—because I forgot to. I'd had two tests the previous day and had had one test that day. I also had a game. I was prepared for it, but I wasn't prepared for the people who would show up.

I was in the locker room getting ready when Paige came in.

"Grey, he showed up," she said.

"The guy from the café?" Quinn asked.

"Yes, Quinn. I forgot to tell Declan."

"You better do it tonight, because this guy got you flowers," Paige said.

I could kill Allie. Any other time I wouldn't care about what she did, but things are different now. I have secrets to keep.

"Great. Let Alex know I forgot to say something to Declan. And try to get him to tell Declan before the end of the game."

"Grey, come on. We need to get out on the court," Quinn said, pulling me to the door.

"Tell him, please!" I yelled.

I tried looking for Alex when we got to the court, but I only saw Travis. He waved and smiled down at me. That's when I saw Alex, Declan, and Jack walking toward the others.

I hope he didn't see that.

"Okay, girls, let's win this one. You can do it! Go out and play hard!" Coach Greer yelled as we ran onto the court.

Quinn served, starting the game. Things went back and forth for a while. It was tied at two sets apiece. The score was tied in the last set, and we were trying for the win. The other team got the return, and now they were trying for the win. Julia set me up, Quinn went down, and then I spiked the ball for the kill.

We needed to get the next two points to win the game. Julia scored the first one and Amy made the last point we needed to win. We all went crazy. It was our first win of the season. We weren't that bad of a team; we weren't great either, but a win was a win. I'd take that any day.

I was heading to the locker room when I saw Travis coming down the stands toward me. I rushed inside to avoid him.

"You can't avoid him the whole time, Grey," Quinn said.

"I know. I'll tell him now." I put my shoes on.

"Maybe not in that outfit." She giggled.

I forgot to change my shirt. I hurried to grab whatever clothes I had in my bag. I found Declan's jersey. Perfect. I threw it on and grabbed my bag—and Quinn.

"Come on, I need you next to me."

We walked out of the locker room and there he was, waiting outside the door. Everyone else was at the far end of the hall. *Could this night get any crazier?*

"Hey! Great game. I see you used my move," Travis said.

"That was *your* move?" Quinn asked, looking at me.

"Yeah, I taught her when we played in gym back home. She was short, so she needed an advantage."

"Well, then. I thank you." Quinn smiled.

"Oh, these are for you," he said, handing me a bouquet of

daisies and roses.

"Thanks, Travis, but I should tell you, I'm seeing someone."

"Well, that's okay," Travis said. "Maybe he needs some competition."

"I don't think so. He's very special to me. You're only here for the break," I said. "It's best we stay friends, okay?"

"Deal. As long as we can hang out," he replied.

I remembered I'd always had fun with Travis. Why would that have changed?

"That's fine," I said. "Come on, you can come to the café with us."

We were walking to the lot when I saw Declan arguing with Alex. *Man, he's mad. I need to talk to him.*

"Guys, I'll meet you at the café," I said. "And Quinn, can you please go with Travis in his car so he doesn't get lost?"

She agreed and walked with him to his car. I walked over to the Jeep and asked Alex to leave for a minute. I grabbed Declan and kissed him until he had to pull back for air.

"Well, I guess I needed that."

"He's an old friend from Billings. He's just visiting. I've already set the rules. And he knows I'm taken."

I kissed him again.

"Hold on a minute, before you put me in a place to stop you." He pulled back. "You need to go celebrate a great win, Shakespeare."

"You're crazy. You know that?"

"I know I'm crazy about you," he said, pulling me closer.

We started to kiss again.

"I would like to eat sometime tonight without getting sick!" Alex yelled.

"Sorry, man. She's too irresistible." Declan pulled away. "I'll meet you there, okay?"

I left the flowers in the car except for one white rose I got out of from the bouquet. Walking into the café, I saw Quinn in the back. I sat down and put the rose on the table in front of me. Paige just shook her head and laughed. She knew what I was up to.

"Hey, guys, did you order yet?" I asked.

"No, we were waiting for you, girl," Travis answered.

He'd started to get up to sit next to me when they walked in and made their way to our table.

"Hi, I'm Declan. And you must be Travis. Nice to meet you, man," Declan said as he tried to shake Travis's hand. Travis ignored him and turned to Alex.

"Hey, Alex. Long time, no see."

"Travis, it's been a couple of years. Are you visiting?"

"Yup, I'm staying with my uncle for a couple of weeks, then back to Billings."

Travis turned and smiled at me. Declan noticed and quickly sat down, then put me on his lap.

"You can chill out, you know. I'm not going anywhere," I said as I moved his hair from his face.

Declan put the rose on the table so he could grab my hand, and then kissed me.

"I know, but this is fun."

He squeezed me.

"Whatever." I shook my head. "I need to sit to eat."

"You *are* sitting. And I'll feed you. Now enjoy the company like I am, please."

I think he's enjoying this too much.

"You know I am," he whispered.

I just shook my head again, as did Paige and Jack. Declan was making sure everyone knew I was taken, especially Travis. Sometimes Declan's protective side was nice—until it turned into full blown jealous insanity. I would have to keep an eye out, but that night we were focused on celebrating the win.

The rest of the week flew by, and we made plans to head to the club later that night. Declan had actually invited Travis, which was a little shocking, but I think he was keeping an eye out. And what better way for Declan to do that than to invite Travis along? We were meeting everyone at the club around seven o'clock.

I got dressed and ran to Alex's room to help him pick something out to wear.

"You're wearing that outfit again?" he asked.

"Yeah, Declan likes it, and it's easier to dance in than jeans. Here, wear these pants and this shirt."

"Thanks, Grey."

"Anytime, Alex. Listen, don't be so eager. Try to have fun tonight. I know you've been under a lot of pressure, what with the lessons and the family stuff."

I walked back to my room to grab my coat. As soon as Alex came down, we left. It took about an hour to get there, which gave him time to relax.

"So you look pretty decent tonight. Now you just have to relax. You don't have to dance," I said. "I got a table again."

"Thanks, again. I'm trying."

"We don't expect much. Just be the Alex we all know and love."

"I'll try my best," he said as we pulled up to the garage and parked.

When we got to the club, we realized we were the last ones to arrive.

"This line is bigger than last time." I said

Emery nodded.

"No problem for you, right?" Travis laughed.

He had started to walk toward me when Declan grabbed my waist and pulled me to the door.

"Hey, Ty." I said, waving to the bouncer as he pulled the rope back.

"Hey, Grey. Head on in."

"You are amazing," Declan whispered.

We walked in and I saw Scott coming toward us.

I hope he'll be nice. That's the last thing I need tonight.

"Hey, sweetie. I'm glad you came back. This must be the lucky guy." He turned to Declan and stared at him. "You treat her right, okay?"

"I will." Declan gulped.

"Scott, stop," I said. "He treats me wonderfully. He took me to London for Valentine's Day to see a play."

I grabbed Declan's hand and smiled.

"That's my kind of guy. Good for you, man."

"Declan," he said, correcting him.

"Well, good for you, Declan. Now enjoy yourselves. Let Mark know if you need anything."

I started walking to our table.

"You definitely have some pull around here," Declan said to me.

"Whatever. I'm going dancing. Enjoy."

I headed to the middle of the floor. Paige and Emery soon followed. We danced for a while and I lost track of time like I always did when I was having fun.

"So Alex doesn't dance?" Paige asked.

"No, he has two left feet!" I yelled over the music. "He came to my lessons, but he pretty much watched most of the time. I think he came for the girls."

"Declan, too, but at least they're behaving."

I felt like she was hiding something but brushed it off.

They lowered the music and announced there was going to be a dance contest. Just my luck—I knew Travis was behind me. I knew what he wanted, and I had to remain calm. Travis was one of two guys who had been in my class and we'd seemed to hit it off right away. Of course my mom pushed the dancing thing a little, and she had me enter contests, which I hated doing at the time.

"So, partner, you ready to tear up the floor?"

Travis grabbed me around the waist.

"Sure. We'll wipe the floor with them," I said, moving his hands away.

We walked to the center of the floor, alongside four other couples. I looked over at our table to see shocked faces. Alex didn't seem to be, though. He knew Travis had been my partner in class when I used to take dance lessons.

The problem at that moment was that Travis and I only danced well when it came to salsa. Our instructor had liked to throw a little spice in there every once in a while. We'd learned traditional styles, but the instructor had focused more on raw, street-style moves.

Just like old times. Great. Alex heard me and I saw him smile. I couldn't help but smile a little at the thought.

It was a long night, but it got more intense when we became one of two couples left in the contest. I walked over to the table to grab a drink of water. Declan's face was priceless. I leaned in and whispered in his ear. He laughed, then kissed me before I headed back out to the floor.

The music started. We began slowly and then worked our way up. The DJ lowered the music and started to speak.

"Well, it looks like we brought the street and a lot of heat to the floor tonight. I haven't seen dancing like that in a while. I say it's a tie."

I grabbed my coat, said bye to Scott and Mark, and headed outside for some air. Everyone else met me outside except for Travis. *I hope we didn't lose him already.* I had started looking around when Quinn came over.

"He drove himself. He decided to stay."

"That's good," I said. "He'll have fun."

I put my coat on and headed to the garage.

When we got to the cars, Quinn pulled out first. We followed them back to town. I waved as we passed them. We pulled up the drive of the Watt's house andparked.I got out of the Jeep. Paige pulled up behind us and got out.

"Alex, what are we doing at the Watt's house?"

"They spend too much time in our house, so it's a change of scenery."

Alex walked toward Paige and I followed them inside.

"Where are your parents?" I asked.

"They left this morning. They're gone for a week and a half, visiting relatives."

"Lucky me," I mumbled to myself.

Paige gave us the tour of their house. Their house was similar to ours, but it had fewer rooms and wasn't as old. Everything seemed to be made of cedar, not oak, which was interesting. Paige's room was by the stairs at the front of the house, and Declan's room took up the back of the house. Their house was quaint, but the downstairs and along the wall that went upstairs, it looked like a natural history museum.

Her room was simple. She had a large, mahogany, sleigh bed, a desk, and a large dresser. The walls were a natural beige color, and her curtains, that flowed to the floor, were a grayish-brown.

I walked down the hall to Declan's room. The walls in his

room were a darker beige, almost taupe. He also had a large bed at the far end of the room. There was a small sofa next to the door and to the right, was a closet like mine. He had no dresser, but there were several shelves for his clothes. On the room's back wall, there were three large windows that overlooked his backyard, framed photos in between each one. I didn't stop to look at the pictures because something else caught my eye. I walked in further, toward his bed. He had a gray comforter and pillows. I chuckled a little at the color. *Typical.* On the nightstand next to his bed was the framed photo and the rose I had given him. I couldn't help but smile.

I looked up and noticed an odd-shaped piece of art above his bed. It looked very old and brittle. I took off my boots and climbed on the bed to get a closer look. I was afraid to touch it. It looked so fragile that it might crumble if I did. It was silver, but it was a little tarnished.

I couldn't take my eyes off of it. It was beautiful. The continuous knots that formed an intricate and never-ending pattern—it was beyond words. I didn't even notice when he climbed up behind me. He wrapped his arms around my waist and rested his chin on my shoulder.

"It's as beautiful as you are."

He kissed my neck. I closed my eyes and sighed. He tightened his hold and continued down my shoulder.

"It'll be yours someday, you know." he said.

I opened my eyes and turned around to look at him.

"What?" I said.

It was all I could get out.

"I'm not going anywhere, and if I have my say, you'll have this totem for a long time. It's been in my family for as long as I can remember." He smiled.

"Not, not now," I stuttered, because I was a little more than freaked out.

"I know not for a while, but it'll happen. So don't be so shocked."

He continued where he left off. I couldn't comprehend what had just happened, but I knew I wasn't going anywhere without him. I stopped thinking and just acted. I reciprocated his advances.

I woke up and turned to see the time. I remembered I wasn't in my room, but the clock was there, next to the bed on the night-stand. It was only five o'clock in the morning. I rolled back over and curled up next to him. He was still asleep. I laid there watching him. He looked happy and at ease, the way I always liked him to be—"content" was a good word for it. As I put my head on his chest, he grabbed me and pulled me closer. I kissed his chest and closed my eyes.

I heard a knock at the door and Alex's voice. I was still sleeping when he got up to open the door. I heard it close and then the two of them walk down the hall. I rolled over and buried myself under the comforter. I didn't want to get up. That's when I heard the door open again.

Why can't I go back to sleep?

Paige jumped into the bed and I turned over.

"Good morning," she whispered.

"Hi, can we go back to sleep, please?" I pleaded.

"Sure. Whatever you want."

She rolled over on to her other side.

I heard the door again.

"What is this, a party?" I said.

"What?" I heard Declan laugh. "I leave for two minutes and she's mad. Thanks, Paige."

"She's grumpy in the morning." Paige got up. "I'm taking a shower and you should get up. I'll buy breakfast. Come on."

"Fine," I said. I rolled out of bed with the blanket still wrapped around me. "It's cold in here."

They just laughed as I headed to the bathroom with Paige.

"You can use this one and I'll use my parents. I grabbed some of your clothes last night. They're on my bed," she said as she walked out.

"Thanks."

I quickly showered and walked to her room to get dressed, then dried my hair. I picked up the blanket and walked back to Declan's room.

"Here's your blanket back."

"Come here," he said.

He pulled me into his arms.

"I love you, Grey."

"I love you, too, Declan." I kissed him. "Now let's get something to eat."

He followed me downstairs, where Paige and Alex were waiting.

"It's about time," Alex mumbled.

I just headed toward the door. Paige handed me my coat.

We got to the not-so-aptly-named café and sat at a table in the back. Tyler brought us some menus.

"Someone looks happy this morning."

He chuckled as he walked back to the counter. I looked at Declan and he smiled. I gasped as he leaned in closer.

"Nothing happened. Relax, Grey. I told you it's not the right time."

He kissed my cheek. I took a deep breath and relaxed.

I'm glad for that. Nothing happened, and he wasn't going to let it. That's definitely a good thing for now.

We had just finished eating when I saw Evan walk in.

"Hey, guys," he said. "Can I speak with you for a minute?"

Alex and I followed him outside and waited for him to start talking.

"Okay. You guys are old enough and you're smart. I need to go out of town until next Sunday morning. I'll be gone all week with Grams and Allie. They'll be visiting with some relatives while I'm at the conference. I figured you didn't want to come. But *no* parties."

"Sure, Evan. No problem," Alex smiled.

"Grey, no accidents," Evan begged.

"I'll lock the knives away," I muttered.

"Not funny, Grey." Alex said.

"I'll see you guys next Sunday." Evan said.

He hugged us good bye. Evan and Alex looked at each other and I knew they were talking about me. I wish I knew what they were saying.

"You're leaving now?" I asked.

"Yup, see you later—and be good. No parties!" he shouted as he got into his car.

We waved and went back inside to finish up.

"What was that about, Grey?" Paige asked.

"Well, we've got the house to ourselves until next Sunday."

I heard Declan drop his fork on the plate. His expression was priceless. But it made me squirm a little.

"You guys are alone all week?"

I wondered what he'd meant by that. Maybe nothing. so I let it go.

"Yup, all alone—but no parties," Alex answered.

I sensed there was more to their conversation.

"Come on. Let's head home," I said, grabbing Declan.

We switched cars and headed back to our house. We would invite everyone over later that night. Evan had said no parties, but he hadn't said we couldn't have friends over. Thankfully, Grams had stocked the kitchen before they left.

CHAPTER TWENTY-THREE

HOUSE GUESTS

We'd invited everyone over for dinner, and I had just finished preparing everything and the roast was in the oven. I had a couple of hours to kill, so I went to Evan's office to look for a book to read.

I grabbed one of the many photos albums off the shelves instead. I sat at his desk, looking through the photos. They were of Evan and my mom when they were teenagers. They were mostly of vacations at the lake with family and friends.

I grabbed another album and opened it. This one was my album. It was hard to look through, because there were a lot of pictures of me with my parents. And there was also a few of me with someone I didn't recognize. I'd blocked out anything that had to with my past before my dad passed away because he and I were so close. It was hard to think of him without crying, so I shoved it way back in my memory, locked it away, and I tried not to think about it.

I heard a thud and noticed a book on the floor. I put the album away and picked the book up off the floor. There was no name or title on the front cover, and I thought that was weird. I opened it and started turning the pages. There was nothing there. They were blank.

"Grey, are you here?" Alex called from the door.

I didn't answer. I stood up as he walked toward me.

"Where did you get that book?" he asked.

"I was at the desk and it fell off the shelf." I looked at him, confused. "Why are the pages blank?"

He grabbed the book and put it back on the shelf.

"It's just a ledger that belongs to Evan."

I knew he was lying. He wasn't that good at it. He knew something and I was going to find out what.

"But why is it blank?" I asked again.

"He just got it. Why don't you go finish dinner? Or meditate or something before everyone gets here?"

He walked me out of the office and toward the kitchen. I checked the roast and it was done, so I took it out to rest. Alex was acting weird and I couldn't figure out why. He was all jittery and on edge. It was like the garden all over again. I wasn't allowed in the garden without Grams, and now it was the office without Evan. When I wasn't allowed to do something, I wanted to figure out why I couldn't, and how I could get down to the secrets.

I felt a little drained somehow, so I decided to go relax for a bit or meditate.

"Alex, I'm going upstairs to lie down for about thirty minutes or so."

"Okay!" He called from downstairs.

I walked up the stairs to my room and closed the door behind me. I sat on my bed and began to think about the book.

"Mom?" *I can't believe I'm doing this.*

I felt a slight twinge against my temples, but this was different from before, somehow more gentle.

"Yes, Grey? What's wrong?" she answered.

"Do you know anything about that book that fell off the shelf?"

"No. What book?"

Okay, that answered *that* question—it hadn't been because of her—but what did happen? The book hadn't fallen by itself. My head was starting to hurt.

"Grey, what book fell?" she asked.

"It didn't have a title or a name on it. Alex said it was Evan's."

"Oh, I don't know. What did it look like?"

"It had leather binding, green, with manila colored pages, but they were all blank."

She didn't answer me for a while, so I thought maybe she had disappeared again.

"Mom?"

"Yes, I'm here. No, I don't know that book. It was probably a new ledger."

Okay, now I know she's keeping something from me, because I never said it was new or a ledger, but I'll play along for now.

"Thanks, Mom. I know you tried."

"How are things otherwise? I hear you're cooking and meditating," she said, changing the subject.

"Yeah, a new skill I picked up thanks to Declan. I'm good, and school is fine. Grams has me do the meditation to refocus my abilities, and cooking, to focus my mind."

I could play this game too.

"I'm glad, sweetie. I have to go, but remember you are special and your gifts are great."

"I do, thank you."

Just then I thought I heard someone in the hallway upstairs. I opened the door, but no one was there. Maybe I'd accidentally moved something without thinking. I needed to get more sleep, because I was starting to hear things. I'd turned around to go downstairs when I heard a door open. *I know I didn't do that.* I turned back and saw that Allie's door was open. *I know I can talk to spirits, but seeing them is a different story.* I was beginning to get a little freaked out. I walked down the hall to see if anyone was in the room.

"Mom, is that you?"

She didn't answer. Then I heard a faint creaking noise in her room. I knew it was a bad idea, especially after watching so many horror flicks. It would be the time when the knife-wielding maniac would close the door and kill me.

Okay, bad image to have in my head before I walk in.

I stepped across the threshold, seeing a small opening in the wall by her bed. Another passage. I wondered where it went. I crawled through to find myself in a small hallway. I walked until I came to a spiral staircase. I felt strange; not tired, but drained again. It was like someone or something was taking all my energy. I descended the stairs and started down a narrow corridor, feeling weaker as I progressed farther into the darkness. It led nowhere. It was a dead end. *Not good, Grey. Not good.*

I hurried back toward the stairs, but I tripped and fell into the wall, which caused another door to open. *Man, this house is crazy.* I stood up, noticing that my leg was cut. *This is just great.*

I limped down the hall to another door and I found myself under the deck. *These passages get better and better,* I thought to myself. Now my count was at seven. I had to show Allie. I walked up the stairs to the deck, still tired and now bleeding.

I heard Alex talking to someone at the front door and then I heard Declan and Paige calling my name.

"Guys, I'm out here!" I called.

"Where have you been?" Alex was freaking out. "You were gone for an hour."

I was only gone twenty minutes. Maybe he got the time wrong? He was waiting for my answer.

"In the garden," I lied.

I couldn't tell him I was stuck in a passage way, being zapped of all energy.

"A what?" he asked.

"I was in the garden," I repeated.

"Fine, Dec and Paige are here."

I saw Paige on the balcony. She ran to the stairs, yelling that I was on the deck.

"Hey, your brother was freaking out because he couldn't find you."

She hugged me, and that's when I felt a jolt of energy stream through my body. It felt like she was giving me a piece of her, and as soon as it happened, I began to feel more like myself.

"I'm fine. I was in the garden."

I walked to the kitchen to finish making dinner. I grabbed the plates from the cupboard and placed them on the counter. I was getting the silverware when I heard a noise behind me. I turned, but no one was there. *I am officially going crazy.* I turned back to get the knives and I heard the noise again. I quickly turned around to see Declan jump back.

"Grey, be careful with those knives," he said, grabbing them from my hands.

"Sorry."

My hands started to shake a little. I started to carve the meat.

"Grey, let me do that."

"I got it, Declan," I snapped at him.

"Your hands are shaking. Are you okay?"

He took the knife from my hand and hugged me. I felt a shiver down my back and I pulled away from him and ran up to my room. That had never happened before either. I figured he would follow me.

This is not good. I am going crazy. I'm hearing things that aren't there. This is getting too weird.

I tried to light the candle several times before the wick finally took the flame.

"Grey, open the door. Are you okay? Talk to me."

Declan sounded panicked.

"I'm fine. Give me a minute and I'll be right out."

"I'll be on the stairs waiting for you."

I closed my eyes and tried to calm and center myself. I realized I couldn't stay there and talk to myself with him right outside the door. I walked into the closet, candle in my hand, and down the passage to Evan's office.

"Mom?"

"Yes, sweetie?"

I placed the candle on the edge of the desk.

"Did you show me a passage in Allie's room?" I asked.

"No," she replied.

I needed more information about her appearances.

"Okay, so. Mom, do you watch me sometimes?"

"No, I can only communicate with you. I can't watch you. I come only when you call me or when you need me. My abilities don't work that way. I only knew a couple of people who could. Why?"

"No reason. Thanks."

I blew the candle out and exited the office without the answers I needed. I was walking to the front door when Alex caught me.

"Grey, where are you going?"

"I'm going to get the door."

"No one is there."

The doorbell rang and he stared at me.

"How did you do—"

"Do what?"

The doorbell rang again.

"I'll be right there."

Declan came down the stairs as I opened the door.

"Hey, guys. Nice to see you." I said.

Alex kept staring at me. I felt Declan wrap his arms around me and it felt weird. Something was up, but I couldn't pinpoint it. The amount of pressure in my head had multiplied. What the heck was going on?

"Are you okay?" He kissed me. "And how did you get down here?"

Alex closed the door and brought everyone out to the deck.

"I need to talk to you," I said.

I pulled Alex into Evan's office, closed the door, and I walked him to the far wall.

"This is how I got down here," I said, pointing to the wall.

"What? It's a wall."

I pushed it open to reveal the stairs.

"Whoa! Another passage,"

He walked through.

"Yeah, Paige knows about this one."

I walked in and immediately I felt a strange vibe, like something wasn't right. He closed the wall and kissed me. There was that awkward feeling again. It wasn't the kiss, or him, but the room. I stopped him.

"What's wrong?" he asked, pulling me closer, and the feeling got more intense.

"This doesn't feel right," I said.

He let go of me and walked back through the wall. *Oh, crap. He thought I meant us.* In my head, I ran through my prior actions.

"Damn it!" I yelled.

I ran out after him. I got out the front door in time to see him speeding down the drive. Paige came running out, looking at me. She must have sensed something; we seemed to be in sync more as of late.

"What happened?" she asked.

"Outside, now," I demanded.

I pulled her out and closed the door.

"What?"

"This is going to sound crazy."

I started pacing like a crazy person. *Maybe I'm going crazy after all.*

"Grey, sit down. You're freaking me out."

She pulled me down onto the stairs.

"Get a grip, and breathe."

"I'm sorry."

"It's fine. Spit it out," she said as she went to hug me.

"I've been hearing noises. I know this is an old house, but these noises are different." I stopped to breathe. "The doors are opening by themselves. I think someone is watching me, and every time I feel a shiver. Then, in Evan's office earlier, a book fell off the shelf, but it only had blank pages."

I didn't tell her about the jolt from her hug or the fact that I was feeling more drained by the minute.

"Okay, but what happened right now?"

"I had a strange feeling while Declan and I were in the passageway and he was kissing me. It felt different somehow, and I stopped him. I told him it didn't feel right, and this was right after I told him I needed to talk to him."

"Aw, he thought you meant you guys, not the place."

"I wanted to talk to him about the strange things going on, but he didn't wait for me to explain."

"I know where he went," she said. "Here are the keys to my house. Go now."

"Paige, don't wait. Just go ahead and eat. Everything is done."

"Don't worry about us. Go take care of this."

I ran as fast as I could down the drive and toward their house. When I turned up the Watt's drive, I saw his Jeep. I ran up to the porch, taking two steps at a time. When I unlocked the door, I could hear glass breaking upstairs. I ran up to his room.

"Declan."

"Grey, please, I can't take this anymore."

He put his hands over his face. I ran to his side and sat down on the bed next to him.

"Declan, please listen to me."

"Grey, please leave."

"No."

I needed to explain myself and he was going to listen.

"I don't need you to explain anything. Now please go. I need to be alone."

I grabbed him and wanted to force him to listen, but he pushed me away. I fell onto the floor.

"Please, Grey. Don't make it worse."

As I was getting up I noticed my photo on the floor. The glass was shattered and the photo was scratched. I wasn't sure what came over me, but I started to cry. He didn't comfort me. He only helped me to the door.

"Please leave now."

I stumbled down the stairs and out toward my house. I felt weak and exhausted. It started to rain; of course, that was just my luck. I wandered toward my house with no idea of time or my own existence. It was like I was somewhere else. I had no energy left and I felt so zapped, like someone was sucking it out of me. I walked around toward the back of the house and saw no one was on the deck. *They must have gone inside whenever it had started to rain.*

I walked to the garden and sat next to my roses. They were wilting, both of them.

It was entirely my fault. There was nothing I could do.

"Grey!" Alex yelled from the deck. He must have heard my thoughts.

Again I heard faint sounds of someone calling my name, but I didn't respond.

"Grey, are you okay? You're so pale," Alex said.

He saw the state the roses were in as he lifted me up by my arm.

"What happened to them?" he asked.

My body slumped against his shoulder. He picked me up and carried me to the deck. Paige was in the doorway when he came up the stairs.

"I think we should call it a night," Alex said.

"That might be best. I'll tell everyone else." Paige said.

He took me up to my room and sat with me until I fell asleep.

When I woke up, he was right next to me, waiting, with a concerned look on his face.

"Grey, what happened?" Alex asked.

"I don't want to talk about it."

I heard creaking noises coming from the hall and I cringed.

"Can you let me sleep? But please don't leave." I asked.

I heard the creaking again. I covered my ears and shut my eyes. Maybe that would help. Alex hesitated, but then I heard the door close and his footsteps as they went down the stairs. I rolled back over and cried when I heard the sound of tires as he peeled out of the drive. I knew exactly where he was going. I hoped that he would get the answers I needed.

I heard Alex and Paige outside my door.

"Hey, wait," I heard him say. "Come on."

"What happened with him, Alex?"

"Your brother is a jerk. I'm sorry, but I punched him. Maybe that will knock some sense into him."

"You what?!" she said, shocked. "Alex, he's your best friend."

"I don't know anymore. I don't know who that was in that room, but it wasn't Dec."

I heard them open my door. Alex walked into my room and sat down next to me.

"Grey, how are you doing?"

"Please leave me alone," I responded.

"Grey, please come with us now," Paige said as she came toward the bed.

Alex turned to look at her. It seemed like he thought she was crazy to suggest moving me anywhere right now.

"She needs to get out of this house, Alex. Trust me."

"Grey, come on. Let's go."

Alex picked me up and carried me out to the Jeep.

"Alex, he's not going to be there, not after what just happened."

"Fine," he said reluctantly.

We drove back to Paige and Declan's house, and sure enough, Declan's Jeep was gone. Paige had been right. We got out of the car and went inside the house.

"Take her upstairs to his room. I'll clean it up while she's sleeping so I can watch her."

Alex took me upstairs and put me down on Declan's bed. I curled up under the comforter. The woodsy smell enveloped me, and I felt relieved. I heard them both cleaning up the glass that had shattered everywhere. They were done fairly quickly. Paige leaned down and kissed my head.

"You'll be fine here," she said. "Get some sleep. We'll be right downstairs if you need anything."

I heard the door close. That's when I cried myself to sleep.

It was dark in the room when I woke up and the moonlight was streaming in through the windows. I rolled over and hugged his pillow.

I love him so much. How could this happen again? I need him. He's my soul and my life. Why didn't he let me explain? I'm really starting to freak out now. What is going on in my house to scare me like that?

Then I remembered I had never been there by myself; I was always with Evan, Grams, or Paige. Were they protecting me in some way? I felt the safest and most secure when Declan was with me.

My protectors are gone. I'm vulnerable. I need him to come back to me— so much so that I can actually feel his touch. Please, let this be real. Let him be here with me now.

I took a breath and sighed.

"I'm here," he whispered.

I rolled over to kiss him, and I didn't stop.

"Grey, this isn't the right time. Please come here."

"Declan, I'm so sorry."

I reached up to touch his face.

"You didn't do anything wrong. I did. I hurt you, and I was wrong. I can't believe the things I said to you. They were so hurtful."

I could feel his tears on my hand.

"Your brother was right," he continued. "I don't deserve you. I'm a jerk." He touched my face with his hand. "I should have listened to you instead of reacting the way I did. I don't know what came over me."

"You're not a jerk. You may be stupid, but you're not a jerk."

I put my head on his chest and he embraced me.

"What you said to me yesterday, Declan, it broke me. It was like I lost half of myself."

"I'm sorry, truly sorry."

"You need to promise me something," I told him.

"Anything. Please tell me what you want."

He held me tighter.

"Declan, if something happens from here on out, you need to let me explain things first before you react. I need you with me, so please do this simple thing for me."

"I will," he whispered. "I promise."

I kissed him, but he stopped me again. He got up and I heard the lock click, and then felt him climb back into bed.

"We need to be alone. No distractions," he said, pulling me to his chest.

"We have all week to work this out. I don't feel safe at home alone without you or Evan there. I'll be here until Evan returns home."

"I'm not going anywhere."

He slept next to me all night. I was beginning to feel the safety and security he gave me again, but it was coming slowly. It wasn't like the instant reaction I'd had when Paige held me. It was different, and somehow not enough.

I heard him get up, and then his slow footsteps as he walked across the room to the door. I could hear him talking to Paige, and when he came back to the bed I could make out her silhouette as she stood in the doorway. He leaned down to kiss me on the forehead.

"I'll be right downstairs. I'm coming back soon, so try to sleep," he said.

He kissed me again. He walked toward the door and closed it behind him.

I rolled over and tried to sleep, but I felt the urge to hear what was going on downstairs. I tiptoed to the door and opened it a crack so I could listen to them.

"This is the book that Grey was talking about with Paige," I heard Alex say.

"Why is it blank?" Declan asked.

"It's not. Watch," Alex said to them.

I heard the book close and then rustling of the pages.

"Whoa! How did you do that?" Paige asked.

What did he do? I couldn't see. I needed to see what was going on, but I couldn't chance moving so I just continued to listen.

"This is the Parker family grimoire," Alex told them.

"So only you can read it. But what about Grey? Why can't she read it?" Declan asked frantically.

"Don't worry, Dec. She's still a Parker, but she hasn't been taught how to read it yet. That's why the pages appear blank to her."

"Why would *this* book fall off the shelf instead of a different one?" Paige asked, curious.

"Someone was trying to tell her something, but I haven't figured it out yet. She was looking at old photo albums when the book fell. They must be connected, but I don't know how yet."

"What does it mean?" Declan asked.

"Grey revealed a new ability the other day I don't know if it's temporary or not. It had to be transferred or shown to her some-how, but I haven't figured that out yet either."

"Why would it show up now?" Declan asked.

"I don't know, but something happened to bring this person into the house. She's vulnerable right now because she knows about her abilities but hasn't been properly trained to use them. As Paige pointed out, her training is what will protect her."

What gift did I acquire the other day? Did I get something else from my dad? Is that why he's been coming around? Dad, you need to help me out here, please.

"The gift was my brother's," I heard a deep voice say. "I think he's causing the turmoil while your grandmother and Evan are gone."

"Dad," Alex whispered.

How was he here? I thought I could only hear Mom? And how could Alex hear him?

"Yes, son, it's me. We need to keep Grey safe right now."

"Mr. Parker, how are you here?" Declan asked him. "We don't possess this type of communication."

"Ah, you must be Declan. Grey thinks of you often. I'm glad you've protected her thus far."

"Thank you, but that doesn't answer my question," Declan stated.

"What are you talking about, Mr. Parker?" Paige interrupted.

"Please call me Barclay, Paige." He paused. "Your brother was chosen for Grey. They're both marked. Didn't your parents tell you this?"

"No, not really," she answered.

"What does that mean, Dad," Alex interrupted. "And how are you here now?"

"Alex, you and your sister are special, and so are your abili-ties, but your sister is more powerful than anyone knows yet. This power of hers needs to be controlled or it will consume her. You needed to be joined by others with the same talents and abilities. The Watt twins were the ones who were marked for each of you. That's why your mother brought you back here, and why you two are drawn to them."

My mom knew all along that we needed to be here, but couldn't tell us the reason before she died. Now I was learning the importance of why we'd come back.

"And to answer your other question, I'm here because of Grey. She possesses the power of communication like your mother and I did."

"So you're here because Grey is who's making it happen?" Paige spoke softly.

"Yes, Paige. She was given this gift at birth. Her mother transferred it to her."

I gasped suddenly and I think they heard me, so I ran to the bed and hid under the comforter.

"She knows. I need to go now, but you must put that book back and keep her here until Evan returns," he told Alex.

I heard footsteps coming up the stairs.

"Go return that and I'll stay with her. Paige, you go with him," Declan said. "She and I need time alone."

I heard the door lock and he walked over to the bed, climbed in, and held me.

"Thank you," I whispered.

"You don't need to thank me for anything, Grey," he said, holding me tighter.

"I do. I need to thank you for being with me and keeping me safe."

"I told you that listening to others' conversations might get you in trouble."

"With who?" I laughed.

"Grey, please."

"But you wouldn't have found out the truth unless I *did* listen,"

I said, and kissed him.

"I know, so *I* should say thank you to *you*. You need to rest. I'll be here."

I rested my head on his chest as he tightened his hold on me.

My days were getting mixed up. I *did* know that I needed to take a shower, because I couldn't remember the last time I had. Alex and Paige had gone to the store to pick up some food for us, and I think Declan was downstairs.

I walked down the hall to the bathroom. The door was open, of course, and Declan was in the shower—same situation as before, different house. I leaned against the door frame and stared at him. I could see his blurred figure through the etched glass. I turned away before he caught me.

I sat on the floor outside the bathroom. He walked out to find me there, waiting.

"Grey, what's wrong?"

He had a towel wrapped around his waist and he was dripping water on the floor.

"I was waiting so I could take a shower," I said, looking at the floor.

"You could have used my parents' shower."

"Oh, I didn't know. But you're done, so I'll just use this one."

He helped me up. I could feel my pulse racing. *I need to go now before someone crosses a line.*

"That's a good idea," he responded.

He walked to his room. I sometimes wished I could keep just *some* thoughts to myself, but in this instance I agreed with him.

I climbed in the shower and let the water calm my nerves. I must have been in there for a while, because the mirrors were completely fogged up. I shut off the water, climbed out, and grabbed a towel from the closet.

I decided to let my hair air dry again. I wrapped the towel around me and walked back to his room to grab my clothes that

Paige had brought from the house.

I took out some jeans and a shirt and I dropped my towel to get dressed. Then I heard a noise behind me. *Not again.* I turned to see Declan standing in the doorway of the closet. I quickly picked up the towel and held it against my body.

"I-I'm sorry. I thought y-you had gone downstairs already," I stuttered.

He stood there speechless, and before I could grab my clothes, he'd crossed the room, closed the door, and locked it.

"Declan, I'm really sorry."

He put his fingers on my lips to silence me. He grabbed me and pressed his lips roughly against mine. It was intense, and I couldn't help but throw my arms around him, which caused my towel to drop again—and things got a lot warmer.

He picked me up and moved me to the bed. I pulled him up and started to turn him onto his back. I parted his lips with mine and then slowly moved down his neck.

He took off his shirt before he pulled me back down. Our bodies became intertwined, and the atmosphere became even more intense, hotter.

I might need another shower if this continues.

He'd started to remove his pants when I heard a knock at the door. He abruptly stopped and jumped up to answer it.

"What?" he said, breathing heavily.

"Dec, are you okay?" I heard Paige say.

"Go away, Paige."

He walked to the sofa and sat down, then picked up my clothes and started throwing them on the bed.

"Get dressed, please."

I could tell he was still irked—and not because of Paige's disruption. He seemed different, and I was starting to notice it.

He quickly threw on his shirt as I reached for my clothes. He opened the door and I could hear him head downstairs. I saw that

Paige was still standing in the doorway. She walked in to see me in bed, pulling up my jeans.

"I'm so sorry, Grey. I didn't know," she said, trying to apologize as she sat down on the bed.

"I guess you knocked on the door at the right time, Paige."

"Are you serious?"

"I am. You stopped him. Because he wasn't going to," I told her. I got up and pulled my shirt over my head.

"Whoa, okay." She took a breath. "You know, I need to take you to lunch. Let's go."

"But, Paige, what about Alex and Declan?"

"No, just us. You'll be safe now. Come on."

We walked down the stairs and toward the front door.

"Where are you going?!" Alex called from the living room.

"I'm taking Grey to lunch. She'll be fine. She needs to get out for a little while," Paige said as she eyed Declan.

We left the house and drove to Wicked Brew Café. Tyler was working and Quinn was out with Jack.

"Hey, Grey. Are you feeling better?" Tyler asked.

"Yes, thank you," I replied as he smiled and handed me a cup of tea.

"You need to eat something before we go back. I think you should stay in my room," Paige told me.

"No, I'll be fine. You worry too much."

I knew she was right, but it was just the timing of it all. Tyler brought us our sandwiches and we ate in silence.

As she drove up the drive I saw Declan and Alex waiting for us.

This doesn't look good for me.

I got out, pacing myself as we walked toward the porch. Paige grabbed me before I got to the first step.

"Think about what I said, Grey."

She walked in the house.

"Think about what?" Alex and Declan said at the same time.

"Nothing. I'm going back to bed," I said. "I'm a little tired."

I walked past them and up to Declan's room.

He followed behind, of course, and closed the door once we were inside the room. We sat on the bed, holding hands for a few minutes before he started to speak.

"She doesn't want you in here with me, does she?" Declan asked.

"Yes, but I told her it would be fine." I said.

"Listen, Grey, I'm sorry," Declan said. "I don't know what came over me. Well, I know what—*why*—but what was happening was inappropriate anyway."

"You did what came naturally to you. Don't apologize," I said as I touched his face. "But come on, Declan, this body? *Please.*"

I laughed and he leaned in to whisper in my ear.

"Yes, and only yours. Now lie down. Get some sleep. I'll be back later to see if you want dinner."

"I love you, Declan."

"I love you, too, Grey."

He kissed me.

The rest of the week passed by quickly. Evan, Grams, and Allie came home and Alex told them everything that had happened. Evan had Alex bring me home right away. We pulled up in front of the house and Declan walked me inside.

"Grey, come into my office, please," Evan said, grabbing my arm. "Declan, she's fine. You can wait in the kitchen with Alex."

Declan kissed my hand and reluctantly let me go. He hesitated to leave, but Alex pulled him to the kitchen as Evan closed the door.

"Grey, Alex and Paige told me what happened here. I think it's time to start your lessons—early."

"Why now? What's made you change your mind, Evan?"

"Sean happened. He's been trying to bring his chaos into your life because you're vulnerable right now."

"But why? I don't understand."

"He's your godfather. You two were close until the accident. He wants to continue to cause pain to your father, and he can only do it through you right now."

"He's been watching me?"

"Yes. That's why we're always with you. As long as your father is around, Sean won't harm you."

"But what about Declan?"

"Grey, he's as gifted as you are, so he knows how to protect you. That's why he's always here when we aren't. He didn't know that Alex couldn't help you with this one."

"So when do I start?"

"Tomorrow. Go get some sleep. Be ready, because there's no turning back."

"I will. Thank you."

I walked up to my room and sat out on the balcony.

"Grey, I'm here to help you."

"Thanks, Dad."

"You are ready." He sighed. "We made the right choice with Declan, didn't we?"

He hesitated, and I wondered if there was someone else they had considered. I quickly pushed that from my thoughts.

"You did. And I thank you for that," I said.

"Grey, remember you are special. And your gifts are great."

"I know."

I looked out at the garden and saw Grams smiling at me. The next day, I would be ready to take my position within our family— but first I had to get some much-needed sleep.

ABOUT THE AUTHOR

An avid lover of Shakespeare and a hopeless romantic, J.T. Carroll enjoys reading, and lives in woodsy western Massachusetts with her family and two crazy dogs. She has a love of the outdoors, and can often be found roaming nature with a camera in hand.